W9-BCN-628

PRAISE FOR *THE RINGWORLD THRONE*

"*The Ringworld Throne* is vintage Niven; which is to say, it's weird, wild, and inimitable, and it juggles huge concepts of time and space that no one else can lift."
—Charles Sheffield

"Larry Niven is one of the giants of modern science fiction. With *The Ringworld Throne*, he just grew even taller."

—Mike Resnick

"In *Throne* Larry's vast Ringworld—with three million times the surface of the Earth—once more comes alive with adventure while Puppeteer, Kzinti, Grass Giants, Machine People, Gleaners, Vampires, Ghouls, and Pak Protectors all make life interesting again for Louis Wu."
—Donald Kingsbury

THE
RINGWORLD
THRONE

LARRY
NIVEN

A DEL REY® BOOK
BALLANTINE BOOKS
NEW YORK

A Del Rey® Book
Published by Ballantine Books

http://www.randomhouse.com

LIBRARY OF CONGRESS CATALOGING-IN-PUBLICATION DATA
Niven, Larry.
   The Ringworld throne / Larry Niven.
      p.   cm.
   "A Del Rey book."
   ISBN 0-345-35861-9
   I. Title.
   PS3564.I9R56   1996
   813'.54—dc20   95-47882
                                                             CIP

Text design by Holly Johnson

Manufactured in the United States of America

First Edition: June 1996

10 9 8 7 6 5 4 3 2 1

For Robert Heinlein

CONTENTS

CONTENTS

THE
RINGWORLD
THRONE

Prologue

THE MAP OF
MOUNT ST. HELENS

A.D. 1733	Fall of the Cities (Puppeteer Experimentalist regime introduces superconductor plague to Ringworld)
A.D. 2851	First contact: *Lying Bastard* impacts Ringworld
A.D. 2878	*Hot Needle of Inquiry* leaves Canyon
A.D. 2880	*Hot Needle of Inquiry* reaches Ringworld
A.D. 2881	Ringworld stability restored

A.D. 2882

The Hindmost danced.

They were dancing as far as the eye could see, beneath a ceiling that was a flat mirror. Tens of thousands of his kind moved in tight patterns that were great mutating curves, heads cocked high and low to keep their orientation. The clicking of their hooves was a part of the music, like a hundred thousand castanets.

Kick short, kick past, veer. One eye for your counterpartner. In this movement and the next, never glance toward the wall that hides the Brides. Never touch. For millions of years the competition dance, and a wide spectrum of other social vectors, had determined who would mate and who would not.

Beyond the illusion of the dance loomed the illusion of a window, distant and huge. The Hindmost's view of *Hidden Patriarch* was a distraction, a ground-rules hazard, an obstacle within the dance. *Extend a head; bow—*

The other three-legged dancers, the vast floor and ceiling, were projections from *Hot Needle of Inquiry*'s computer memory. Dancing maintained the Hindmost's skills, his reflexes, his health. This year had been a time for torpor, for recuperation and contemplation; but such states could change in an instant.

One Earthly year ago, or half of the puppeteer world's archaic year, or forty Ringworld rotations . . . the Hindmost and his alien thralls had found a mile-long sailing ship moored below the Map of Mars. They had named it *Hidden Patriarch* and set sail, leaving the Hindmost behind. The window in the Hindmost's dance was a real-time view from the webeye device in *Hidden Patriarch*'s fore crow's nest.

What the window showed was more real than the dancers.

Chmeee and Louis Wu lolled in the foreground. The Hindmost's servants-in-rebellion both looked a bit the worse for wear. The Hindmost's medical programs had restored them both to youth, not much more than two years ago. Young and healthy they still were, but soft and slothful, too.

Hind kick, touch hooves. Whirl, brush tongues.

The Great Ocean lay beneath a sea of fog. Wind-roiled fog made streamline patterns over the tremendous ship. At the shore the fog piled like a breaking wave. Only the crow's nests, six hundred feet tall, poked above the fog. Far inland, far across the white blanket, mountain peaks burst through, nearly black, with glittering peaks.

Hidden Patriarch had come home. The Hindmost was about to lose his alien companions.

The webeye picked up voices.

Louis Wu: "I'm pretty sure that's Mount Hood, and Mount Rainier there. *That* one I don't know, but if Mount St. Helens hadn't blown her top near a thousand years ago, that might be it."

Chmeee: "A Ringworld mountain doesn't explode unless you hit it with a meteor."

"*Precisely* my point. I think we'll be passing the map of San Francisco Bay inside of ten hours. The kind of wind and waves that build up on the Great Ocean, you'll need a decent bay for your lander, Chmeee. You can start your invasion there, if you don't mind being conspicuous."

"I like conspicuous." The Kzin stood and stretched, claws extended. Eight feet of fur tipped everywhere with daggers, a vision out of nightmare. The Hindmost had to remind himself that he faced only a hologram. The Kzin and *Hidden Patriarch* were 300,000 miles distant from the spacecraft buried beneath the Map of Mars.

Whirl, forefeet glide left, step left. Ignore the distraction.

The Kzin sat again. "This ship is fated, don't you think? Built to invade the Map of Earth. Pirated by Teela after she became a protector, to invade the Map of Mars and the Repair Center. Now *Hidden Patriarch* returns to invade the Earth again."

Within the Hindmost's crippled interstellar spacecraft, a rising, cooling wind blew through the cabin. The dance moved faster now. Sweat soaked the Hindmost's elegantly coiffed mane and rolled down his legs.

The window gave him more than visible light. By radar he could see the great bay, south by the map's orientation, and a crust of cities the archaic kzinti had built around its shore. The curve of a planet would have hidden that from him.

Louis said, "I'm going to miss you."

For a few moments it might be that his companion hadn't heard. Then the great mass of orange fur spoke without turning. "Louis. Over there are lords I can defeat and mates to bear my children. *There* is my place. Not yours. Over there, hominids are slaves, and they're not quite your species, either. You should not come, I should not stay."

"Did I say different? You go, I stay. I'm going to miss you."

"But against your intellect."

"Eh."

Chmeee said, "Louis, I heard a tale of you, years ago. I must learn the truth of it."

"Say on."

"After we returned to our worlds, after we gave over the puppeteer ship to be studied by our respective governments, Chtarra-Ritt invited you to make free of the hunting park outside Blood-of-Chwarambr City. You were the first alien ever to enter that place other than to die. You spent two days and a night within the grounds. What was it like?"

Louis was still on his back. "Mostly I loved it. Mostly for the honor, I think, but every so often a man has to test his luck."

"We heard a tale, the next night at Chtarra-Ritt's banquet."

"What did you hear?"

"You were in the inner quadrant, among the imports. You found a valuable animal—"

Louis sat bolt upright. "A white Bengal tiger! I'd found this nice green forest nesting in all that red and orange kzinti plant life, and I was feeling kind of safe and cozy and nostalgic. Then this—this lovely-but-oh-futz *maneater* stepped out of the bushes and looked me over. Chmeee, he was your size, maybe eight hundred pounds, and underfed. Sorry, go on."

"What is it? Bengal tiger?"

"Something of ours, from Earth. An ancient enemy, you could say."

"We were told that you stepped briskly past it to pick up a branch. Confronted the tiger and brandished the branch like a weapon and said, 'Do you remember?' The tiger turned away and left."

"Yah."

"Why did you do that? Do tigers talk?"

Louis laughed. "I thought he might go away if I didn't act like prey. If that didn't work, I thought I might whack him on the nose. There was this splintered tree, and a hardwood branch that looked just right for a club. And I talked to him because a Kzin might be listening. Being killed as an inept tourist in the Patriarch's hunting park would be bad enough. Dying as whimpering prey, *nyet*."

"Did you know the Patriarch had set you a guard?"

"No. I thought there might be monitors, cameras. I watched the tiger go. Turned around and was nose-to-nose with an armed Kzin. I jumped half out of my skin. Thought he was another tiger."

"He said he almost had to stun you. You challenged him. You were ready to club him."

"He said stun?"

"He did."

Louis Wu laughed. "He had an ARM stunner with a built-up handle. Your Patriarchy never learned how to make mercy weapons, so they have to buy them from the United Nations, I guess. I set myself to swing the club. He *dropped* the gun and extended his claws, and I saw he was a Kzin, and I laughed."

"How?"

Louis threw his head back and laughed, mouth wide, all teeth showing. From a Kzin that would have been a direct challenge, and Chmeee's ears went quite flat.

"Hahahahah! I couldn't help it. I was tanj lucky. He *wasn't* about to stun me. He'd have killed me with one swipe of his claws, but he got himself under control."

"Either way, an interesting story."

"Chmeee, a notion has crossed my mind. If we could get off the Ringworld, you'd want to return as Chmeee, wouldn't you?"

"Little chance that I would be known. The Hindmost's rejuvenation treatment erased my scars, too. I would seem little older than my oldest son, who must now be managing my estates."

"Yah. And the Hindmost might not cooperate—"

"I would not ask!"

"Would you ask me?"

Chmeee said, "I would not need to."

"I hadn't quite realized that the Patriarch might accept the word of Louis Wu as to your identity. But he would, wouldn't he?"

"I believe he would, Speaker-to-Tigers. But you have chosen to die."

Louis snorted. "Oh, Chmeee, I'm dying no faster than you are! I've got another fifty years, likely enough, and Teela Brown *slagged* the Hindmost's magical medical widgetry."

That, the Hindmost thought, was quite enough of that!

"He must have his own medical facilities on the command deck," the Kzin said.

"We can't get to those."

"And the kitchen had medical programs, Louis."

"And I'd be begging from a puppeteer."

Yet an interruption might infuriate them. Perhaps a distraction?

The speech of the puppeteers was more concise and flexible than any human or kzinti tongue. The Hindmost whistle-chirped a few phrases: *command* [] *dance* [] *drop one level in complexity* [] *again* [] *go to webeye six* Hidden Patriarch [] *transmit/receive* [] *send visual, sound, no smell, no texture, stunner off.* "Chmeee, Louis—"

They both jumped, then rolled to their feet, staring.

"Do I interrupt? I desire to show you certain pictures."

For a moment they simply watched the dance. The Hindmost could guess how silly he must look. Grins were spreading across both faces; though Louis's meant laughter and Chmeee's meant anger. "You've been spying," Chmeee said. "How?"

"Look up. Don't destroy it, Chmeee, but look above your head at the mast that supports the radio antenna. Just at the reach of your claws—"

The alien faces expanded hugely. Louis said, "Like a bronze spiderweb with a black spider at the center. Fractal pattern. Hard to see . . . hard to see where it stops, too. I thought some Ringworld insect was spinning these."

The Hindmost told them, "It's a camera, microphone, telescope, projector, and some other tools, too. It sprays on. I've left them in various places, not just this ship. Louis, can you summon your guests?" Whirtle: *command* [] *locate City Builders.* "I have something to show you. They should see this, too."

"What you're doing, it looks a little like Tai Kwon Do," Louis said.

Command [] *Seek: Tai Kwon Do.*

The information surfaced. A fighting style. Ridiculous: his species never fought. The Hindmost said, "I don't want to lose my muscle tone. The unexpected always comes at the most awkward times." A second window opened among the dancers: the City Builders were preparing a meal in the huge kitchen. "You must see—"

Chmeee's claws swiped at the puppeteer's eyes. Window Six blinked white and closed.

Kick. Weave past the Moment's Leader. Stand. Shift a millimeter; stand. Patience.

Avoid him they might. They had avoided him for ten hours now, and for half an archaic year before that; but they had to eat.

The wooden table was tremendous, the size of a kzinti banquet. A year ago the Hindmost had had to turn down the olfactory gain in the webeye, for the stench of old blood rising from the table. The smell was fainter now. Kzinti tapestries and crudely carved frescoes had been removed, too bloody for the hominids' taste. Some had been moved to Chmeee's cabin.

The smell of roasting fish was heavy on the air. Kawaresksenjajok and Harkabeeparolyn were doing things in the makeshift kitchen.

Their infant daughter seemed happy enough at one end of the table itself. At the other end, the raw half of a huge fish awaited the Kzin's pleasure.

Chmeee eyed the fish. "Your luck was good," he approved. His eyes roved the ceiling and walls. He found what he sought: a glittering fractal spiderweb just under the great orange bulb at the apex of the dome.

The City Builders entered, wiping their hands. Kawaresksenjajok, a boy not much past adolescence; Harkabeeparolyn, his mate, some years older; both quite bald across the crowns of their heads, their hair descending to cover their shoulder blades. Harkabeeparolyn picked up the baby and gave it suck. Kawaresksenjajok said, "We lose you soon."

Chmeee said, "We have a spy. I thought as much, but now we know it. The puppeteer placed cameras among us."

The boy laughed at his anger. "We would do the same to him. To seek knowledge is natural!"

"In less than a day I will be free of the eyes of the puppeteer. Kawa, Harkee, I will miss you greatly. Your company, your knowledge, your skewed wisdom. But my thought will be mine alone!"

I'm losing them all, the Hindmost thought. Survival suggests that I build a road to take them back to me. He said, "Folk, will you give me an hour to entertain you?"

The City Builders gaped. The Kzin grinned. Louis Wu said, "Entertain . . . sure."

"If you'll turn off the light?"

Louis did that. The puppeteer whistle-sang. He was looking through the display, watching their faces.

Where the webeye had been, now they saw a window: a view through blowing rain, down past the rim of a vast plate. Far below, pale humanoid shapes swarmed in their hundreds. They seemed gregarious enough. They rubbed against each other without hostility, and here and there they mated without seeking privacy.

"This is present time," the Hindmost said. "I've been monitoring this site since we restored the Ringworld's orbit."

Kawaresksenjajok said, "Vampires. Flup, Harkee, have you ever seen so many together?"

Louis asked, "Well?"

"Before I brought our probe back to the Great Ocean. I used it to spray webeyes. You're seeing that region we first explored, on the highest structure I could find, to give me the best view. Alas for my view, rain and cloud have obscured it ever since. But, Louis, you can see that there is life here."

"Vampires."

"Kawaresksenjajok, Harkabeeparolyn, this is to port of where you lived. Can you see that life is thriving here? You could return."

The woman was waiting, postponing judgment. The boy was torn. He said a word in his own language, untranslatable.

"Don't promise what you can't deliver," said Louis Wu.

"Louis, you have evaded me ever since we saved the Ringworld. Always you speak as if we turned a blowtorch hundreds of thousands of miles across on inhabited terrain. I've questioned your numbers. You don't listen. See for yourself, they still live!"

"Wonderful," Louis said. "The vampires lived through it!"

"More than vampires. Watch." The Hindmost whistled; the view zoomed on distant mountains.

Thirty-odd hominids marched through a pass between peaks. Twenty-one vampires; six of the small red-skinned herders they'd seen on their last visit; five of a bigger, darker hominid creature; two of a small-headed variety, perhaps not sapient. All of the prey were naked, and none were trying to escape. They were tired but joyful. Each member of another species had a vampire companion. Only a few vampires wore clothing against the chill and the rain. The clothing was clearly borrowed, cut to fit something other than what wore it.

Vampires weren't sapient at all, or so the Hindmost had been told. He wondered if animals would keep slaves or livestock . . . but never mind. "Louis, Chmeee, do you see? Here are other species, also alive. I even saw a City Builder once."

Louis Wu said, "I don't see cancer and I don't see mutations, but they must be there. Hindmost, I got my information from Teela Brown. Teela was a protector, brighter than you and me. One and a half trillion deaths, she said."

The Hindmost said, "Teela was intelligent, but I see her as human, Louis. Even after her change: human. Humans don't look directly at danger. Puppeteers you call cowards, but not to look is cowardice—"

"Drop it. It's been a year. Cancers can take ten or twenty. Mutations take a whole generation."

"Protectors have their limits! Teela had no notion of the *power* of my computers. You left me to make the adjustments, Louis—"

"*Drop* it."

"I will continue to look," the puppeteer said.

The Hindmost danced. The marathon would continue until he made a mistake. He was pushing himself toward exhaustion; his body would heal and then grow strong.

He had not bothered to eavesdrop through the aliens' dinner. Chmeee had not slashed the webeye, but they would not speak secrets in its view.

They need not. A year past, while his motley crew was still trying to settle the matter of Teela Brown and the Ringworld's instability, the Hindmost's flying probe had sprayed webeyes all over *Hidden Patriarch*.

He would rather have been concentrating on the dance.

Time enough for that. Chmeee would be gone soon. Louis would revert to silence. In another year he, too, might leave the ship, leave the Hindmost's control. The City Builder librarians . . . work on them?

They were lost to him already, in a sense. The Hindmost

controlled *Needle*'s medical facilities. If they saw that he used his power for extortion, they saw nothing but the truth. But he had been too direct. Chmeee and Louis had both refused medical attention.

They were walking briskly down a shadowed corridor, Louis Wu and Chmeee. Reception was poor in so little light, but they wouldn't see the web. The Hindmost caught only part of the dialogue. He played it back several times afterward.

Louis: "—dominance game. The Hindmost *has* to control us. We're too close to him, we could conceivably hurt him."

Chmeee: "I've tried to see a way."

Louis: "How hard? Never mind. He left us alone for a year, then interrupted himself in the middle of an exercise routine. Why bother? Nothing about that broadcast looked urgent."

Chmeee: "I know how *you* think. He overheard us, didn't he? If I can return to the Patriarchy, I won't need the Hindmost to recover my properties. I have you. You do not exact a price."

Louis: "Yah."

The Hindmost considered interrupting. To say what?

Chmeee: "By my lost lands he controlled me, but how did he control you? He had you by the wire, but you gave up your addiction. The autodoc in the lander was destroyed, but surely the kitchen has a program to make boosterspice?"

"Likely enough. For you, too."

Chmeee dismissed that with a wave. "But if you allow yourself to grow old, he has nothing."

Louis nodded.

"But would the Hindmost believe you? To a puppeteer . . . I do not insult you. I'm sure you speak the truth, Louis. But to a puppeteer, to let yourself grow old is suicide."

Louis nodded, silent.

"Is this justice for a trillion murders?"

Louis would have broken off conversation on another night. He said, "Justice for us both. I die of old age. The Hindmost loses his thralls . . . loses control of his environment."

"But if they lived?"

"If they lived. Yah. The Hindmost did the actual programming. I couldn't go into that section of the Repair Center. It was infested with tree-of-life. I made it possible for *him* to spray a plasma jet from the sun across five percent of the Ringworld. If he didn't do that, then *I* can . . . live. So the Hindmost owns me again. And that's important, if *I'm* the reason he doesn't own *you*."

"Exactly."

"So show Louis an old recording and say it's a live broadcast—"

The wind was rising, gusts drowning the voices. Chmeee: "What if . . . numbers . . ."

". . . Hindmost to drop it . . ."

". . . brain is aging faster than the rest of you!" The Kzin lost patience, dropped to all fours and bounded away down the deck. It didn't matter. They were out of range.

The Hindmost screamed like the world's biggest espresso device tearing itself apart.

In his scream were pitches and overtones no creature of Earth or Kzin could hear, with harmonics that held considerable information. Lineages for two species barely out of the veldt, down from the trees. Designs for equipment that would cause a sun to flare, then cause the flare to lase, a cannon of Ringworld scale. Specs for computer equipment miniaturized to the quantum level, sprayed across the Hindmost's cabin like a coat of paint. Programs of vast resiliency and power.

You twisted rejects from half-savage, half-sapient breeds! Your pitiful protector, your luck-bred Teela, hadn't the flexibility or the understanding, but you don't even have the wit to listen. I saved them all! I, with software from my ship!

One shriek and the Hindmost was calm again. He hadn't missed a step. *Back one, bow, while the Moment's Leader engages the Brides in quadret: a chance to get a drink of water, badly needed.* One head lowered to suck, one raised to watch the dance: sometimes there were variations.

Was Louis Wu going senile? So quickly? He was well over two hundred years old. Boosterspice had kept some humans hale and sapient for half a thousand years, sometimes more. But without his medical benefits, Louis Wu might age fast.

And Chmeee would be gone.

No matter. The Hindmost was in the safest place imaginable. His ship was buried in cubic miles of cooled magma near the center of the Ringworld Repair Center. Nothing was urgent. He could wait. There were the librarians. Something would change . . . and there was the dance.

Part One

THE
SHADOW
NEST

Chapter One

A WAR OF
SCENTS

A.D. 2892

Cloud covered the sky like a gray stone plate. The yellow grass had a wilted look: too much rain, not enough sun. No doubt the sun was straight overhead and the Arch was still in place, but Valavirgillin hadn't seen either for twenty days now.

The cruisers rolled through an endless drizzle, through high grass, on wheels as tall as a man. Vala and Kay rode the steering bench; Barok rode above them as gunner. Barok's daughter Forn was asleep under an awning.

Any day now—any hour—

Sabarokaresh pointed. "Is that what you've been looking for?"

Valavirgillin stood up in her seat. She could just see where the vastness of grass turned to a vastness of stubble.

Kaywerbrimmis said, "They leave this pattern. We'll be seeing sentries or a harvesting party. Boss, I don't understand how you knew they'd be Grass Giants here. I've never been this far to starboard myself. You, you're from Center City? That's a hundred daywalks to port."

"Word came to me," Valavirgillin said.

He didn't ask more. A merchant's secrets were her own.

They rolled into the stubble and turned. The cruisers rolled faster now. Stubble to right, shoulder-high grass to the left. Far ahead, birds were wheeling and diving. Big dark birds: scavengers.

Kaywerbrimmis touched his handguns for reassurance. Muzzle-loading, the barrels as long as his forearm. Big Sabarokaresh eased back into the turret. The top of the payload shell housed the cannon, and that might be needed. The other wagons were swinging left and right, covering Kay's wagon so that he could investigate in safety.

The birds wheeled away. They'd left black feathers everywhere. Twenty big birds, gorged until they could hardly fly. What might feed so many?

Bodies. Little hominids with pointy skulls, lying some in stubble, some in uncut grass, stripped of most of their meat. Hundreds! They might have been children, but the children among them were even smaller.

Vala looked for clothing. In strange terrain you never knew which hominids might be intelligent.

Sabarokaresh dropped to earth, gun in hand. Kaywerbrimmis hesitated; but nothing sudden popped out of the grass, and he followed. Foranayeedli popped a sleepy head through the window and gaped. She was a girl of sixty falans or so, just reaching mating age.

"Since last night," Kay said presently.

The smell of corruption wasn't strong yet. If Ghouls hadn't arrived before the birds, then these victims must have been slain near dawn. Vala asked, "How did they die? If this is local Grass Giant practice, we want none of it."

"This could've been done by birds. Cracked bones, see?

But cracked by big beaks, for marrow. These are Gleaners, Boss. See, this is how they dress, in feathers. They follow the harvesters. The Gleaners hunt smeerps, firedots, anything that digs. Cutting the grass exposes the burrows."

—Feathers, right. These feathers were black and red and purple-green, not just black. "So what happened here?"

Forn said, "I know that smell."

Beneath the corruption: what? Something familiar, not itself unpleasant . . . but it made Foranayeedli uneasy.

Valavirgillin had hired Kaywerbrimmis to lead the caravan because he was local, because he seemed competent. The rest were his people. None had ever been this far to starboard.

Vala knew more of this place than any of them . . . if she was right about where she was.

"Well, where are they?"

"Watching us, maybe," Kay said.

Vala could see a long way from her perch at the bow of the cruiser. The veldt was flat, the yellow grass was chopped short. Grass Giants stood seven and eight feet tall. Where grass stood half their height, could they hide in that?

The traders pulled their cruisers into a triangle. Their midday dinner was fruit and roots from stores on the running boards. They cooked some local grass with the roots. They'd caught no fresh meat.

They took their time. Most hominids were more approachable after feeding. If Grass Giants thought like Machine People, they would let strangers eat before they made contact.

No ambassador came. The caravan rolled on.

Three cruisers rolled sluggishly across the veldt with no

animal to pull them. Big square wooden platforms rode four wheels at the corners; the motor, centered aft, turned two more drive wheels. The cast-iron payload shell rode ahead of the motor, like an iron house with a fat chimney. Big leaf springs were under the bow, under the steering bench. A savage might wonder at the tower on the payload housing, but what would he think if he had never seen a cannon?

Harmless.

Shapes the color of the golden grass, shapes too big to be men: two big humanoids watched from the crest of a far hill. Vala saw them only when one turned and loped away across the veldt. The other ran along the crest, toward where the cruisers would cross.

He waited in their path, watching them come. He was nearly the color of the golden grass: golden skin, golden mane. Big. Armed with a great curved sword.

Kaywerbrimmis walked to meet the giant. Valavirgillin set the cruiser following him like a friendly ridebeast.

Distance put strange twists in the trade dialect. Kaywerbrimmis had tried to teach Vala some of the variations in pronunciation, new words and altered meanings. She listened now, trying to make out what Kay was saying.

"We come in peace . . . intend to trade . . . Farsight Trading . . . rishathra?"

The giant's eyes flicked back and forth while Kay talked. Back and forth between their jaws, Forn and Vala and Kay and Barok. The giant was amused.

His face was hairier than any Machine Person's! Pretty Forn's jawline fringe of beard just growing, just long enough to take a curl at the corners. Vala's was turning elegantly white, two points at the chin. Other hominids were too often distracted by Machine People beards, especially on the women.

The giant waited out Kay's chattering, then strode past

him and took a seat on the cruiser's running board. He leaned against the payload shell and immediately jerked away from the hot metal. Recovered his dignity and waved the cruiser forward.

Big Barok held his post above the giant. Forn climbed up beside her father. She was tall, too, but the giant made them both look stunted.

Kaywerbrimmis asked, "Your camp, that way?"

The giant's dialect was less comprehensible. "Yes. Come. You want shelter. We want warriors."

"How do you practice rishathra?" It was the first thing any trader would want to know, and any beta male, too, if these were like Grass Giants elsewhere.

The giant said, "Come quick, else learn too much of rishathra."

"What?"

"Vampires."

Forn's eyes widened. "That smell!"

Kay smiled, seeing not a threat, but an opportunity. "I am Kaywerbrimmis. Here are Valavirgillin, my patron, and Sabarokaresh and Foranayeedli. In the other cruisers they are Machine People, too. We hope to persuade you to join our Empire."

"I am Paroom. Our leader you must address as Thurl."

Vala let Kay do the talking. Grass Giant sword-scythes had too little reach. Farsight Trading's guns would make short work of a vampire attack. That should impress the Bull, and then—business.

Grass Giants, scores of them, were pulling wagons filled with grass through the gap in a wall of heaped earth.

"This isn't normal," Kaywerbrimmis said. "Grass Giants don't build walls."

Paroom heard. "We had to learn. Forty-three falans ago the Reds were fighting us. We learned walls from them."

Forty-three falans was 430 rotations of the star patterns, where the sky rotated every seven and a half days. In forty falans Valavirgillin had made herself rich, had mated, had carried four children, then gambled her wealth away. These last three falans she had been traveling.

Forty-three falans was a long time.

She asked or tried to ask, "Was that when the clouds came?"

"Yes, when the old Thurl boiled a sea."

Yes! This was the place she sought.

Kaywerbrimis shrugged it off as local superstition. "How long have you had vampires?"

Paroom said, "Always there are some. In this last few falans, suddenly they are everywhere, more every night. This morning we found nearly two hundred Gleaners, all dead. Tonight they will hunger again. The walls and our crossbows hold them back. Here," said the sentry, "bring your wagons through the gap and prepare them to fight."

They had *crossbows?*

And the light was going.

It was crowded inside the walls. Grass Giant men and women were unloading their wagons, pausing frequently to eat of the grass. They looked up as the Machine People moved among them; they gaped, then returned to work. Had they ever seen self-propelled cruisers? But vampires were a more urgent concern.

Already men in leather armor lined the wall. Others were heaping earth and stones to close the gap.

Vala could feel the Grass Giants staring at her beard.

She could count roughly a thousand of them, as many women as men. But women outnumbered the men among Grass Giants elsewhere, and she didn't see *any* children. Add a few hundred more, then, for women tending children somewhere in the buildings.

A great alien silver shape strode down the slope to meet them.

It lifted its crested helm to reveal a golden mane. The Thurl was the biggest of Grass Giant males. The armor he wore bulged at every joint; he looked like no hominid Vala had ever seen.

"Thurl," Kaywerbrimmis said carefully, "Farsight Trading has come to help."

"Good. What are you, Machine People? We hear of you."

"Our Empire is mighty, but we spread through trade, not war. We hope to persuade your people to make fuel for us, and bread, and other things. Your kind of grass can make good bread; you might like it yourselves. In return we can show you wonders. The least are our guns. These handguns, they'll reach farther than your crossbows. For close work we have flamers—"

"Killing-things, are they? Our good luck that you have come. Yours, too, to reach cover. You should move your guns to the wall now."

"Thurl, the big guns are mounted on the cruisers."

The wall stood twice the height of a Machine Person. But Valavirgillin remembered a local word. "Ramp. Thurl, is there a ramp that leads up the wall? Will it carry our cruisers?"

The day's colors were turning charcoal-gray. It was starting to rain. Far above these clouds, the shadow of night must have nearly covered the sun.

And there wasn't any ramp, until the Thurl bellowed his orders. Then all the huge males and females broke from their labor and began moving earth.

Vala noted one woman climbing, guiding, shouting. Big, mature, with a voice to shatter rocks. She caught a name: Moonwa. Perhaps the Thurl's primary wife.

Metal payload shell and metal motor, and wide timber running boards a hand thick: a cruiser was heavy. The ramp tended to crumble. The cruisers went up one by one, with the wall brushing their right sides and ten Grass Giant males lifting and steadying on the left. How would they get the cruisers *down*?

The top was as wide as a cruiser wheelbase. Sentries guided them. "Face your weapons starboard-spin. Vampires come from there."

The wagonmasters placed their vehicles, then met to confer. Kay asked, "Whand, Anth, what do you think? Shrapnel in the cannon? They might bunch up. They often do."

Anthrantillin said, "Have the giants gather some gravel. Save our shot. This will be handgun work, though. Spread out?"

Whandernothtee said, "That's what the giants want."

"Me, too," Kaywerbrimmis said.

Vala said, "The Grass Giants have crossbows. Why are they worried? Crossbows won't have the reach of guns, but they'll outreach vampire scent."

The wagonmasters looked at each other. Anth said, "Grass eaters—"

"Oh, no. Elsewhere they're considered scary fighters," Whand said.

Nobody answered.

Whandernothtee's cruiser and Anthrantillin's rolled off in opposite directions. They were almost invisible in the rain and dark before the Grass Giant warriors stopped them.

Kaywerbrimmis said, "Barok, you on the cannon, but keep your guns handy. I'm on handguns. Forn, reload." She was too young to be trusted to do more. "Boss, do you like the flamer?"

Vala said, "They'll never get that close. I throw pretty good, too."

"Flamer and fistbombs, then. I hope we do get to use the flamer. It'd help if we could show them another use for alcohol. Grass Giants don't need our fuel, they pull their own wagons. Vampires aren't intelligent, are they?"

"The ones near Center City aren't."

Forn said, "In most languages it's *vampires*, not *Vampires*. They take the prefix for animals."

Language wasn't Kay's interest. "Do they charge, Boss? One big wave?"

"I only fought vampires once."

"That's one more than me. I hear stories. What was it like?"

"I was the only survivor," Valavirgillin said. "Kay? Just stories? Do you know enough to use towels and fuel?"

Kay's brow furrowed. "What?"

—and Vala's head whipped around at a sentry's bass call.

All was shadows now, and a sound that might be wind through taut cords, and the whisper of crossbows. The Grass Giants were being chary of their bolts. Bullets weren't replaceable, either, where there was no client race to make more.

Vala couldn't see anything yet. For the Grass Giants it would be no darker, but these plains were their home. A crossbow whispered, and something pale stood up and fell over. The wind picked up . . . that wasn't wind.

Song.

"Look for white," Forn called unnecessarily. Kay fired, changed guns, fired.

It was well that the cruisers were spaced far apart. The

flash of their handguns was blinding. Vala thought it over, while the fire balloons in her eyes faded. Then she rolled under the cruiser and pulled the flamer and the net bag of fistbombs after. Let the cruiser shield her eyes from the flash.

And the cannon?

They were firing around her. Her sight was back. There, a pale hominid shape. Another. She could see twenty and more! One fell, and the rest backed away. Already most of them must be beyond crossbow range. Their song plucked at her nerves.

"Cannon," Barok commented, and she closed her eyes just as he fired.

Fire was trying to light in the stubble. There were pale bodies, six . . . eight. Thirty or forty vampires stood in plain view, still in gun range, she thought.

Why would men with crossbows fear vampires? Because nobody had ever seen so many vampires together!

It was bizarre, insane. How could so many feed themselves?

High Rangers Trading Group had died in a tower in a deserted city, forty-three falans ago. High Rangers had fought no more than fifteen, that night. Killed no more than eight. All the rest had died, and only a fluke had saved Valavirgillin.

She remembered the song wafting up from the street. The vampires pale, naked, beautiful. The terror. High Rangers had fired from tenth-floor windows, and posted sentries down along the stairwell. One by one the sentries had disappeared, and then—

Kay said, "The wind's blowing right."

Barok said, "Cannon."

She clenched her eyelids against the flash. Barok's cannon roared, then one from farther away, barely heard.

Barok's voice was faint. "They could circle."

"They're not sapient," Kay said.

To left, another distant cannon fired. To right, another.

Vampires carried no tools, wore no clothing. Reach into the lovely wealth of ash-blond hair on a vampire's corpse: you would find too much hair around a small, flat skull. They built no cities, formed no armies, invented no encircling movements.

But the warriors on the wall were buzzing among themselves, pointing, firing bolts into the dark to spin and starboard and antispin.

"Kay? They've got noses."

Barok looked down. Kay said, "What?"

"They don't have a battle plan," Valavirgillin said. "They're just avoiding the smell of fifteen hundred Grass Giants served by a primitive sewer system. It's the same smell that brought them here! When they get upwind of that, the smell won't bother them anymore. And then *we'll* be downwind from *them*."

"I'll get Whandernothtee to move his cruiser around," Barok said, and ran.

Vala bellowed after him. "Cloth and alcohol!"

He came back. "What?"

"Pour fuel into a towel, just a splash. Tie it around your face. It keeps the scent out. Tell Whand!"

Kay spoke from overhead. "I still have targets here. Boss, they're not in throwing range. *You* go tell Anth to move. Tell him about towels and fuel. Then the Grass Giants might not know, either. Boss? Remember I wanted to show them some use for fuel?"

Idiot. She splashed a towel for herself and took two more with her. This could turn urgent.

In the dark, with a drop on either side, she had to watch her footing. It had stopped raining. The song of the vampires rode the wind. She breathed alcohol fumes from the towel around her face. It made her dizzy.

She heard distantly, "Cannon." Closed her eyes, waited for the roar, walked on toward a square shadow. She called, "Anthrantillin!"

"He's busy, Vala." Taratarafasht's voice.

"He'll be very busy, Tarfa. The vamps are circling round. Get your towels out, splash them with fuel, tie them over your mouths. Then move the truck a sixth around the arc."

"Valavirgillin, I take my orders from Anthrantillin."

Fool woman. "Get the cruiser into place or you can both tell it to the Ghouls. Get a towel on Anth, too. But first give me a fuel jar for the giants."

Pause. "Yes, Valavirgillin. Do you have enough towels?"

The fuel jar was heavy. Valavirgillin was terribly conscious of the weapons she wasn't holding. When the big shape loomed before her, she was embarrassingly relieved.

The Grass Giant didn't turn. "How goes the defense, Valavirgillin?"

Vala said, "They're circling us. You'll smell them in a minute. Tie this—"

"*Fowh!* What stink is that?"

"Alcohol. It moves our cruisers, but it may save us. Tie this around your neck."

The guard didn't move, didn't look at her. He wouldn't insult an alien guest. So: *Valavirgillin has not spoken.*

She didn't have time for games. "Point me toward the Thurl."

"Give me the cloth."

She threw it to him underhand. He snorted in disgust, but

he was tying it around his neck. He pointed then, but she'd already seen the shine of the Bull's armor.

The Bull looked at the cloth in her hands even as he backed away from the stink. "But why?"

"You don't *know* about vampires?"

"Stories come to us. Vampires die easily enough, and they don't *think*. As for the rest . . . should the cloth cover our ears?"

"Why, Thurl?"

"So that they cannot sing us to our deaths."

"Not sound. Smell!"

"Smell?"

Grass Giants weren't idiots, but . . . they'd been unlucky. First somebody has to live through a vampire attack. Even if a child survives, he won't know why the adults all went away. She, Kay, *someone* should have raised this subject, no matter the rush.

"Vampires put out a mating scent, Thurl. Your lust rises and your brain turns off and you *go*."

"The stink of your fuel, it cures the problem? But isn't there another problem? We hear of you Machine People and your empire of fuel. You persuade other hominid species to make alcohol for your wagons. They learn to drink it. They lose interest in work and play and life itself, anything but the fuel, and they die young."

Vala laughed. "Vampire scent does all of that before you can take a hundred breaths." Still, the Thurl had a point. *Do we want crossbowmen drunk while vampires circle the wall?*

"Is fuel better? Try strong herbs?"

"When can you pick these herbs? I have fuel now, not tomorrow."

The Bull turned from her and began bellowing orders. Most of the males were on the wall now, but women began running. Bales of cloth appeared. Women climbed up the wall and along the top to the cruisers. Vala waited with what patience she could muster.

The Bull roared, "Come!" He entered an earthen building, the second largest.

It was fabric stretched over the top of a dirt wall and one central pole. Here were tall heaps of dried grass, but other plants too, a thousand scents. The Bull crushed leaves under her nose. She shied back. A different leaf; she sniffed gingerly. Another.

She said, "Try all of those, but try fuel too. We'll find out what works best. Why do you store these?"

The Bull laughed. "Flavoring, these, pepperleek and minch. Woman eats this, makes her milk better. Did you think we eat only grass? Wilted or sour grass needs something for taste."

The Bull gathered armfuls of plants and strode out bellowing. She could have heard his roar in Center City, she thought. His voice and the women's, and presently the scuff of their big feet as they climbed.

Vala retrieved her fuel bottle and climbed after.

From the top she watched the big shadows, warriors motionless, women moving among them distributing impregnated towels. Vala intercepted a big, mature woman. "Moonwa?"

"Valavirgillin. They kill by *smell*?"

"They do. We don't know what smell protects best. Some men already have alcohol-scented towels. Leave them those, give the Thurl's plants to the rest. We'll see."

"See who dies, eh?"

Vala walked on. The alcohol fumes were making her a little giddy. She could handle it, and for that matter her towel was nearly dry.

This morning Vala had been thinking that Forn was mature enough to practice rishathra, or perhaps to mate straight off. Forn had beaten that prediction. She could hardly be remembering the smell of vampires. She'd recognized the scent of a lover!

That old scent of lust and death was into Valavirgillin's nose and nibbling on her brain.

The Grass Giant warriors were still shadows amid the moving shadows of women. But . . . they were fewer.

The Grass Giant women had noticed, too. Breathy screams of rage and fear; then two, four, ran down the embankment shouting for the Thurl. Another ran the wrong way down, moaning, out onto the stubbly field.

Vala moved among the remaining defenders, sloshing fuel on towels. Women, men, whoever she could find. Haste would kill. Fuel would protect. Herbs? Well, the smell of the Thurl's herbs might last longer.

In every direction she could see pale hominid shapes. So little detail. You had to imagine what they looked like; and with the scent tickling your hindbrain, you saw glorious fantasies.

They were closer. Why wasn't she hearing guns? She'd reached Anthrantillin's cruiser. Up onto the running board. "Hello? Anth?"

The payload shell was empty.

She used the trick lock and climbed into the payload shell.

All gone. No damage, no trace of a fight; just gone.

Soak a towel. Then: the cannon. The vampires were bunching nicely to spin. Bunching around Anth or Forn or

Himp, somewhere down there? It didn't matter. She fired and saw half of them fall.

Sometime during that night she heard a repeated whisper of sound. "Anthrantillin?"

"Gone," she said, and couldn't hear her own voice. She screamed, "Gone! It's Valavirgillin!" and barely heard that. Her bellow, his bellow, reduced to whispers by the cannon's ear-shattering roar.

It was time to move the cruiser. The vampires had pulled way back here, they'd learned not to bunch, but she might find fresh prey elsewhere. Guns weren't needed on the starboard and spin sides. Upwind from the vampires, crossbows would reach them.

"It's Kay. Are they all gone?"

"Yes."

"We're low on firepower. You?"

"Plenty."

"We won't have any fuel come morning."

"No. I set all mine out and told the women about it. I thought—Moonwa, the Grass Giant who was forcing towels on the warriors—teach her to use the cannon? Do we want—"

"No, Boss, no. Secrets!"

"Take too long to train her anyway."

Kay's head rose into the cannoneer's chamber. He pulled out a jug of gunpowder, hefted it with a grunt. "Back to work."

"Do you need smallshot?"

"Plenty of rocks." He looked at her. Froze. He set the jug down.

She slid down. They moved together.

"Should have soaked that towel again," she said unsteadily. It was her last coherent thought for some time.

He, not Vala, *Kay* wriggled out of the door and splashed into mud in a blowing rain. Vala followed, to snatch him back.

He ripped her shirt off. She pressed herself against him, but he howled and ripped it again, and turned in her arms, and turned back with two dripping half shirts and pushed one into her face and one into his own.

She breathed deeply of alcohol fumes. Choked. "All right."

He gave it to her. He tied the other around his own neck. "I'm going back," he said. "You'd better fight your gun alone. Under the—"

"—circumstances." They laughed shakily. "Are you safe? Alone?"

"Have to try it."

She watched him go.

She should never. Never. Never have mated with another man. Her mind, her *self* had washed away in a tide of lust. What would Tarb think of her?

Mating with Tarablilliast had never been so intense.

But now her mind was flowing back. She *was* mated.

She lifted the towel to her face. The alcohol went straight to her head and cleared it, unless that was an illusion. She looked along the wall and saw big shadows, too few, but some. Hominid shapes in the black fields were also fewer, but very close. They were taller, more slender than her own species. They sang; they implored; they were bunched almost beneath the cruiser.

She climbed up and loaded her cannon.

Chapter Two

RECOVERY

A pale light was growing, lighter to spin. The song was over. Vala hadn't heard a crossbow twang in some time. Vampires had become hard to find.

Unnoticed, the dreadful night had ended.

If she had ever been this tired, exhaustion must have wiped the memory clean. And here was Kaywerbrimmis asking, "Do you have any smallshot left?"

"Some. We never got our gravel."

"Barok and Forn were both gone when I got back to the cruiser."

Vala rubbed her eyes. There didn't seem to be anything to say.

Whandernothtee and Sopashintay came up leaning on each other. Whand said, "What a night."

Spash said, "Chit liked the singing overmuch. We had to tie him up. I think I put too much fuel, in his towel. He's sleeping like . . . like I would if I could just—" She hugged herself. "—just stop jittering."

Sleep. And several hundred Grass Giant males were expecting— "I couldn't handle rishathra now," Vala said.

She'd put off the memory of mating with Kay. That could have consequences.

Kaywerbrimmis said, "Sleep in the cruisers. At least for to-night. Hello—" His hand on her shoulder turned her around.

Company. Nine Grass Giants and a suit of silver armor had come among them. You could see their exhaustion, and smell it. The Thurl asked, "How is it with you Machine People?"

"Half of us are missing," Valavirgillin said.

Whand said, "Thurl, we never expected so many. We thought we had weapons for anything."

"Travelers tell that vampires *sing* us to our doom."

Kay said, "Half of wisdom is learning what to unlearn."

"We were prepared for the wrong enemy. Vampire scent! We never guessed. But we've set the vampires running!" the Thurl boomed. "Shall we hunt them through the grass?"

Whand threw up his arms and staggered away.

Vala and Kay and Spash looked at each other. If Grass Giant warriors could still fight . . . Whand was done, used up, but *someone* had to stand up for the Machine People.

They trailed the warriors down into the wet stubble.

Shapes stirred at the foot of the wall. Two hominids, na-ked. Crossbows and guns swung around. Arms batted them aside, voices barked. *No! Not vampires!* A big woman and a little male were helping each other to stand.

Not vampires, no. A Grass Giant woman and— "Barok!"

Sabarokaresh's face was slack with a terror too deep to touch surface. He looked at Valavirgillin as if she were the ghost, not he. Half mad, dirty, exhausted, scarred, alive.

I thought I was tired! Vala thumped his shoulder, glad to feel him solid under her hand. Where was his daughter? She didn't ask. She said, "You must have quite a tale to tell. Later?"

The Thurl spoke to the crossbowman, Paroom. Paroom led/pulled Barok and the Grass Giant woman up the slope.

The Thurl moved at a trot, away from the wall, to starboard-spin. His people followed, and then the Machine People. A night of sleepless terror and wild mating had left them all without strength.

They passed vampire corpses. None of their beauty survived into death. A Grass Giant stopped to examine a female skewered by a crossbow. Spash stopped too.

Vala remembered doing that, forty-three falans ago. *First you smell rotting flesh. Then the other scent explodes under your mind—*

The Grass Giant lurched clear. He stayed head down, vomiting, then slowly straightened, still hiding his face. Spash straightened suddenly, then wobbled toward Vala and hid her face against her shoulder.

Valavirgillin said, "Spash. You haven't *done* anything, love. It feels like you want to mate with a corpse, but that's not your *mind* talking."

"Not my mind. Vala, if we can't examine them, we can't learn about them!"

"It's part of what makes them so scary." Lust and the smell of rotting meat do not belong together in one brain.

Vampires near the wall had crossbow bolts in them. Farther out, they were chewed by balls or smallshot. Vala saw that Machine People had scored as many kills as a hundred times as many Grass Giants.

Two hundred paces beyond the wall, they weren't finding vampires any more. Dead Grass Giants lay naked or half clothed, gaunt, with sunken eyes and cheeks, and savage wounds in their necks, wrists, elbows.

That slack face . . . Vala had seen this woman run out into the dark hours ago. Where were the wounds? Her throat seemed untouched. Left arm thrown wide, wrist unmarred; right arm across her body, no blood on the rucked-up tunic . . . Vala stepped forward and lifted her right hand.

Her armpit was torn and bloody. A Grass Giant man turned and wobbled back toward the wall, retching.

Big woman, small vampire. Couldn't reach her neck. Spash is right, we have to learn.

Farther along, bright cloth lay near the grass border. Vala began to run, then stopped as suddenly. That was Taratarafasht's work suit.

Vala picked it up. It was clean. No blood, no ground-in dirt. Why had Tarfa been brought so far? Where was she?

The Thurl had outrun his party by a good distance. He'd almost reached uncut grass. How much did that armor weigh? He scrambled up a ten-pace-high knoll, then paused at the top, waiting while the rest straggled up.

"No sign of vampires," he said. "They've gone to cover somewhere. Travelers say they can't stand sunlight . . . ?"

Kay said, "That tale's true."

The Thurl continued, "Then I'd say they're gone."

Nobody spoke.

The Thurl boomed, "Beedj!"

"Thurl!" A male trotted up: mature, bigger than most, eager, indecently energetic.

"With me, Beedj. Tarun, you'll circle and meet us on the other side. If you're not there I'll assume you found a fight."

"Yes."

Beedj and the Thurl went one way, the rest of the Giants went the other. Vala dithered, then followed the Thurl.

The Thurl noticed her. He slowed and let her catch up.
Beedj would have waited, too, but the Thurl's gesture sent
him on.

The Thurl said, "We won't find live vampires hiding in
the grass. Grass grows straight up. Night slides across the sun,
but the sun never moves, not anymore. Where can a vampire
hide from sunlight?"

Vala asked, "Do you remember when the sun moved?"

"I was a child. A frightening time." He didn't seem frightened enough, Vala thought. Louis Wu had been among these
people; but what Louis had told Valavirgillin, he didn't seem
to have told them.

It's a ring, he said. *The Arch is the part of the ring you're not
standing on. The sun has started to wobble because the ring is off
center. In several falans the ring will brush the sun. But I swear
I will stop it, or die trying.*

Later the sun had stopped wobbling.

Beedj was still jogging, stopping here and there to examine bodies; swinging his sword to cut a swath of grass to see
what it hid; eating what he cut as he resumed his patrol. He
was burning more energy than the Thurl. Vala had seen no
challenge between them—easy command and easy submis-
sion—but she became sure that she was watching the next
Thurl.

She nerved herself to ask, "Thurl, did an unknown hominid come among you claiming to be from a place in the sky?"

The Thurl stared. "In the *sky?*"

He could hardly have forgotten, but he might hide secrets.
"A male wizard. Bald narrow face, bronze skin, straight black
scalp hair, taller than my kind and narrow in the shoulders
and hip." Fingertips lifted and stretched the corners of her
eyes. "Eyes like *this.* He boiled a sea hereabouts, to end a
plague of mirror-flowers."

The Thurl was nodding. "It was done by the old Thurl, with this Louis Wu's help. But how do you come to know about that?"

"Louis Wu and I traveled together, far to port of here. Without sunlight the mirror-flowers couldn't defend themselves, he said. The clouds, though, they never went away?"

"They never did. We seeded our grass, just as the wizard told us. Smeerps and other burrowers moved in well ahead of us. Wherever we went, we found mirror-flowers eaten at the roots. Grass doesn't grow well in this murk, so at first we had to eat mirror-flowers.

"The Reds who fed their herds from our grass in my father's time, and fought us when we objected, they followed us into new grassland. Gleaners hunted the burrowers. Water People moved back up the rivers that the mirror-flowers had taken."

"What of the vampires?"

"It seems they did well, too."

Vala grimaced.

The Thurl said, "There was a region we all avoided. Vampires need refuge from daylight, a cave system, trees, anything. When the clouds came, they feared the sun less. They traveled farther from their lair. We know no more than that."

"We should ask the Ghouls."

"Do you Machine People talk to Ghouls?" The Thurl didn't quite like that idea.

"They keep their own company. But Ghouls know where the dead have fallen. They must know where the vampires hunt, and where they hide during the day."

"Ghouls only act at night. I would not know how to talk to a Ghoul."

"It's done." Vala was trying to remember, but her mind wasn't working well. Tired. "It's done. A new religion pops up, or an old priest dies, and then it's a rite of ordeal for the new shaman. The Ghouls must know and accept what rites he demands for the dead."

The Bull nodded. Ghouls would carry out funeral rites for any religion, within obvious limits. "How, then?"

"You have to get their attention. Court them. Anything works, but they're coy. That's a test, too. A new priest won't be taken seriously until he's dealt with the Ghouls."

The Bull was bristling. "*Court* them?"

"My people came here as merchants, Thurl. The Ghouls have something we want: knowledge. What do we have that the Ghouls want? Not much. Ghouls own the world, Arch and all, just ask them."

"Court them." It grated. "How?"

What had she heard? Tales told at night; not much in the way of business dealings. But she'd seen and talked to Ghouls. "Ghouls work the shadow farm under a cluster of floating buildings, far to port. We pay them in tools, and the City Builders give them library privileges. They'll deal for information."

"We don't *know* anything."

"Nearly true."

"What else have we got?" The Thurl said, "Oh, Valavirgillin, this is nasty stuff."

"What?"

The Thurl waved about him. In view were nearly a hundred vampire corpses, all lying near the wall, and half as many Grass Giant dead scattered from the crossbow limit to the uncut grass.

Beedj was examining a smaller corpse. He saw he had her attention, and he lifted the head so that Vala could see its face. It was Himapertharce, of Anthrantillin's crew.

A shudder rippled along Vala's spine. But the Thurl was right. She said, "Ghouls must feed. More than that: if these thousand corpses were left to lie, there would be plague. All would blame the Ghouls. The Ghouls must come to clean up."

"But why will they listen to me?"

Vala shook her head. It felt stuffed with cotton.

"What then, *after* we know where the vampires lair? Attack them ourselves?"

"The Ghouls might tell us that, too—"

The Thurl broke into a run. Vala saw Beedj waving, holding—what? At that moment he shook it violently, then flung it away, and hurled himself in the other direction. Where it fell, it writhed and went quiet, though Beedj was howling.

It was a living vampire.

Beedj called, "Thurl, I'm sorry. It was alive, wounded, just the bolt through its hip. I thought we might talk to it, examine it—anything—but—but the smell!"

"Calm yourself, Beedj. Was the smell sudden? You attack, it defends?"

"What, like a fart? Sometimes controlled, sometimes not? . . . Thurl, I'm not sure."

"Resume your patrol."

Beedj's sword slashed viciously at the grass. The Thurl walked on.

Vala had been thinking. She said, "You must set a delegation among the dead. A tent, a few of your men—"

"We'd find them sucked empty in the morning!"

"No, I think it's safe for tonight and tomorrow night. The vampires have hunted this area out, and they'd smell their own dead. Even so, arm your people and, mmm, send men and women together."

"Valavirgillin—"

"I know your custom, but if the vampires sing, best your people mate with each other." Should she be saying this? She surely would not have spoken thus before other Grass Giants.

The Bull snarled, but "Yes. Yes, and what the Thurl does not see did not happen. So." The Thurl beckoned at Beedj. He asked Vala, "Will Farsight Trading join us?"

"We should support you. Two species in need will speak louder than one." Farsight Trading could roll away from most problems, but not *this*. They'd poured most of their fuel into towels.

"Three species, then. Many Gleaners died the night before last. The Gleaners will wait with us. Should we be more yet? Vampires must have hunted among the Reds."

"Worth a try."

Beedj came up. The Thurl began talking much faster than Vala could follow. Beedj tried to argue, then acquiesced.

"We should sleep during the day," Vala said. Her body was crying for sleep.

Something closed on her wrist. "Boss?"

She jerked awake. Her squeak was intended as a scream. She rolled away and sat up and—it was only Kaywerbrimmis.

"Boss, what have you been telling the Bull?"

She was still groggy. She needed a drink and a bath or— that rattle, was it rain? And a flash and boom that was certainly thunder.

She'd pulled off her filthy clothing before she slept. She slid out of the blankets, out of the payload shell, into the cool rain. Kay watched from the gun room as she danced in the rain.

Consequences. Traders didn't mate. They shared rishathra with the species they met, but mating was something else. You didn't get a business partner pregnant, and you didn't engage in sexual dominance games, and you didn't fall in love.

But in far realms, among strange hominids, you couldn't shun each other, either.

She beckoned and shouted, "Wash with me. What time is it?"

"Coming on dusk. We slept a long time." Kay was pulling off his clothes in something like relief. "I thought we'd need this time to arm against vampires."

"We'll do that. How's Barok?"

"Don't know."

They drank, washed each other, dried each other, and were reassured: the mating urge could be resisted.

The rain stopped. You could see wind driving the last flurries across the stubble. Swaths of navy-blue sky showed through blowing broken clouds, and a sudden narrow vertical line of blue-white dashes.

Vala gaped. She hadn't seen the Arch in four rotations.

By glow of Archlight she could see patterns in the grass stubble. An arc of pale rectangles. A tent erected within the arc. Grass Giants moved back and forth, and a handful of much smaller hominids moved with them. On the rectangles . . . sheets? They were laying out bodies.

"Did you tell them to do that?"

"No. Not a bad idea, though," Vala said.

In Anthrantillin's deserted cruiser they found Barok with a woman twice his size. He seemed abnormally subdued, but he was smiling. "Wemb, my partners Valavirgillin and Kaywerbrimmis. Folk, this is Wemb."

Kay started to say, "I would have thought—"

Barok's laugh was not quite sane. "Yes, and you would've been right, if you would have thought we slept!"

Wemb cut in. "Sleeping here, together, protects each against intent of the rest, against *yet more rishathra*. We were lucky in each other."

Groping through his exhausted mind, Barok found another thought. "Forn. You never found Foranayeedli?"

Vala said, "She's gone."

Barok's body rippled, an uncontrollable shudder. His hand closed on Vala's wrist. "I shouted down at her. 'Load!' Nothing. She was gone. I stepped out to look for her, to stop her if she followed the singing. Stepped out and my mind turned off. I was at the foot of the wall and the rain was hammering me into the ground. Someone stumbled into me. Knocked me in the mud. Wemb. We, rishathra isn't a strong enough word."

Wemb took him by the shoulder and turned him toward her. "Shared love, or even mated, but we *must* say *rishathra*, Barok. Truly we must."

"—Tore our clothes away and rished and rished, and our minds seeped back to us with not a heartbeat to spare. A half circle of those pale things was closing on us. The rain must have washed away some of the scent. I saw crossbows lying all around us. Grass Giant warriors have been stumbling down the wall all night long, dropping crossbows and anything else they're carrying—"

"We picked up crossbows," the Grass Giant woman cut in. "I saw Makee lying dead with a vampire in his arms and a bolt through both of them, and his quiver dropped beside him. Picked up the quiver and dumped it and pushed a handful of bolts at Barok and shot the nearest vampire. Then the next."

"At first I couldn't cock the crossbow."

"Then the next. Is that why you were screaming? We never talked till after."

"Scream and pull. Scream for strength," Barok said. "Your cursed tools aren't built for tiny little Machine People."

Vala asked, "You were out there all night?"

Wemb nodded. Barok said, "When the rain started to slack off, I got us towels. There were heaps of towels." His grip was painful. "Kay, Vala, we saw why."

"Warriors walked past us," Wemb said. "I shot Heerst in the leg, but he just kept walking, following the singing. Vampires came up to him and pulled the towel off his face and led him away. He's my son."

"If something is covering your face, they pull it off! Heerst was using fuel in his towel. Rain washes it out. We looked for towels that had— Wemb?"

"Pepperleek. Minch."

"Yes, those kept their scent. They kept us alive, the towels and the rishathra. Any time it was too much for us, we rished. And crossbow bolts. The guards were dropping their swords and crossbows but not their quivers. We had to go looking. Rob the dead."

"I saw what I didn't understand," Wemb said. "I should tell the Thurl. Vampires rished with some of us, then led them away into the high grass and farther. Why keep them alive? Are they still alive?"

Vala said, "The Ghouls might know."

"Ghouls keep Ghoul secrets," Wemb said.

The clouds had closed again. In the dark Barok said, "I shot the vampire who was leading Anth away. It took two bolts. Another picked up the song, and I shot her. Anth followed a third woman, and by that time he was out of range.

They led him into the grass. I never saw him again. Should I have shot *him?*"

They only looked at him.

"I can't keep vigil with you," Barok said. "I can't face rishathra now. My head is too— I don't know if I can make you see—"

They squeezed his arms and tried to assure him that they understood. They left him there.

Chapter Three

THE

GATHERING

STORM

The tent huddled beneath the wall, but faced outward into an arc of gray sheets.

The corpses were laid head-to-head, two giants to a sheet, or four vampires. Giants had found Anthrantillin and his crewman Himapertharee and laid them out on one sheet. Taratarafasht and Foranayeedli must be still missing. Another sheet held six tiny Gleaner dead.

The giants had nearly finished making their patterns. Tiny hominids moved about them, not helping much, but carrying food or light loads. All wore sheets with holes in them for the head to poke through.

A Grass Giant could lift a vampire with no difficulty. It took two to carry a dead giant.

But Beedj was carrying a dead Grass Giant woman across his back. He rolled the woman off his shoulders to slump across a sheet, perfectly placed. He took her hand and spoke to her sadly. Vala changed her mind about disturbing him.

Two women finished laying out more vampire dead. One approached. "We rubbed pepperleek along the rims of the sheets. Stop small scavengers," Moonwa said to the three Machine People. "Big scavengers we can crossbow. Ghouls won't have to fight for what's theirs."

"A polite notion," Valavirgillin said. Tables would have raised the dead out of a scavenger's reach; but where would Grass Giants find wood?

"What can I do for you?" Moonwa asked.

"We've come to keep vigil with you."

"The battle cost you too much. No Ghouls come on the first night. Rest."

Vala said, "But it was my idea, after all."

"Thurl's idea," Moonwa informed her.

Vala nodded and carefully didn't smile. It was a social convention, as in *Louis Wu helped the Thurl boil a sea.* She waved toward the little hominids. "Who are these?"

Moonwa called, "Perilack, Silack, Manack, Coriack—" Four small heads lifted. "—these are more allies: Kaywerbrimmis, Valavirgillin, Whandernothtee."

The Gleaners smiled and bobbed their heads, but they didn't come up at once. They moved off to where Grass Giants were carefully stripping their sheets off inside out, well away from the dead and the tent, then picking up scythes and crossbows. The Gleaners stripped off their contaminated sheets, then hung slender swords behind their backs.

Beedj approached, sheetless and armed. "Towels under the tent. We rubbed minch on them," he said. "Welcome to all."

Gleaners stood armpit-high to Machine People, navel-high to Beedj and Moonwa. Their faces were hairless and pointed; their smiles were wide and toothy, a bit much. They wore tunics of cured smeerpskin with the beige fur left on, lavishly decorated with feathers. On the women, Perilack and Coriack, the feather patterns formed smallish wings. The women had to walk with some care to protect them. Manack and Silack looked much like the women. Their clothing showed greater differences; feathered, but with arms free to swing. Or fight.

Rain spattered down, just enough to send the Machine People into the tent. Vala saw grass piled thickly on the floor. Grass for bedding and to feed the Grass Giants. She stopped her companions until they had taken off their sandals.

Already it was dark enough that Vala could barely see faces. Rishathra was best begun in the night.

But not on a battlefield.

"This is a bad business," Perilack said.

Whandernothtee asked, "How many have you lost?"

"Nearly two hundred by now."

"We were only ten. Four are gone. Sopashintay and Chitakumishad we left on guard above us with the cannon. Barok is recovering from a night in hell."

"Our queen's man went with the Thurl's woman to bring other hominids to bargain. If the—" The little woman's eyes flickered about her. "—lords of the night do not speak, other voices will join ours tomorrow."

Legend told that the Ghouls heard any word spoken of them, unless—some said—during broad daylight. The Ghouls might be all about them even now.

Kay asked, "Would your queen's man truly rish with his traveling companions?"

The four Gleaners tittered. Beedj and Moonwa boomed their laughter. A little woman—Perilack—said to Kay, "If the Grass Giant women would notice. Size matters. But you, you and we might make something happen."

Perilack and Kaywerbrimmis looked at each other as if both taken by the same notion. The little woman took Kay's elbow; Kay's arm brushed the Gleaner's feathers. He suggested,

"I expect you accumulate these faster than you can use them?"

She said, "No, the skins spoil quickly. We can trade a few, not many."

"What if we could find a way to delay the spoilage?"

From time to time Valavirgillin would catch a foul whiff of battlefield stench and snort it out. But the smells weren't reaching Kaywerbrimmis. Not him! Kay was into trader mode. His mind was in a place where win and lose were a matter of numbers, where discomfort was an embarrassment one could not afford, where an empire survived because one hominid's trash was another's ore bed.

Full night had fallen. But by the faint flash of an arc of daylit Arch, she saw Beedj's broad grin. She asked the Grass Giant, "Have you watched bargaining sessions?"

"Some. Louis Wu came when I was a child, but agreements were all between him and the old Thurl. The Reds made peace with us thirty falans ago; we parceled up habitats. Twenty-four falans ago we gathered with the Reds and Sea People, shared maps. All peoples have learned things about the new territory. But all find Grass Giants awkwardly large."

A polite disclaimer would not be believed. Vala reached up to grasp elbows with the Grass Giant. She'd been listening for Ghouls in the night, but the only sound was the rain.

The clouds had closed. It had become full dark.

One of the Gleaner men asked, "Should we only wait? Would they find that more polite?"

Manack, wasn't it? Hair thicker around the throat, as if he were an alpha male and Silack a beta. In a good many hominid species, one male got most of the action; but Vala didn't know that about Gleaners.

Vala said, "Manack, we're *here*. In their habitat. You may even consider that we've come to entertain the lords of the night. Will you share rishathra?" To Beedj she quickly added, "Beedj, this is for size, to leave me larger. I expect Whand will go with Moonwa first . . ." Though Kay and Perilack, she noticed, were no longer talking business. Philosophies differ.

To rish with a Gleaner male was no more than foreplay.

Rishathra with the Thurl's heir was something else again. It had its pleasures. He was big. He was very eager. He was very proud of his self-restraint, though it was right at the edge of his control. He was *very* big.

Kaywerbrimmis was having a wonderful night, or seemed to be. He was sharing some joke or secret with Moonwa now. Good trader, that one; a generally good man. Vala kept looking in his direction.

They'd mated. Vala couldn't get her mind out of that mode . . . shouldn't try, really. It was a good mind-set for a rishathra party. Still.

Mating is a matter of order. Eons of evolution have shaped many hominid's mating responses: approach, scents, postures and positions, visual and tactile cues. Culture shapes more: dances, cliques, styles, permitted words and phrases.

But evolution never touches sex outside one's species, and rishathra is always an art form. Where shapes don't fit, other shapes might be found. Those who cannot participate can watch, can give ribald advice . . .

Can stand guard, for that matter, when a trader's body or mind needs a rest.

The night was almost silent, but not every whisper was

wind. Ghouls should be out there. It was their duty. But if for any reason word hadn't reached them of a corpse-strewn battlefield, then those sounds might be vampires.

Vala perched on a stool three paces high and sturdy enough for a Grass Giant. The night was warm enough for nakedness, or *she* was, but loaded guns were on her back. Before her was blowing rain and little else to see. At her back any excitement had died for the moment.

"We and the Grass Giants, we love each other, but we're not mere parasites," one of the Gleaners was saying. "Wherever there once were mirror-flower forests, there are plant eaters now, prey that can feed us. We forage ahead of the Thurl's people. We probe, we guide, we make their maps."

Manack, that was. He was a bit small to accommodate even a Machine People woman, and inexperienced; but he could learn. The proper attitude was easy for some. Others never learned it.

Mating has consequences. A hominid's response to mating is not of the mind. Rishathra has no consequences, and the mind may remain in command. Embarrassment is inappropriate. Laughter is always to be shared. Rishathra is entertainment and diplomacy and friendship, and knowing that you can reach your weapons in the dark.

"We hope to make our fortunes," Kay was saying. "Those who extend the Empire are well-treated. The Empire grows with our fuel supply. If we can persuade a community to make fuel and sell it to the Empire, the bonus would let each of us raise a family."

Moonwa said, "Those rewards are yours. Your client tribes face something else. Loss of ambition, loss of friends and mates, delusion and early death for any who learn to drink your fuel."

"Some are too weak to say, 'Enough.' Moonwa, you *must* be stronger than that."

"Of course. I can do that tonight, now. *Enough, Kaywer-brimmis!*"

Vala turned to see white grins large and small. Beedj said, "I wore one of your fuel-wetted towels last night. It made me dizzy. It threw my aim off."

Kay gracefully changed the subject. "Valavirgillin, will you return to Center City, mate and raise a family?"

"I mated," she said.

Kay suddenly had nothing to say.

He didn't know!

What had he been thinking? That he and she would become formal mates? Valavirgillin said, "I made myself rich with a gift from Louis Wu of the Ball People." How she had done that was nobody's business, and illegal. "I mated then. Tarb's parents were friends of my family, as is usual with us, Moonwa. He had little money, but he's a good father, he freed me to engage in business dealings.

"I grew restive. I remembered that Louis Wu suggested . . . no. *Asked if* my people make tools from the sludge that remains after we distill alcohol. *Plastic,* he said. His talking thing would not translate, but I learned his word. He said it means shapeless. Plastic can take any shape the maker likes. That sludge is useless, nasty stuff. Clients might be grateful if we had a reason to haul it away for them.

"So I funded a chemical laboratory." She shrugged in the dark. "Always it cost more than anyone expected, but we got answers. There are secrets in that goo.

"One day most of my money was gone. Tarablilliast and the children are with my sire-family, and I am here, until I can feed them again. Coriack, are you ready to take guard?"

"Of course. Hold the thought, Whandernothtee. Vala, what's out there?"

"Rain. I glimpse something black and shiny, sometimes, and I hear tittering. No smell of vampires."

"Good."

Moonwa had lapsed into Grass Giant language and was making jokes that set Beedj roaring. In the gray light of morning the Gleaners spoke together, waved at the brightening land, then more or less fell over in a pile.

"Do you think they came?" Spash asked nobody in particular, and he stepped out of the tent.

Whand said, "I don't care. Let's sleep."

"They came," Spash said.

Vala stepped out.

It was moments before she realized that one sheet was empty. Which? Far left . . . six Gleaner dead. The rest were untouched.

Beedj came forth briskly, swinging his scythe-sword. More Giants were coming down the earth wall. They conferred, then fanned out to explore, looking for evidence of what the Ghouls had done.

But Vala climbed up the wall to sleep in the payload shell.

At midday she woke ravenous, with the smell of roasting meat in her nostrils. She followed the smells down to the tent.

She found Gleaners and Machine People together. The Gleaners had been hunting. The fire they had made to cook their kills, Barok and Whand had used to make bread from local grass.

"We eat four, five, six meals in a day," Silack told her. "Pint says you eat once a day?"

"Yes. But a lot. Are you finding enough meat?"

"When your men came down to eat, ours went to hunt more. Eat what you see, the hunters will be back."

The flatbread was a good effort, and Vala complimented the men. Smeerp meat was good, too, if a bit lean and tough. At least the Gleaners didn't have a habit found in other hominids: changing the flavor of meat by rubbing it with salt or herbs or berries.

Vala wondered about breeding smeerps in other places, but all traders knew the answer to that. One hominid's local bounty was another's plague. With no local predators to restrict their numbers, smeerps would be eating somebody's crops, breeding beyond their food source, then vectoring diseases when starvation weakened them.

Meanwhile she had eaten everything in sight. Gleaners and Machine People alike were watching her in amusement. Silack said, "Heavy exercise last night."

"Did I miss anything?"

Kay said, "The Ghouls were active. There aren't any dead Grass Giants between the wall and the tall grass. Beedj found neat piles of bones in the grass. They didn't touch the vampires. Saved them for tonight, I guess."

"Considerate of them." With their dead gone, the Grass Giants' mourning was over, except . . . "More considerate if they would take the rest of our dead. Anything else?"

Silack pointed.

It wasn't raining now. The clouds formed an infinite flat roof, way high. You could see a long way across the veldt. What Vala could see was a sizable beast-drawn wagon plodding toward Grass Giant domains.

Five great big-shouldered beasts. More than that high-sided wagon needed, though it was big.

"It will be here well before dusk. Even so, if your species can sleep in spurts, you will have time."

Vala nodded and climbed up the wall to sleep some more.

Paroom was riding in the guide seat beside a much smaller red-skinned man. Three more Reds rode in the enclosed space beneath.

They stopped the wagon just under the wall, near the opening. They lifted a thing out of the wagon bed. Vala squinted, trying to see something almost invisible. Her mercenary instincts raced along her nerves, gibbering.

At the Fall of the Cities, flying vehicles were the most common of fallen objects. This curved transparent sheet was the kind of thing people found in fallen cars. Most were shattered. This one looked intact. Its value must be immense!

The Reds came forward, carrying it at the corners. Each carried a sword nearly as long as himself, hung from his back in a leather sheath. They wore dyed leather kilts and leather backpacks, men and women both, though brighter colors adorned the women's. Their teeth were pointed, all of them, a double row of canines.

Valavirgillin, Kaywerbrimmis, Moonwa, the Thurl in full armor, Manack, and Coriack waited to greet them. The group had been pruned a little.

"Thurl, this is a window," one Red male said solemnly. "It is a gift from the Marsh People, who cannot go from where they live. They beg that we shall ward them from the spreading plague of vampires. The Marsh People cannot flee, for only the marsh gives them life."

Valavirgillin caught the Thurl's questioning look. "We know species like that," she said. "Marsh, desert, one side of a mountain, a forest that is all one kind of tree. Their bellies have changed to accept only one food, or they cannot survive cold or heat, or too little moisture in the air, or too much. But this is a magnificent gift."

"It is. We will do what we can for the Marsh People," the Thurl said. "These, our allies, were able to reach us . . ." and the Thurl made introduction, speaking slowly, pronouncing the names of Gleaners and Machine People with varying accuracy.

"I am Tegger hooki-Thandarthal," the Red male said. "This is Warvia hooki-Murf Thandarthal. We travel with Anakrin hooki-Whanhurhur and Chaychind hooki-Karashk." The other two Reds had moved away to tend to the loadbeasts.

The Thurl asked, "How do your people deal with rishathra?"

"We cannot," said Warvia, and did not amplify.

Paroom grinned, and Vala grinned back, picturing the male Grass Giants' disappointment. The Thurl as host spoke for all, as protocol required, but briefly. What point in enlarging upon a guest's skill at rishathra, for a species that couldn't do that at all? Tegger and Warvia merely nodded when he fell silent. The other Red males were not even listening. They were examining the vampire corpses lying on one sheet, and chattering at high speed.

Tegger and Warvia looked much alike. Their red skins were smooth; their faces were hairless. They wore kilts of soft leather with decorative lacing. They were as tall as Machine People, but much thinner. Big ears stood out from narrow heads. Their teeth seemed to be not filed, but grown that way. Warvia had breasts, but almost flat.

"We never hear of so many vampires found together," Warvia said.

"You killed an army," Tegger said. "Vampires lie every-where. Your neighbors must be glad."

Warvia asked, "The Ghouls, have they come?"

The Thurl said, "An army of vampires came the night before last. An army was gone when the shadow withdrew from the sun. You have seen the dead they left behind, but our own dead have gone with the Ghouls. They were half as many or a bit more, plus a hundred of Gleaners and four of our Machine People. The vampires are a terrible foe. Welcome to you."

"We have seen nothing of the terror," Tegger said. "Young hunters disappear. Our teachers lose their skill, we said, or some new hunting thing has found us. Paroom, if we did show disbelief, forgive us."

Paroom nodded graciously. The Thurl said, "What we knew of vampires was half false. The Machine People empire came in time to help us."

Vala was beginning to realize that no other Grass Giant *could* say such a thing. To disparage the tribe was to disparage the Thurl. "We must show you our defenses," he continued, "but have you eaten? Should you cook while there is still light?"

"We eat our meat uncooked. We like variety. Grass Giants eat no meat, but what of Gleaners and Machine People? May we share? Let us show you what we have."

They had five loadbeasts and the cage atop their wagon. The thing in the cage felt their gaze and roared. It was a beast as massive as a Grass Giant, and a killer, Vala realized. She asked, "What is that?"

"Hakarrch," Tegger said with visible pride. "A hunter of the Barrier Hills. Two were sent us by the Gardener People for our sport. Hunted outside its familiar terrain, the male still killed one of us before we brought it down."

It was a brag. *Mighty hunters we are. We hunt the lesser hunters, and we'll hunt your vampires.* Vala suggested, "Perilack, shall we sample this? Not tonight, but tomorrow at our one meal."

The Gleaner woman said, "Bargain. Warvia, tonight you may kill a loadbeast. Tomorrow and after, let us play host. We will feed all until the—" Shadow's edge had bitten a piece from the sun, but the light was still bright. "—eaters of the dead deign to speak. You'll want to taste smeerp meat."

"We thank you."

The fire had become the only light: not enough light to cook, but the cooking was over. Of the other Reds, Anakrin hooki-Whanhurhur was an old man, wrinkled but still agile. Chaychind hooki-Karashk, another male, was badly scarred and had lost an arm in some old battle.

They had brought a gift of their own, a sizable ceramic jug of a strong, dark beer. Not bad at all. Vala saw Kay react, too. *Let's see how Kay handles it.*

Kay exclaimed, "Do you make this yourselves? Do you make a lot?"

"Yes. Do you think of trade?"

"Chaychind, it might be worth moving if it's cheap enough—"

"Tales of the Machine People are not exaggerated."

Kay looked flustered. Too bad, but Vala had better step in. "Kaywerbrimmis means that if we can distill enough of this, we would have fuel for our cruisers. Our cruisers carry weapons and can carry much more. They move faster than loadbeasts, but they cannot move without fuel."

"A gift you want?" Chaychind asked, while Tegger exclaimed, "You would boil our beer for fuel?"

"Gifts for the war. All must contribute. Grass Giant fight-ers, Gleaner spies, your fuel—"

"Our eyes."

"Ah?"

"We know of no species that can see as far as any Red Herder."

"Your eyes. Our cruisers, our cannon, our flamers. Can you contribute three hundred manweights of beer to the war against the vampires? It would distill to thirty manweights of fuel. We carry a distilling system simple enough to be copied."

Warvia exclaimed, "That's enough to souse whole civiliza-tions!"

But Tegger asked, "What size of manweights?"

Hah! Vala said, "Your size." Tegger had asked the obvious question, but it implied agreement . . . and a Machine People manweight would have been a sixth higher. "I'm thinking of taking two cruisers. Leave the third here. Let the Thurl fuel the third cruiser."

"Whand and Chit can supervise that," Kay said.

"Oh?" She'd wondered why both were absent.

"They've had enough, Boss. Spash is wavering, too. So's Barok."

"Any foray would be to murder selves," red Warvia said, "unless we can know our enemy. Have the Ghouls spoken?"

The Thurl said, "Some bodies are gone," and shrugged.

"We're paying for our good manners," Vala said. A trader must know how to project her voice on demand. "The bodies we guarded from vermin, the lords of the night will take last. They took our Gleaner dead because they died a day earlier." The night would hear her.

Tonight Kay and Whand were on the wall with Barok, watching over them with the cannon. Spash and Chit had traded places with them.

This night looked to be less exhausting, but less joyful, too. The Gleaners and Machine People and an undersized Grass Giant woman named Twuk tried to get something going. The Thurl kept his armor on. The four Red Herders watched gleefully from beyond touching distance, and chattered in their own language, and it all sort of fell apart.

The Reds weren't unfriendly. They might be a little stiff around the Thurl himself, but around others they were relaxed and talkative. Spash and three Reds were trading stories now. The Reds had considerable experience with hominids, despite their handicap.

Vala listened idly. The Reds were guided by their diet. They ate live meat, and they were herder-gourmets. Herding one life-form, rarely two, was easier than trying to keep several types of meatbeast together. The Red tribes mapped their routes to cross each others' paths, to trade feasts.

They traded stories, too, and met hominids in a variety of environments. Now they were speaking of two types of Water People, apparently not the same two Vala was familiar with.

The fourth Red, Tegger, was on watch with Chit.

The Thurl was asleep in full armor. He clearly wasn't interested in rishathra, or Ghouls, either, Vala thought.

Sopashintay lay propped against a tent pole. "I wonder what it's like inside the wall tonight," she said.

Vala considered. "The Thurl's out here. Beedj is in there, on defense. 'What the Thurl does not see did not happen.'"

Spash came up on an elbow. "Where did you hear that?"

"From the Thurl. The beta males are doing a lot of mating, I expect, and some fighting, too. I suppose we're missing all the fun—"

"Again, in my case," Spash said.

"—but they wouldn't rish anyway if they can mate. And I can use the rest."

"So can the Thurl. He sleeps like a near-dormant volcano," Spash said.

Chit looked at the women and smiled, and stepped lightly out of the tent. A dense mist cloaked the night. Chit picked up a bone from dinner and threw it. Vala heard a tiny muffled *tock*.

A silver bulk was at her shoulders, sensed but never heard. The Thurl sniffed, while his hands cocked a crossbow without sound or effort. He said, "They are not near, vampires or Night People. Chitakumishad, did you see anything? Smell anything?"

"Nothing."

The Thurl seemed exceedingly alert for one who had been sleeping moments ago. He pulled his helm closed and stepped out. A Grass Giant guard, Tarun, followed him.

Spash said, "I had it wrong, didn't I? But why—"

Vala whispered, "Reds. They're the ancient enemy, and they're all around him. That's why he kept his armor on, and that's why he pretends to sleep. Bet on it."

In the morning there were no dead between the wall and the tall grass, save for those that lay on sheets. The Ghouls had taken Vala at her word, it seemed.

Chaychind asked of nobody in particular, "Where shall we turn the hakarrch loose?"

Coriak looked at Manack. The Gleaner female said, "Just

short of the tall grass, but let me tell my companions first. Vala, will your people hunt, too?"

"I think not, but I'll ask."

She spoke to the others. None were eager. Machine People did eat meat, but predator meat generally had a rank flavor. But Kay said, "We'll look timid if someone doesn't join the hunt."

"Ask some questions," she told him. "That thing looked dangerous. The more you know, the less often you get killed."

He'd never heard the proverb. He stared, laughed, then said, "We want to bring it to less than *once?*"

"Yes."

She slept through the hunt. At midday she woke to share in the meal. Kaywerbrimmis bore a single slash along his forearm, the fool. Vala bound it with a fuel-soaked towel. Hakarrch meat had a flavor of cat.

The dead were fewer, but the stench of them hovered about the tent, and the dreadful night was coming.

The Ghouls would take her at her word, she thought. *The bodies we guarded from vermin, the lords of the night will take last.* Tonight.

Chapter Four

THE PEOPLE

OF THE

NIGHT

When shadow had nearly covered the sun, Vala found the Gleaners and Reds around a fire. The Gleaners were eating; they offered to share. The Reds had eaten their kills as they were made.

A fine rain began to sizzle on the coals. The negotiators retreated into the tent: Valavirgillin, Chitakumishad, and Sopashintay for the Machine People, three of the Reds, the four Gleaners. Anakrin hooki-Wanhurhur and the Thurl and a woman Vala didn't know were already inside.

Stale grass had been replaced with fresh.

The Thurl spoke, his powerful voice cutting through all conversation. "Folk, meet my negotiator Waast, who has a tale to tell."

Waast stood gracefully for so large a woman. "Paroom and I went to starboard two days ago, on foot," she said. "Paroom returned with these Reds of Ginjerofer's folk. I followed on foot with a guard of Red warriors, to speak to the Muddy River People. The Muddy River People cannot join us here, but they may speak of our sorrows to the Night People."

"They'll have the same trouble we did," Coriack said.

(Something was tickling at Vala's attention.)

Waast sat. To the Reds she said, "You cannot practice rishathra. But mating?"

"It is not my time," Warvia said primly. Anakrin and Chaychind were grinning. Tegger seemed angry.

(The wind.)

Many hominid species were monogamous, exclusive of rishathra, of course. Tegger and Warvia must be mates. And the Thurl was saying, "I must wear my armor. We know not what might visit us."

Too bad. They might have gotten some entertainment going.

(Music?)

Spash asked uneasily, "Do you hear music? That isn't vampire music."

The sound was still soft, but growing louder, almost painfully near the upper end of her hearing range. Vala felt the hair stir on her neck and down her spine. She was hearing a wind instrument, and strings, and a thuttering percussion instrument. No voices.

The Thurl lowered his helm and stepped out. A crossbow was in his hand, pointed at the sky. Chit and Silack stayed at either side of the door, their weapons readied. Others in the tent were arming themselves.

Tiny Silack walked backward into the tent. The smell came with him. Carrion and wet fur.

Two big hominid shapes followed, and then the much bigger Thurl. "We have guests," he boomed.

In the tent it was almost totally dark. Vala could make out the gleam of the Ghouls' eyes and teeth, and two black silhouettes against a scarcely brighter glow, Archlight seeping through clouds. But her eyes were adjusting, picking out detail:

There were two, a man and a woman. Hair covered them almost everywhere. It was black and straight and slick with the rain. Their mouths were overly wide grins showing big spade teeth. They wore pouches on straps, and were otherwise naked. Their big blunt hands were empty. They were not eating. Vala was terribly relieved, even as she resisted the impulse to shy back.

Likely enough, none but Valavirgillin had ever seen one of these. Some were reacting badly. Chit remained in the door, on guard, facing away. Spash was on her feet, not cringing, but it seemed the limit of her self-control. Silack of the Gleaners, Tegger, and Chaychind all cringed away with wide eyes and open mouths.

She had to do something. She stood and bowed. "Welcome. I am Valavirgillin of the Machine People. We've waited to beg your help. These are Anakrin and Warvia of the Red Herders, Perilack and Manack of the Gleaners, Chitakumishad and Sopashintay of the Machine People—" picking them out as and when she thought they had recovered their aplomb.

The Ghoul male didn't wait. "We know your various kinds. I am—" something breathy. His lips didn't close completely. Otherwise he was fluent in the trade dialect, his accent more like Kay's than Vala's. "But call me Harpster, for the instrument I play. My mate is—" something breathy and whistling, not unlike the music that was still playing outside. "Grieving Tube. How do you practice rishathra?"

Tegger had been cowering. Now he was beside his mate, instantly. "We cannot," he said.

The Ghoul woman half hid a laugh. Harpster said, "We know. Be at ease."

The Thurl spoke directly to Grieving Tube. "These are

under my protection. My armor may come off, if you can speak for our safety. After that, you need only have care for my size." And Waast only smiled at Harpster, but Vala could admire her for the nerve that took.

The Gleaners were in a line, all four standing tall. "Our kind does practice rishathra," Coriack said.

Vala longed for her home. Somewhere she would have found food for her mate and children, and as for her love of adventure, a person could set that aside for a time . . . too late now. "Rishathra binds our Empire," Valavirgillin told the lords of the night.

Harpster said, "Truth was that rishathra bound the City Builders' empire. Fuel binds yours. We do practice rishathra, but not tonight, I think, because we can guess how it would disturb the Red Herders—"

"We are not so fragile," Warvia said.

"—and for another reason," Harpster said. "Do you have a request to make of us?"

They all tried to speak at once. "Vampires—"

"You see the terror—"

"The deaths—"

The Thurl had a voice to cut through all that. "Vampires have devastated all species in a territory ten daywalks across. Help us to end their menace."

"Two or three daywalks, no more," Harpster said. "Vampires need to reach shelter after a raid. Still, a large territory, housing more than a ten of hominid species—"

"But they feed us well," Grieving Tube said gently, her voice pitched a little higher than her companion's. "The problem you face is that *we* have no problem. What is good for any of you is good also for the People of the Night. The vampires feed us as surely as the lust for alcohol among your client species, Valavirgillin. But if you can conquer the vampires, that serves us, too."

Did they realize how much they had revealed in a few breaths of speech? But too many others were speaking at once, and Vala held silence.

"For your understanding," Grieving Tube said, "consider. Manack, what if your queen had a quarrel with the Thurl's people? You might persuade us not to touch any dead who lie near the Thurl's walls. Soon he must surrender."

Manack protested, "But we and the Grass Giants—we would never—"

"Of course not. But Warvia, you and the old Thurl were at war fifty falans ago. Suppose your leader Ginjerofer had begged us to tear apart any Grass Giants who came to kill their cattle?"

Warvia said, "Very well, we understand."

"Do you? We must not side with any hominid against any other. You all depend on us. Without the People of the Night, your corpses lie where they fall, diseases form and spread, your water becomes polluted," the Ghoul woman sang in her high-pitched breathy voice.

She had made this speech before. "We forbid cremation, but suppose we did not? What if every species had the fuel to burn their dead? Clouds still lid this sky forty-three falans after a sea was boiled. What if that were the smoke of the burned dead, a stench growing richer every falan? Do you know how many hominids of every species die in a falan? We do.

"We cannot choose sides."

Chaychind hooki-Karashk had been flushing a darker red. "How can you speak of siding with vampires? With animals!"

"They don't think," said Harpster, "and you do. But can you always say that so surely? We know of hominids just at the edge of thinking, several just along this arc of the Arch. Some use fire if they find it, or form packs when prey is large and formidable. One strips branches into spears. One lives in water; they cannot use fire, but they flake rocks for knives. How do you judge? Where do you draw the line?"

"Vampires don't use tools or fire!"

"Not fire, but tools. Under this endless rain vampires have learned to wear clothing stripped from their prey. When they are dry, they leave it like garbage."

The Ghoul woman said, "You see why we should not rish with you, if we must refuse your other desires." Grieving Tube did not see, chose not to see, the mixed emotions that statement generated.

Well, she must try something. Vala said, "Your help would be of immense value, if you had reason to give it. Already you have told us the reach of vampire depredations, and that they must return to their lair, that they have one single lair. What else could you tell us?"

Harpster shrugged, and Vala winced. His shoulders were terribly loose, like unconnected bones rolling freely under his skin.

She continued stubbornly, "I have heard a rumor, a story, a fable. The Machine People hear it where vampires are known. You must understand that to our client species far from Center City, there's no real explanation of how all these vampires appeared so suddenly."

"They have a high breeding rate," Harpster noted.

Grieving Tube said, "Yes, and clusters of them split from the main body to find other refuges. Ten daywalks was *not* too large a guess."

The others, even Chaychind, were letting Vala speak. Vala said, "But a less sensible explanation spreads, too. The victim of a vampire will rise from the dead to become a vampire himself."

"That," said Harpster, "is purest nonsense!"

And of course it was. "Of course it is, but it explains how the plague spreads so rapidly. See it from the viewpoint of a—" Careful now. "—Hanging Person widow and mother." Hanging People were everywhere. Vala set one hand on the beam overhead, lifted her feet to hang, and said, "What is to be done, lest my poor dead Vaynya become my enemy in the night? The lords of the night forbid us to burn the dead. But sometimes they permit it—"

"Never," said Grieving Tube.

Vala said, "Starboard-spin from Center City by twelve daywalks, there are memories of a plague—"

"Long ago and far away," Harpster snapped. "We designed the crematorium ourselves, taught them how to use it, then moved away. Years later we returned. The plague was beaten. The Digging People still cremated, but we persuaded them to leave their dead again. It was easily done. Firewood was scarce."

"You see the danger," Vala said. "I don't believe locals have started burning vampire victims yet—"

"No. We would see plumes of smoke."

"—but if one client species begins, the rest might follow."

Grieving Tube said sadly, "Then of course we'd have to do a deal of killing."

Valavirgillin throttled a shudder. She bowed low and answered, "Why not begin now, with vampires?"

Grieving Tube mulled it. "Not so easy, that. They, too, command the night . . ."

And Vala's eyes closed for an instant. *Now it's a problem, a challenge, and lesser species must see you solve it. Now I have you.*

The Ghouls had cleared the grass away from a sizable section of tent floor. They were drawing in the dark, tweetling at each other in their own high-pitched language. They argued over some feature none other could see, and settled that, and Harpster stood up.

"When the shadow withdraws, you may examine these maps," Harpster said. "For now let me only describe what you would see. Here, spin by port by two and a half daywalks, the ancient structure of an industrial center floats two tens of manheights above the ground."

"I know of a floating city," Vala said.

"Of course, near your Center City, a collection of free buildings linked. Floaters are rare enough these days. We think this one made machinery for the City Builders. Later it was abandoned.

"Vampires have lived beneath the Floater for many generations, for hundreds of falans. The perpetual shadow is perfect for vampires. Locals moved out of their reach long ago. Peaceful travelers and migrations were warned to avoid it. Warriors must look to themselves in that regard.

"This range of mountains to port and antispin of the Shadow Nest stands between there and here. It formed a barrier for the mirror-flowers. Hominids on the far side came to call it the Barrier of Flame, for the fire they could sometimes see playing along the crest.

"The flowers would ultimately have crossed the crest and burned out the Shadow Nest in their usual fashion. Vampires wouldn't be safe from *horizontal* beams of light. But then the clouds came."

Heads nodded in the dark. Harpster said, "The vampires' range expanded by a daywalk. Grieving Tube is right, the damage is worse than that. Their population has grown, and hunger drives families of vampires into other domains."

Valavirgillin asked, "Can you blow away the clouds?"

Both Ghouls hooted laughter. Grieving Tube said, "You want us to *move clouds?*"

"We beg."

"Why do you think we could do such a thing as move clouds?"

Over the rising sounds of throttled laughter Valavirgillin said, "Louis Wu did that."

Harpster said, "Omnivore Tinker. Not odd as hominids go, but from off the Arch, from the stars. He had tools to prove what he said he was, but we do not know that he made clouds."

The Thurl spoke. "He did! He and the old Thurl boiled a sea to make these clouds above us—"

"Then go to him."

"Louis Wu is gone. The old Thurl is gone."

"We cannot move clouds. Our embarrassment is great." Harpster laughed. "What can we do that you cannot do yourselves?"

The Thurl said, "We will use your maps, much thanks to you. I will lead an army of whatever species will fight. We will destroy this nest of vampires."

"Thurl, *you* cannot go," Grieving Tube said.

Harpster questioned. Grieving Tube began to explain, but the Thurl would not wait. "I am protector to my people! When we fight, I fight at the head—"

"In armor," the Ghoul woman pointed out.

"Of course!"

"You must not wear armor. Your armor keeps your smell. You, all who fight, you must wear nothing. Bathe where you find water. Wash every surface of your cruisers and wagons. Can't you see that the vampires must not smell you?"

Vala thought, *Oh.*

"The bottleneck is the fuel," Chitakumishad was saying. "The Reds make a beer, it can be turned into fuel—"

"Go to your war by way of the Red pastures. We can send them the design for your distilleries by a secret means, tomorrow. Let them make fuel there while you make fuel here from your own stills and rotting grass. You will confront the Shadow Nest no more than a falan from now."

Chit nodded, his own mind busy with plans. "Fuel to take two cruisers there and back—"

"You must cross the Barrier of Flame. I think your cruisers can do that. There are passes."

"Takes more fuel."

"Fuel to explore, or for towels or flame throwers, would come out of what you have. What of it? Only in victory will you need fuel to return here, and then your third cruiser can meet you, or you may leave one behind."

"Travel in mated pairs," Harpster said. "Grieving Tube and I will travel together. Thurl, we know your customs, but from time to time your tribe divides. Do it that way. Tegger, you and Warvia believe you can resist the vampires. It may be so, but what of these others? Let them mate when they must, and not rish with bloodsuckers. Anakrin, Chaychind, you have no mates. You should go home . . ."

And the arguments began. No hominid here would uncritically accept a Ghoul's plan for their war. But Vala remained silent and knew how much she had won.

They're with us. They really are. And they'll bathe . . .

Chapter Five

THE WEB
DWELLER

No telling how long the wizard had been there. The older children had gone into the Great Wood to compete at catching birds. The boy Parald threw with conspicuous grace; his net kept its shape longest, flew the farthest, though he'd caught only two. Strill was thinking how to speak to him, when she chanced to look up.

The wizard was out on the river, floating far above the silver water, on a thick coin-shaped support not much wider than a man is tall.

They shouted, beckoning him down. When he noticed them, he stopped his stately progress among the treetops, then descended gradually. He smiled and spoke in an unknown tongue. He was bald over most of his body, but that wasn't rare among visitors.

They led him home, talking all the way. Some of the boys tested his knowledge with insults. Strill disapproved, and presently knew she was right.

The wizard never did learn their speech, barring a few basic words like "flup" and "rishathra," but he wore a necklace that spoke like a teacher before they reached the village.

Anyone of a strange species might be a teacher. A wizard who flew, who was served by a magical translator, must have a good deal to teach.

Nine years now, since he'd left Kawaresksenjajok and Harkabeeparolyn; ten since Chmeee departed for the Map of Earth. Eleven years since they'd set sail aboard *Hidden Patriarch*. Twelve since their return to the Ringworld. Forty-one years since Louis Wu and his motley crew first touched down, cocooned in stasis, at 770 miles per second.

The first hominids they'd found had been small, furry religious fanatics.

These chattering youths were of that or a similar species. They were chin-high to Louis Wu and covered with fluffy blond fur, and wore kilts of muted browns. They threw their wonderfully patterned nets with wonderful skill, in this maze of bare trunks beneath branches spread like the caps of mushrooms.

They were friendly. Every species around the Great Ocean was friendly to strangers. Louis was used to it.

The oldest girl asked, "What shape is the world?"

Quiet fell and heads turned. Was it a test? "I should ask rather than tell, Strill. What shape *is* the world?"

"A circle, the shape of infinity, the Web Dweller says. I don't understand, though. I see an arch, like—" Strill pointed. There were small conical roofs below, sprouting among the trees: a sizable village strung along the river's vastness. Upstream was an arch like the oft-rebuilt St. Louis Arch, broad at the base, narrowing as it rose. "—like the Upstream Gate."

So that was all right. "The arch is the part of the ring you're not standing on," Louis said. *Web Dweller?*

He was walking with one proprietary hand on the stacked cargo plates as they floated alongside him.

There were *millions* of these in the Repair Center beneath the Map of Mars. He'd welded some needed items to the topmost floating disk. These included handholds, a seat back, a bin for spare clothing and another for food, and a little attitude thruster, a spare part for the Hindmost's probes. And . . . well, he'd found that already in place after the battle eleven years ago. It was Teela Brown's medkit.

Furry adults and small furry children saw the bird catchers returning early. Most stayed with their tasks, but a man and a woman waited at the arch to greet them.

Strill cried, "He's a wizard! Kidada-sir, he says it's a ring!"

The man glanced at the floating plates. He asked, "Do you *know* this?"

Louis said, "I've seen it. I'm Louis Wu of the Ball People."

It shouldn't have meant anything to them, but the Elders gaped and the children ooohed.

The woman said, "Louis Wu of the Ball People?" Age had put white in her golden fur, and more of that in the man's. Their knee-length kilts were elaborate tapestries that would have been valuable in any culture. "I am Sawur and this is Kidada, both of the Council, both of the Weaver Folk. You are from nowhere on the Arch, yes? The Web Dweller has vouched for your power and wisdom."

"Web Dweller?" How could anyone have known of him here?

Kidada said, "The Web Dweller is certainly of another world. It's got two heads! And servants like itself in uncountable numbers."

Aw, tanj. "What else did the Web Dweller have to say?"

"It showed us pictures from far up the Arch, so it says."

"What did you see? Vampires?"

"Strange humanoids living in darkness, and an alliance of many kinds of people come to attack them. Can you tell us of those?"

"I know something of vampires. The Web Dweller may know more, but I haven't spoken to him in thirty-six falans."

"How do your folk manage rishathra?" Sawur asked, and there was suppressed giggling.

Louis grinned. "As best we can. Yours?"

"We Weavers are said to be very good with our hands, and visitors speak well of the touch of our fur. One must ask, shall we wash?"

"Good idea."

Weavers, they called themselves.

Their village—*city*—was nowhere crowded, but it seemed to go on and on, spilling up and down both sides of the river, sprouting among the trees of the vast forest. Their houses were wickerwork shells shaped like low mushrooms, not unlike the trees.

Louis was being led toward a vertical cliff of bare pale rock. Kidada said, "See you water running down that cliff face? The baths are below. Sunlight warms the water as it flows, a little."

The pool was long and narrow. Low tables bore little heaps of embroidered kilts. Sawur and Kidada added theirs to a heap. Three parallel furrows ran through the hair across the old man's buttocks, old scars rimmed with white fur, leading Louis to wonder about local predators.

Weavers were already bathing themselves. Children and the elderly seemed to gravitate together; postadolescents separated out, but rarely formed pairs. Louis had learned to look for such patterns.

The water was muddy. He didn't see any towels. He set his clothing—Canyon style camping garb and backpurse, from two hundred light-years away—on a table, and stepped in. When in Rome . . .

It wasn't all that warm, either.

Now all the ages mixed as the Weavers gathered around the visiting alien, the teacher. Newly met species always had the same questions.

"My companions and I steered our great ship to the shore of the Great Ocean, forty falans ago. We found desolation. Long before any of you were born, Fist-of-God raised the shore forty manheights along twenty thousand daywalks of shoreline . . ."

Confusion. Louis's translator would translate Sol system measurements into the Ringworld's thirty-hour day, seventy-five days to a falan; but daywalks and manheights varied by species. Louis floated on his back, treading water while they spoke of distance, time, height. No hurry. He'd done this dance before.

"People to spinward remember Fist-of-God in their legends. Something bigger than any mountain struck the floor of the world from underneath at hellish speed, thirty-five hundred falans ago"; A.D. 1200, by Louis's best guess. "It pushed the land up and then ripped through as a fireball. You can see the mountain it made from here, a hundred thousand miles away, and the deserts all around it. The shore of the Great Ocean moved a thousand miles seaward. All the patterns of life changed . . ."

The water was armpit-deep, shallower at the end where the children gathered. A kind of dance was going on here: not a courtship game, but the women around Louis were of mating age, and men their age were hanging back. Ring pattern. A rishathra dance?

His eye kept snagging on Strill's attentive look and wonderful smile. They all had questions. The same questions always. But Louis had seen the glitter of bronze on the bare cliff above his head. The fractal spiderweb was out of a Weaver's reach, and the water flowing down the rock wasn't washing it off.

So he spoke for an unseen audience. "We had to stay with the ocean or we'd have had nothing to eat. We spent two falans cruising along the shore, and finally we realized we were in a river mouth. We continued upstream. The fertility has returned to the soil along the Shenthy River valley. We've been in this vast river valley for thirty-five falans. My City Builder friends left me at a village downstream, twenty falans ago."

"Why?"

"They have children now. But I continued upstream. The people are friendly everywhere. They like hearing my tales."

Sawur asked, "Why does that surprise you, Louis Wu?"

He smiled at the older woman. "When a visitor comes to your village, he probably doesn't eat what you eat or sleep where you sleep or feel quite comfortable in your house. An alien doesn't compete with his host. And he might have something to teach. But the Ball People are all one species on all the worlds. A visitor can be bad news."

A moment's uncomfortable silence followed. One of the brawny boys settled behind Strill broke it. He called, "Can you do this?" He reached around his back, one arm above, one below, and clasped wrists with himself.

Louis Wu laughed. Once he could have. "No."

"Then you should have your back washed," the boy said, and they all moved in.

The great thing about the Ringworld was its variety. And the great thing about variety was that rishathra wouldn't work at all if it required an elaborate dance.

"How do your folk manage rishathra?"

"If you will state your gender—"

"How long can you hold your breath?" Sea Folk.

"No, but we like to talk about it."

"We cannot. Don't be offended." Red Herders.

"It was thus we ruled the world!" City Builders.

"Only with sapient species. Here, solve this riddle—"

"Only with nonsapient species. We prefer not to become involved."

"May we watch you with your companion?" Louis had once had to explain that Chmeee was not a hominid, and was male besides. He wondered how much the Weavers knew about the bronze spiderweb above their heads. They were pairing off now, but not mating in public. How would Weavers rish?

Sawur led him out of the water. She squeezed a liter of water from her brown and white fur, with Louis's help. When she saw he was shivering, she wiped him down with his shirt.

Louis could smell roasting bird flesh.

They dressed. Sawur led him into a circle of woven wicker cages. "Council House," she said of one. Birds were roasting above a barbecue pit. The smells were wonderful. Birds and a huge fish, tended by . . . "Sawur, those aren't Weavers."

"No. Sailing Folk and Fishers."

One Weaver of middle age was tending the pit with the

help of seven aliens. They weren't all of the same species. Two males had webbed hands and broad flat feet, and oily straight hair slicked along their bodies in a smooth curve. The other five, three men and two women, were burly, powerful versions of the Weavers, with altered jaws. Close enough that they might still mate, maybe. All seven were wearing the fantastic Weaver kilts.

The big Fisher, Shans Serpentstrangler, made introduction. Louis tried to remember their names. His translator would retrieve them, if he could remember even a syllable. Shans explained, "We trade for cloth, yes? We compete. When Hishthare Rockdiver and I offer to broil this monster fish the Sailors catch downstream, the Sailors offer, too. Afraid we talk to Kidada, learn something needful. Get a lower price."

"Meanwhile we argue over how to cook our fish." That was the Sailor, Wheek. "Kidada at least gets his birds the way he wants."

"I'd say those birds are done," Louis said. "I can't guess about the fish. When did you start?"

"It will be perfect in a hundred breaths," Shans said. "Cooked on the down side for the Sailors, warm on the up side for us. How do you like it?"

"Down side."

The Weaver population half dried themselves and came to eat. The birds came off the hot rocks and were torn apart. The fish continued to cook. Louis would find his own vegetables, tomorrow.

And they talked.

The Weavers' nimble fingers wove nets to catch mid-sized birds and beasts of the forest; but they wove cloth for river traffic. Peekaboo clothing, hammocks, fishnets, belt pouches and back pouches, a variety of things for a variety of species.

Fishers and Sailors traded up and down the river, carrying Weaver kilts, smoked and salted fish, salt, root vegetables . . .

It was shop talk. Louis eased out of that. He asked Kidada about his scar, and was told of a fight with what sounded like a monster bear. Weavers withdrew: they'd heard the tale. Kidada told a good tale, though from the sound of it, the scar should have been in front.

At sunset all the Weavers seemed to melt away. Sawur led him to a ring of tents, their feet crunching in dry brush.

Sailors and Fishers remained in conversation around the dying coal bed. One called advice after him: "Don't wander. Only the Night People walk these paths at night."

They stooped under the edge of the wicker cage. Sawur rolled against him and fell asleep at once. Louis felt a moment's irritation; but species differ.

Sleeping in a strange place hadn't bothered Louis in falans . . . no, in years. Nor sleeping in a strange woman's arms, nor rubbing against fluffy fur . . . like sleeping with a big dog . . . nor both together. But knowing the Hindmost's eye was near, *that* kept him awake for some time.

Sometime in the night, he dreamed that a monster sank teeth into his leg. He woke holding back a scream.

Sawur spoke without opening her eyes. "What is it, teacher?"

"Cramp. In my leg." Louis rolled out of her arms and crawled to the door.

"I get cramps, too. Walk." Sawur was asleep.

He limped outside. The side of his calf was shrieking. He hated muscle cramps!

The daylit arcs of the Ringworld reflected far more light

than Earth's full moon. The medical kit would give him medicine for a cramp, but it didn't act any quicker than just walking it off.

His foot crunched dry twigs.

Low dry brush surrounded the guests' huts. Friendly as they were, the Weavers must have some way to discourage thieves. This dry stuff might be their defense.

The cramp had eased, but he was wide-awake. His cargo plates floated outside the guest hut. He pulled himself aboard. He crossed the brushy barrier without a sound, weaving among the tree trunks.

Not a bit nocturnal, these Weavers. No sign of any of them. Sleeping like the dead, how would they catch a thief? The visiting aliens had retired, too. Lanterns lit the bow and stern of a long, low sailboat he hadn't noticed earlier.

In a minute or two Louis was floating silently above the pool, lit by Archlight real and reflected.

Motion within the cliff . . . and a light blazed in his face.

Louis squinted, cursing. He looked into the glare . . . through a window with fuzzed-out edges, at an impressive cinder cone capped in what seemed dirty snow. On any world, that would be a volcano. Here it could be a meteor crater punched from below. It looked very like Fist-of-God, crowned with vacuum and naked Ringworld floor structure.

A message from the Hindmost?

Once the puppeteer knew Louis was moving up the river, he could have moved his probe ahead. He'd sprayed a spy device on this rock cliff, and others elsewhere, no doubt. He'd talked to the Weavers . . . easy enough, but why bother? What did he *want*?

Something spat from the crater, twice, thrice within ten seconds.

"Six hundred and ten hours ago," said a familiar contralto. "Watch."

The view zoomed on the three objects. Lens-shaped space-craft, big. Kzinti design, Louis thought. They stopped just above the peak, then began their descent, two or three meters above the glassy crater wall.

"The warcraft are moving quite slowly. Let me show you fast-forward," the Hindmost said. The warcraft moved briskly downslope. Beyond and below, cloudscape jumped into streamlined motion. "In two hours, twenty minutes at just under sonic speed, they had covered fourteen hundred miles. For kzinti, amazing restraint. Then they diverged, thus—"

The cloudscape and the saucers jerked to a near stop. Two veered off at right angles; the third continued straight on.

White light blinked. Then the scene was as before, but the three ships had a blobby, half-melted look, and they gleamed like mirrors. They began to descend . . . to fall.

"Stasis fields. They stopped your beam," Louis said.

"Worrisome, Louis. Wrong twice within five seconds. Is your brain deteriorating?"

"That can happen," Louis said equably.

The Hindmost said, "Those beams were intense. Vast energy flux was trapped inside the stasis fields before they formed."

"But—"

"You and Nessus survived a similar attack because *we* design defense mechanisms to react *quickly*! Those kzinti warcraft are nothing but bombs now. And that was the Ringworld Meteor Defense, but I did not use it."

"Yah, right."

"Observe." The view jumped . . . a view of the magnified sun, darkened to something tolerable. From the fluid storm a plume rose in fast-forward motion. Higher, straight toward the camera . . . hundreds of thousands of miles. A brighter shock wave was rising from its base. It lashed out along the plume and was suddenly terribly bright.

"A superthermal laser effect, definitely the Ringworld Meteor Defense, Louis. But not mine."

The Hindmost *would* lie. But would he shoot down an invading ship?

"Louis, I'm not shooting down invading spacecraft! I want to contact them. A hyperdrive motor could free me from this place!"

"I buy that, I guess, but— Hindmost, do you think someone is in the Repair Center with you?"

"I do not believe my defenses have been breached. Louis, there are two Great Oceans."

It took Louis a moment to see what the Hindmost meant.

A single Great Ocean would unbalance the Ringworld. The water involved would mass as much as a major Jovian moon. There had to be two, on opposite arcs; and there were.

The Hindmost's crew had found a Repair Center in one Great Ocean, under the Map of Mars. The other ocean they had never explored at all.

And it was across the Ringworld's diameter. The Ringworld was sixteen light-minutes across. Sixteen minutes at lightspeed before a second Repair Center could *see* invading ships coming through Fist-of-God. Eight minutes more to begin to affect the sun. More time—an hour? Two?—to stretch a plume of plasma some millions of miles out from the sun, then cause it to lase. The terrible sword of light would be another eight minutes on its way.

Two hours and twenty minutes was a plausible guess. Louis said, "Stet. You'd best assume there's another Repair Center on the far side of the Ringworld Arch, and a protector inside."

"Why a protector? Mind you, Louis, I think so, too."

"A protector would find a way in. If a hominid got in somehow—a breeder—he'll be a protector by now. The other Repair Center must be infested with tree-of-life, like ours was. Is this what you wanted me for? You know almost as much about protectors as I do, and it's dead of night here, so my brain may not be fully functional."

"Age, too, may have affected your brain. We do need to talk, and I have more to show you. Louis, shall I appear to the Weavers and acknowledge your power? Or shall I not?"

"Thoughtful of you, but that may be out of our hands." The locals slept, but Fishers or Sailors must have seen this glare, and who could know when a Ghoul was nearby?

Actually . . .

The Hindmost missed Louis's sudden grin. He said, "These Weavers seem hospitable."

"Every species around the Great Ocean is friendly if you watch your mouth."

"What news of our companions?"

"Chmeee took an assault vehicle to carry his gear. Didn't you have a webeye on that?"

"He buried it," the Hindmost said.

Louis laughed.

"He can unearth it if he has need. What of the City Builders?"

Louis said, "Kawaresksenjajok and Harkabeeparolyn had two children to raise and another on the way. I won't say we were bored with each other, but . . . futz. I put them off at a village downstream from here, with one of the assault boats. They're teaching there and along the far shore. How are you?"

"Not presentable. Louis—" Three silver blobs bouncing down the slope of Fist-of-God were replaced by a glare of snow, a mountain ridge in broad daylight. A green outline blinked around two dots crawling through a cleft in the ridge. "—let me direct your attention to these. Ten years ago I showed you—"

"I remember. Is this the same view?"

"Yes, as of three days ago, taken from the rim of a floating structure above a vampire nest."

"Is this what you've been showing the Weavers?"

"Yes." The view zoomed. Those were great crude six-wheeled vehicles, possibly powered by steam. One of them was turning back, upslope. The view zoomed on the other, on the driving bench. "These are Machine People?"

Louis looked. "Right. Note the beards. Looks like Machine People vehicles, too. Hey . . ."

"Louis, my computer's recognition program—"

"That's Valavirgillin!"

Chapter Six

SNOWRUNNER'S PASS

The Barrier of Flame had been given a low, eroded look.

None but Valavirgillin would see mountains that way. Louis Wu of the Ball People had taught her to view the world as a mask. He and his weird companions had looked up into its black underside, where seas were bulges, mountain ranges were chains of pits, and tremendous pipes carried seabottom flup under the world and over the rim wall to become spill mountains.

Some entity had *carved* the Barrier of Flame to suit esthetic whims. Had carved passes through the range for the convenience of travelers. Various Red tribes and their herds had followed the retreating mirror-flowers across Snowrunner's Pass. Two of these same Reds now guided the cruisers.

Night was biting an edge from the sun as the cruisers crossed the crest of Snowrunner's Pass. None of them had seen blue sky in many falans. They gloried in it. Unbroken clouds spread below them. There was snow on the ground, not deep, but enough to cause the wheels to slide. Vala had trouble steering. To left and right the mountains flamed, raw sunlight reflecting from snowfields.

Below and behind the driving bench, Waast was telling

someone unseen, "We didn't see snow when we crossed here. The mirror-flowers burned it all away."

Her bulk had half hidden Tegger. He said, "Mirror-flowers don't like clouds. They burn anything that moves. Waast, is it good to separate the wagons this late in the day?"

"One must decide," Waast said firmly.

The Red Herder frowned. "Of course the pilot gives the orders. But, look you, mates have been separated. Valavirgillin and Kaywerbrimmis. Grieving Tube and Harpster, too. Kaywerbrimmis and Chitakumishad are both *male*. What if vampires come? Warvia and I are safe separated. Beedj is with you, Paroom is with Twuk, Manack is with Coriack, but what of the rest?"

Vala steered Cruiser One down the long slope, pretending not to listen. This was how a Red Herder expressed his dissent, by letting it be overheard. *Mates!* The next turn put her in sight of a wide brown river.

The Reds were of a monogamous race, and mated. They didn't like being separated; but two cruisers need two guides. Kay and Vala must part too: two cruisers need two drivers. But she and Kaywerbrimmis were not mated!

And here came Pilack pelting after her ahead of Cruiser Two. Vala choked the fuel line and let her cruiser stop.

Gleaners could run like the wind. Pilack looked up at her, grinning, for a moment in which to catch his breath. He said, "Kaywerbrimmis wants to go farther up."

She looked back. Left of the pass the crest rose gently enough. Kay would be above the snow line, and he'd have a view.

"Shall we wait?"

"Kay says don't wait. Stop the cruiser if you find danger. We'll have you in view. We'll come."

"Aye."

Pilack ran away. Uphill, Kay's crew were offloading cargo.
Tons of it. Without Paroom and Twuk, it would have taken
forever. A few tenbreaths later Cruiser Two was in motion,
with Kay on the steering bench and the rest of the crew walking behind, except for the Ghoul, of course. Grieving Tube
would not wake till halfnight.

Now a curve took them out of sight.

Cruiser One carried Valavirgillin and Sabarokaresh, Waast
and Beedj, Manack and Coriack, Tegger, and Harpster. They
stayed out of the payload shell. The payload shell had never
been so clean, so scentless. The Ghoul Harpster would have
liked the darkness; but he made do with the rest taking their
turns under the awnings, on blankets spread along the running boards.

The Machine People on Cruiser Two were both male. She
and Kay had dithered about taking Chitakumishad. They'd
have preferred Spash, but nobody would risk Spash's life while
she was pregnant. And Chit had had to be tied up during the
vampire attack, but he was clever and skillful with tools.

They'd be all right. There was always rishathra.

Cruiser One was beneath the cloud deck now. The dark-
ening day signaled a sun half shadowed. And what was happening down there at the river? "Tegger, give me your sight.
The river?"

Gleaners were nearsighted; they could barely see beyond
their toes. Machine People had good eyes. But none had eyes
like the Reds. Tegger scrambled up onto the steering bench,
peered under his hand; then climbed to the cannon tower,
higher yet.

"Vampire. Two of them. They're hideous, Vala. Do you
hear anything?"

"No."

"I think they're singing, Vala. And . . . a black thing is coming out of the water. What do River People look like?"

"Wet black. Your size, but compact, streamlined—"

"Short arms and big hands with webbed fingers? Legs likewise? They've lured one out. Now one vampire is moving downstream. Wrong gender, maybe, I can't tell from this far away. How fast can we get down?"

"Not that fast." Not fast enough for rescue. They were closer now. Vala could see two pale shapes and a black. One pale shape ambled away down the shore. The black waddled to the other white, who enfolded it in its arms. Moments later the white hurled itself backward onto the mud.

The squat black shape approached again, arms outstretched. The white backed away fast on its skinny buttocks. Recovered its courage, or its hunger; got up and accepted the other's embrace.

Black rubbed against white. Vala heard a squall like a mountain cat's as the pale shape tore itself free and ran away along the shore, upstream.

The black shape couldn't catch up. It stopped and cried, a desolate honk.

"How fast?" Tegger asked again.

"We'll be down before halfnight, in time to wash. Then we'll test our defenses, I think. Best if Cruiser Two stays high. Manack, you listening? Coriack?"

"I hear," Coriack said. "Cruiser Two stays high till dawn."

"Go tell Kaywerbrimmis. Then stay with Cruiser Two! I don't want you alone on the slopes when night falls."

Beedj was up and walking ahead and to the right, his crossbow cocked. Barok was tending the cannon. Tegger perched above him.

The black hominid lay inconsolable on wet river mud.

It presently rolled over and saw the descending cruiser. It waited.

Manack dropped from the running board and ran ahead. Vala's gun was in her hands, ready.

A vampire sang.

The music was unmistakable, thrilling along her nerves. Manack came to a jarring stop. Vala could see no target. The River Person waddled toward the bushes.

The second vampire stepped timidly out to meet it. Male, it was. It raised its arms imploringly. With the scent and the music going wild in her head, Vala fired.

The bullet struck beneath its armpit, slamming the vampire violently away. In the near-dark its blood was as red as any hominid's. Vala caught a stronger whiff of its scent; she raised the towel and inhaled pepperleek.

Manack was hanging back. The River Person cast itself on the body. The vampire spasmed in agony, then relaxed.

Vala pulled the cruiser alongside both. Passengers were dropping from the running board.

Slick black hair, short thick arms and legs, wide hands and feet, streamlined body . . . clothing. The River Woman's torso was covered with some other creature's brown fur. She looked up, then pulled away from the vampire male with visible effort.

"Greeting," she said. "I am Wurblychoog—" a liquid flow of syllables and a trace of smile. *You can't pronounce that.*

Vala said, "Greetings, Wurble. Valavirgillin. Why didn't the vampire kill you?"

"This," the woman said, and her hands waved down her barrel body. The garment was stiff around her throat. The sides were smooth leather, the hair shaved off. The rest, chest and back, were fur taken from some water beast.

She said, "We take a jell from a floating predator in Lake Deeps, half a daywalk across land. The jellfisher stings fish to eat them. The sting is in the jell. We smear an otter fur vest with jell, then shave off the fur where our arms lie when we swim. Vampires don't like the sting, but after, must . . . must . . ." She turned to Manack. "Can swim, little courageous one? Can hold breath for a little while?"

"I would drown," said Manack.

The River Woman told Vala, "Homeflow tribe has only four vests. Vampires bar us from shore, many falans now. If from time to time one of us wears a vest and lets a vampire embrace her, she may teach them to leave River People alone. Then we can hunt the shore for a time."

"You show great courage."

"I show my courage for Borubble, to take him for my mate."

"And get some vampire scent on yourself, too," Waast leered.

"Shubble flup! This is not to speak of. You, red one, can dive deep for only a few tens of breaths?"

Tegger shook his head. He was tired of the question. The River Woman sighed. "We hear rishathra. Never practice. Must mate! Will tell Borubble the good news. Will tell him visitors come, too. Stay here on mud flat, see vampires coming from a long way."

She was across the mud and into the water before Vala could frame an intelligent reply.

Water could hide threats other than vampires. The whole team bathed with edged weapons in hand. Afterward Barok went upstream with the Gleaners to fish. Vala envied him a little, but she must remain to set up defenses.

Cruiser One spent the night on the mud flat. No visitors came, vampires or River People.

It was all going very smoothly, Vala thought. Very much according to prediction and plan. That worried her.

Three nights ago they had put a final shape to their plans.

Four Reds had come to the war. Warvia and Tegger had stayed, but two unmated males, Anakrin hooki-Whanhurhur and Chaychind hooki-Karashk, had been persuaded to return to Red territory carrying instructions that might be the saving of them all. Whand had had enough of vampires, and it seemed he and Spash had gotten pregnant. They would stay to refuel Cruiser Three. That left Valavirgillin and Kaywerbrimmis, the remaining drivers, split up to command two cruisers.

They'd chosen the teams early, then argued about it every night since.

Raking through a mountainous Grass Giant midden for several days had not improved the Machine People's standing with these tribes. Vala was sure of that. But Grass Giant dung had yielded many barrels of saltpeter crystals.

The relief map outside the wall had become elaborate and wonderful. Only at halfnight and halfday was there light for Ghouls and the other species to work together on it; but they'd had a falan, seventy-five days, to do that. Dirt was replaced with colored clays. Once witnesses agreed on the shape of the land, they'd baked it hard under coals, and afterward used colored sand to mark possible routes for the cruisers. They were still moving those lines when night fell, and all retreated inside.

The vampires didn't come every night, but they came in swarms.

Vampires didn't learn, didn't communicate. Moonwa had

mounted the Marsh People's curved window in the starboard-spin curve of the wall. The vampires attacked from starboard-spin, and warriors of four species killed them with guns and crossbows, firing around the edge of an invisible shield.

Vala had learned crossbows that way, several nights running. She loved the false sense of invulnerability . . . false, because the window would not stop vampire scent.

The main building was a near-dome, fabric stretched over the top of a dirt wall, with a central pole. It was awesomely big, but awesomely crowded. Fifteen hundred Grass Giants—more women than men, a great many children, infants everywhere—made a stench rich enough to slice with a scythe-sword.

Wemb was in a cluster of wives. They were feeding her by hand, feeding themselves, too, and Wemb seemed to be enjoying it. Barok waved at her, and she waved back without getting up. Recovering nicely, Vala thought, from the night she and Barok had spent down among the vampires.

Barok would ride with Cruiser One. Vala had wondered if he would drop out of the game with Whand and Spash, or chase down the vampires who had taken his daughter.

Grass Giants were big, but they could stand crowding. For Machine People, Vala discovered, the problem was to avoid getting stepped on.

The Reds were prickly. Grass Giants steered clear of them.

If Reds and Machine People were feeling overmatched, why weren't the even smaller Gleaners intimidated? But they'd found strategies that seemed to work. Some were playing with the children, some were grooming adults. Their nearsighted eyes found insect parasites with precision.

The Thurl pulled himself free of a ten of wives. He asked

Vala, courteously and with no malice, "Do you have what you wanted of the shit pile?"

So, it was time to reveal a secret. "Yes, we thank you. When we mix the crystals with the sulfur and charcoal the Reds are gathering, we will have what propels our bullets."

"Ah," the Thurl said, hiding surprise.

He could not make gunpowder: he still didn't know the proportions, Vala told herself. But now he knew that this was no mere Machine People perversion.

Into the quiet, vampire music insinuated itself, and quiet became silence.

But now the vampires' song had a rising instrumental accompaniment. First it matched the vampire music. Vala had learned to pick out the harp, the grieving tube, the whistling tube, the thutter. Now the Ghoulish music skirled away, jarring with the vampire song, drowning it, while the thutter in the background played faster and faster, pulling heartbeats along. And now there was no vampire song at all.

Next dawn they'd been rolling. By night they camped on a bluff above a river. The vampires left them alone.

They reached Ginjerofer's herds early on the second day. The Reds had fuel waiting. Charcoal and sulfur they had imported from far away, trading away their own wealth, with little yet to show for it.

Night covered the sun before the cruisers were loaded. The Reds made camp around the cruisers. When the vampires came, the cannon fired over the heads of Red sharpshooters. By dawn the vampire dead numbered forty or more.

Cruisers carried trade goods, and Vala made gifts; but forty vampire dead were what bonded these species together.

The third day carried them through Snowrunner's Pass. The length of a daywalk varied by difficulty of the terrain, by altitude and slope and species; but Vala thought they'd covered two honest daywalks. They could reach the vampires' refuge by midday tomorrow, if they were crazy enough to travel so directly.

In the morning Cruiser Two came rolling down. Warvia rode above the cannon housing, beneath a sheet awning.

Twuk called cheerily, "Waast! Is it so, that Snowrunner's Pass is the easiest through the mountains?"

"When Reds and Ghouls agree, who can doubt?"

"Vampires think so, too!"

Cruiser Two was noisy with victory. Even Grieving Tube's dark head lifted into the light, squinting, and grinned grotesquely before it sank back. Vala didn't notice Warvia's silence, then. Red Herders were rarely merry.

The din roused others. Vala saw wet black heads surfacing in a line along the shore. The River People came no farther, and Vala let them be, while Kay, Chit, Twuk, Paroom, Perilack, and Silack told their interwoven stories.

Kaywerbrimmis parked Cruiser Two on a knob of rock above the pass. The view was of unbroken clouds, not what Kay had hoped for, but he would wait. All had bathed in the streams they crossed, twice in three days. If they were not scentless, at least they'd tried.

(They weren't scentless now, grinning and touching and

word-wrestling to be next to speak. Vala could guess something of how the night had gone.)

Darkness flowed over them. Vampires began to stream through the pass. Grieving Tube, on watch, alerted the rest.

Cruiser Two's heavy cargo, still piled in the pass, must have carried a scent. Kay sighted the cannon starboard of that point and waited. He killed twenty with three blasts.

The vampires left the pass empty for a while. Then they'd begun darting across. Kay's passengers used the chance for target shooting, but otherwise let the vampires through. Bolts and bullets could be recovered, but not gunpowder.

They bunched up again later. Kay used the cannon again, and stopped almost at once. "They had prisoners, Vala. Big slow guys with big hands and big shoulders, wide-bodied women a head shorter, both of 'em with yellow hair blooming out around their heads like mushrooms. Warvia saw them best. Warvia?"

Warvia roused herself. "We know the Farming People. Herbivores. They grow and tend root vegetables and keep animals, too, in partnership with Red Herder tribes who defend them. We didn't see any Reds last night."

Paroom: "They weren't bunched up and they weren't trying to escape. They were each with their own vampire, ah, companion. I couldn't get a clear shot. We shot a few that didn't have company—"

Twuk: "They sang at us. Grieving Tube played along. That scared them!"

Kay: "I couldn't use the cannon because of the prisoners. Not that we were any help to them. What under the Arch would vampires want with prisoners?"

Tegger said, "Herds."

He spoke almost absently; he was studying Warvia, who

would meet nobody's eyes. Still, it was an ugly thought. Double-ugly: it implied uncomfortably high sapience in vampires.

"The wind," Kaywerbrimmis said, "was cold and wet and clean in our nostrils until the night was half gone. The vampires started crossing again, and these didn't have prisoners. They ran. Maybe the smell of their own dead made them nervous. It was fine shooting. Then the wind shifted around and we smelled them, too."

Grieving Tube was looking out from under the awning, listening, though her face was deep in shadow. "I would have hunted them, Kay," she said. "Our music confuses them, freezes them."

Kay's eyes were on Vala. "Whatever. I invited Grieving Tube to join me in rishathra." Unspoken: *the Ghoul woman was about to join the vampires!* "She played, we danced. Warvia accused me of abandoning the fight, but the rest got the idea quick enough—"

In the general laughter, Harpster's tenor whisper sounded clear. "How was he?"

Grieving Tube: "Inspired. Paroom, too."

"We all—" Kay stopped suddenly, for no more than a heartbeat, but Vala knew at once. "We all joined in. You understand, Vala, we had them backed up at the pass. As soon as we stopped shooting, they flowed through like a wide river. The smell of them, we could have chopped it into bricks to sell to the elderly."

Tegger was looking up at his mate. Warvia's silence disturbed him, Vala thought, but he hadn't noticed anything more ominous. Kaywerbrimmis said, "I think the Thurl gave us Twuk because she's small. Inspired decision." Twuk smiled brilliantly at him. Warvia was looking into far distances, her face like stone.

"Two-tenths of night passed this way, I think. Then the wind swung around. I didn't notice right away: the vampire scent was gone, but we had our own smells by then. But Chit saw—"

Chit: "Vampires trying to creep upon us across the ice. They're not much darker than snow themselves."

Kay: "The wind went gusty and stayed that way. They'd get a whiff of us and look around, and we were conspicuous, I guess."

Paroom: "Ten tens of them."

Kay: "Toward morning they stopped coming entirely. We left a carpet of vampires dead in the pass."

Twuk: "There's nothing under the Arch like the stink of a hundred vampire corpses. They do avoid their own dead."

Vala: "Might keep it in mind."

Twuk: "We collected our cargo and our bolts and bullets at halfdawn. Vala, I think we *saw* the Shadow Nest."

"Tell it."

"Warvia?"

The Red woman didn't look down. "From spin the light of day flowed toward us while we were still in dark. We were exhausted, but I was at my post, here on the cannon tower. The clouds parted. I saw two black lines. Hard to tell how far, hard to tell how high, but a black plate with structures above, high in the center and glittering silver, and its black shadow parallel below."

"Not much more than what Harpster told us," Vala said, probing.

A flash of anger, throttled. "I could see the silver curves of the river, this river, flowing into the shadow."

"We know of the Shadow Nest." A new voice heard from: a glossy black shape of uncertain gender and uncertain age slid out of the water and stood erect on the mud. "I am

Rooballabl. Welcome to the Homeflow; have free passage of us. I speak the Tongue better than most. I'm told none of you will rish?"

"Not underwater, Roobla," Vala said with regret. That *would* be a coup. "Shadow Nest?"

"The Shadow Nest is a cave without walls. A black roof fifteen hundred paces around, with open sides. Vampires have lived and bred below since before any of us were born."

Harpster spoke without emerging from the awning. Only Vala heard. "Fifteen hundred paces around would be less then five hundred across, in Water People paces. Two hundred for Grass Giants, three for the rest of us. Three hundred paces in diameter, as we were told."

Vala asked, "Roobla, how high is that roof?"

Rooballabl exchanged a quick sequence of honks with someone still in the water. Then: "Fudghabladl doesn't know." More honking. Rooballabl said, "Low enough to block rain even in high wind. Understand, only Fudghabladl has been there."

"What's the Homeflow like under the Shadow Nest? Can vampires swim?"

A gabble of honking voices. One came forward—white fringes on his head and along where his jaw would have been—and chattered at Rooballabl. Rooballabl said, "We must hug the bottom when we pass through. None of us go anymore. The water is a sewer, sometimes a *whonkee*." Unknown word. "Vampires never swim."

Unseen, Harpster spoke. "*Whonkee*, path of the dead." Vala nodded.

Warvia swung down into the cannon enclosure.

Vala watched Cruiser Two while the discussion ranged. Warvia didn't emerge. And where was Tegger?

The River People had observed the vampires for generations, but from their own viewpoint. Vampires sporadically rolled corpses into the Homeflow, hundreds at a time, from ten to twenty species including their own. A turn later there would be a glut of fish. That used to be worth knowing . . . but old Fudghabladl hadn't been near the Shadow Nest in twenty falans or more. Fishing aside, nothing that lay beyond was worth traversing the Shadow Nest.

Vala dropped her voice. "Harpster. Corpses rolled into the Homeflow are lost to you, aren't they?"

"Fish eat them, and Fishers eat the fish, and in the end all is ours."

"Flup. You're being robbed."

"Vala, vampires are animals. Animals don't rob."

Rooballabl: "None but the River People may come to the Shadow Nest and leave alive. Why do you ask these things? Why are you here, so many species?"

Beedj spoke before Vala could. "We go to end the vampire menace. We will attack them in their home. Hominids who cannot travel have supported us."

The River People discussed that. Vala thought she saw silent laughter.

Maybe not. Rooballabl said, "Valavirgillin, we think we saw a Ghoul among your number."

"Two of the Night People travel with us. Others parallel our path as friends. They don't like sunlight, Roobla."

"Ghouls and vampires are all People of the Night."

Did Rooballabl mean they were allies? "They compete for the same prey on the same terrain. Truly, it's more complicated than that—"

"Are you sure they stand with you?"

For all of a falan, Vala had wondered at the Ghouls' motives. She said, "Yes, quite sure."

"We could not travel with you."

"No."

"But if you will roll your wagons along the Homeflow, we can travel alongside, Fudghabladl and I. Tell you things. Take vests, teach our lessons downstream."

They began working out details. This was unlooked-for luck, and Vala knew she must pursue it, though Tegger and Warvia were nowhere to be seen.

Chapter Seven

WAYSPIRIT

Tegger knelt with his back to a big pale rock, his heels under his buttocks, quite still. The scrub was all around him, hiding him.

This was how Reds hunted. And Tegger was hunting through his mind, seeking Tegger. His hands played idly with his sword, honing the edge.

Thoughts played over the surface of Tegger's mind. If he let them go deeper, he'd be thinking of Warvia. He knew he couldn't face that.

The water's steady roar had him nodding. He would not hear any creature approaching. Perhaps he would smell it, or see motion in the scrub around him. His sword was defense enough.

All the action was at the shore. At some point the negotiations had become a swimming party.

A sword could be used on oneself. Just turn it around. Jump from the top of a rock? The thought merely skimmed the surface of his mind.

"Tegger hooki-Thandarthal."

Tegger jumped and was on the rock, his blade swinging in

a full circle before his mind caught up. *Vampires don't speak. What . . . ?*

A voice just louder than the river, so low that Tegger might have imagined it, said, "I cannot harm you, Tegger. I grant wishes."

No living thing was in sight. Tegger asked, "Wishes?" Had he been found by a wayspirit?

"I was a living woman once. Now I help others in hope of making a better self. What would you have of me?"

"Want to die."

Pause, then, "Such a waste."

Tegger heard a rasp of effort deep beneath the whisper. Somehow he could not believe that his sword would be fast enough. He said, "Wait."

"I wait." The whisper was much closer now.

Tegger had twice spoken without thinking. Now: he had evaded a quick death. Did he want that? But if wishes could be granted . . .

"Something happened last night. I want it not to have happened."

"That cannot be."

Every man on Cruiser Two, whatever his shape, chemistry, diet, had mated with Tegger's mate. *They* have to die, he thought. But the women? . . . All who know. Warvia, too, he thought, even as his mind was rejecting the notion.

They did this to Warvia, to me. It was the vampires! Shall I kill half of us with a wish? Undefended, the rest would die. Ginjerofer's tribe— He saw, suddenly, how the Red tribes would fall before an expanding vampire plague. Men and women, unable to trust one another, would separate in rage. Families and tribes would disintegrate. Vampires would take them one by one.

Tegger said, "I would have you kill every vampire under the Arch."

The whisper came. "I have no such power."

"What power have you?"

"Tegger, I am a mind and a voice. I know things. Sometimes I see things before you do. I never lie."

Useless creature. "Wayspirit, your good intent exceeds your means. What if I wish for a fish to eat?"

"I can do that. Will you wait?"

"I will, but why?"

"I must not be seen. I could much more quickly tell you how to get your own fish."

True, the shore was very active. "Do you have a name?"

"Call me what you wish."

"Whisper."

"Good."

"Whisper, I want to kill vampires."

"So do all of your companions. Will you rejoin them?"

Tegger shuddered. "No."

"Think what you will need. By now you must know that the vampire's power reaches farther than your sword—"

Tegger moaned, his head bowed low, his hands over his ears. The whisperer waited him out, and presently said, "You will need defenses. We should make a list."

"Whisper, I don't want to talk to any of them." He was beginning to remember that for a falan of nights among the Thurl's people, he and Warvia had tried to explain why their monogamous nature made them superior to the lure of the vampire. It made the other species irritable.

Whisper said, "The first vehicle is abandoned save for Harpster. Harpster sleeps. Even if he wakes, he will not disturb you. Take what you will need."

Vala was wishing she could get into the spirit of the thing.

The water was cold. You had to stay active to stay warm. Everyone seemed to be washing each other. Discussions involving physiognomy or rishathra could be answered by pointing. Chitakumishad and Rooballabl were trying to work out an arrangement that would leave Chit's mouth above water. Beedj and Twuk were watching and making suggestions. Any parasites had been washed away, but Gleaners were good at finding a phantom itch.

Barok turned, grinning. His hands took Vala's shoulders and firmly turned her around. He scrubbed her back briskly with some scratchy sea-vegetable thing.

It was all wonderfully friendly, as it can be among species who don't compete for the same needs. All would be well if only Warvia and Tegger would come running out of the payload shell, hand in hand.

She looked over her shoulder. The river sounds would drown her lowered voice. "Sabarokaresh, I need your help. You and Kaywerbrimmis and Chitakumishad."

Barok continued his work. "What kind of help?"

"Come with me when I look inside Cruiser Two."

His hands stopped then. He looked around. "I don't think we should disturb Chit."

"No. Do you think he'll get that to work?"

"Might drown himself. There's Kay over there. Unusual view."

Kaywerbrimmis was lying on his belly, mostly in the water, drawing maps in the mud with his fingertips. An unidentifiable River Person was advising him. Vala pulled herself up on his other side and asked, "Learning anything?"

"Maybe."

"Give me a few breaths of your time, me and Barok?"

He looked around, studied her face, decided not to ask. Jumped to his feet and was pulling her along, as naked as she and Barok. There was no chance for Vala to go to her piled clothes.

She might have liked going naked, if the rain would ease off. Was clothing really that dangerous? But it wasn't just a matter of keeping clean. A vampire might learn that there was blood underneath the scent of woven cloth or cured leather.

It wasn't her clothes she wanted. It was her pack.

A pack would look incongruous on a naked woman.

. . . Oh, no doubt it would be all right.

When the three were out of anyone's earshot, Vala asked, "Kay, how did Warvia act—"

"Rished with all of us."

She stepped up onto the running board. "Bother her?"

"It did. A few times she tried to go outside. Maybe just to get clear of us, maybe to go to the vampires. They would have had her anyway. She's wrong about being immune."

"Kay, nobody believed that—"

"*Warvia* did. I *couldn't* let her out. Come daylight, we tried to calm her down." He was talking through clenched teeth. "No good. Maybe a woman. Or someone who wasn't there. Could get her talking."

"I'll try," Vala said. She opened the trick lock and entered the payload shell.

It wasn't quite dark. Light glared down from the gun tower. Vala sniffed at the ghosts of old cargoes and waited for her eyes to adjust.

Gunpowder. Minch and pepperleek. Great masses of grass

for Twuk and Paroom. Soap: strange stuff made by a species far to starboard. She sniffed for old stenches, the fear-sweat of people hiding from attackers, agony of the wounded; but those had been cleaned away. There was no smell of blood.

She climbed the ladder to the cannon. No sign of Tegger.

Kaywerbrimmis touched her ankle. She half sobbed, "Oh flup, oh flup, I was so sure we'd find everything covered with blood! Tegger must have guessed, and how could Warvia lie to him? *Warvia!*"

Warvia's feet dangled listless before the cannon slot. Vala pulled herself half through the opening. "Warvia, where is he?"

Warvia made no answer.

"Well, how's he taking it?"

Warvia spoke. "Dead inside."

"Warvia, cherished ally, nobody really thought you'd be immune to vampire scent."

"I thought he'd kill me," Warvia said. "It never even crossed his mind."

"Can we do anything for him?"

"He wants to be alone, I guess."

"For you?"

"So do I."

Vala slid down the ladder.

"He can't lose us," Kaywerbrimmis said. "He can follow the river, follow the wheel ruts. Maybe he just wants some time to digest what's happened. Rethink."

She nodded in the gloom.

"Vala, we should get the wagons moving."

"I'll take the tail position." While the rest got Cruiser One ready to roll, maybe she could search out Tegger. She didn't believe it. "Keep a close eye on Warvia. Or shall I take her?"

"Take her. You're the boss, and she's got the best eyes—"

"That isn't—"

"It's a decent excuse. But she might talk to you because . . ." He stalled.

"Because she hasn't rished with anyone in Cruiser One."

"Just so."

"You're a male, Kay—"

"Boss, I just can't guess how Tegger's feeling now. This doesn't *happen* to Reds."

Tegger dropped silently from the cannon mount. No living thing was in his sight, and he jumped when a voice whispered from far too close to his ear. "Do you have what you need to travel?"

Tegger remained crouched. He whispered, "Towels and a pepperleek. Soap. Clean clothes. My sword. I'm following the river, so I won't need the canteen, so I filled it with fuel. That can be useful stuff."

"Not for drinking, I hope."

"Fuel burns." *None of your business!*

"Is it random killing you plan? Or something more organized?"

"I don't *know* anything. They live under a factory city, a big floating structure. Whisper, if we—"

"If you."

"If I can't destroy their refuge, I accomplish nothing. If I don't . . . if I can't do something . . . large?"

"For your honor?"

"Yes. What Warvia did—I am nothing now. I must make myself something."

"Wish."

"To destroy the Shadow Nest."

"You shall."

"Make it fall. Crush them underneath."

"That could be difficult."

"Difficult?" Tegger shouldered his pack. He noticed three naked Machine People entering Cruiser Two. That was harmless, but they might search the other cruiser next. Tegger eased away into the bush.

He spoke to himself, or to the empty air. "Difficult. It's impossible! I can't invade a vampire nest. If I could get above them, onto that floating factory—but I'd have to fly."

Whisper: "What is Valavirgillin hiding?"

Huh? "Machine People have their secrets," Tegger said.

Whisper: "She knew that you and Warvia would succumb to the vampire lure. Still, she hopes that her little army can win. Does she know something that nobody else does?"

Tegger's mind was trying to shut down; the moan was rising in his throat. *They'd hear him. Find him.* His mind, he must not lose his mind to his body's hysterics. *Think.*

His first coherent thought in some time was that he had just heard Whisper's first *real* command, however phrased.

Louis Wu of the Ball People had visited Ginjerofer's tribe. Valavirgillin knew him, too . . . knew him better, since rishathra was among her skills. Had Louis Wu revealed something to her?

And he'd seen her naked, moments ago.

"She must have left her pack with her clothes. Whisper, where are Valavirgillin's clothes?"

"Look along the shore . . . there. The pack is on the mud flat but you could reach it with a stick."

"Whisper, I'm not a thief. I only want to look."

The voice whispered, "What if Valavirgillin hides knowledge that would help her companions?"

"Information is property."

Silence answered.

"Am I mad?" he asked himself. This wayspirit had done nothing Tegger's own mind couldn't do. What had happened to him might drive anyone mad. Was there a Whisper?

Warvia had suffered a shattering shock. What was she feeling? The horrifying truth was that she might be as crazy as him.

And Tegger was creeping through the brush like some predator, his prey a leather pack that didn't belong to him.

Stop, listen for rustling brush, for Whisper or for his companions. Nothing.

He must already be lunatic, to suspect the Machine People woman. This was truly Valavirgillin's war. She had involved the Ghouls, where a megalomaniac would have kept command for herself. Valavirgillin's weaponry was worth their lives . . .

But here was her clothing, washed and tossed over bushes, and her backpack hung here, too. He could look.

He need not show himself. His blade had the reach. He slid its point under the strap and fished the strap to him, and slid backward on his belly into the bushes.

The pack opened out flat, like many he'd seen, but unlike those, this had a good many pockets. Leather on the outside; some very finely woven stuff as a lining. Her firestarter was as good as his own, traded from some distance away. Blanket, fancy canteen (empty), a box containing damp soap, bullets and an empty handgun.

The gun: for Tegger it might be the difference between life and death. Between thief and—there was no word for what he and Warvia were now, but every hominid knew the word *thief*.

"Lunatic," he said. He was trying to put things back as

he'd found them. Could he get the pack back without being suspected?

He whispered into the silence. "I do not hold title to Machine People gunpowder. Stealing that secret would be *stealing*," and he rolled the pack closed, and open again. Something had felt *cold*.

The lining: it was *cold*, the cold fading under his touch.

He rubbed it in his fingers. Its weave was too fine to see at any distance. It had layers, several layers.

He separated a layer out and pulled. Threads of a less robust material separated, and the layer detached.

It was filmy stuff, very fine. He could see no way to put it back. What was it?

What was Whisper's interest?

He stuffed it into his kilt. That was less likely to be searched than his pack. He wrapped Valavirgillin's pack. His blade set it back on a branch, perhaps the right branch.

His erstwhile companions were all up and down the beach and into the bush. Maybe they were hunting him. He'd best be on his way.

Tegger knee-walked through brush until the brush petered out. Then he ran on bare mud, hidden in a mist growing gradually denser.

The river was broadening, and so was the mud-flat shore. The cruisers were out of sight.

Tegger wasn't worried about River Folk. Folk whose eyes must see through air and water both would have trouble identifying him. They couldn't swim as fast as he could run, and they could hardly walk at all. How would they inform the cruisers? He was outrunning the news of himself.

Tegger was on his own.

The knowledge was a tearing in his chest. Though four alien species had been his allies and friends, he gave them little thought. His grief was for Warvia. Never since their mating, never since his childhood or hers, had they been separated for more than a few days.

The world must change before he could ever face her again.

The river changed as he ran. Sand. Pebbles. A stand of trees dug in all over a bare rock cliff, nearly to the water. Narrow rapids here, and he had to climb a cliff side to get around them. Three vampires and an infant, huddled in the meager shadow of an overhanging cliff across the river, watched him run away from them and didn't give chase.

As the day passed, he ran.

Chapter Eight

FOR NOT

BEING

WARVIA

It had been raining since midday. Valavirgillin tried to find paths over bare rock, but there was mud everywhere. Tilting, skidding, never quite toppling over, the wagons moved downstream toward the Shadow Nest.

When night bit an edge from the sun, Vala already had the military high ground picked out.

The river was four hundred paces wide here. Rooballabl and Fudghabladl should be safe enough. The cruisers filled their water tanks, then rolled up toward the crest. These nearer mountains were foothills to the Barrier of Flame, but that highest one would do.

The cruisers slipped and tried to slide off cliffs. Would rain slow vampires the way it was slowing her? She should have camped earlier.

But they still had daylight when they reached her chosen position.

She set the cruisers back-to-back, not too close, cannon facing out. Those who must cook their food, cooked under an awning while they still had light. Warvia had shot some creature big enough to share with the Machine People. In the last light they washed, then piled their towels a distance from the cruisers.

The Gleaners retired. They didn't like rain and they needed their sleep. The rest talked or slept or merely waited.

Vala would have welcomed the Ghouls' advice. They were perched on a bare granite peak overlooking the Shadow Nest, talking in their own tongue, with their backs to the doused fire and the company. Valavirgillin saw two only, but she seemed to hear several voices.

The other hominids were letting the Machine People do most of the talking. So be it. Vala said, "Any vampires that get this far should be exhausted from the trek uphill. Our smell is all on the towels. It'll distract them. They'll be easy meat."

Give me your thoughts. What have I missed?

Barok said, "Vampires would be coming *back* from where they hunt. They won't expect to hunt this close to their nest. There's no prey left."

"We'll see."

Chit said, "When they come, they come in hordes."

"Reminds me," Kay said. "I scooped up three barrels of river gravel, Vala. Want some? We still have to use powder, but we can save our shot."

"Good."

"How's Warvia?"

Warvia said, "Warvia hooki-Murf Thandarthal can speak for herself, Kaywerbrimmis. Warvia is in health. Have you seen sign of Tegger?"

Vala said, "I found some things missing. Survival stuff, enough to fill a backpack, all from Cruiser One. Tegger must be the quickest thief alive." Her backpack had been disturbed too, but nothing seemed to be missing. That, she didn't mention.

"Next question. What do we do tomorrow? Harpster? Grieving Tube?"

"Come and see," said Grieving Tube.

Vala climbed the rock. It was nearly flat on top, and cold to the touch. She saw that Warvia had followed her; she reached down and pulled the Red woman after her.

Downstream, the Homeflow split and split again. Her gaze followed the main channel to where it dipped into shadow. The floating factory was ominously close, and huge.

Grieving Tube was almost scentless, smelling only of wet fur. She said, "Valavirgillin, can you see beneath the Floater? Do you see dangling loops, near side, right of center?"

It was as Tegger had described it, a disk that bulged upward in the middle. Beneath . . . beneath was shadow, and a sense of restless motion about the edges.

"No," Vala said.

"Yes," said Warvia. "I'll sketch it, come day."

The Ghoul said, "Warvia, that dangling helix is a ramp wide enough for heavy machinery. There are cogs along one edge, so that machines need not slip, and stairs along the other. No eyes have seen these things in many generations. The description you hear is more than twenty lifespans old, stored in a library far to spin, given me some days ago at the Thurl's fort."

Given how? But communication was a Ghoul's secret, and what Vala cared about was — "You have *maps* of the floating thing?"

"Yes, from before the Fall of the Cities, before so many things stopped working. Details only reached me yesterday, while we were above the clouds."

"That's—"

"It doesn't touch the ground," Warvia said.

Grieving Tube said, "I was afraid of that."

Harpster said, "None of us have been this close in a very long time. There was no point before Louis Wu boiled a sea, and after it was too dangerous—"

Vala broke in. "Warvia? The ramp doesn't touch?"

"I'm having trouble with distances, Valavirgillin, but it's hanging in midair. The bottom of the ramp straightens out flat like a shovel blade, but twice as high as those vampires around it."

"We did not expect this," Grieving Tube said. "Our chosen path would have been to force a way onto the Floater. Then vampires would have to come to us along a narrow way. They prefer to swarm. They might even have to face raw daylight, that high."

Vala was holding tight to her temper. Long practice made that surprisingly easy. "I see. But we can't reach it?"

"I see no way," Harpster said, "but there are more minds here than ours. Let us set them thinking."

Running through fog and mist, running from his life, his eyes always where his feet would fall, Tegger would not have seen any threat. But he smelled it, gasped it in, as if the memory of Warvia punched him in the face. He stopped, caught his balance, reached over his shoulder and was armed.

Fingers brushed his face. He slashed waist high, forward and back, before ears and eyes caught up.

Her song peaked in a squeak of agony. He poked out at throat level. The song ended. Tegger clapped his hands over his ears and ran.

And ran.

He knew that smell! She was behind him, dying, but with her scent in his nose he saw her more clearly than his pounding feet. The leather cloak she wore was too big for her, and in tatters, and she spread it like wings to show her nakedness. Her song was piercingly sweet. She was slender and very pale, perhaps adolescent, her hair thick and white, the points of her canine teeth visible past her red lips.

Vampire! Night after night they sang outside the Thurl's wall. Tegger was stronger than their lures. He'd said so over and over. But that drifting scent was older yet, for it was Warvia's scent during the friendliest part of her cycle; only stronger. His heaving breath was driving it out of his nose, out of his mind, and he ran—

—out of the mist, and slowed to a stop.

For most of a falan he'd studied the map, the relief map they'd shaped and fired outside the Thurl's compound. Now it was as if he were an ant viewing it at eye level.

He crept uphill to put a boulder between himself and the creatures around the Floater, before he looked again.

An ant looking at an anthill. It was far away still, but a Red's eyes are good. Those were human shapes interacting in what seemed human patterns. They moved as if at work or gathered in little social groups. Some carried burdens that their posture said were babies. They moved in and out of the black shadow that lay beneath a huge disk, a mass like a full-sized city floating above them.

The Ghouls had called it a factory complex, but Tegger couldn't help but think of it as a City Builder city. A vampire city, now.

He could see no more than twenty vampires, even including the few down at the river, but there must be thousands in the shadow of the Floater. If it fell, it would crush most of them. Shrapnel spraying horizontally would take out most of the rest, Tegger thought.

He could see something hanging down, like an unsupported spiral staircase. He couldn't see the bottom. Maybe he could climb that.

How to reach it? As best he could judge through the drifting fog, the floating city was twelve hundred paces downstream along a wide mud flat that the Homeflow had carved into multiple channels. The main channel flowed under the city, but many channels went around. Here and there along the river vampires had come into daylight to drink.

Too close to the Shadow Nest, channels flowed around both sides of some tremendous thing, a tilted square plate obtrusively artificial and half buried in the mud. Some relic from the Fall of the Cities, no doubt. Vampires nearby didn't seem to be avoiding it.

A pity he couldn't swim. Could he hide beneath the water and move downstream that way? Or would he freeze? Or were there vampires too close, and would the smell be too much for him? For the vampire woman's scent was still in his mind if not his nose.

Were there River People about? He was willing to ask for help.

Mist blew across his view, a fine rain washed him, and a voice in the mist whispered in his ear. "So you really were as strong as you thought."

Tegger snorted. *An unarmed woman: no challenge, mere murder.* His mind shied from what the dying vampire had taught him of himself, and fastened on another puzzle. "How did you get ahead of me, Whisper?"

Silence.

Tegger was coming to believe that Whisper was a machine, something left over from before the Fall of the Cities. Or else a wayspirit who had dreadful secrets. Whisper didn't answer questions about Whisper.

Ask instead— "Is there a way to make the Floater fall on the Shadow Nest?"

The whisperer said, "I know of none."

"My father told me. The City Builders made lightning to flow through silver threads for their power. We could turn it off! Find the threads, rip them out!"

Whisper said, "Floater plates don't use power to float, though power was needed to make them. They were made to repel the scrith, the floor of the Arch, and that is what they do."

It was impossible, then. It had always been impossible. In some bitterness Tegger said, "You know so much. You hide so much. Are you a Ghoul?"

Silence.

One might consider that distance means nothing to a wayspirit. Or that a madman's imagination is as quick as thought. Or if Gleaners run faster than Reds, faster than Tegger at a dead scared run, then something else might run faster than Gleaners.

But Ghouls could not. Whatever else he was, though Ghouls were as elusive as Whisper, Whisper was not a Ghoul.

The mist drifted, revealed and concealed. It was full dark, or very near. Through gaps in the clouds Tegger could catch an occasional vertical blue-white glare, the Arch still unchanged, whatever happened to his universe.

The activity beneath the floating mass was increasing, Tegger thought. It was certainly growing darker. Vampires would be waking. Tegger said, "We should hide."

"I see a place, but it might not help you."

"Why not?" Tegger asked, and was instantly aware of the sweat running freely down his arms. Much of that was rain; still, his own smell would attract vampires for a daywalk's distance.

He waited while the mist closed in—and heard no more from Whisper. On hands and toes, then, he moved down to the river. He drew his sword before he waded in. No telling what lived in the brown water. If a fish brushed him, he might find his dinner.

He stopped as water brushed his kilt. Valavirgillin's rag, should he get it wet?

He pulled it free of his kilt. It was filmy stuff, very finely woven, very strong. He'd seen his hand through it earlier, though it was too dark now. He'd noticed it because it was cold; but it wasn't cold at all an instant after he stuffed it in his kilt. During a halfday of running he'd forgotten all about it.

He let a corner dip into the river.

It wasn't dissolving. Good. But the upper corner in his fingers was as cold, instantly, as the river washing past his legs.

He submerged himself. Rubbed himself with moss, climbed out fast, dried himself fast. Running had kept him warm in the wind and rain, but he wasn't running now. There was a poncho in his pack, and the firestarter.

Vala's cloth was like a pipe for heat and cold. What would happen— "Whisper, what if I put a corner of Valavirgillin's cloth in a fire? Would it burn? Would it be too hot to hold?"

There was nowhere Whisper might be on this bare mud.

His own mind told him he'd be crazy to build a fire. Hominids used fire. Vampires, no matter how stupid, would learn to seek fire. Still, he couldn't help but wonder.

He toweled his face, and pulled the towel away in time to see six vampires running at him across the mud.

They didn't sing. They didn't posture, didn't implore with their bodies. They came fast. Tegger snatched up his sword.

A sword didn't frighten them. They were pacing each

other, spreading out a little, attacking as a pack. Tegger ran to the left and slashed, slashed. Two fell back with haphazard wounds, enough to put them out, Tegger thought, but he was too busy to look. The other four had him encircled.

He half rested, turning in a step-stop motion, his sword held vertical, reversing himself, reversing. He and his friends had played this game with sticks when they were children. Their elders had fought Grass Giants this way.

Two wounded were crawling away, uphill toward the shadow. The remaining three men and one woman circled him.

He hadn't known—none of the vampire hunters had known—that when vampires outnumbered their prey six to one, they didn't bother with lures or song or even scent. They just attacked.

He must reach the cruisers, if he lived. Tell them. Even if he must face Warvia again. Warvia.

The vampires didn't seem to be in any hurry. No reason why they should be. More were trickling down from the Shadow Nest. More yet would be returning from the lands beyond the mountains. Darkness was falling.

"Whisper!" he screamed. "Hide me!"

Nothing. The rain had stopped. He was on a wide mud flat. This time there really was no place for a wayspirit to hide.

The scent. It wasn't strong, but it was getting into his head and it wasn't coming out. He remembered the other vampire, remembered killing her, killing her for not being Warvia. His mind was going, and there was no reason why he should wait.

And the woman spread her arms for him, imploring.

Tegger jumped backward, turning, sword swinging. Yes! The men were coming at his back, converging while she held his mind prisoner. His blade swiped across their eyes—he

missed the second clean—came back and stabbed economi-
cally into that one's throat. He jabbed back blindly at where
the woman should be. She slammed into him with his sword
through her to the hilt, knocking him off balance, her teeth
slashing at his biceps. He curled her away one-handed. He
could hear himself screaming.

One man was crawling backward, leaving his life's blood
behind. One seemed blinded. The third brushed blood from
his eyes and saw Tegger as Tegger reached for him. Then
Tegger's hands were on his throat and Tegger's weight was
driving him into the mud.

The rest was a fog. The man gripped Tegger's shoulders
and tried to pull Tegger close to his teeth. Tegger shook him
like a rat while he strangled him. The woman had almost
reached the river when Tegger reached her and took back his
sword. He stepped too close to one who should have been
dead, felt teeth close in his ankle, stabbed down and kept
walking. The blinded one came toward him, sniffing. Tegger
took three swings with a blade dulled as blunt as a club, before the head came off. He could hear himself snuffling like a
sick herdbeast.

In the shifting fog he could see shapes moving down from
the Shadow Nest.

The pack, don't forget the backpack. Good. Where now?

"Whisper! Hide me!"

Whisper spoke, but not in a whisper. "Run toward me!"
The voice was a whipcrack command with just a trace of
speech impediment, coming from far downstream, straight
toward the Shadow Nest.

Tegger ran. He was a hundred paces along when the voice
spoke again, much closer now. "Out into the river!"

Tegger veered left, into the water, toward the voice of
Whisper. Was there something out there? In the rain and the

dark was a shadow on the fog, a shadow too big to be solid. And a strip of darkness . . . an island?

Vampires couldn't swim, or the Water Folk would have known it. Tegger was a plains dweller; he had never tried to swim.

It was ankle deep, knee deep . . . Pause a moment to get his pack on his back. No kilt. He'd left it. Sword: into the sheath on his back. He'd need his arms to swim, if hominids swam like Rooballabl, if Reds could swim at all. And he ran on. Knee deep, knee deep . . . and out.

"Here," said Whisper, from far away. "Go to the downstream end."

He'd crossed thirty paces of knee-deep river to reach a shallow bulge of dark mud that did not really deserve the name of *island*. Vampires were piling up on shore. One, then another, stepped into the water and came toward him.

Downstream he went, running over mud, beneath a shadow too big to be anything but fog patterns. Wondering if vampires could fight while water impeded their feet. This might really be the best place for a final stand.

He did not shy from dying. *I killed a vampire woman for not being Warvia*, he'd told himself. But when he killed the six, it felt like he was killing Warvia over and over, killing her for what she'd done in the night, and he gloried in it.

If he killed more vampires, he would lose Warvia even in his mind.

As his feet pounded across the mud, the monstrous shadow shifted. It was too rigid. Was solid, suddenly, and alongside him. He lashed out at it with his sword, and whacked *something*. He rapped it with his fist.

Not a fog pattern. It was flaky and a bit springy, like layers of hammered metal.

He'd seen this thing from much farther away. It was a

tilted plate with square corners, obtrusively artificial, fifteen paces by fifteen paces if half of it was under the mud. It stood out of the mud at an angle of forty degrees. The mud had piled up against it.

There were notches along the rim, big enough to attach cables. A thick post stuck up from the center. At one of the visible corners was what looked like a pulley. If there had been a cable, it was gone.

The highest corner bulged.

(Whisper was silent. Whisper spoke rarely. It might be Whisper expected him to work things out on his own, Tegger thought. But why?)

There was no smell of vampires here.

At the fall of the cities, hundreds of falans ago, vehicles were said to have rained out of the sky. Most of those were gone, buried or corroded out of existence. Sometimes you could find the shell of a floating car, and curved sheets of stuff as transparent as water, usually broken: windows. Sometimes something bigger.

Like a big plate for carrying cargoes too big to fit into a car.

The fog concealed, revealed. The plate's highest corner bulged like soap bubbles stuck together—faceted—and as with soap bubbles, you could see in. One facet was crazed as if crawlerwebs covered it. Others were clear.

When Tegger tried to climb, the plate was too smooth and too slippery with rain and mud.

He'd better do something. He didn't doubt he had outrun this latest wave of vampires, but even wading, they'd catch up. Tegger backed up several paces, then ran at the plate.

Halfway up he ran out of momentum. He dropped, arms and legs spread wide. The mud didn't reach this high. It wasn't metal, or it was covered metal: a gritty surface, offering traction even under a rain slick. He crawled.

The bulb was a single bubble, part windows, part painted metal. What was clearly a door hung by one hinge. Tegger's fingers found an edge of the opening and pulled himself up and in.

He looked down to see a vampire below him. She looked back, watching him.

Now two. Now four.

Tegger reached down for the hanging door. His thrashing foot went through something crunchy. He ignored that. He lifted the door—it wasn't heavy—pulled it into place and looked for a way to lock it. There was clearly a lock, but he couldn't make it work.

Now the vampires began to climb, and slip, and climb again.

The door wouldn't stop them. The slope might. Otherwise this bulb would become their larder.

"Whisper? What next?" he asked, expecting nothing.

Nothing. He must have left Whisper down there. With the vampires. Funny, but he couldn't make himself worry for Whisper's safety.

Tegger took off his pack. He wanted light, and there was no harm now in setting a fire. He struck his firestarter until he had a blaze.

He studied the crunchy stuff for a moment. He'd seen the bones of prey and of cattle, and he knew the feel of his own bone structures. His foot had punched through some ribs, it seemed.

The pilot had been of an unknown species, bigger than a Red, burly, with long arms. Its clothing was mere shreds of no particular color. The skull had fallen too easily, as if its neck was broken when the carrier hit the mud. It had the massive jaw of an herbivore.

A hominid skeleton. Imagine that. The Ghouls had never come for it.

At the fall of the cities the Night People must have been gorged and busy beyond imagination. When they found they couldn't climb this wreck to reach the corpse in the control bubble, they'd given up. Nothing else would be climbing up here—they must have reasoned—to find an abandoned corpse and upbraid the untidy Ghouls.

In the dazzle of the firelight he couldn't see the vampires below. The shell glowed around him. One curved window was not covered with webs, as he'd thought, but shattered; the pieces still stuck together. Others were intact.

Before him were toggles just big enough for his fingertips, that slid horizontally or vertically. There was a little door as big as his two spread hands, and another twice that size, but neither would open. There was a wheel on a post that Tegger found he could push in all six directions, though that took both hands and all of his strength. He moved all of the toggles, right or left or up or down, whichever way they'd move. None of them did anything.

His tinder was running out, and there was nothing here to burn.

If Warvia were here. She'd figure this out.

If Warvia were here. He'd tell her he never doubted her. She hadn't chosen to break their marriage, she'd been overwhelmed by a smell that entered below her mind and clamped down on the soul. How long had he been hearing that vampire song? The light was going, and now he could see a triangular face peering longingly in at him.

Animal. Brain half the size of his. If she ever realized what the door was, he was dead. But the real danger, Tegger knew, was a scent that would have him tearing it free himself. He shouted, "Whisper!"

She shied from his scream, just for a moment, then answered with her song.

He drove his fist into one of the little doors with all his strength.

It popped open. The compartment behind it wasn't large, but he found what he needed: a thick book full of dry sheets of thin stuff that would burn.

The vampire woman—*women*—shied back from the light. Two women now, and a man, too, all trying to balance above him on the shell. Waiting.

He held a burning sheet above the compartment. There was the book—he was tearing up a thick book of maps—and a paper bag filled with dry mold, and a peculiar dagger which he took, and nothing else.

So he smashed the other door. It hurt, but the door popped open.

This recess was no deeper than one joint of a finger. What showed was entirely cryptic, a maze of tiny knobs. The guts of a City Builder machine, Tegger thought, and he looked for silver threads linking the little knobs. He had been told that they were what carried power. He was disappointed not to find them.

He touched two of the points with his fingertips.

The muscles in his arms spasmed hard and threw him back in the seat. For a long moment he couldn't remember how to breathe.

Was this what lightning felt like? Power! But it would kill him.

He lit another paper and held it above the recess.

Some of the little knobs were linked by slender lines of dust. His own touch had disturbed the rest.

It was as if something linked in his mind. Tegger pulled out Valavirgillin's cloth. The peculiar dagger didn't have an edge, only a flattened point. He used his badly blunted sword's edge to cut a narrow strip from the cloth.

He should lay it along one of those lines of dust.

He brushed it, the little strip of Vala's cloth, quickly across the knobs. Lightning flashed up his arm, jolting him just for an instant.

The smell . . . he couldn't fight it forever . . . but he'd fight it for now, the vampire that sang in his mind. He glared at them and tried to think.

Glove? He pulled his towel out and tried gripping the strip through that. No good. He could grip the peculiar dagger through it, though. He could drop the strip of Vala's cloth into the recess, and push it around with the point of the dagger until it mated two knobs.

He couldn't see what suddenly glowed; it was outside the cabin. Three vampires suddenly lit up like suns. They yelped and tried to leap away from the light. Two slid away down the plate; the man dropped off the edge.

Reflected light was still pouring in. He didn't need the fire anymore.

He left the first strip in place. He cut another strip from Valavirgillin's cloth and began testing that. His teeth hurt from being clenched. He could hear his whimpering, and know how badly he wanted to throw himself out that door and follow two vampire women down to the mud. But *Warvia, Warvia, I did it! I made the lightning flow!*

Now, why didn't he have anything but light?

It might be, he thought, that light was only the easiest

part of City Builder tech, the part that lasted the longest. Or the part that used the least power, and too little power remained for any of these other unnamed wonders . . . But Tegger didn't believe that. He'd felt the shock. Wherever it came from, there *was* power. And it was driving the vampires back.

The old skull was so clean. Something had claimed the meat. If not Ghouls, then birds? The big empty sockets seemed to be looking at him.

He set it in the larger compartment, but changed his mind about closing it. He said to the ancient pilot, "You think you had a bad day? I had a day nobody would want to live through. You had maybe a hundred breaths . . ."

But it must have felt like forever to the pilot, he thought. Falling out of the sky, maybe in a cloud of smaller vehicles, maybe screaming for help through a voice-sender that didn't work anymore, as every part of his wonderful flying hauler went dark and dead.

Ah!

Tegger began sliding every toggle that would move. When the lights died, he slid that one back.

Yes! Every sliding thing was on full power when this thing fell, and in his experimenting he had turned each of them off. Everything but the lights! The hauler must have fallen in daylight!

And the next thing Tegger caused to happen was a sputtering, and a smell of something burned. He feared he had destroyed something.

But the next was a wind in the control bubble, which carried the vampire scent out and away and left his head clear and cold. And then he screamed in triumph.

He twisted himself around to look down the length of the cargo plate. It was hard to pick out the vampires. The lights seemed to be to either side of his bubble; they cast shadows, and vampires like shadows. He thought he saw five, and guessed at twice that. But they would come no closer.

Time, now, to remember hunger; to wonder if anything nested in here. The outside was too bare. He'd have to wait for full day and catch a fish. It seemed he would live through the night.

Where was the power, the lightning, coming from? He couldn't guess.

He cut another finger-length strip and began trying that.

Chapter Nine

FAMILIAR

FACES

Through the window in the cliff, Louis studied the weathered woman in weathered clothing. She was steering a steampowered vehicle downslope, with a similar man beside her and a small red man perched above her head. "Three days ago?"

"Ninety hours exactly."

"If that's Valavirgillin, she doesn't look good."

"Neither do you, Louis. Perhaps she's been neglecting her boosterspice?"

Louis ignored the dig. "She's gotten old. Eleven years . . ." Louis himself had lived eleven years without the bioengineered seeds that kept a human being from aging. Vala had never touched the stuff. Was it really Valavirgillin?

It *was*. He'd rished with the woman!

"This skews the odds a bit, doesn't it, Louis?"

"She must be tens of thousands of miles starboard of where I left her. What would she be doing there?"

"Attacking a vampire enclave, I believe. It's her, isn't it? Have I made my point? If I show you ten healthy hominids, they could be ten survivors out of a thousand dead. But I show you a woman you knew before the radiation storm, and clearly in present time. What are the odds now?"

Louis shifted on the water-smoothed boulder he'd chosen for a seat. "Is this present time, Hindmost?"

"Forty hours ago."

Louis asked what he had refused to ask for eleven years. "Are you claiming Teela lied? *Why?*"

"She acted on insufficient knowledge. With enhanced intelligence comes enhanced arrogance, and she never did have good sense, Louis. She could have done what I did, with my computers to play with. Louis, Teela never grasped how closely I was able to guide the plasma plume we ripped from the sun. I set it flowing directly into the attitude jets on the rim wall. The plasma never played across the main Ringworld surface. The radiation she feared . . . of course it was well above background level."

"The rim," Louis said. He was beginning to believe.

"Yes, the rim, of course."

"And how do you suppose the Spill Mountain People made out?"

"Along five percent of the rim wall, I suppose I must have killed a great many."

Ten million, a hundred million people of a kind Louis Wu had never met. Several species, maybe.

Nonetheless Louis said, "Hindmost, I believe I owe you an apology."

The Hindmost chimed. *Making sure it's in his records,* Louis thought. Then, "Another matter. Notice the man in lookout position. Red Herder?"

"Yah. Little red carnivores, lived not that far from the rim wall. Very fast runners they were."

The great wagon suddenly zipped downslope, fast-forward, dodged boulders at Mach 5 in a storm of streaming cloud-shadows, and was lost in a maze of rocks. "I lost the wagons for a time," the Hindmost said. "Fifteen hours later I picked up this."

A small red man ran down a river shore, Mach 12 for sure. Louis laughed. "They're not *that* fast."

"It's the same man?"

"I can't tell. Slow him down."

The red man slowed to something an Olympic runner might hope for. Louis said, "Looks like him."

"Infrared," the Hindmost said. A pink shadow glowed through the fuzzy-edged window in the dark cliff, running along a black river amid glowing rocks. A brilliant green cursor pointed. "This?"

A running pink shadow, and glimpses of another. The Red ran steadily. Some warmer shape flitted from cover to cover, flashed between rocks—"Slow that down!"—now through brush, *now* where was it? Reds ran fast, but this thing was keeping up with the Red while hiding most of the time.

Louis couldn't get any notion of its shape.

"Louis, we watched the burning of three Patriarchy ships. I suspect a protector," the Hindmost said. "Might we have another protector here?"

"Why not just a Ghoul?"

The red dots streaked away in fast-forward, then shifted to normal light. The Red Herder ran alone. Near him there was a suggestion of sporadic motion, and the man's eyes were constantly shifting.

Something popped up in front of him. His sword came out—

Pause. And the Hindmost's cursor pointed. "Red Herder. Vampire. Do you see anything else?"

"Give me infrared."

In infrared Louis found *five* glow spots. In normal light . . . The cursor pointed. "Red Herder. Vampire. This and this are Ghouls. See."

Louis remembered Ghouls; though they were hidden in brush and shadow, he knew their lanky shape.

But the fifth glow was hiding even from the Ghouls. Louis could make out a hand smaller than a Ghoulish hand, nearly hairless. An old man's hand, arthritic, with knobby knuckles.

Protector? "Why would a protector bother?"

"Unknown. But see this." Fast-forward. The vampire woman fell dying. The Red ran, stopped, splashed in the river, and was suddenly fighting half a dozen vampires. The recording went dead slow. The Red's sword swept around . . . a woman was uncoiling herself at his back . . . a hand slapped her ankle.

The hidden one was mud-colored, plastered with mud. Its knotted hand only just touched her, closed and released. The woman swiped with her claws at nothing she could see; returned to the attack, and died on the red man's sword.

"Minimalist," Louis said. A rustling sound was trying to find his attention.

"Secretive," the Hindmost said.

The Red Herder ran along mud. Vampires converged . . . and they all faded into distance.

"He's out of my instrument's range. I lost him for a time. I nearly lost the hidden one, too, and that concerns me. Look."

The camera viewpoint swung back along the river, caught a splash, then moved fast upslope and into shadow.

Louis said, "I don't—"

"Here, again, in infrared. The lurker is nearly invisible."

"Yah. He was underwater, of course, shedding heat. Where's he going? Into the vampire nest?"

The sequence ran again, light-enhanced. *Splash:* something emerged from water and ran upslope in jerky, random fashion. *Pause:* not a good view, but the shadow was clearly hominid. *Run:* up into shadow, gone.

"That was the last I saw of it. Clearly it is not a vampire. It guards the Red Herder, and perhaps his companions, too, avoiding notice at all costs."

In a crunching of brush the Fishers and Sailors were lining up along the pool to stare at Louis Wu afloat in midair; or else at a window in a rock cliff, a view of distant daylit mountains.

Louis asked, "What else have you got?"

"Nothing of interest since three hours ago."

"Hindmost, my brain really *is* dying for lack of sleep."

The Hindmost said, "Wait. This *thing*—"

"Is thirty-five degrees up the curve of the Arch, five and a half minutes away at lightspeed. Can't hurt you. You're right, though, it's a protector."

"Louis! You must accept medical help."

"You don't have medical help. You put the 'doc on the lander, remember?"

"The crew cabin kitchen has a medical menu. Louis, it can make boosterspice!"

"Boosterspice doesn't make a man well. It only makes him young."

"Are you—"

"No, I'm not sick. But humans *get* sick, Hindmost, and I

keep remembering *why* we don't have a full working 'doc. Chmeee and I, we didn't volunteer for this work. You thought we might refuse to operate the lander. So you put the autodoc in the lander, and Teela flamed it."

"But—"

"Leave the window running. I don't want anyone to think we're hiding something from them." Louis stood and turned away.

"Louis, I weary of your not listening to me!"

Louis took two more steps. But he'd refused to listen to the Hindmost for eleven years, and he found apologizing tanj awkward . . . so he turned back and resumed his seat on the boulder. "Speak," he said.

"I have my own medical facilities."

"*Oh*, yes." The Hindmost would surely be protected against any concievable accident or malaise. Nessus had lost a head and neck on their first visit, and Louis had seen it replaced. "Surgery for a Pierson's puppeteer. What would that do for a human?"

"Louis, this technology was of human origin. We bought it from a Kzin law enforcer on Fafnir, but it appears to have been an ARM experiment of more than two hundred years ago, stolen from Sol system. The system uses nanotechnology to make repairs inside the cells themselves. No second was ever built. I've had it modified to heal humans or kzinti or my own kind."

Louis was laughing. "Tanj, you're careful!" Most of what was aboard *Needle* was of human manufacture, and what wasn't had been carefully hidden. If the Hindmost were caught while abducting his crew, he wouldn't implicate the Fleet of Worlds.

"Pity I'll never see it."

"I can move it to the crew deck."

Louis felt cold running up his spine like river water. He said, "You're not serious, and I'm too tired to think. Good night, Hindmost."

Louis parked his stack of plates next to the guest house. Dry brush rustled as he stepped down. He spoke to the night, not loudly.

"When you're ready to talk, I'm here. And I bet you're wearing an embroidered kilt."

The night had no answer.

Sawur barely stirred when he crawled into the tent. He fell asleep at once.

Chapter Ten

STAIR STREET

A whiff of corruption pulled her half awake. Pointed fingernails pressing hard into her elbow pulled her the rest of the way. Vala sat up with a yelp. Harpster ducked below the gun she managed not to fire.

"Valavirgillin, come and see."

Flup. "Are we attacked?"

"You would smell vampires. I'm surprised they haven't come to look at us. Perhaps they're distracted."

Vala stepped out onto the running board.

Rain was falling in fat drops. The awning kept her half dry, but visibility was low. Lightning played to antispin-starboard, the direction of the vampires' stronghold. Lightning and something else. Downslope, toward the river, a steady white light.

After all their talk, had Tegger lit a fire? But fire wasn't quite that color, and fire would have flickered.

Grieving Tube was above them on the rock, on sentry duty. Harpster said, "Will you wake Warvia?"

"Yes." Vala slipped into the payload shell. No point in waking anyone else, but Warvia could see details; she might even see something that would tell her this was Tegger. "Warvia?"

"I'm awake."

"Come and look."

Rain came and went at random, permitting glimpses of the light. The glow wasn't a dot, she saw presently; it was a tilted line.

The light blinked off, then on again. Warvia said, "Tegger likes to fiddle with things."

"Is it him?"

"How would I know?" the Red woman snapped.

They watched. By and by Harpster said, "Light could keep away the vampires, if it's bright enough."

Warvia was slumped against a rock, asleep. Vala said, "Wake me if something changes. I'll be out here, but I want a blanket." She started to climb into the payload shell, thinking, Get two. One for Warvia.

The light began to jitter. Vala paused to watch.

Then a bright dot separated from the tilted line and went straight up.

The hauler was shuddering, shaking, trying to tear it-self apart. Tegger clung to the seat as he would have clung to Warvia. Could he free a hand to pluck the strip of Vala-cloth away from the contacts?

Did he want to? The shaking wasn't killing him, only jarring his teeth.

What was doing this? Some half-ruined motor? Or else a motor doing just what it was told to, trying to lift a cargo hauler, along with the riverbed it was buried in.

And while his mind toyed with such notions, Tegger's fingers toyed with toggles.

Flup, that was the lights again. That one didn't do anything, nor that one. That one turned the wind off, then back on. An ominous grating sound from somewhere below had been the response to this one, but now it did nothing.

Something protruded from the shadowed recess where the skeleton's knees would have gone. A big two-pronged handle . . . that didn't move under his hand.

Tegger gritted his vibrating teeth, gripped the chair with his knees and the handle with both hands and *pulled*.

Nothing. Fine. *Push*.

Push and *twist*.

It lurched under his hands, and his head banged hard into the controls. He was being hurled into the sky.

The twist of cloth! Get it out of there— He dared not let go of the chair, and perhaps that was a good thing. Dark as the night was, he could see the riverbed dwindle. A fall from this high would kill him.

If he could free a hand or a toe from its death-grip on the chair . . . there must be a way to steer this . . . bubble. As the river wheeled past him he glimpsed a half-buried square plate with a notch missing at the high corner. He'd torn the control bubble loose from the hauler.

Then he *was* falling. He felt it in his belly. Falling, falling, *surge*, twenty to thirty manheights above the river and moving inland. Moving toward the City.

A way to take control, there *must* be a way—

Did he trust Whisper?

Whisper had led him to the cargo hauler. Whisper had put Vala-cloth into his hands. What would Whisper have done if Tegger hadn't experimented on his own? But Whisper had never suggested he steer the hauler—or its ripped-away control bubble, either—anywhere but where he was going now. The damaged machine was going home to its aerial dock.

So, Whisper's minimal guidance was taking him where he wanted to go. To trust Whisper was to let it happen. But he didn't know Whisper's nature and had never known Whisper's motives . . .

Rain running down the windows had Tegger half blind. By flickering lightning and glimpses of Archlight he saw a flat-topped mass approaching. He could see no motion. Wait, the rain was swirling, wheeling . . . suddenly he was in a cloud of screaming birds.

Could vampires fly? But even in the rainy dark he knew them. Bluebelly makaways, no different from the makaways of his own turf. Wingspread greater than his spread arms; good gliding ability; raptor beaks. Maks were meat eaters, big enough to carry off a herder boy. He'd never seen so many together.

He couldn't navigate through that. He kept his hands where they were, gripping the chair back.

The birds withdrew to a wheeling pattern.

The window bubble had come to rest, still in midair.

Plainsman that he was, Tegger had once boarded a barge to trade stock with another tribe. He was familiar with docks. He was floating a manheight from the edge of what might have been a riverside dock hung in midair. Floating boats would ride against this buffer rim. Those cables hanging over the rim would tether them. Cargo in those big buildings, behind those vast doors . . .

The birds were losing interest, returning to roost. Makaways weren't nightbirds.

The bubble's doorway was facing out from the dock. Was there at least a way to turn it around? Maybe if he twisted something . . . Tegger was reluctant to experiment this high in the air.

What *should* be happening here? The hauler might be waiting for the City's signal to land. Might be sending a signal of its own. Maybe one of those cables was supposed to reach out and secure the hauler, pull it in. But none of it was going to happen, because the dock was as dead as anything else that had died in the Fall of the Cities.

The door hung loose, as he'd found it.

Pack. Sword.

Tegger eased out into a light rain, feet on the hanging door's wobbly rim, *jump* to the bubble's slippery top, flatten and cling. The birds wheeled closer, looking him over.

Tegger crept forward on his belly, down the slope of the bubble. A little farther, hands and knees now, a bit more, knees forward, feet braced, slipping, *jump*.

He landed flat, banging his chin, his legs kicking in open air.

The dock felt like soft wood.

He'd have stayed but for the shrieking of the birds as they dropped toward him. He rolled over, pulled his sword and waited. When one came close enough, he slashed.

"He must have found some City Builder thing, something like an old car. Made it work. He's up there." Warvia stared fiercely at the light that blazed at the edge of the floating factory.

Her faith was stronger than Vala's. Vala asked, "What do you see?"

"I can't see past the light. There are big birds wheeling around it. I think I saw him jump—"

The light sank. Faster. Flashed painfully bright and was gone.

"He jumped," Warvia said positively. "Vala, I'm about to fall over. I'll give you a better description come daylight."

"Can we do anything?"

"Vala, I'd do anything to reach him."

"Grieving Tube, any thoughts?"

The Ghoul shook her head.

"We'll have to wait. I don't know any safer spot for the cruisers, and the view is lovely. Dig in here, wait and watch."

Makaways preferred live prey, but they would eat carrion. Makaway meat had a nasty taste.

Tegger felt much better after he had devoured the bird. Take away hunger, disperse the rutting scent of ten thousand vampires, give him a flat surface to rest ... The wind was cold, this high. Tegger pulled a poncho from his pack and wiggled into it.

The cold, the aches, the troubles of a nightmare day began to recede ... and sleep was a vampire with its teeth in his throat. He dared not sleep in the open. He looked about him in woozy panic.

The huge door on that storage cube was surely too heavy to move. Too heavy for anyone, and wildly wasteful of power ... ?

Around a corner from the huge door was a door not much taller than Tegger.

A kick sent it springing back at him. He went into darkness, found something resilient to climb, and slept.

He clung to sleep, fearing what his memory would tell him. Memory came anyway; but it was wavering light on his eyelids that snapped him awake.

Sunlight flooded through the man-sized doorway. It faded even as he was climbing down from a mountain of bales that smelled weakly of vegetable rot. Stuff to be turned into cloth? Foodstuffs would have been in a worse state.

He stepped outside.

Broken cloudscapes swept sluggishly overhead. Sunlight swept in vertical beams along the dock. Tegger didn't see any birds until he crept to the edge on hands and knees and looked down.

The windowed bulb that had carried him here was below him, crushed. He wasn't going home that way ... hadn't planned to.

Myriad birds wheeled with spread wings in the sunlight, dropping to snatch up—what? Makaways in such numbers must be finding plenty of prey. A whole ecology would be feeding off what the vampires left, off whole populations of drained corpses.

There might be nothing but birds up here.

No, wait: here was some kind of web on the vertical face of the dock, facing outward, to starboard. He had to lean far over to see it.

The threads were bronze when the light fell right; otherwise nothing could be seen at all. Size was hard to judge because of the way the web divided itself into nothing at the edges. It might be as wide as a Grass Giant was tall. The motionless black dot at the center might be the webspinner ... dead of starvation. Tegger hadn't seen an insect since he left the ground.

Birds and a webspinner implied insects, but the birds might have eaten the insects. Tegger wondered if he would starve. At best he faced a time limit. As if he hadn't known that already!

What he'd been thinking of as the "City" was unfamiliar in nearly every detail. Tegger didn't have names for most of what he could see. The City sloped upward in irregular geometries, and peaked at the center in a vertical tube.

Tegger began running.

There was no fear in him now. It was just a way of exploring. He ran, and the dock, eight manheights wide, ran away before him. Now it narrowed, but continued, two manheights wide: not a dock anymore, but merely the rim of the City.

Rim Street. Structures lined it. Some had doors. Here and there an alley ran out of sight between windowless bulks. Rounded, doorless shapes had ladders running up their sides.

The rain resumed. Tegger had to watch his footing now, but the surface was rough beneath his feet, and the rain was running off into a gutter along Rim Street's inward edge.

He was not much more than warmed up when he saw an anomaly, a wide street becoming flights of steps, and on either side—

Tegger stopped. Dwellings? He knew the Thurl's tents and Ginjerofer's much smaller tents; he'd seen permanent dwellings kept by more sedentary hominids. He'd never seen anything like these brightly painted square houses. But they were houses, with manheight doors, and trees arrayed about them, and *windows.*

Later. He ran on.

There were no more houses along Rim Street. He saw Brobdingnagian shapes, rectangular solids, distorted eggs, forests of tubing, great flat and curved metal webs. His mind wasn't making much sense of what he saw. Get a rounded picture, that was it; go for detail later.

He was looking at the City, not at the landscape beyond. But he had the river in view again, and a line of rocky bluffs—

The cruisers!

No species had better distance vision than a Red Herder, and no natural shape could pass for a Machine People cruiser. He couldn't be wrong. He'd found Valavirgillin's caravan on that rocky peak.

Most of the expedition seemed to have gone off. He saw no sign of life until one of two specks stood up to stretch. Grass Giant sentries? Tegger stepped to the edge and waved like a man trying to fly.

Would they see him?

Not here, against all these confusing shapes. But if he could put the sky behind him . . .

All in good time. The cruisers would keep.

Surprises were not easy to come by when you recognized *nothing.*

Rim Street opened out, widened. Far ahead, that was the door he'd kicked open last night. And here at the port-spin end of the docks, a street ran off at a right angle. A dark-mouthed street eight manheights wide, angling steeply down, where everything else ran uphill toward the City's center.

He turned right.

He was running into darkness.

He slowed. The stench would have stopped anyone. Death and corruption, and something under that, something familiar. A bit of night vision was coming now. The street curved off to the right, still descending . . .

He ran out faster than he'd gone in.

What he'd seen as a spiral staircase last night was far larger than he'd realized. Big enough for four cruisers moving abreast, he thought. For vampires too, this was the way up.

Tegger looked into the darkness and knew that he would have to go there. And wait while his eyes adjusted. And look into the Shadow Nest, and see what looked back.

But not yet. Tegger ran on.

Docks and storage ... great silvered tanks ... here, sunlight flashed off windows. Short streets and wide stairs, skewed as they rose, windowed houses rising tier after tier to what might be a great eyeball.

He'd reached Stair Street. Tegger began to climb.

The houses had bands and patches of dirt around and between them. For most of Stair Street's length the wide dirt patch stretching out from the front door of one house was the flat roof of the house below.

Some of these plots were flooded. Some had been washed away or reduced to sand by hundreds of falans of rainfall. Here grew tall grass; here grew nothing. There were dead trees, fallen trees, live trees, fruiting trees. Here a straggling line of pomes ran from the topmost house nearly down to Rim Street. They looked planted, at first; but two topmost pome trees were dead, and the bottommost were just beginning to produce head-sized fruit. Tegger pictured tens of thousands of spherical pomes rolling downhill over hundreds of falans, seeding this whole slope from one tree.

Here was a window—flat, not like a vehicle window, as big as the Thurl's bed. Awesome. Its surface was murky. Tegger peered through it, but the interior was dark.

Next door, a huge tree had uprooted and cracked the wall

of a house. This house, too, had one great window facing the earthen plot. Tegger picked up a chunk of fallen rubble and tried to smash it. It was the rubble that cracked.

But the cracked wall. Might he squeeze through that opening?

Yes.

The place was big by Tegger's standards: larger than a tent. The scale was larger, too: not quite Grass Giant size. A chair he sat in left his feet dangling.

He found an oval bed on the other side of the picture window. Five skeletons on the bed. Three adults, two children. They were a friendly group and seemed at peace. One more, child size, was off the bed, reaching for a door.

The space behind that door looked very dark.

He used rotted bedding to make a torch and went in.

No windows here. There were furnishings . . . controls? Levers that would wiggle, anyway, above spouts that came out of the wall. Two were at either end of a tub with a drain in the bottom. Water spouts, but no water ran from them.

Tegger continued his search.

Another windowless room. Another skeleton, adult size, lay near a shallow opening with tens of tiny knobs inside. More controls—Tegger thought, reaching for his pack—like the recessed control panel in the hauler.

Towel. Wedge-bladed knife. Strips of Vala-cloth already cut. He began pushing them into place.

Nothing, nothing, nothing . . . a miracle happened.

Light. A point in the ceiling was blazing too bright to look at.

Tegger got out of there.

Lights were shining throughout the house. Tegger left them that way. It surprised him that there was still power. Where did it come from? Thunderstorms? Power was directed lightning . . .

He moved up the line of houses, faster now, looking through windows. Here and there he saw skeletons. Always inside. Bodies outside were gone, meat for birds.

There were scrubby grasses, some he knew as edible to hominids. Plants too weird to be anything but ornamental. Unless that one with big purple leaves . . . ?

He dug a bit, pulled, and found fat roots. Cloudy River Delta Farmers would eat those boiled.

These were miniature farms!

Tegger settled himself cross-legged on the roof edge of a plot of earth, slumping within his earth-colored poncho, letting the rain wash over him like just another lump on the landscape.

These little patches of dirt were farms no longer. The plants were no orderly array of crops. Untended since the Fall of the Cities, likely enough. But was it not strange that in this restricted space the occupants would seed croplands too small to feed a smeerp?

Tegger found it more than interesting. He hadn't been nibbled by pests last night. Maybe he'd climbed out of their reach. Maybe nothing lived here save for the makaways who foraged below. But if there was anything like a food chain up here, it would begin with growing plants.

So, he would hunt.

What else was worth noting here?

Vines had grown from two narrow strips of soil to engulf

the house behind him and tear it down. Windows and their frames had buckled. He could see furniture ruined by rain.

The houses were flat surfaces and right angles. But Stair Street was crowned by a dome of window-stuff as big as two or three houses. He'd compared it to an eyeball, but he was only seeing reflections of white clouds. It had no color of its own. The tube that was the City's peak loomed above even that.

He was among the topmost houses; and they were the biggest, with the widest of garden/farms. It seemed the City Builders liked a view.

The wilderness before and below him was almost a perfect square. The center was an empty pool in the shape of a scallop shell. Four trees had been planted at the corners, but rain had carved runnels, undercut one of the trees and felled it. Its roots poked into the air beyond the roof's edge.

Tegger liked the pool. It might have been some Cluster Islands grotto. Its rounded bottom was smooth blue City Builder stuff, and there were stairs leading in. There was even a running waterfall, a spout in the pile of boulders at one edge. He could see where the outflow from the waterfall, and the rain, all ran into a drain at the bottom and disappeared.

There was dirt in the pool, too, but it didn't belong. There wasn't enough. It had washed in. Still, plants had taken root and were cracking the blue bottom.

A pool for swimming. Why? Stairs to get out: you could drown otherwise. Maybe City Builders swam; maybe Homeflow River Folk came visiting.

But having built it, why leave it empty?

Nothing was happening among the patches of plants. Tegger supposed he would have better hunting during halfnight. Between light and dark was an active time for things that were used to evading predators. Maybe he could chase something into the pool, trap it there.

Meanwhile—he dropped to the grass, then walked into the pool.

Mud had half choked the drain. It had not quite hidden the cover.

A round drain and a pipe below. A round cap the size of his spread fingers, on a hinge, with a rusted chain hanging from it. Tegger could see where it ought to lead, up there at the edge. You'd stay dry while you pulled the chain to open the cap.

He tried to close the cap. It resisted. He leaned his weight on it and the hinge snapped. He set the loose cap on the drain. It stayed. He watched as the pool began to fill.

Chapter Eleven

GUARD

DUTY

WEAVER TOWN, A.D. 2892

Daylight was glowing on his eyelids. Louis tried to roll over, then stopped. He'd wake her.

His memory oozed into place. *Sawur. Weavers. Shenthy River valley. Hindmost, vampires and vampire killers, a hidden protector* . . .

She turned in his arms. Gold and silver fur; thin lips. Her breasts were near flat, but prominent nipples poked through the fur. She was awake in an eyeblink. Bare black eyelids made her brown eyes look huge.

Sawur studied him to verify that he, too, was awake. Then—he hadn't asked, but he had guessed. Morning was Sawur's time for rishathra, and Louis needed this in the worst way.

The worst way. She certainly sensed something wrong. She pulled back two inches to see his face. "Do you hunger in the morning?"

"Sometimes."

"*Something* is distracting you."

"Something was. Is. Sorry."

She waited to be sure he had no more to say, then, "Will you teach today?"

"I should go looking for plants I can eat. We're omnivores. Our guts need roughage. Hey, the older children go hunting—"

"Yes, we'll go with them," Sawur said. "They'll learn more from you in the woods than they would from me in a hut. Here, this would be your parting gift, but you need it now."

From a corner she pulled something with straps. Louis took it into sunlight to admire it. It was intricately embroidered weavework, a valuable gift: a backpouch.

He found remains of last night's fish in the ashes of the barbecue, wrapped in leaves. It made a good breakfast.

He caught up to Sawur trying to herd a score of children all in one direction while she lectured on plants, fungus, animals, and animal spoor.

Yesterday he'd seen fleshy arrowhead-shaped leaves on a purple stalk, growing at the bases of the trees. Something like that grew downstream, and those leaves had been edible.

Ordinarily an omnivore could watch what other hominid species ate and try that himself, try eating whatever another hominid found safe. He couldn't do that among strict carnivores.

Then again, what he found need not be shared. If it was poisonous, there was the medkit. Eat one thing at a time and check himself. If it was mildly poisonous, he might have to eat it anyway for roughage, for potassium, for whatever scarce substance he wasn't getting.

The children watched as he tested this and that, chewed this, threw that away, put this or that in his backpouch. Sawur tried to help. She pointed out a poisonous twining plant before Louis could hurt himself, and a blue berry the birds liked, that tested clean and tasted of lemon. A fungus the size of a dinner plate tested positive for allergies . . .

They reached a pond a little ahead of the children. Sawur slowed him with a hand on his arm. The water was flat and still. His knees and back protested as he knelt.

His hair . . . he'd never seen it like this, laced with white strands. His eyes were lined at the edges. Louis saw his age.

In an agony of regret, he thought, Like this! I should have dressed like this at my two hundredth! Everyone at the party would have freaked!

Sawur grinned at him impishly. "Were you hoping that Strill would come to you?"

Louis stared at her, then laughed with surprise. Sawur hadn't been seeing his age, but her own! He was saved from answering: the children were crowding around them again.

There was something Louis wanted to know. He could learn by teaching. He picked out a blond-furred net thrower who was fighting hard to attract Strill's attention. "Parald, do you know that all humans were once alike?"

They had heard of such. They didn't quite believe and they didn't quite disbelieve.

Louis drew in the mud: *Homo habilis*, life size, as best he could render him. "*Pak* breeder. Our ancestors lived on a planet like the world I was born on, a ball, but much closer to the center of our whorl of stars," and he drew a barred spiral, the galaxy. "We're out here. The Pak lived in there." He couldn't draw the Pak world. Nobody had ever seen it. "A plant grew there called 'tree-of-life.' "

He began to alter *Homo habilis*, giving him a swollen misshapen head, swollen joints, wrinkled and folded skin, tooth-less jawbones grown through the gums into a bony beak.

"You're turning from children into adults," he told them. "When all humans were alike, before there was a Ringworld, there were children, and adults to make more children, and a third shape to protect them both. Adults didn't have minds then. When an adult got old enough he would eat tree-of-life—"

"She," Parald said, and giggled.

Stet, their generic pronoun was female. Louis said, "Then *she* would sleep, and change as she slept, like a butterfly. Her sex would fade away. Protector men and women look alike. Her jaw would grow to replace her teeth, her brain case would expand, her joints would expand to give the muscles greater leverage, her skin would become thick leather armor. When the change was over, she would be smarter and stronger, and she would care for nothing except to protect her children. Protectors fought terrible wars over whose children would survive."

Strill asked, "Why doesn't it happen to us?"

"There's an element almost missing from the soil beneath the Arch. The virus that makes protectors can't live without it. But in a cavern under one of the islands on the Great Ocean, tree-of-life still grows with the virus in the root.

"The terrible thing about a protector is that she'll do any-thing to give an edge to her own relatives. Whoever built the Ringworld locked the tree-of-life up so nobody could reach it. It grows in artificial light in great plantations beneath the Map of Mars. But somebody must have got to it—"

"That's what scares the Web Dweller!" Parald crowed.

"Right. He thinks he's found a protector on the other Great Ocean, and another halfway up the Arch to antispin, and maybe more at work on the rim wall. The Web Dweller isn't related to any human protector. By instinct they would call him an enemy. He controls the Meteor Defense in the Repair Center. With that he can burn whatever he likes, anywhere on the Arch.

"So who should we be afraid of? The Web Dweller or the protectors?"

The children shivered, and giggled, and then began to talk.

Louis listened and learned. They knew of protectors. War was only a rumor to them, yet the rumor came clothed in protector-shaped armor. All hominids seemed to carry that shape in their minds, as heroes or monsters, as Saint George or Grendel; as designs for armor among the Grass Giants and as pressure suits on the spaceport ledge.

After much argument, the children seemed to side with the Hindmost. Strangers didn't compete, didn't steal, didn't rape; and what could be stranger than the Web Dweller?

Presently they all ran off to swim in the lake.

Plants here reminded Louis of another plant with a fat root like a beet. He began digging. Sawur watched for a bit, then asked, "Well, Luweewu, can you feed yourself?"

"I think so. It isn't the style of life whereby a man gets fat," he said.

"And are you glad you came among us?"

"Oh, yes." He was barely listening. A decision he'd made eleven years ago was unraveling.

"But you wanted Strill."

Louis sighed. Strill would have been a delight, but even Sawur, mature at forty-odd Earth years, was as close as he wanted to get to child molesting.

He said, "Strill is beautiful. Sawur, if Strill had come, it would have been bad news. I can tell how wealthy a culture is from the woman who shares her tent with me. I'm the prize here, whatever my real value—"

"High."

"—and you claimed me. But if people are starving, or beset by predators, or at war, they try to guess what prize *I* want. Then I find some glorious young woman in my bed and I know we have a problem."

"But *you* would not."

"No, I mean they might need more than ideas." He'd given away two of his cargo plates to people along the river who needed heavy lifting power. He didn't want to tell Sawur that, so he only said, "Knowledge is like rishathra. You have it, you give it away, you still have it. But I've had to give away tools."

"What made you so twitchy this morning? Protectors?"

Louis dropped a root into his pack. Now he had four. "You know about protectors?"

"Since I was a little girl. In the stories they are heroes, but at the end of time their battles destroy Arch and world together. Kidada and I don't tell those stories anymore."

"These are heroes," Louis agreed. "The ones on the rim wall, they're repairing motors that hold the Arch where it belongs. Another has been repelling invaders. But protectors can be a bad thing. The Web Dweller's records suggest that protectors destroyed all the life on Home, on one of our ball worlds. It was part of a war between protectors who wanted more turf for their breeders."

Sawur asked, "Do you trust the Web Dweller's records?"

"They're very good."

"Shall we swim?"

In mid-afternoon the boys killed something like a small antelope. The children cut a pole to carry it down to the village, with Louis marching at the fore end. It was pleasant to be the strongest man, and not all that uncommon. The average Ringworld hominid was smaller than Louis Wu.

The Swimmers had moved on, but the Sailors and their ship were still in port. They'd caught a few fish and started the fire. By halfnight the antelope was nearly done.

Half seen between the huts, tonight the window in the cliff showed the Ringworld edge-to-edge, a checked blue and white band with black sky along either edge.

Where in tanj were the fearless vampire hunters?

Louis set his assortment of roots to roast at the edge of the coals. Children and adults were abuzz with questions.

"It's the Arch," he told them. "Tonight the Web Dweller must be looking all the way across to the opposite edge. See, there's the edge of the sun itself, and that's part of one of the shadow squares that hide the sun at night. All that patchy white is clouds. No, you can't see them moving. If they moved as fast as that, the wind would blow the landscape right off the scrith foundation! Those glittering dots and curves and lines, if you can make them out, those are seas and rivers."

"He's showing the stars larger, too," old Kidada said. "What's that moving one? And, Louis, what is the Web Dweller trying to tell you?"

Off the edges of the Arch, all of the bright stars were adrift. The brightest was moving crosswise to the rest. Louis had been watching it. It slowed as it approached the rim wall. It was *on* the rim wall, turning a stretch of the rim into a brilliant blue-white line . . . and it went out.

Louis said, "He's trying to tell me that another invader has come under the Arch."

Parald sliced off meat and passed it to Kidada, then Sawur, then a sudden crowd. Wheek offered Louis a fish on a stick. Weavers and Sailors took their meals and moved through the huts to the cliff side.

I show you the Ringworld invaded; come and talk. I do not show you Valavirgillin alive or dead; you must ask.

Louis accepted a slice of antelope and, eating two-handed, followed Parald.

The Weavers sat on tables and the sand, watching. Sawur made room for him on a table.

Within the webeye window, a shadow square crossed the sun. Details became clearer, sharper.

Brilliant light flared on the rim wall. Over the next several minutes the point moved inward, above the Ringworld surface; dimmed; blurred; went out.

Dull stuff, but they watched. Louis wondered if Weavers would become addicted to passive entertainment.

The clouds were moving now. Vast wind patterns showed their shapes in fast-forward. A tiny pale hourglass sucked streamlines at both ends: a hurricane on its side, a meteor puncture hole.

Fast-forward, a solar prominence rose past the rim of the shadow square. A shock wave of green brilliance rose up the plume. Then a burning green star delicately touched the rim wall at the point where the earlier star had rested. The green star walked off the rim and blurred as it intersected clouds.

As the last sliver of sun vanished overhead, the Weavers all streamed off to their huts, chattering in excitement punctuated by yawns. Louis watched in astonishment. These Weavers were *really* diurnal.

Before the Hindmost could decide to speak in front of them, Louis strolled back to the fire. He raked two roots out of the coals.

One was acrid. One wasn't bad. He didn't always eat this well.

The Sailors had remained. One came to join him. "That show is for you, isn't it?"

Louis looked back. Within the Hindmost's window, the green star had gone out.

"I don't know what to say to him," Louis said. "Wheek, did he speak to you?"

"No. He frightens me."

The Hindmost's message seemed clear enough. Fusion drive: invading spacecraft. ARM and Patriarchy and the Fleet of Worlds all knew of the Ringworld. Each had had time to mount expeditions. Or the invader might be a returning City Builder craft, or someone else entirely.

The automatic Meteor Defense wouldn't react if an invader moved slowly. Some entity was *actively* killing ships.

The killer had a problem, too. Lightspeed. The invader had landed light-minutes from the second Great Ocean, but the attack had come hours slow. A solar plume must be ejected, the superthermal laser effect must propagate along the plasma, and it all took time; but there was still that lightspeed delay. The prey might still escape.

The Hindmost would be *extremely* eager to find a hyperdrive ship undamaged.

Low music was playing through distant branches. Wheek had gone to his boat. Louis raked a third root from the fire. He slit it, then pushed on the ends to open it. Live steam, and a smell not too different from a sweet potato.

He wondered if he'd found wild tree-of-life. No matter.

The soil wouldn't have enough thallium; the plant wouldn't support the virus that caused the change; and cooking would kill it anyway. Louis took his time eating, then went toward Sawur's wicker hut.

The music seemed to grow louder. Strange stuff, with qualities of wind and humming strings. He stopped outside Sawur's wicker hut to listen.

The music stopped. A voice said, "Will you not speak to the Web Dweller?"

"Not tonight," Louis said, and looked around him. The voice was a child's, with a bit of a speech impediment. Tonight was foggy, but Ringworld nights were bright, and he should have seen *something,* Louis thought.

"Will you show yourself?"

A nightmare rose out of low brush, too near. Lank hair covered its body, the color of the night. Big spade teeth forced an exaggerated grin. Long arms, big hands; a miniature harp in one hand.

The Ghoul seemed male, but a kilt hid that. Sparse facial hair, flat chest: a child, boy or girl.

"Nice kilt," Louis said.

"Nice backpouch. Weaver work is loved all through the Shenthy River valley."

Louis knew that: he had seen Weaver work tens of thousands of miles downstream. He asked, "Do you do security work for the Weavers?"

"Sec . . . ?"

"Guard their possessions by night."

"Yes, we stop thieves."

"But you're not paid for normal, ah . . ."

In lieu of answer—*was* there a word for garbage disposal plus funeral service?—the child blew into the handle of his harp while his fingers played across the holes and tweaked the strings. He played a tune on his tootling, twanging instrument, then held it out. "Do you have a name for this?"

"Illegitimate child of a harp and a kazoo. A kazarp?"

"Then I am Kazarp," the Ghoul said. "Are you Louis Wu?"

"How—"

"We know that you boiled an ocean, far up the Arch—" Kazarp pointed. "—*there*. You vanish for forty-one falans, and we find you here."

"Kazarp, your communications are awesome. How is it done?" Louis didn't expect an answer. Ghouls had their secrets.

"Sunlight and mirrors," Kazarp said. "Was the Web Dweller your friend once?"

"Ally. Not friend. It's complicated."

The pointy-faced hominid examined Louis. Louis was trying to ignore the smell of a carrion eater's breath. The child asked, "Would you have spoken to father?"

"Maybe. How old are you?"

"Near forty falans."

Ten years. "How old is your father?"

"A hundred fifty."

"In falans I'm about a thousand," Louis Wu said. He decided that the child was too easy to notice. A distraction? Was his father eavesdropping?

Well, then, how to tell this? Should he? Louis said, "The Web Dweller, the big cat, two City Builders, and me. We saved everything under the Arch."

Kazarp said nothing. Some wanderers must be great liars, Louis thought. He said, "We had a plan. But it would kill s-s-some ... it would kill *many* of the people we were trying to save. I'm as guilty as I thought the Web Dweller was, and

I hated him for it. Now I find out that the Web Dweller saved many more than I realized."

"Then you must thank him. And apologize?"

"I did that, Kazarp. Kazarp, I expect we'll talk again, but my species needs sleep. If your father wants to talk, a Ghoul could certainly find me." Louis knelt to enter the wicker house.

"Did it leave a bad taste?"

Louis laughed. A Ghoul might well know all about bad taste! *But that voice wasn't Kazarp.*

He stepped back outside. He said, "Yes."

"Still, you swallowed what you must. Now the Web Dweller must decide. A valuable alliance, a breach of manners— you're a thousand falans old? How old is the Web Dweller?"

"Even guessing makes my head hurt."

The child had settled cross-legged and was playing background music to the voice that spoke from nowhere. The adult's voice said, "We live perhaps two hundred falans. If your misunderstanding only cost you forty or fifty falans, for such as you it must be worth repairing."

"Oh, the City Builders were refugees, and killing doesn't bother Chmeee! But *I'm* still guilty. *I* consented. I thought we killed all those people to save the rest."

"Be joyful."

"Yah." He couldn't ask even a Ghoul to consider the numbers involved. No sane mind could grasp them. *Hominids of varying intelligence inhabit the Ringworld, invading every conceivable ecological niche. Cattle, otters, vampire bats, hyenas, hawks . . . Roughly thirty trillion, with a margin of error bigger than all known space.*

We can save most of them. We will generate a solar flare and turn it on the Ringworld surface to bring heated hydrogen fuel to the few remounted attitude jets on the rim walls. Lose fifteen hundred billion to radiation and fire. They would die anyway. Save twenty times as many.

But the Hindmost's advanced, adaptable programs had exercised fine control over a plasma jet bigger than worlds. The Hindmost *had not* killed fifteen hundred billion. Not at all.

But Louis Wu had consented to their deaths.

He said, "That region of the Repair Center was infested with tree-of-life . . . with the plant that changes hominids into something very different. Kazarp says you're about the right age to become a protector. I'm seven times that old. The virus in tree-of-life would kill old Louis Wu.

"So I sent the Web Dweller in alone to cause their deaths. Otherwise I would have *seen* how many didn't die. I took all those lives, and the only apology I could make was to die."

"But you're not dead," the hidden voice said.

"Dying. With the medkit on my cargo plates, I might get as much as another falan."

The child's music broke in discord, and the night was silent.

Tanj! He had longevity and he'd thrown it away, but these people had never had the choice. Just how ill-mannered had he been?

The adult said, "And you gave up his friendship."

"The Web Dweller doesn't exactly have friends. He bargains very exactly, and his aim is always to make himself safer. He intends to live forever, whatever that takes. That bothered me then. It bothers me now. What *will* it take?"

"Your alliance? Does he have something to gain from you?"

"A traveling pair of hands. A life to risk that isn't his

own. A second opinion. He can offer *me* another hundred twenty falans of life." And that was scary.

"Could he do that for, let us say, me?"

Offer longevity to a Ghoul? "No. His systems, the programs to heal him or me or the big cat, he must have designed and built them before he left home. He can't *get* home. *I* stopped that. And if he could, why not just stay?"

And he thought further: *He's got a program to repair humans and a program for a Kzin. For a Ghoul he'd have to write a new program. What my life would cost me is already too much, but what would it cost to write a treatment program for yet another species? And if Louis Wu asked him to save a Ghoul, then why not a Weaver next? A City Builder? A . . . ?*

Impossible.

The hidden Ghoul had accepted that . . . or else he was thinking that some wanderers were mad. Kazarp was playing again. Louis said, "When I thought I'd murdered so many people . . . I decided to age and die in traditional fashion. How bad could it be? People have done that since there were people."

"Luweewu, I would give all I have to be a hundred falans younger."

"The Web Dweller can do that for me . . . for my species. He can do it again when I get old again. Demanding anything he likes of me, each time."

"You could refuse, each time."

"No. That's my problem exactly." Louis peered into the dark. "What shall I call you?"

The music of the kazoo-harp suddenly had a bass accompaniment. Louis listened for a time. A wind instrument? He could not guess its shape.

"Tunesmith," he decided. "Tunesmith, it's been helpful talking with you."

"We should speak of other things."

"Ships and shoes and sealing wax, and—"

"Protectors."

What did the Ghoul heliograph net know of protectors? "But I'm groggy. Tomorrow night," Louis said, and crawled inside to sleep.

Chapter Twelve

WEANING
VAMPIRES

Tegger had expected the window-dome to be some kind of weird dwelling, but it wasn't. There was no obvious way to lock the door. The interior was all one big room, and that was a stairway too big even for Grass Giants: concentric semicircles of steps. And tables, a dozen light tables on skids.

What *was* this? he wondered. If a hundred or so hominids sat on those steps, they'd have one fine view of the factory city and lands beyond. A conference room? He tried it himself for a bit, then moved on.

Doors at the top of the last step. Beyond, darkness. Tegger lit a torch.

This was not a room to live in. It was all flat surfaces, and thick doors that had little windows in them and little boxes inside.

When in doubt, he thought, keep looking. Three big water basins with drains. A flat table of wood now warped. Hanging from a hundred hooks, metal bowls and dishes with long handles. Behind a panel above eye level Tegger found something he recognized: tiny knobs joined by fine lines of dust.

He began replacing the dust lines with strips of Vala-cloth.

A light came on.

Six channels he'd laid; one light. What did the others do?

There were more doors to the back. Tegger took up his torch and passed through.

Storage here: doors, drawers, and bins. The ghosts of old smells were pleasant enough. Plants. They didn't smell like food, but they probably were. Tegger searched out dried plant residues, but found nothing that even a Grass Giant would eat.

They sat on those semicircular steps and *ate?*

Maybe. Tegger went back into the lighted room. It seemed warmer . . . and he still didn't get it until he tried to lean on one of the flat surfaces.

Red Herders don't yell when hurt. Tegger hugged his burnt arm, teeth bared in pain. Then, after careful thought, he began to spit on flat surfaces.

Twice, his spit sizzled.

The doors to two of the boxes were hot to the touch.

He was in some kind of chemical plant. Maybe another hominid could understand this better than he.

The peak of the City was a great squat tube with a wasp-waist constriction. A helical stair took him to the rim. Tegger looked about him like a king.

What he'd missed before, leapt at him now that he'd reached the tallest point in the City.

Every roof was the same color!

The flat tops of rectangular solids, the curved tops of tanks, were all a glittery gray. Some had symbols painted on the gray in narrow lines. The only exceptions were the houses along Stair Street, where flat places were soil and pools, and—yes—the *stairs* were glittery gray.

But the sides of things were of all colors. Industrial shapes were not so much decorated as labeled. There was script Tegger didn't recognize, square and curved and scrawly. There were simple pictures.

The old City Builders could fly. Why not label the tops of things, too? Unless this gray surface had—was . . . Flup, he almost had it.

Work on it. Meanwhile . . . He was standing at the rim of a tremendous tube, ten manheights tall and about that wide. Tegger looked down inside, a much greater distance than ten manheights. The reek of ash and chemicals was faint, but he wasn't imagining it. Here was a chimney big enough to burn whole villages.

This alone might be reason enough to set a factory floating. The smoke from such a burning might hover for years before drifting away, but at least it would rise first! Irritated neighbors might be pacified. Then again, how would neighbors reach a floating industrial center to make their complaints?

He'd been climbing stairs and exploring houses for a quarter of the day, but the cruisers hadn't moved. Valavirgillin must have chosen that peak as a defensible position. Sentries shifted on the rock, watching the river, watching the Shadow Nest and its floating roof.

Tegger dropped his poncho to expose the unmistakable color of his skin. At the rim of the tallest point of the City, he raised both arms and waved.

Warvia! By the power of our love, and Valavirgillin! By the power of the cloth I stole, I've reached this place. Here I will accomplish something, somehow. Somehow!

Had he been seen? He thought they were pointing at him . . .

Well, then.

The City rolled away below him. He was able to find the dock, to orient himself from that. The houses and stairs ran from just below him down to Rim Street, along both sides of a zigzag line. That line was nearly opposite the docks.

Most of what he saw, he still didn't understand. But ...

Cisterns. Sixteen huge cylindrical tanks were open to the sky, evenly spaced about the City. He had to guess that those tanks were intended to hold water. The houses and window-dome, at least, would need water. But the cisterns were empty, every one of them. Like the pools along Stair Street. All empty.

After the Fall of the Cities, citizens would have nothing to carry them down. Some must have gone down the ramp. When the vampires moved in, that option closed. They were marooned.

They would need water. There was the river; there must be pumps. Why else position a factory above a river? But the pumps had likely stopped working, and the rain hadn't started yet.

But they'd drained the City's water. Why had they done that? Were they already crazy?

Whisper was gone, and his own mind wasn't enough. He had to get the cruisers up here, somehow.

He slept in the window-dome that night, on one of the steps. It seemed safe, and he loved the view.

At halfnight several hundred vampires streamed away from the Shadow Nest, up the Homeflow and into the mountains. As the last edge of sun disappeared, their numbers rose into the thousands.

Vala's people reacted variously to that many vampires passing that closely. The Gleaners simply missed it: they *had* to sleep at night. Vala rapidly realized that she couldn't use Grass Giant sentries at night. Anyone could see their courage, but anyone could smell their fear . . .

Except Beedj. How did they train a budding Thurl? Was it something she could use, too? She sent the rest to bed and relied thenceforth on her own people and the Ghouls.

Whatever their frustrations, they were learning a great deal about vampires.

The second night was ending; and now, in driving rain, beneath a black lid of cloud, the vampires straggled home. Their numbers were thinned a bit, Harpster said, and they had a few tens of prisoners. They had been more quarrelsome going out.

The Ghouls reported structures in the Shadow Nest. There were huts or storage shacks; many had fallen down. Something mountainous stood in mid-river. The Ghouls couldn't see the top of it; their angle was too high.

They could see no way up save for the spiral ramp.

There was a midden, a garbage dump off to port-antispin of the Shadow Nest. It must have been growing for ages, a mountain of vampire and prisoner corpses, until even Vala could see it once it was pointed out. It was too close to the Shadow Nest to be of use to Ghouls.

There was no place beneath the floating factory that the vampires didn't go.

It was full light now, and the procession of vampires had become a trickle. "When that stops, we're going back to the river," Vala said.

"We need our sleep," Harpster said.

"I know. You stay here."

"We're ripe for bathing and we need to learn. We'll sleep under the awning. Wake us at the river."

Valavirgillin rolled the cruiser along the riverbank. There was no way to hide anything so large, and she didn't try.

Flashes of daylight came and went, and flurries of rain. The Shadow Nest loomed ahead, too near. None of her companions could see into the blackness below the ancient hulk; but when the shifting black clouds closed their own lid over the land, Vala could see motion around the shadow's edges. Some vampires, at least, were active.

It was midday. Valavirgillin kept a wary eye on the weather. If it got too dark, the vampires would be out and hunting.

The tilted plate loomed across the sluggish brown water. It looked hard to reach. Vampires seemed safely distant. Vala stepped out onto the river mud.

Two black heads surfaced well out into the water and swam toward them.

It was best to introduce oneself repeatedly to aliens who might not see differences in individuals. "I am Valavirgillin—"

"Rooballabl, Fudghabladl. The river is shallow here. Your cruiser might safely roll as far as the island. It would be more difficult to attack you."

"—Warvia, Manack, Beedj." Barok and Waast were tending the cannon. "We're not planning to stay. Roobla, there was activity around here last night—"

"The Red companion you asked us to look for, we have seen him. We could not come near, but we saw him fight and we saw him fly. Fudghabladl says that he had a companion. I never saw one—"

Warvia burst out, "Companion? Where would Tegger find a companion? *Was it a vampire?*"

"I saw no companion, no kind. Fudghabladl's sight fails. Tegger talked to himself from time to time. He came to look at this tilted flying thing. Six vampires jumped him. They did no courting, they simply attacked."

Rooballabl sounded petulant, as if the vampires had broken a rule. Vala nodded. *Worth knowing.*

Beyond that, the River Folk had seen not much more than Warvia had seen from the cruisers. When the tale was told, Vala asked, "Are you safe here?"

"We believe so. We learn, too. Do you know that prisoners live in the Shadow Nest?"

"We saw prisoners brought through the pass," Warvia said.

"Some roam free," Rooballabl said. "We did not come near those, but we watched. Never were more than two or three loose at once."

"What species?"

"Two big ones went to eat river grass, then back under the shadow. Grass Giants, I think. Many vampires came to meet them. The vampires fought. Some ran away and the rest fed upon the Grass Giants. The Grass Giants did not survive. But we saw Farmers of the Spin Delta region pull up roots and boil and eat them, and return alive."

Fudghabladl spoke. The River Folk chatted a bit, then Rooballabl translated in spurts. "Fudghabladl watched a Red woman. She spent half a day hunting, but badly. She had no patience. She came back again and again to the shadow and her vampire. He would send her again. Late in the day she caught a leaperbuck drinking, jumped it and broke its neck. Pulled it back to the shadow. Three vampires shooed the rest off. These three drank the beast's blood, then they rished with the Red, then the Red ate of the leaperbuck. She was very hungry."

Vala tried not to see the hot rage and shame in Warvia's face. She asked Rooballabl, "Did you see any of my species?"

More River Folk chatter. Then, "One, a young woman, goes guarded by a vampire male. Valavirgillin, what success for you?"

"We've seen Tegger waving at us. He's up there, alive and active. I still don't see how we can get ourselves up. I don't see how else we can do anything."

"What did you expect?"

Warvia half snarled, "The *Ghouls* had a *plan*. The ramp they want doesn't go all the way down."

Vala half expected angry comments from under the awning, but the Night People held their peace.

"It must have reached the ground once," Rooballabl said. "What else could it be for?"

When the city worked, there had been flying cargo craft, but rolling craft must have been cheaper, and surely there were cargoes too heavy to float. "I expect the Fall of the Cities brought the vampires," Vala said.

Beedj asked, "How?"

With her eyes on the misty outline of the Shadow Nest, Valavirgillin let her mind roam and her tongue follow. "A center of industry could hardly permit vampires to nest in their basement. So, somehow they kept the vampires out, but when the cities fell, it stopped working. Vampires look for shadows. They moved in. One night the vampires went up the ramp. They didn't get everyone, so by the next night the refugees had pulled up the ramp—"

Again Beedj asked, "How?"

Vala shrugged.

Rooballabl's voice was like bubbles popping in mud. "Ask instead, why? They built a tremendous hanging road for cargoes too big even for this great floating plate. Why would anyone build it to move, to lift? Such a—vertical bridge—would be difficult to build, and easily damaged if it also had to lift. We understand weight and mass a little, I think."

Rooballabl was right, and Vala was irritated. "I don't know the answer. How about a war between people who could fly and people who couldn't? You'd want to pull up the bridge, so to speak."

Her crew looked at each other. Beedj asked, "Do any of you have old records of such a war?" None spoke. "Rumors, then?"

"Forget it," Vala snapped.

Manack asked, "Why build the ramp to lift? Why not just lift the city a little?" Alien or not, he saw something in Vala's demeanor and added, "Never mind."

The sky was black and pouring rain when Tegger walked into the shadow.

He lit a torch when he could, but the light didn't travel far. It lit a featureless circle of the road down. He was walking into a roar like a rainstorm. He edged to the right side and found a rib-high curb. Peered over and saw nothing.

They must have seen him. They might not like the torch, but it certainly made him conspicuous. He was carrying nine more. What would happen if he dropped one?

Instead, he leaned far over the curb and hurled the torch onto the loop of road below him. He looked over to be sure it still burned, then walked a little farther down the ramp. He'd come somewhat more than a full turn.

Now he could let his night vision develop.

These odors reminded him of the nights he and the others had spent waiting to speak to the Ghouls. The sounds were like the Thurl's tent at night: domestic sounds, murmurs, sudden quarrels, all in an alien language, all above a sound like a waterfall. What he imagined below him must be worse than the reality . . .

Tegger looked over.

The bottom of the spiral ramp was high off the ground.

Something inside him saw that as funny. He could see pale triangular faces looking up, and that was funny, too. Tegger began to giggle.

Deep into shadow, water fell in a vertical river, a waterfall of tremendous scope. All the rain falling on the City was pouring onto some huge dark mass, and thence into the Homeflow.

He was at the edge of the City. The waterfall must be near or at the center, but the roar was loud even here. It was pouring onto, *into*, a vast, intricate structure, then into the Homeflow via lesser falls and streams. Tegger could see little but dark-on-dark, but . . . here was a fountain of such size as nobody but an ancient City Builder would even consider.

The Homeflow ran around the fountain on both sides. Here it seemed to be confined in concrete. Where the concrete ended, near Tegger's perch, was rapids. Water falling from the City, adding its momentum to the Homeflow itself, had cut a deep canyon. Only its walls showed in the blaze of daylight around the City's edge.

And of course there were vampires everywhere.

Most were asleep, cuddled in family groups. Wait, now . . . that was a Machine People, wasn't it? Hard to tell in the dark. A woman, despite the mustache; she had breasts. And no clothing. She was the center of a circle of vampires.

It looked to Tegger like they were protecting her from other vampires: from thieves. Four of adult size, two small enough to be children, and the infant in one woman's arms: enough to guard her.

Machine People had been taken during the attacks on the Thurl. Tegger continued to watch.

The baby woke and attempted to suck.

The woman half woke. She gave the baby to the Red woman. Oh, flup, the Red was putting it to her neck!

Tegger let himself slump against the curb, in the dark. He hadn't eaten in some time, but old bird meat was trying to rise again.

Why do vampires collect prisoners?

How do vampires wean their babies?

Tegger didn't want to know anymore.

Sometimes the trick is to set a problem aside. Tegger had almost reached the light above him when it all came together in his mind.

Water. Ramp. Lights. Vampires below, stranded City Builders above. The cruisers!

There was more to be learned, but Tegger knew what he had to do *now*. And afterward . . . ultimately he'd have help.

All over the floating industrial structure, lights were going on.

Valavirgillin was hurting for lack of sleep. Soon she would seek her bed. But they were so beautiful.

Her mind drifted.

Food was running low in the heights. Grass was scarce; prey was scarce and agile. The Gleaners were finding enough to eat. The River Folk had found fish, enough and to spare. Cruiser One had brought whole basketfuls back. Fish would feed anyone but the Ghouls and Grass Giants. Machine People would need something more than fish, but not yet.

A few vampires were hunting around the Shadow Nest's garbage dump. They must be hungry, Vala thought, but they were having some success. Warvia reported scavengers no Red had ever seen before. Perhaps Ghouls killed competing scavengers where they could.

Fudghabladl had said they rolled corpses into the Home-flow. The vampires' numbers must have been smaller then. Now they stacked them away from the river. Scavengers came for the bodies, and starving vampires hunted them for their blood.

The cruisers were once again parked back-to-back, with sentries on duty. Vampires had ignored them on the first night. *They've had the whole day to watch us. As we watched them.*

In a day or two the stored grass would be gone. The giants would have to forage in the lowlands, in daylight only, with companions to guard them. The Ghouls might find forage, too. Vampire prisoners must die during the trek home.

Grieving Tube spoke. "Power cannot be made to flow without certain unusual materials."

Valavirgillin didn't jump, didn't look around. "I know."

"Unusual. Some wire must have survived the Fall of the Cities, or else come under the Arch afterward. Where would a Red Herder find such?"

"In my pack, I think," Valavirgillin said. Ghouls know all secrets. "A good thing for Tegger. He would have died at the river."

"Yes."

Into the silence Valavirgillin said, "Louis Wu left me a stack of—it has a long name—*superconductor cloth.* I traded it to the City Builder families of a floating city. They used it to repair their lights and water condensers.

"So, I was rich. I took Tarablilliast for my mate. I bore three children. I invested in a project to make what Louis Wu described. *Plastic.* Tarablilliast has never criticized me for wasting our money." Never but once, she remembered. "After all, it was my wealth. He brought little to the mating."

"This *plastic.*" Grieving Tube's pronunciation was the exact imitation of Valavirgillin's. "Does it have a name in our tongues?"

"I think not. Louis described stuff that could be made from the nasty residue after one makes fuel. Scentless. Taking any shape. He showed me one or two plastic things. Otherwise, I was guessing.

"Tarbavala Labs has produced results . . . answers . . . nothing we can sell. Tarb and our parents are taking care of our children while I scramble for money to keep our concerns going. I thought a trading expedition would serve me. Persuading hominid cultures to make alcohol commands a bounty. Trade is wealth on top of that."

"How long have you been gone?"

"Nearly ten falans."

"Too long?"

"I don't know. I've *mated.* Tarb never bargained for that." Vala shook her head. "I need sleep."

"I will watch."

Chapter Thirteen

SAWUR'S
LAW

WEAVER TOWN, A.D. 2892

Louis was alone when he woke, and hungry. He pulled on his zipsuit and walked out through crackling brush.

The village seemed empty.

There was warmth in the ashes of last night's fire. He found the last of his roots and cut it open. It was almost like eggplant. Not a bad breakfast.

Noonday sun—of course—but it *felt* like noon, like he'd wasted half the day. He boarded his cargo stack and went up for a look around. There they were, instantly obvious: Comet Sawur leading a tail of children through the upstream arch.

He caught them leaving the arch, left the cargo stack and joined the tail.

They walked along the river. Louis drew maps of the Ringworld for them, and spoke of its builders and its age and its fate, and tried to tell them which parts were guesswork. He drew the double superconducting toroids they'd found re-mounted on the City Builder spacecraft: Bussard ramjets taken from their mountings on the rim wall. He did not speak of what it had cost him to fuel the rest.

Some of the boys had disappeared. Now they were back. They'd found hundreds of bird nests perched in forked trees. The entire horde ran off, and Louis and Sawur followed slowly.

Sawur said, "I cannot work out your sleep pattern."

"I talked long last night with two whom you may never meet."

"People of the Night? They're said to know all and to rule everything under the Arch. The dead belong to them. Louis, we have guested visitors who speak to such folk, but why do you?"

"I'll talk to anyone," Louis admitted. "Sawur, I enjoyed it. I may have learned a little. I think the child wanted to talk and her father didn't move fast enough to stop her. Then Tunesmith gave away more than *he* knew, and now I *almost* know how their empire communicates over all that vast distance along the Arch."

Sawur's jaw sagged. Louis said hastily, "*Not* my secret to tell, Sawur, not even if I knew it. Even so, they don't know everything. They've got problems, I've got problems—"

"You do, yes," she said sharply. "You wouldn't wake this morning, but you were talking to your dreams. What torments you, Louis?"

But they had nearly walked into an explosion of small nets.

The children had crept around the grove, surrounded it. Now the nets were flying. In an hour they had caught an amazing number of pigeon-sized birds.

Weavers seemed to have no interest in eggs, but Louis collected a dozen. They looked and felt like slick plastic, like free-fall drinking bulbs with no nipple. Worth a try.

In mid-afternoon they were back in the village. While the

children plucked the birds, Louis and Sawur went off alone. They sat on a flat rock and watched the older Weavers building the fire.

Sawur asked again, "What torments a teacher?"

Louis laughed. Teachers don't have torments? But how to explain to a Weaver . . . ?

"I made a fool of myself, long ago. It must have taken the Web Dweller four or five falans just to realize *how* stupid I've been, *why* Louis Wu wasn't talking to him. But we're talking now, and that's not the problem.

"Sawur, the Web Dweller captured me and Chmeee to be his servants. Very reprehensible, of course, but he has gifts to pay for such a theft. He has seeds to be chewed to make an old hominid young, or a Kzin."

Sawur nibbled her lip. "Well. He can. Will he?"

"For value received. And he has a device, an autodoc. It can heal serious wounds, scars and missing limbs. Likely it can repair damage even boosterspice won't touch.

"Sawur, to rebuild a man requires *extreme* medical techniques. If he can build me young, I believe he can build me docile. Chmeee and I both made poor slaves. The Hindmost can make me a better servant. A perfect servant. Until the night before last, I had an excuse for keeping myself *out* of his machines. Now I don't."

Sawur asked, "Have his machines had you before?"

That was a good question. "He had me in frozen sleep for two years. He may have done some medical work on me. He could have done anything he wanted."

"But he didn't."

"I don't think he did. I don't feel any different."

Sawur was silent.

Louis laughed suddenly, turned and hugged her. "Never

mind. I cut his hyperdrive motor apart! He can't go back to the stars, and that's why he had to save the Arch. If he made me a servant, he made me a bad one."

Sawur stared, then laughed loud. "But Louis, you trapped yourself, too!"

"I'd made a promise." To Valavirgillin of the Machine People. "I said I'd save the Ringworld or die trying."

Sawur was silent.

"He thought he had a wirehead." Louis heard the gap in translation: *wirehead* had no equivalent in Sawur's tongue. "He thought I would do anything he asked for electric current through the pleasure center of my brain ... as a Weaver might sell her freedom for, say, alcohol? He didn't know I could throw it off. He knows now."

Sawur said, "So, what if he makes you young and docile? But what if you first determine that you will ignore his commands?"

"Sawur. *He can change my mind.*"

"Ah."

Louis brooded for a time. Presently he said, "I'm clever and agile and the Web Dweller knows it. If he made me a better servant, I might become stupid or slow. I can tell myself he'd be a fool to alter me very much. It's hellishly tempting. I'm afraid I'll believe it, Sawur."

"Would he keep a promise to you?"

Another good question.

Nessus, rejected by his species ... Nessus the mad puppeteer had demanded that the Hindmost mate with him, should he return from the Ringworld. The Hindmost had agreed. And *kept* the covenant.

But that was a bargain between equals ... no, it wasn't. Nessus had been presumed mad, mad for centuries.

Throughout known space, puppeteers had kept their contracts with a variety of species.

He'd forgotten Sawur; he jumped when she spoke. "You've given me my youth and snatched it away, if I believe your crazy dream. But I'll tell you this," she said with a whip in her voice. "The older I am, the more I would give to be young again. If you don't ever intend to deal with the Web Dweller, that's one thing. If you do, then the last thing you want is to wait until you're old and sick."

She was, he decided, dead right.

That night they cooked their meat—and the Sailors their fish, and Louis his eggs and a river weed he'd found edible—and went to sit beneath the cliff.

Louis found himself looking for Tunesmith in the brush. There was no sign of the Ghoul, but he would be listening.

The floating industrial park had been lifeless when last Louis had seen it. Now the Hindmost's webeye window showed it blazing with lights.

"You've got me," Louis said to the empty air. "I have to know how that happened."

The view jumped—

Chapter Fourteen

INVASION

Pointed claws rested on her wrist. She whispered, "Grieving Tube?"

"Harpster. My mate wakes others. Valavirgillin, you must see."

It seemed she'd only just closed her eyes. Vala rolled out of her blanket. She didn't say, "This had best be important." Other species had their priorities; traders had to learn them.

Black night and rain. The Shadow Nest was a blurred constellation. Harpster had returned to the cruiser. Waast and Beedj came out, then Barok. Barok asked, "What is it, Boss?"

"I can't see anything."

Warvia came up beside them. "It's murky down there, Valavirgillin."

"I know."

"The ramp. Vala, you really can't see? It isn't just the ramp. The whole city has settled a little. Flup, Manack was right!"

The folk in Cruiser Two spilled out all at once, gaping, chattering. They saw no more than Vala did. But Harpster was at Warvia's side, saying, "Not our imagination. The vampires are trying to jump to the ramp. It's still too high for them—"

"They'll have it in not too many breaths."

"It's Tegger!" Warvia screamed. "He did it!"

"But they'll be pouring up the ramp!" Vala wondered, Is this real? Nobody could see the change but Warvia and the Ghouls, and even they wouldn't claim that the ramp was *down*.

"Board!" Valavirgillin bellowed. "Anyone not aboard gets left! Board your vehicles and arm yourselves! We're going up!"

Tegger lay on his belly, looking over the edge of the dock. He didn't see many vampires. It wasn't good hunting territory for them. Their only prey were the besotted prisoners under the shadow. A few starving rogues hunted out here, vampires desperate enough to try to trap animals for their blood.

It was dark down there and rain blurred the view, but the cruisers were unmistakable. They rolled slowly. Mud and sand sucked at their huge wheels.

Four vampires swarmed onto the first cruiser, quick as Gleaners, and climbed toward the driving bench.

Gleaners dropped from the turret, towels across their mouths, swords in hand. Paroom stepped from aft, swinging some kind of mace. In a moment the invaders became imploring suitors. Another moment and two were dead, the others in flight, and Paroom's long mace caught one in midair . . .

A shock traveled lightly up Tegger's spine. He had been waiting for that.

He'd spent most of the day finding circuitry panels, opening them, testing what their circuits did. He'd learned to recognize the styles of panel that controlled lighting. Here was the panel that controlled the dockside lights. He'd already placed twists of Vala's cloth. He flicked two switches and the dock lit up like daylight.

With his eyes tightly closed, Tegger felt his way to Ramp Street and into the darkness. He paused for a bit to get his night vision back. Then he looked over.

He'd felt the shock as the ramp touched bottom.

Vampires were moving up the successive turns of the ramp. There weren't many. Perhaps their noses told them how little awaited them: one little lone Red Herder, and no other prey at all.

Tegger set to the patient work of lighting a torch. When he had it flickering, he set it aside and looked down again.

Roughly thirty young adults and adolescent children were climbing toward him in no great hurry. What were they thinking? *Here's a road where no road was, but there's no scent of prey. Follow it, but best not be first. Light, oh my, it hurts—* They were piling up a level below him, their arms hiding their faces. Tegger wondered if the dockyard lights would hold them.

The scent billowed into his face.

Reflex said *Do something!* And reflex called him down, but he couldn't. Couldn't. He whipped the torch around his head and hurled the fireball a level below. All the pale faces ducked away, and most of them were running back down the ramp. A few were trapped between the torch and the dockyard lights.

Tegger fled.

At the dock's edge he leaned over empty space and sucked great lungfuls of clean air.

The cruisers were close now, two or three hundredbreaths away.

Vampires were harrying them, more with every breath

that passed. Warriors lined the running boards. Gleaners jabbed spears between the pillars of Grass Giant ankles, while Grass Giants fired crossbows at more distant targets. Tegger heard, very faintly above the whisper of the river, the duet the Ghouls were playing from the cannon towers.

No gunfire? Had Valavirgillin ordered silence to delay alerting the nest? But the vampires' numbers were growing; the nest was waking to an invasion.

The river flowed into darkness, and the cruisers followed.

—Darkness. It was black as sin below him. Vampires would see just fine. Ghouls on the driving benches might be able to shout directions, but the rest would be blind.

There *was* something he could do. He'd need nerve. And his sword.

Valavirgillin drove with a hand for the tiller and another for her gun. Barok rode the bench with her, facing backward. She was breathing pepperleek through a towel. The Thurl had been right from the first: herbs were more effective than fuel.

A white face popped up and she fired two-handed, and had the tiller again before the cruiser could veer. Other guns began firing. Barok took her gun and handed her another, loaded.

The noise drove the vampires back, and the cruisers rolled into darkness.

The floating factory glowed above her like a constellation. She could see little below its edge, but she knew where the ramp was, and she aimed for that.

How well would these reject vampires fight now that only they could see? She was driving into a black stench like all the graveyards under the Arch. Disgust should be a defense, but it wasn't. It wasn't. As always, the real enemy here was a growing urge to mate in the middle of a war.

Harpster interrupted his eerie music to shout, "Boss! Left! Left, then hook around right and onto the ramp. Boss, there are vampires on the ramp!"

Vala turned left, into blackness.

The cruisers were holding their own. The shadows they fought were children, maimed and halt, elderly, pregnant: all who hadn't departed in the stream of hunters. In the dead of night they were at their peak of alertness. Vala had considered waiting for dawn. But dawn would have brought the hunters back, however exhausted, in all their strength and numbers; and these she fought now would have had half the night to reach Tegger.

Meteors fell ahead of her.

Vampires, crouched waiting between Vala and the ramp, skreeked and rolled aside. Fireballs fell—torches—and some went out, but six still burned. Tegger's gift.

She was on the ramp, and Cruiser Two right behind her, and vampires coming from all sides. One popped up on the bench. Vala blasted it away and set the gun aside. The cannon roared: a wind of fire and pebbles swept the ramp clean ahead of her.

Behind her, light suddenly blazed as if the sun had fallen from the Arch. In the terrible glare, vampires hid their eyes and froze, sitting birds. Guns and crossbows banged and twanged all around her.

The bench shook. Vala whirled around with vampire scent driving her crazy and only her empty gun for defense. A distorted Machine People face looked back at her. Forana-yeedli, looking quite crazy, gripped the bench with all four limbs and her teeth.

Vala kept driving.

Round and round. A shadow in the light semaphored both arms. One hand brandished a sword. She drove into the light.

Red Tegger—naked: why?—stepped aside to let the cruisers past.

She saw Warvia leap from the cruiser. The shock when she impacted Tegger sent his sword flying. Warvia's tunic flew after it. Vala hardly needed to hear the shouts of her companions: it was celebration time, rishathra time.

Someone must keep her wits long enough to guard them.

Vala pulled up in the white light of the dock. She heard fighting. *Vampire?* No, she heard speech . . .

Foranayeedli had found her father. They were screaming mortal insults at each other.

Vala tried to judge if they would kill each other. There was a moment in which they paused for breath. Vala touched their shoulders—get their attention, back up *fast*, talk *fast*—"Forn, *no*, Barok, *really*, it was *my* fault. *Our* fault. Any of us could see what would happen. Can't we share the blame?"

Father and daughter looked at her, shocked.

"You should not have been together when vampires came. I should have parted you. I was wrong. Don't you understand, we *all* mated. We couldn't help it. Chit and Kay are pregnant. Barok, they *still* don't know about you and Forn, do they?"

Barok mumbled, "Don't think so."

"But we can't go home!" Forn wailed.

"Rish with someone," Vala said.

"Boss, don't you see—"

"*Now*, silly girl. Paroom looks distractable. Get it out of your *blood* so you can *think*. Go!"

Forn suddenly laughed. "What about you, Boss?"

"I've got to button this up. Barok, find Waast—" But that was Waast's voice. Waast had been found, and by more than one male. "—or someone. Go." She pushed them in opposite directions, and they went.

Next? The Reds seemed reconciled. That might even last. Tegger must know the power of the vampire scent by now. The scent still fizzed through Vala's brain and blood, but she'd known it far stronger, and resisted. Well, not resisted, exactly . . .

A pale child stood before her, half her size, squinting, mutely beseeching.

She stepped toward it.

A crossbow bolt sprouted in its chest. It squawled and ran wobbling into shadow.

Vala turned. It was Paroom. She said, "I thought I'd use the gun butt. It was too young to put out a scent."

The Grass Giant accepted that. "We may have brought more than one rider. I haven't seen any but that child."

"Check the tunnel?"

"I found four vampires dead by blade. Tegger's prey, I think."

"That'll help."

"One of them had all her teeth knocked out. And . . . what did you say? That's right, vampires don't like the stink of their own dead. They won't go past."

"Then . . . we made it. We're safe."

"Good enough," Paroom said, and folded her in his arms.

The party was ending.

Vala didn't want to notice. She was wrapped in sexual congress with Kaywerbrimmis. It should be safe. She'd be doing it anyway, but after what he'd been through this past halfnight, she thought, no male could still make a child.

The sun was a blurred silver in the gray-white clouds. All

four Gleaners were asleep in a pile. The Ghouls had dropped out early and crawled under an awning. The Grass Giants had begun exploring each other, outside the rishathra pattern—as she and Kay were—and Tegger and Warvia were talking, just talking.

Kaywerbrimmis relaxed in her arms and was fast asleep.

Vala disengaged herself, rolled Kay's tunic and pushed it under his head. She strolled—limped—down the dock toward the Reds, alert for body language; but they didn't seem unwelcoming.

She said, "Tell it, Tegger. How do you lower a floating factory?"

Tegger grinned in pride, and so, Vala believed, did Warvia. He said, "It's a puzzle. You'll see the pieces all around you. There are swimming pools and cisterns, and every one of them was empty when I got here."

Vala waited.

"City Builders were stranded here after the Fall of the Cities. I've seen their bones. We know vampires moved into the shadow. They must have come up the ramp. What would you have done?"

"We talked about lifting the ramp somehow."

Tegger nodded happily. "Every cistern empty. But the Fall of the Cities came long before Louis Wu boiled a sea. They *had* to have a water supply, but the vampires scared them more. So they let all that mass of water run out, and the city went *up*."

"So you plugged all the cisterns—"

"There were some big metal sheets at the dock. I used them for plugs."

"—and waited for the rain to fill them up, and the city went *down*."

"Yes."

"Thank you for the light."

Tegger laughed. "Heh, I thought you'd like that. I lit all my torches and dropped them over. Then I poured a canteen's worth of fuel down on the fire."

"And now what?"

Tegger said, "Now we're where we can do something, and now I've got fifteen bright friends to work something out."

Vala nodded. Tegger didn't have an answer, but he'd done miracles already.

Chapter Fifteen

POWER

In the blaze of full day, Tegger led them up Stair Street to show them his discoveries.

He found it frustrating. Warvia would dive into houses, jungles of ornamental plants, and half-filled swimming pools, then rush back with questions. Tegger couldn't follow her; he must keep to the pace of the rest. Gleaners were even faster than she was, and they got into places no Red would fit, then came sprinting back to chatter at the Grass Giants.

"Here, these grasses ought to serve you," Tegger told Waast, while she was the only Grass Giant handy. She took the handful, smiled at him and, chewing, followed Perilack and Silack into a collapsing house. "I haven't seen any plant eaters," he told Coriack. "I looked for droppings. Nothing. Oh, we'll find something to eat. There're webspinners if nothing else. Did we bring any insect eaters?" He was talking to Valavirgillin now. "You'd think there must be animals to eat the plants, but I haven't been able to catch anything but birds, and I haven't *seen* any insects."

Vala asked, "Carrion?"

He guessed her meaning. "Old dry bones. The Ghouls

won't eat until *we* starve. But I did find these. Pomes, a whole line of pome trees. Here."

Vala broke a pome apart and began to eat. They'd feed Machine People, yes, for a while. "Tegger, what do these factories make?"

"I found a warehouse full of cloth. Maybe they make that here. Vala, I haven't really looked yet."

Vala was interested in the factories. With her pack full of Louis Wu's magic cloth, she might get some motors working. Even if she couldn't, if everything had deteriorated too far, she might still find wonders made before the Fall of the Cities, stacked in factories or warehouses, still waiting to be shipped.

But Tegger himself must be starving. Her people had to be fed *now*. Look for profit later. After she found some way down!

The little party trickled up Stair Street to the bubble at its top, and in.

What Tegger found mysterious was clear enough to Machine People. Barok smiled and led them up the giant stairs and into the back. "Banquet hall," he pronounced. "City Builders are omnivores who cook. They like a lot of variety. Look at all this equipment!"

Tegger said, "It's all boxes and surfaces that get hot."

"Yes, and a table for chopping stuff."

Above Stair Street was only the chimney and its spiral stair. Warvia was on the rim of the chimney, kicking her heels in space, looking down on the floating factory city and the lands beyond. She seemed indecently happy.

"I can see our River Folk waving. *Rooballabl!* Hey, any of you, come up here and show them we made it! They'll think I'm just Tegger."

Vala climbed the spiral stair to meet her, past a bronze

web clinging to the stone. The women edged around the rim to leave room for those who followed: Coriack, Manak, Paroom, Barok. Tegger stopped to study the web, then climbed to join them.

There is something about being at the top of . . . well, anything . . . that puts one in command.

Practically speaking, Vala could see nothing of what was most interesting: vampires swarming in the Shadow Nest below and the regions nearby. But far into the mountains, sluggish pale streams flowed through the passes. Flowing along the Homeflow they became individual dots: vampires returning in their thousands.

The river and the snow-crested mountains glittered in patchy sunlight. Close in, two squat black manshapes stood against the glitter. Vala and the others waved. Reassured, Rooballabl and Fudghabladl sank beneath the water.

But she could see all of the factory complex. Tegger had left lights burning everywhere. A broken line of green ran down Stair Street. Green showed nowhere else; none near the chimney. What would a webspinner eat?

The flat tops of warehouses and factories, the curved tops of tanks, were all a glittery gray. The only exceptions were the houses along Stair Street, where the flat places were soil and pools, and the *stairs* were glittery gray.

Paroom asked, "Valavirgillin? See those gray roofs?"

"Well?"

"I wondered why the lights still work. Everything that's flat-on to the sun is that same glittery gray. That stuff must be storing sunlight."

Tegger said, "Yes!"

Paroom smiled. "Bothered you?"

"Yes, but it's obvious once you—Let's see, they can't have

been getting much light through these clouds, but none of the power was used before I got here. Hundreds of falans. That means—"

"Could run out. We'd better turn the lights off in the daytime."

"The hauler plate was that color, before I tore the cab loose. *That's* why it could still lift. So lightning is sunlight . . . turn them off? Paroom, what are we saving power *for?*"

"I don't know," the Grass Giant said, "but I don't like waste. Leave the lights on around the dock, though, where the vampires come up. That's *my* thought."

Tegger shrugged. Suddenly he looked exhausted. Warvia led him away, murmuring in his ear.

The rest of the party weren't finding anything note-worthy. Presently, like tourists on holiday, they trickled back to the cruisers. Most of them were ready to fall over.

Gleaners *had* to sleep at night. All four looked alert enough now, at midday, the only members of the foray team who did. Vala set Manack and Coriack on guard. Then she crawled under an awning.

Forn was there, fast asleep, not just from exhaustion, poor girl, but loss of blood, too. She looked peaceful, though. Vala dipped a towel in fuel and washed the angry-looking wounds on Forn's neck. Then she spread a blanket and lay down.

When Beedj came in she only closed her eyes against the light.

Beedj spread a double armful of fresh-cut grass in what space was left, and curled himself into it. He murmured, "Clever, what Red Tegger did."

"Yub," said Vala.

"Maybe we can go further with that."

"Mm?"

"Boss, we can collect more water. Bash holes in the roofs of all those factories, storage tanks, whatever. Anything that isn't a roof, seal it so water doesn't run out. Spread cloth for funnels. Let it rain. A sea of water! This factory-thing would sink even farther, wouldn't it? Crush the vampires."

Could he be right? Vala was too tired to think . . .

"No."

"Who speaks?"

"Foranayeedli. It isn't flat under here, Beedj. There's a structure as big as Administration in Center City."

"Oh flup, that's right, you were *living* down there. What kind of thing is it, Forn? Like a statue or like a building? Something we could crush?"

Forn began to answer. Vala crept out into daylight, pulling her blanket along, and into the darkness of the payload shell. She spread her blanket and—

A voice said, "Valavirgillin, this is a good time to look into the Shadow Nest."

Harpster. "I don't smell you."

"We explored before we slept. There's a row of houses— you saw?—and pools. Delightful. And grass to roll ourselves dry."

"Appreciate it. Harpster, this is a good time to sleep."

"Night People sleep, too, Boss. In daylight. I'd rather sleep." One sharp claw pricked her side for emphasis. "So do vampires. They'll be torpid. We can just push them off the ramp. What I'm really after is the light conditions. Shall I take some Gleaners and go down?"

Vala tried to think. "I put two on guard. Take Silack and Perilack. Take Kaywerbrimmis," because he'd had *some* sleep, and they'd want a variety of viewpoints. "Ask Beedj." The Thurl's heir would volunteer for anything. Flup! Vala sat up and reached for a gun and alcohol flamer. "And me."

They were eight: two Machine People, Beedj, two Gleaners, Warvia, and the Ghouls. The Ghouls moved ahead of the circle of torchlight cast by Vala's throttled-back flamer. The rest followed, masked and half blind.

Vala was looking at four vampire dead. She should have been watching where she stepped. She stumbled . . . on a handful of vampire teeth, pointed like a Red's teeth. Sure enough, the one woman was toothless, just as Paroom had described her, and . . . not just hacked. Vala shuddered.

Grieving Tube bounded out of sight. Vala drew breath to shout, and Harpster was gone, too. Vala ran instead, flamer held high, and found the Ghouls standing over a male vampire still twitching.

They moved on. Rich and corrupt scents were working their way through the pepperleek she breathed. But her sight was coming back.

The party halted three loops down, two and a half loops above the vampire-infested floor.

A broken circle of daylight lit the Shadow Nest bright enough to hurt.

There was dark soil on either side of the Homeflow, patches each the size of a lord's farm. That was off to port-and-antispin, where the river entered the shadow. Huge mushrooms grew in those plots, and vampires lived under them. Shadow farms. A hundred varieties of fungus might have grown here before the vampires moved in. The monster mushrooms must have been too big to trample.

Directly below was paving similar to the stuff the Machine People used for roads.

"You see, there's quite a lot of light," Grieving Tube said cheerfully.

"I wanted to wait for a wind," Harpster complained.

A wind, yes. Vala felt madness bubbling in her blood. The rich smell of pepperleek had become no more than a spice for the rutting scent. Wind would have blown that away. There must be tens of thousands of them down there, she thought, and they were starting to look up.

Warvia was breathing through her mouth in great gasps. Warvia *knew* her will could be broken. Kay was edging away from Vala: no distractions needed *now*. The others looked all right. Try to concentrate! That center structure . . .

The fountain was many things. There were windows in the side that faced the ramp, and small balconies without railings, and outside stairways: probably offices rather than domiciles.

Partway around, a flat space faced rising concentric arcs, something like the steps in the feeding dome. Seats. That had to be a stage! Piles of rotting stuff at the corners might have been a curtain; collapsing flat structures must be props; a flimsy wall, fallen, showed a honeycomb of backstage structure. Valavirgillin wondered if others would recognize it for what it was.

Water poured from above, a waterfall surrounded by shadowy giants, and wound through and around every part of the structure. Standing statues of City Builder Folk poured water from great bowls. Water flowed down the back of the stage, a permanent backdrop. Thus watered, vividly hued mushrooms still grew behind the office structures. It all flowed down through a maze of pipes and channels to meet the Homeflow.

Forn was right. That mountain of masonry was as big as a

civic center. It wouldn't support the mass of a floating factory, maybe, but it would stand against any mass of water *this* group could collect.

"All right. All right. We can't lower the factory on them," Perilack said. "What if we move it sideways? Something's holding it here. What if we could set it loose? Let it slide away with the vampires all running after it. Wouldn't they make great targets?"

Grieving Tube said, "She's at least partly right. Something holds it here, some—" She went off into her own language, and so did Harpster. Vala turned back. Even the Ghouls might not be able to set a floating city adrift.

Harpster dropped back into the Tongue. "—like at the bottom of a bowl, a low spot in the realm of magnetic power. We could *tow* the floater out of it if we had enough power, but with two steam cruisers? Flup, I wish you people had never heard of Louis Wu."

Statuary, lines of windows, a stage, a sculpted flow of water. "What's missing?" Vala asked herself.

Grieving Tube heard. "Boss?"

Vala said, "Tell me what you see."

The Ghoul woman obliged. "Offices. Public affairs, I bet. They put it all down here so they wouldn't have to invite political entities topside. The stage is for speeches and conferences, but it's a stage, too. This was a social center."

Harpster said, "I'd like to see around the other side."

"What do you think you'd find?" Vala asked.

"I think . . . a podium. This one's for plays, it's not really right for speeches, or music for that matter. I bet somebody got an award for the way he worked the fountain into it all. Think how beautiful it would be if we could clear the vampires out."

"*Got* it," Vala shouted. "*Lights!*"

The Ghouls' eyes glowed at her.

"Lights! Plays, music, speeches, bureaus of this and that, award-winning sculpture?" Vampire song rose high at the sound of Valavirgillin's shout, but her warriors were listening, too. "Nobody but a Ghoul would expect all that to be played in the dark! Warvia, Tegger must know where the lights are."

Warvia was fully awake now. "He'd have turned them on."

"Flup."

"Boss, the switches might be down here."

"Flup. That'd be nasty."

Harpster said, "I see it." He was pointing up. "Warvia, that group of statues right at the top? City Builder warriors three manheights tall. They're all carrying spears . . ."

Vala could see vague hominid shapes up there, but nothing more. The ring of daylight didn't reach that high.

"It's just one great black spot to me," Warvia said.

"They're there," Grieving Tube said. "That top one—"

"Bigger than the rest. Spear as thick as my leg, and it doesn't have a point, it just goes right up into the roof. It's a pipe for the power. Sorry, Boss."

"Flup! Not water pipes? Of course not, they've got infinite water. All right. But we'll search topside first because it's easier. Get Tegger to show us what he found. Then look where he didn't."

Warvia refused to let them wake Tegger. "Boss, he showed you everything he knows!"

Harpster and Grieving Tube dropped out early. Nobody could expect Ghouls to guess where an alien hominid would put light switches!

The rest of the warriors spread through the city. Valavirgillin cut a sheet of Louis's cloth, once a priceless secret, into strips and gave them away like confetti. They played with the boxes and switches Tegger had showed them, and presently had the city blazing to rival the cloudy daylight.

Thin strips of glittery gray ran from the glittery-gray rooftop patches, down the sides of buildings. Several of the party followed those lines to where they converged. When Twuk brought Valavirgillin to see, she found a hole near the city's center that was as wide as a Ghoul's leg. She stirred traces of dust she found inside, and sniffed her finger. She couldn't be sure that it was ruined superconductor; but Vala didn't doubt what they'd found.

She hated what had to come next, but there was no help for it. The channel could be two tens of manheights high. Vala cut all of her remaining sheets of Louis Wu's cloth into strips, knotted them together, tied the resulting rope to a chunk of wall and lowered it into the hole until it went slack.

What was it touching, down there at the bottom of a statue's spear haft? It *might* be an unbroken line of power. She'd done what she could. Now she used torn branches to move the top end of her line to where all the channels of silver-gray joined. That patch was flat. There was nothing to tie her line to, but she could weight it with a block of rubble only three Grass Giants could lift.

The clouds darkened and presently sent forth a steady rain. The explorers bore what they could of that, then came trickling back to the dock area. Each looked into Ramp Street. The Grass Giants were the last to give up. The others told them what they'd found, but the Grass Giants had to look, too. The Shadow Nest remained in shadow.

Chapter Sixteen

WEB OF

SPIES

A shadow crossed the light, falling on his closed eyelids.
Tegger was just close enough to waking to enjoy the warmth, the relaxation, the sense of Warvia's back against his chest and belly, the smell of her hair. If he let himself wake further, he'd be thinking of hunger.

Hunger. How was he to feed Warvia? The carrion birds had fled from noise and alcohol fumes and heroes. There were vampires—he shied from a sick memory—but what was here for carnivore Reds?

Drive the vampires away. Descend. Hunt.

In daylight all shadows were vertical. Night must have fallen, and these must be dockyard lights. Who would be moving past at night? Tegger opened his eyes.

Two furry backs moved in and out of the light, moved away down Rim Street.

Tegger slid away from Warvia. He found a blanket and covered her. Harpster and Grieving Tube were turning into Stair Street. Tegger followed, stalking.

Ghouls were a secretive bunch. They had the right to their secrets; but Reds were stalkers.

The Night People moved in a glare of artificial light. The rest of Vala's crew had found switches Tegger missed. Night was their element, but tonight it was the Ghouls who were half blind. Would it bother them? Ghouls must depend a good deal on scent.

The houses along Stair Street were staggered. There was plenty of cover. Tegger hid behind solid masses, trees and walls, staying well back. Where were the Ghouls?

Coming out of a shattered window, softly complaining in their own speech. Tegger had found a whole family of skeletons in that house. Were the Ghouls sniffing out carrion? They'd find nothing but bones.

At the top of Stair Street they moved into the bubble-shaped banquet hall. Nothing for them there, either, Tegger remembered. He waited in an empty pool, his eyes just above the rim.

They came out, and continued up into shadow. The City's apex, the chimney, was still dark. Would they climb it to view their domain? But as Tegger eeled up crooked Stair Street, he did not see shadows rising against the sky. He grew more cautious still.

The sound he heard then was loud. Metal was being tormented.

He climbed a ladder and peered over the top of a chemical storage tank, his shadow lost in a maze of pipes.

The Ghouls were at the base of the chimney. It was still too dark to see what they were doing. He heard brick being cut in rhythmic fashion, cut by a saw. He dropped from the ladder and began weaving closer.

It wasn't food they were seeking. What, then? He edged from behind a radiator wall, and Grieving Tube took him by the wrist.

He most carefully didn't reach for his sword. He whispered, "It's Tegger."

Grieving Tube called, "It's Tegger!" She grinned into his face and said, "You slept through some of this. Valavirgillin is sure there must be lamps focused on the structure below us. Only need to be turned on. We think so, too, but switches are down there."

"What, in the fountain?"

"Fountain, stage, mid-stage command offices, speaking platform. They would want to command the light themselves. Valavirgillin has restored the cable that carries the sunpower."

"They'd want some way of getting down there, too," Harpster said. He had come up quite silently. Ghouls could teach Red Herders how to stalk prey. "I thought we might find a stairway, something for people, for visitors. The ramp isn't it—"

"The ramp is for vehicles. People would feel menaced," Grieving Tube said.

"So we looked for a stairway along the chimney, because we already know it goes pretty far down, but Grieving Tube has a better idea."

Tegger said, "That chimney goes down to a furnace."

"It goes to furnaces all over the city. Channels off to all sides, down inside. We looked." Harpster grinned with great square teeth. "Coming? Or would you prefer to stalk us?"

Tegger said, "There's not much entertainment up here, and not much distraction to a hungry Red."

Harpster said, "You solved that one. You ate—"

"Come, then," Grieving Tube said hastily, "we will divert you." She walked downstep toward the dining place, away from the chimney. Her hand was on Tegger's wrist, her grip unbreakably strong.

"I know what I ate," Tegger said.

"Yes, but who would you tell? Your mate?"

"Yes."

Grieving Tube stopped in the door. "Truly?"

"Of course I must tell Warvia."

Harpster said, "Four vampires on the ramp. You killed three. The remaining woman, you knocked out all her teeth and rished with her, then hacked off a segment of muscle meat. It seems clear you must have eaten it."

Tegger said, "I could see the cruisers below me, running into shadow. I had to get into the ramp to give the drivers light. The smell maddened me, and my hunger maddened me, and I did mad things. But I still dropped the torches and the fuel."

In the end it was Harpster who turned away.

A table or two fell over as they climbed the giant steps. The Ghouls weren't dexterous here. "After the Boss said that about lights," Grieving Tube said, "I got to thinking what else they'd want down there. I thought, food."

Harpster pushed through and waited for the others to follow him.

The big room was stifling hot. "Don't touch anything," Tegger said. "I should have turned those off."

"If you can remember which ones aren't lights," Grieving Tube said.

Tegger nodded. He began plucking Vala-cloth twists from between pairs of knobs, snatching them free in a jolt and sparkle of sunpower.

"People working down below us, in offices," Harpster said. "People sitting in arcs around a stage. People just watching water fall. Would they get hungry? Omnivores get hungry a lot."

"Maybe not just omnivores. Other hominids, too," said Grieving Tube. "Diplomatic relations, it may be."

"It seems the long way around," Tegger said. "Catch food down there on the surface, raise it, grow it, ship it in from farms. What then? Char it, cut it up, mix it with flavorings? Fine. But why carry it up here just to send it back down?"

Grieving Tube sighed. "The Red's got a point."

"Yes, and *we* didn't find anything, but the lighting is fluppy awful in here," Harpster said. "See what you can see, Tegger." He opened another door.

It was the storage chamber Tegger had explored earlier. Lights glowed in the ceiling. Tegger had found doors and drawers at every level, doors an armlength high and smaller, but he hadn't left them open like this. Vala's whole caravan must have been through here.

Storage areas behind the doors, and not much in the storage areas. Dried plants, various kinds, some covered with fungus . . .

Harpster said, "Gleaners and Grass Giants found some dried roots here, not much else. But these lights are blinding, and if we turn them off it's like being buried."

"Harpster? Can't you see in the dark?"

"Night People can see at *night*. By Archlight. Even in a rainstorm it's not *black*."

None of these cupboard doors was even big enough for a Gleaner. "Did you find any more doors?"

"Nothing man-sized."

A cheery voice called, "What about Hanging People?"

Tegger jumped. That was Warvia!

She was looking down at him from above a wall of boxes. "Warvia! Where have you *been*?" he cried.

She laughed, flattered. "Behind you as you left the dock.

When your prey stopped, I bathed in a pool so I could get closer still."

Harpster said, "Prudent. Our sense of smell is better than you might guess. So, shall we invite you into our puzzle?"

She jumped down. On her back was one of Valavirgillin's alcohol flamers. "I heard most of it and solved some of it. Come and look?"

"We follow."

Warvia led them back into the heat. "You know," she said, "the raw foodstuffs probably come up from the docks, up the alleys. Whatever they do to it here, there's probably some chemistry involved, things none of *us* would do to food. But it's food going *down* that has to be in small clumps."

Grieving Tube asked, "Truly? Why?"

Warvia moved among the tables and hot surfaces and doors. "You're watching a play. Or you're playing dominance games for high stakes, water and grazing rights. Or your Thurl is speaking your tribe's future. Down comes your dinner, but it's half a weebler. It's burnt black on the outside and seared dry on the inside, just the way you like it, and there's enough to feed twenty people, but there's twenty-six of you! What now?"

She's worked this out after she had the answer, Tegger thought. She was enjoying herself greatly.

"You fight for your share. Or you try to cut it evenly, but maybe six of you are all trying, too. You forget the play or the shouting match or the speech. The actors grow enraged, or the Thurl. But if individual portions come down, nobody needs to fight," Warvia said.

Here was a little door set into a wall, a thick door with a window in it, showing two shelves in a box. Warvia opened the door and put her hand in—

Tegger shouted, "Hot!"

"I touched the door first, love." She pushed against the back of the box, and the box wiggled. "Watch this." She closed the door and flipped a switch down.

The box dropped away, leaving an empty space behind.

"The door won't open now," she said, and showed them.

Harpster asked, "How far down does it go?"

"It should go to where food's wanted. What you were saying, I never could see why *people* had to go down with the food. So I touched every door, and opened doors that weren't hot, and this was what was loose. Then I had to find someplace to put a strip of Vala-cloth."

Harpster flipped the switch to its middle position, then up. "That box wouldn't hold a man."

"It'll hold me, if we take the shelves out."

It would hold Tegger as easily. Tegger didn't bother offering. Warvia's puzzle, Warvia's choice. Red Herders are territorial.

The shelves came up and out easily. Maybe the old City Builders did sometimes send down a whole burnt weebler or whatever. Warvia tried to crawl into the resulting space and couldn't.

The Night People lifted her bodily into place. On her side, her legs and arms sprawled past the door. On her back, on her face ... but her legs wouldn't fold that far. Tegger thought of tearing the top off the box, to see if there was room above it. What he finally said was, "Even major surgery won't get you in there with weapons too."

"I'd go naked!"

"You don't fit," Grieving Tube said. "This is a box for a Gleaner. Try all you like, Warvia. We are not hurried. Harpster my love, our part here is over. Gleaners don't wake until full day."

The Night People chatted as they walked back to the docks.

Harpster said, "We should send something down ahead of our emissary. A bottle of fuel? Balanced to spill over? In case there are vampires between him and the fuse box. A quick fireball, *poomf*."

Tegger didn't feel like talking, and Warvia spoke not at all. They crawled under their awning and watched Grieving Tube and Harpster slink away.

Then Warvia took Tegger's hand and slid out the other side of the awning. They ran softly to where the docks narrowed to become Rim Street. "We explored while you slept," Warvia whispered. "Follow me."

Tegger said, "I have to tell you about something."

"On the ramp? I heard. You went mad. I went mad. We're still mates. But, love, I do not see how we can go home."

Tegger sighed, relieved that such a nightmare could be solved so easily. "Where, then?"

"I have half a notion. Come."

They ran a zigzag path through a system of alleys, climbed through and along pipes to reach a higher level, working their way up.

Warvia led the way over the banquet hall and down, and farther up, and behind the chimney, and around, on their bellies now, toward a sound of metal being tortured.

The noise stopped.

Warvia gestured him back. She stood and stepped forth. "Very good. Now how will you get it down?"

Harpster and Grieving Tube finished lowering the great ceramic slab onto its back. They had cut it no more than a thumblength thick; it must be quite fragile, Warvia assumed. The front of it was a bronze web of intricate geometric form.

Harpster said, "We do love our secrets. Still, this slab isn't going down unless in a cruiser. We'll have to tell the Boss. So. How much do you know?"

"I saw you cutting it. Looked it over after you led Tegger away. What is it? Why do you want it?"

Harpster said, "We think it's an eye and an ear and maybe other senses, too. We think it belongs to Louis Wu and his off-Arch companions."

"We think they were the ones who recentered the sun," Grieving Tube said. "That would make them immensely powerful. We could tell them how to use that power, if we could communicate with them—"

"But Louis Wu popped into some kind of flying tube. Later our sources saw that tube, or another such, hovering near the Shadow Nest. Night People elsewhere report more such webs. It must be for spying."

Warvia asked, "You'll try to talk to it?"

"We'll try that. If nothing answers, then we'll take it to where it can see what we want seen."

"Tegger and I can't go home," Warvia said carefully. "If we had Night People to speak for us as heroes, we might find entry into another tribe of Red Herders. With that in mind, where do you intend to travel?"

Harpster began to bark laughter. Grieving Tube snapped at him. "Fool! They need not come all the way. Warvia, we— No, tell me this instead. How much shock can you stand?"

Warvia beckoned. Tegger came into view. No point in hiding now, he was laughing too hard. He said, "If you think you can still shock *us*, go ahead and try."

Harpster began to talk.

Chapter Seventeen

THE WAR
AGAINST
THE DARK

Tremendous tilted faces looked out of the rock. Two Red Herders and two even larger Night People spoke secrets none could hear, for an audience—

Louis Wu was the only one laughing.

Louis tore his gaze free of the Hindmost's show. For the locals it must seem that they were watching gods decide their fate.

The Sailing People had run.

He saw no trace of Tunesmith or Kazarp.

Weavers were all about him, but most of them were asleep. Torpid Weaver children were trying to keep their eyes open. Tomorrow they'd know they had dreamed. Louis Wu was alone before these tremendous faces.

He said in Interspeak, for the Hindmost's benefit, "Those Ghouls came a long way to steal a webeye. They really must want to talk to you."

The view changed. For the blink of an eye it became an infrared map of the village pool: black water, faintly glowing Weavers asleep on low tables, the brighter glow of Louis Wu's naked skin . . . and a lacework glow behind him, and another alongside the Council House.

Kazarp and Tunesmith hidden in tall grass. The Ghouls are watching, too. Will they recognize themselves?

Huge faces dimmed. The webeye and its brick backing were being set down in darkness. Now the cliff was only dark rock.

The sun was no more than a sliver of light palely glowing through cloud when Valavirgillin rolled out to see what the commotion was about.

It was about Reds and Ghouls guiding four Grass Giants who were carrying a slab of cut brick down Stair Street. A slab of brick with a bronze web splayed across it. Heavy, from the way they moved. They eased it up to Cruiser Two and set one edge on the running board and rested.

The Ghouls began to talk. The Reds wanted to interrupt, but got little chance.

When all conversation was done, the web and its backing rested on the floor of the payload shell in Cruiser Two. Sleepy Gleaners had come out to join the excitement. Sleepy Ghouls were crawling under an awning. And the way down seemed almost clear.

Somewhere behind black clouds, Valavirgillin thought, shadow must be sliding away to reveal the sun. The only light that reached through the storm was a frenzied dance of lightning.

Four Gleaners and Valavirgillin marched through the rain to the top of Stair Street. They entered the bubble, followed by every hominid save the Ghouls, and climbed the giant steps into that amazing kitchen.

Silack fitted himself into the moving box. Only the other Gleaners knew how he had been chosen over the rest. The flamer fitted easily into his arms.

"Fire it at a wall. Or a vampire, or *anything*," Manack told him. He was jittery, and he held a Machine People handgun. It took both hands. "I'm coming right down after you with nothing but this, and when I get down, I want light. I want to *see* what comes at us. Your first move when the door opens, give me *light*."

They closed the door on Silack and flipped the switch down. There was light enough to watch the line vibrating; noise enough too.

The motor noise stopped.

They waited.

Manack tried to move the switch. It didn't respond to easy pressure. Vala restrained him from using more force.

The switch clicked up by itself, and the line began to vibrate. They waited while the box rose into view.

Silack rolled out and sucked air for a great shout. "Light!" he bellowed. Perilack threw herself at him and hugged him tight. He talked over her shoulder. "Manack, I'm *sorry*, but the panel was *right there*, and I thought I might want to leave fast when I turned the switches on, and flup, was I *right*! I turned on all the lights at once, and the—"

Perilack cried, "They're *on?*"

"*Yes,*" said Silack, and his audience ran away.

Valavirgillin was gasping and staggering as she reached Ramp Street. The Gleaners and Reds were far ahead of her and the other Machine People. The Grass Giants were pounding along behind them.

Ramp Street's lights burned through the rain. They swarmed down the ramp.

There was light below, too, and a traffic jam out of nightmare. Light blazed pitilessly on the great central structure, on stage and windows and running water, and all the space around it. The Shadow Nest was brighter than the murky daylight. Vampires caught in the light were trying to get out. Vampires returning from their hunt were trying to get in.

Silack was shouting, "As soon as the lights came on, the vampires ran every way there was. Two or three tens of them decided the offices were a cave! There's a big space in there that overlooks the stage on one side and the speaking platform on the other—Harpster was right about that—and connects to the offices, too. Vampires were coming at me from three directions. Manack, I propped the door open to the moving box when I got out. Time I got down, I *knew* I didn't want it leaving without me!"

"You greedy flup-sculptor, you!"

"I know, Manack—"

"You took all the glory!"

"—I was very, very glad I still had the box. They came in, I flamed them, I went up."

Murderous fights were developing between vampires who wanted in and those who wanted out. Three turns above, Grass Giants were starting to cheer them on. In a moment they'd be taking bets.

Valavirgillin announced, "Listen up! I'm thinking this is the best time to get out. Most of the vampires are still out hunting, and most of what we've got are blind and confused. If we wait as much as a tenthday, the hunters will be home and we'll have to wait for night. I'm hungrier than that. So we go now!"

If I'm crazy, point it out!

They looked at her in a silence broken only by the shrieking of ten thousand vampires.

"Now!" she bellowed, and her people began to run.

Louis could see three Sailing People peering over the Council House roof. They showed courage, but they weren't seeing any more than Louis was. The window in the cliff had become no more than dark rock. The Hindmost's spy device lay in darkness in the payload shell of a six-wheeled wagon.

The Hindmost said in Interspeak, "I still can hear them, Louis, and smell them."

The dark cliff became a dark window. A Pierson's puppeteer danced, and uncountable others wove a pattern behind him: a dark forest of one-eyed snakes.

Louis was amused. "Dancing in the dark?"

The Hindmost twirled. "A test of agility. Darkness was common enough, long, long ago. Not impossible that the dark might come to any of us."

So: they tested each other for mating privileges, like the Fertility Board on Earth. The Hindmost was honing his skills. But he'd said—"You can hear whom?"

"I can hear Valavirgillin's company. With the door in the payload bay closed, I can still resolve voices. They are organizing to defend the wagons. Now the wagons are in motion, with vampires all about. Would you hear?"

"In a minute. I wonder what our Ghoulish observers make of your dancing."

"The small one shifts position constantly. The larger remains still. Would you capture him?"

". . . No."

"Touch your translator to the core of the webeye. I will transmit."

Louis waded through shallow water to the cliff. It remained a fuzzy-edged doorway to Pierson's puppeteers dancing in dusk. A black dot like a lumpy heart floated unsupported at nose level, and Louis pushed his translator against that.

He heard voices, human shading into animal, bass to tenor and higher, agony and rage and urgency. Once, a cry of surprise and pain, more yelling, then a solid thud as a body fell on the webeye itself. Once, he made out Valavirgillin's voice bellowing orders as she never had in *his* presence. Otherwise it was all a confusion of screaming.

The vampire shrieking dwindled over several minutes. Then, jarring as hell, came a cool, musically persuasive voice that sounded not quite like speech. That stopped suddenly, followed by eerie quiet.

Vala turned them downstream because the upstream direction seethed with vampires returning from the hunt. She kept them moving for a tenthday after they were clear. Slick black heads popped into view on the river: the River People were keeping pace.

Cruiser One was still rolling when Beedj swung the payload bay doors open and rolled inside.

Vala waited.

Something heavy rolled out.

Paroom. They'd been all over him, tearing him to ribbons, while friends hacked at them from above and below. A vampire had slashed Perilack, too. Vala waited.

Beedj climbed up beside her. "Dead," he said. "Perilack doesn't look bad. I washed the scratches with fuel. Does that really do anything?"

Vala nodded, wondering if Grieving Tube and Harpster would be offended . . . would understand why Paroom's body was better left for strangers than for his Night People friends. She said none of that to the Thurl's heir. It was all his own decision.

A meadow stretched away from the river. It looked like good hunting. Valavirgillin kept them in a clump, all the several species, and made them wear towel masks. There were vampires about.

Vala had taken stacks of cloth from the dock warehouses. She gave Rooballabl and Fudghabladl a long sheet of gauzy stuff for netting fish. They were hugely successful, and now there was fish for any who could eat it.

The Grass Giants had found some acceptable river grass. There was prey about. Reds and Gleaners didn't need to wait for fire. The Machine People had a firepot starting to boil, and roots and meat in it.

Her crew was being fed.

Valavirgillin looked her people over while she waited. Tegger looked much better with food in him. Forn and Barok were cooking dinner together. If they shied from body contact, it was hard to tell.

Grieving Tube and Harpster were kneeling twenty manlengths away, and a good thing, because they were eating. The Ghouls had found a hominid of the Farming Folk, perhaps a vampire's captive fallen on the trek to the Shadow Nest. They'd stopped short of actually dragging the carrion into camp.

Vampires still dotted the passes. The excitement around the Shadow Nest drew them. Eventually, Vala knew, she would have to get past that.

Gradually, perhaps only from hunger, Vala's mood darkened. An antic whim set her walking toward the Ghouls.

Grieving Tube saw her coming. She came over to stand not too close. "You haven't eaten yet," she said.

"Soon."

"Your mood will improve. We've escaped, Valavirgillin. We're free, with a tale to tell that no hominid can match."

"Grieving Tube, what have we accomplished here?"

"I don't grasp your point."

"We came. We found our way up. We used up most of Louis Wu's magic cloth. We found our way down. We killed some vampires and drove the rest out into the rain. We've lost one cruiser, and Paroom, and what else can I brag about?"

"We rescued Foranayeedli. You loaded ten manweights of wonderfully preserved ancient cloth into your cruiser."

Vala shrugged. Indeed, she'd reap a profit from what she'd collected from the docks, and not just the cloth. And Forn ... yes.

The Ghoul woman dropped a stripped rib and walked closer. "Boss, we've ended the vampire infestation."

"Oh, Grieving Tube. We drove them out. Now they'll spread to every land around us. The vampire infestation is going to get *worse*."

"They'll be far fewer in a generation," the Ghoul woman said placidly, "in forty to fifty falans. Brag now. Await vindication."

"I don't see why."

"Valavirgillin, you've felt the pull of the vampire musk. No hominid can stand against it, not even a Red Herder. Does it not strike you that they also secrete that scent to lure a mate?"

"What?"

"Vampires secrete their musk when prey is about. When food is to be had, that is a time to breed. When they've found

a cave for refuge, that too is a time to breed, and a cave con-
centrates the musk. It was their mating scent when their ancestors were like ours, and it is their mating scent now. But
we've taken away their refuge and driven them into the rain,
the same rain that hasn't stopped since Louis Wu boiled a sea,
Boss. The rain is washing off their mating scent."

Valavirgillin, thought it over until she believed it. Then
she stood up and whooped. "They'll stop breeding!"

Day was near its end. Before night the cruisers must be
where vampires couldn't reach them. Come morning she
would siphon the fuel from Cruiser Two to move Cruiser One
home.

She said, "And you, you've got the bronze web."

"Somewhere beneath the Arch, Louis Wu can look and
hear through that pattern. There is something we must show
the wizard . . . if the wizard still lives and cares to look, if the
web is still a window."

"You'll have to find your fuel somewhere else," she told
Grieving Tube.

The woman nodded placidly. "We'll make our needs
known. Night People will set fuel dumps all the way to the
rim wall. I suppose Tegger and Warvia told you, they'll travel
with us."

"Not a bad notion. There are Reds everywhere. They'll
find a home."

"Yes."

"How do you propose to buy a trading cruiser?"

She blinked. "Ah, the legendary greed of the Machine
People. Valavirgillin, we need Cruiser Two to end a threat
that endangers all who live beneath the Arch. You know
enough to take my words seriously."

"Seriously, yes, but moving your massive spying thing

formed no part of our agreements." Valavirgillin smiled, remembering the negotiations outside the Thurl's wall. The *effort* with which she'd persuaded the Night People to join her assault on the Shadow Nest! She couldn't have driven them away with a cannon.

"You went to some effort to get Louis Wu's spy thing. You thought to keep that secret from me, I expect, but *how?*"

A Ghoul's shrug looked like she'd disjointed both shoulders. "How were we to know we couldn't just peel the web off and roll it up and walk off? But it's embedded in the brick, and so we must reveal our need. Valavirgillin, we will buy your cruiser." She named a sum. "Payable in Center City, by any local Night People concern, when you return."

"Sold." The money was at the low end of reasonable, and so what? Long before she could return to get it, Grieving Tube would have fuel to simply *take* Cruiser Two. "I may have to explain this to my superiors. Will your people back me up?"

"Your associates may learn as much as I will reveal to you tonight. Some secrets we keep. But let us gorge first, Boss. Isn't your meal prepared *yet?*"

Foranayeedli bellowed two words in Vala's Center City tongue. "Boss! Eat!"

Hunger sank sharp teeth into Valavirgillin's belly. "That's my secret name," she told Grieving Tube; and she went.

Chapter Eighteen

COSTS

AND

SCHEDULES

Even the Sailing People had retired. Now only a pair of heat shadows in grass, and Louis Wu, remained to watch the Hindmost's dance.

The pace was brisk now, but the Hindmost never seemed to run short of breath. "This isn't over, Louis. I heard some of what they told the Red Herders. They spoke of spill mountains and problems with a scrith surface."

"Use the webeye. Ask them where they're going."

"No, I will reserve that one secret. Let them struggle for a time before I speak. Let me see how urgently they want your attention."

"Mine?"

"Louis Wu who boiled an ocean, O Subtlest One. They know nothing of the Hindmost. Louis, you're showing marked signs of deterioration. Do you want medical attention?"

"Yes," Louis Wu said.

The Hindmost said, "Very well. My risk and effort involved in sending you my refueling probe must be compensated. You've had a free hand—"

Louis waved it off. "Don't risk your probe, you might need it. I'll go back the way I came, back down the Shenthy River valley. There are mistakes I don't need to make twice, so it'll go a little faster. I was eleven years coming, I'd be nine years returning, maybe less. It'll give you time to move your 'doc to crew quarters."

"Louis, I have mounted a stepping disk on my refueling probe. In one turn of the Ringworld it can reach you. In an instant you'll be aboard."

"That probe is your fuel source, Hindmost, and I—"

"I have refueled *Hot Needle of Inquiry*, which in any case is still embedded in cooled lava."

"—and I dare not think what price you would ask for its use. Anyway, you'll want to move your 'doc into crew quarters or the lander bay—"

"I have done that." The window shifted, and Louis was looking into the cabin that he hadn't seen in eleven years. A huge coffin occupied what had been his and Chmeee's exercise space.

Well, futz. The Hindmost was eager. Louis said, "I left *Hidden Patriarch* a few thousand miles downstream. Didn't you leave a stepping disk aboard? I can be there in seven or eight falans."

"*Two years?* Louis, matters are becoming urgent. The Ringworld seems infested with protectors."

"Oh?" All innocence was Louis Wu, with a smile beginning deep inside. Yes, it all came down to protectors.

"Before she died, Teela said she had left one living Ghoul protector in charge on the rim wall. I can verify that the Repair Crew is still active."

"Show me," Louis said.

The window in the cliff panned along a wall a thousand miles high.

The rim wall was a frieze: mountain shapes relief-carved into a continuous wall the color of Earth's moon. Bands of night swept along its length, their motion barely visible. Spill mountains stood as tiny cones five to seven miles tall along its base. Along the top of this stretch of the rim wall, twenty faint violet flames pointed toward the stars.

The Hindmost said, "These are the rim ramjets as they were when we first saw them. I was testing a webeye camera, the same that the Ghouls now hold. Here, five years later, six years ago—"

The same view, night again, but the ghost flames had gone out. "The Ringworld was back in place by then," Louis said.

"Oh, yes. But I kept track. Louis, can't you see the attitude jets?" The view zoomed. Now Louis could make out the dark mouths of spillpipes high above the spill mountains, and ghostly shapes much larger than he'd guessed. Pairs of copper-colored toroids circled the tiny wasp waists of twenty-one double cones of fine wire: huge, skeletal Bussard ramjets.

"*Six* years ago?"

"Six before I noticed. Caught up in the dance, I might have lost track for as much as—" Hesitation. "—a falan?"

Lonely to the point of madness, lost in a dance with ghosts. The poor herdbeast, once all-powerful, now all alone, rejected by his kind.

Louis shook it off. "So someone mounted the twenty-first motor, the one we found on the spaceport ledge."

"Yes, but copied it first! Here, less than two years ago . . ." Twenty-three motors, and a twenty-fourth with skewed orientation, not yet mounted. Louis couldn't see what was moving it; he only saw minute adjustments in position.

"My webeye has no more definition than this. But new motors are being manufactured and set in their cradles on the rim wall. Is this not evidence for a protector?"

"More than one," Louis said. "Manufacture, transport, placement, supervision."

Hesitation again. "Louis, some hominids go in herds or tribes, but my records suggest that protectors do not. I believe I could monitor all these activities. So could a protector."

"Mmm. And defense?"

"But a second protector is using the Meteor Defense to destroy invading ships!"

"Stet."

"And what of the unseen creature following the Red Herder?"

"No, I won't give you that one. A Ghoul spying on other Ghouls. Local politics."

"Louis, think. We saw him enter the vampire sanctuary! He must be a protector if the vampire scent doesn't affect him."

". . . Stet. What was he doing in there, do you think?"

"Protecting the Red Herder, it seemed. He may be of that species. Our next sight of him would have been the river, I expect."

"Yah. Self-effacing he was, and you can't do that when you're covered with vampire scent. But we won't see him because your camera is lying in the cargo hold of a—"

"Three protectors, Louis. Six to eight, if your guess is right. War among Pak protectors made a radioactive waste of their own world."

"I see your point," Louis said placidly.

"Protectors of divergent species would leave fragments of the Ringworld falling to interstellar space. Louis, we cannot have two years! I could escape into stasis for the remaining lifespan of the universe. You can't even reach *Hot Needle of Inquiry!*"

"Maybe they'll cooperate," Louis said. "Ringworld hominids do get along. Different species don't use the same resources, and they *all* cooperate with Ghouls. Once you're in that mode, you can get along with anyone."

"There was war between Red Herders and Grass Giants."

"Futz, Hindmost, they both wanted the grass!"

"I feel the situation is urgent."

Louis stretched. His joints creaked, and tendons were protesting even this afternoon's moderate exercise.

"Tell you what," he said. "Send your refueling probe to where I left *Hidden Patriarch*. It'll make a nice big target for you. I'll move back downstream and see if our City Builder friends want to join us again. Eight falans, two Earth years, one of yours. Then, if we can come to an agreement, I'll accept your medical attentions."

The Hindmost said, "Agreement?"

"I'll work out a contract."

"You are in a poor position to bargain."

"Let me know if you change your mind," Louis said. He got up and waded back through the river . . . waiting for the musical scream behind him. It didn't come.

Louis came awake slowly, groggy from lack of sleep. Sawur felt good, moving against him. He asked, "Do Weavers rish at sunglare?"

"By preference, we do."

"Stet." Louis got his arms working and began running his hands through her fur. "Nice."

"Thank you." She stretched along his length. Her fingers caressed his scalp, grooming what hair she could find. They moved easily into rishathra.

It was a *wonderful* lifestyle, in its way.

Presently Sawur pulled back to look at him. "Tired or not, you seem very relaxed."

"I think I've got him."

Night.

"I have formulated a contract," the Hindmost said.

"So have I," Louis Wu said. He held up his translator. "It's in memory, mostly in notes."

"I can't read that. We'll have to work from here." The cliff abruptly glowed with lines of print, black on white, and a virtual keyboard taller than Louis himself.

Their audience murmured appreciatively. Most of the villagers were seated around Louis. Louis wondered what they thought they were seeing.

He'd been making notes toward his own contract all afternoon. To work from the Hindmost's instead of his own would violate a basic principle of negotiation. Louis didn't intend *that*.

But another principle said that a negotiator should never admit to being under a deadline. Louis asked in Interspeak, "How do I work it?"

"Point," the Hindmost said. "Left for cursor, right to type."

Louis tried it, waving his arms like an ambidextrous orchestra conductor. *Mental patterns may require alteration*— Louis deleted that and wrote, *Mental patterns must not be altered for any purpose*. The section on PAYMENT looked reasonable: he was to be charged for work comparable to treatment in hospitals at Sol system, paid off in service not to exceed twelve years.

Hold it—"Boosterspice and standard tech?"

"By no means."

"What then, puppeteer experiments?"

"I've *tried* to describe what I have available, a modified ARM X-program."

"You can't compute the cost of this thing against fees payable at a Sol hospital! Your system would give me another thirty years of life, roughly speaking, wouldn't it? I'll give you seven years of service following my emergence from the 'doc."

"Twelve! Louis, this system will rewrite you to the age of twenty! You'd get another fifty years with no further medical treatment at all!"

"The risks you'll put me through, I'll be lucky to get fifty good *days*, and you know it. That's why I went on sabbatical in the first place. Seven."

"Stet."

Louis pointed with his left forefinger, the cursor. *Time expended shall be computed only for discrete actions taken at the direction of the Hindmost.* "Now what is this flup? What about consultation time? Travel time? Actions done without consulting you because there's no time? Subconscious problem-solving during sleep?"

"Write it in."

"Your motives are questionable. No honest entity would have tried that."

"This is how negotiation works, Louis."

"You're going to teach me how to negotiate? Stet." Louis erased the offending sentence, then typed one-fingered on the air. *Service period shall terminate seven years after acceptance of this contract.* He ignored the squawk of distress. "Now I need a clause to protect me from being altered into a better servant. I don't see anything in here that will do that."

Text added itself. Louis watched for a bit, then said, "No."

"Write, then."

"No. Can you think of any way to get yourself a copy of *my* contract?"

"No."

"It'll have to wait for me to reach *Hidden Patriarch*, then. I'll start tomorrow."

"Wait! Louis, I can easily find you here."

"Hindmost, I think I'll have to insist on your accepting my contract, not yours. If you can't read it, how can you suggest changes?"

"You must read it to me aloud."

"Tomorrow. Now, something else has been bothering me. How long does it take you to shape a plume from the sun and then set off the superthermal laser effect?"

"Two hours, sometimes three. Conditions vary."

"Three ships came through Fist-of-God, near here, and someone blasted them. One landed on the far side of the Ringworld and something blasted *it*. Did that take *longer*? What with all the fast-forward action, I just couldn't tell."

"I will look."

Louis woke late. Sawur and the children were gone. Nothing edible remained from last night. Louis worked near the empty firepit.

No entity or process shall alter Louis Wu's patterns of thought by medical or chemical means nor by any means save persuasion worked while Louis Wu is fully conscious and in his right mind. No agreements made while he is not fully conscious and in his right mind shall be binding.

The period of servitude— Louis crossed out "servitude." *—mutual dependence shall end no more than seven years after acceptance of this contract. Wu shall be entitled to sleep, meals, and* *periods of healing as required. Emergencies interrupting these free times shall shorten the period of mutual dependence at triple time. Penalties for violations . . . vacation periods mutually agreed upon shall extend the period of mutual dependence . . . Louis Wu may refuse any command if in his sole judgment the commission involves undue risk, undue damage to local hominids or their culture or their environment, global damage to the Ringworld, or clear ethical violations.* A few talking points wouldn't hurt.

He'd become ferociously hungry. He knew where to find more roots. Louis rode the cargo stack straight up to seek out a path, and saw children milling in the upland woods across the Shenthy River.

Sawur had found two big mushrooms of different species, and the children had killed a land-going crustacean as big as a rabbit. They watched with interest as Louis wrapped them in leaves and then wet clay. He dug his flash out of the lockbox on his cargo stack. With the flash on microwave, wide aperture, medium intensity, he heated the mound of clay until it puffed steam. Then he carefully locked the flash away. A dangerous thing to leave loose.

"Strill, Parald, keep the rest away from the clay. It'll burn you. Sawur? I want to make you a parting gift."

"Louis, are we to part?"

"The Web Dweller sent his refueling probe to spray the cliff. It must be nearby. I expect he could have it here in a few hours." He hopped off the plates. "Let me show you this now. I'm wondering if it should go to you or to the whole village."

The cargo plate controls were depressions on the rims, and they took some strength to move. Protector strength. Louis jabbed with a slender piece of rod held in both hands. The bottommost plate dropped from his stack and floated an inch above the grass.

Sawur asked, "Will you present it tonight? Give it to the village in charge of me and Kidada. I will be as surprised as any. Show him and me how to work it, but none other, and no visitors."

"Stet."

"This is a magnificent gift, Louis."

"Sawur, you've given me my life. I think. Maybe."

"Do you still doubt?"

"Give me a moment." Louis knocked the clay off one end of his mound. The mushrooms looked and smelled done.

They tasted wonderful. He broke open the rest of the mound and found the crawler done, too. Most of the meat was in the spinnerets, and the children shared those around. The tail made one bite each for him and Sawur.

"That's better. I'm not rational when I'm that hungry. Now look." Louis drew a ring in the dirt. "Light takes thirty-two minutes to cross the Ringworld and come back." He heard the translator converting times and distances.

"Really?"

"Trust me. Eight minutes for a beam from the sun to touch the Arch. Sixteen minutes across, thirty-two to cross and come back. If three starships pop up through a hole *here*, near the Great Ocean, and two and a half hours later they're destroyed, and a ship lands *here* and is destroyed *two* hours later, where is the attacker?"

Sawur studied the sketch, then pointed. "*Here*, across the Arch. The first ships, he needed half an hour just to see them."

"But what if it is attacked *three* hours later?"

Sawur said, "That would put the attacker *here* where you drew the Great Ocean."

"Yah."

When shadow touched the sun, Louis had written a contract that ought to protect him, if a puppeteer would honor a contract.

He presented the cargo plate to Weaver Town while dinner was broiling. They acclaimed him as a mighty magician, a *vashnesht*. Then children wanted to ride the plate while parents were urging caution. Louis showed Kidada the setting that would hold the disk two feet high, low enough to be safe.

He watched Kidada swooping among the houses with Strill whooping in his arms, and hoped that they wouldn't burn the thing out joyriding. One day they'd need it to lift something heavy.

The light was disappearing. Hunters had killed a predator; the meat tasted too much of cat. Weavers took slices and settled to watch the cliff as it came alight. Perched on his stack of cargo plates like a proper wizard, Louis nibbled cooked reeds and a root he'd microwaved in clay.

Puppeteers were dancing in a swirling rainbow. Louis watched with the others, then asked in Interspeak, "Are the pyrotechnics supposed to throw you off?"

"They are for loveliness. Louis, you must come to me."

"How is it with the fearless vampire slayers?"

"I hear only voices. The cruisers have separated. Cruiser Two is gone to starboard with my webeye in the cargo shell. The Red Herders speak of an entity the male calls 'Whisper.' Tegger thinks Whisper has left them. Warvia thinks he dreamed. I think Whisper is our phantom protector. Louis, will you come?"

"We'll have to reach terms—"

"I accept your contract—"

"You haven't seen it!"

"I accept it provided you make no changes from this moment. As you've had no extortionate advantage, you will have written it fairly. My probe will arrive within twelve minutes."

Louis looked at the sky. Nothing was visible yet. "Where will I pop out?"

"In your suite aboard *Needle*."

Suite? It was one compartment, locked, that he had shared with a Kzin! "Contract pays me triple time during emergencies. Shall I arm myself?"

"Yes."

"Sawur, get the children out of the water. Hindmost, land in the stream. Now, I remember crawling through the disk you mounted for refueling. It was pretty cramped."

"I do learn, Louis! I've mounted a full-sized stepping disk on the side of the probe, big enough for you and your cargo plates, too."

Louis thought, *Fortunately I always keep my feathers numbered for just such emergencies.* It wouldn't have meant anything to a puppeteer. From his safe box he withdrew the flashlight-laser and a variable-knife, two powerful weapons. He set the flash for *narrow, short range, high intensity.* He extended the blade by two feet, then brought it back to a foot and a half.

Lose your hold on a variable-knife, the wire blade would cut whatever was close.

A violet-white light peeked above the cliff.

The refueling probe settled on fusion flame. The cavity in its nose, that was the refueling system: a filter to pass hydrogen ions, and a one-way stepping disk no wider than Louis's hips. A much larger stepping disk had been mounted on its flank, a circular plate like an afterthought of a wing.

Weavers oohed and ahhed, then shied back from a wave

of steam. The flame went out. As Louis glided above the probe, it splashed down on its flared motor, then rolled and toppled into the water.

The water dimpled above the stepping disk.

So: it was on. Louis cut the lift and dropped straight in. His peripheral vision caught a shadow leaping after him.

Part Two

"DANCING
AS FAST
AS I CAN"

Chapter Nineteen

THE
KNOBBY
MAN

Hot Needle of Inquiry had been built around a General Products #3 hull, with interior walls to separate the puppeteer captain from his alien crew. Currently the ship was more dwelling than spacecraft. *Needle* couldn't exceed lightspeed because Louis Wu had cut the hyperdrive loose from its mountings, eleven years ago, for reasons that seemed good at the time. The ship itself had been embedded in magma during negotiations with the protector who had once been Teela Brown.

During that period and after, the Hindmost had deployed stepping disks through the ship and the Repair Center and elsewhere, too.

Louis expected to appear in the blocked-off crew quarters. The Hindmost hadn't needed to suggest, maybe hadn't dared to be overheard suggesting, that Louis come in *fast*.

The floating plates came down hard. Louis caught the recoil with bent knees, but he was still knocked off balance. He shouted, "Something's—"

Something's following me! Hindmost— But there was plenty going on *here*.

Thousands of Pierson's puppeteers shifted and swirled and kicked, stage left. It might have been distracting, but it wasn't. Louis and Chmeee had learned to ignore *that* part of the ship. *That* was the Hindmost's, and the wall wasn't glass. It was the invulnerable stuff a General Products hull was made of.

But one two-headed, three-legged alien, his mane curled and bejeweled in formal fashion, was between the kitchen wall and a coffin as big as a transfer booth lying on its side.

A knobby old man in a floppy vest was running at the Hindmost, knees and elbows pumping.

A hidden stepping disk led to the Hindmost's quarters. The Hindmost must be near or on it, Louis thought. He would be invulnerable there.

Instinct must have been too strong. The Hindmost turned his back instead.

It all happened very fast. Louis was still catching his balance. The Hindmost was spinning around, heads splayed wide apart, looking back, binocular vision with a baseline of three feet. Sighting on his target. His hind leg folded forward and shot straight back as the knobby man attacked.

The Hindmost's kick was good, square on target. Louis heard a clank: the knobby man must have been wearing a chest plate. Armor or no, that kick would have knocked a normal hominid into a coma. The knobby man turned with the impact, feet off the floor, one hand on the Hindmost's ankle to borrow its momentum as the Hindmost pulled back for another kick. The knobby man stepped past the hoof and slammed a fist down hard on the puppeteer's bejeweled mane, where the two necks connected to the torso.

That was the Hindmost's skull.

And Louis was bringing the flash around. Too slow, too clumsy, the stunned puppeteer was in the way. Something whacked his right wrist and sent the flashlight-laser flying. A metal ball? Another knocked the variable-knife spinning.

Louis flinched violently away from the spinning wire blade.

The Hindmost was down, curled into a ball, heads and long necks tucked between his forelegs. The floor was ankle deep in water. The fallen flash was submerged, but it sent a thread of light through *Needle's* transparent hull and into the lava beyond.

The wire blade hadn't cut Louis in two. Blind luck. But his hands and wrists felt shattered, he was *way* off balance, and the knobby man was coming at him. *Protector!*

Louis rolled off the stepping disk and into a corner and started to stand up. His right wrist was a sea of pain. The left was only numb.

In the space where he had been, something huge flicked in on all fours. It stood erect, as big as an orange bear, holding a small cannon in one huge hand.

The knobby man spun and ducked and swept Louis's variable-knife past the big intruder . . . the Kzin. The Kzin's weapon flew away with big clawed fingers still attached. The Kzin froze in a crouch, throttling a howl. The knobby man held the flash, too, in a clear threat.

"You don't move," it said. "Web Dweller, you don't move, either. Louis Wu, you don't move. Does your contract call for you to die?"

The knobby man's lips had withdrawn from the gums; the gums had hardened almost to bone, and jawbone had grown through in a jagged pattern. His face was hard, almost a beak. He spoke with a breathy speech impediment, but in Interspeak. How would the knobby man have learned Interspeak? Eavesdropping on the Hindmost?

Contract?

Reality came in waves washing past pain. Eleven years since he'd been in this much trouble. Louis said, stalling, "Yes, under conditions subject to my own sole judgment. Do you accept my contract?"

"Yes," said the knobby man.

Despite what had gone before, that was astonishing.

The Kzin male was bleeding freely from a hand sliced down to one thumb. He was hugging that arm, trying to squeeze arteries shut. His eyes were on Louis. He said, also in Interspeak, "What shall I do?"

"Raise your arm above your head. Keep squeezing the wrist. Squeeze the blood vessels. Don't try to fight. That's a protector. Hindmost, set th— Hindmost! Nap time is over. For all of us."

The puppeteer uncurled. "Speak, Louis."

The black coffin— "Your autodoc, you said you could set it to treat a Kzin?"

"Yes?"

"Do that. Then you can tell me what happened. I'm on triple time, by the way, because this has the authentic feel of an emergency."

The Hindmost wasn't at his best. He said, "Heal an injured strange Kzin?"

"Do it *now*."

"But Louis—"

"I'm under contract! This is for *our* benefit. Can't you see who this must be?"

The puppeteer knelt before the 'doc and began mouthing the controls.

The protector still had the flash and variable-knife. Louis couldn't think of anything to do about that, or the sudden strange Kzin, or the constant flicker of dancing puppeteers in his peripheral vision.

One tanj thing at a time!

The Kzin. "Who are you?"

"Acolyte."

"Son of Chmeee," Louis guessed. He'd forgotten how huge a Kzin male became when you stood next to him. This one couldn't be more than eleven years old, not quite full-grown. "No true name?"

"Not yet. Eldest son of Chmeee. I challenged. We fought. Father won. He told me, learn wisdom. Stalk Louis Wu. Acolyte."

"Aww . . . Hindmost, how long to set the 'doc for Kzin metabolism?"

"Minutes. Give the Kzin a tourniquet."

Louis moved to the wardrobe dispenser, slowly, hands visible to the protector. His right hand and wrist were hugely swollen. He held that arm raised above his head. His left hand felt numb, but it would work, he thought.

The kitchen wall had menus for kzinti and human cuisine, diet supplements, allergy suppressants, clothing, and more. Louis hadn't seen pharmacy menus, but he didn't doubt they were there. The Hindmost had found him as a wirehead. He would not have shown him how to access recreational chemicals.

Louis dialed *Sol/Nordik/formal* and a selection of cravats. Resisting temptation, he chose an orange and yellow pattern that would look good on a Kzin. Not even his eyes moved toward the Slaver digging tool he'd taped under the dispenser port a lifetime ago.

The smell of the Kzin was faint. Acolyte must have washed himself scentless, to stalk him, Louis Wu thought. His orange fur bore three parallel ridges across the belly. Otherwise he wore Halloween markings: both ears tipped with bitter chocolate, nearly black; a broad chocolate stripe down the back, a smaller chocolate comma down his tail and leg. He was shorter than Chmeee, seven feet even, but just as wide: a hybrid. His mother would be of the archaic kzinti from the Map of Kzin.

Acolyte sat down, bringing his arm in reach. Louis bound the thick wrist with his tie, using his left hand and his teeth. The blood slowed to a dribble.

The Kzin rumbled, "Who is my attacker?"

"Tanj if I know, but if I had to guess . . . Hello, knobby man?"

"Speak."

"The Hindmost and I, we both guessed that a protector must be in the Repair Center. You've been shooting down invading ships. The timing made it obvious you were working from here. The Hindmost left stepping disks all over the place. A protector might reprogram a disk to link with this one as soon as it was turned on . . . ?"

"Yes."

"Then pop through just ahead of me. Finicky timing. You needed me for a distraction, and you counted on puppeteer reflexes. That's interesting, isn't it, Hindmost? You had an instant to escape, but you used it to kick?"

"That old argument. Very well, I reflexively turned my back to fight—you win."

Louis grinned. The pain wasn't so bad now, but he was drunk on endorphins. He said, "Acolyte. This is a protector. Look him over. They all have that knobby look, and they're all brilliant and dangerous."

"Looked like just another hominid." The Kzin shook his great furry head.

"How long did you watch me?" Louis asked.

"Two days now. I thought, learn from you before I show myself."

"Wisdom?"

"Father spoke of you. He believes he learned what he has of wisdom from you, and so can I. But one of the scavengers saw me."

"The boy?"

"Yes. You named him Kazarp."

"I talked to his father, too."

"The boy and I, we talked. His father was not far, listening, thinking he hides. I spoke what I knew of you. I don't know secrets worth hiding. I did not speak of the Hindmost."

"How does he think we got to the Ringworld, then?"

"You mean Arch? I said you brought a ship. I did not speak to Kazarp of instant transportation. Didn't believe Father. When you linked the transfer booths—"

"Stepping disks. Transfer booths are what we use in known space and the Patriarchy. They're a lot less sophisticated."

"—stepping disks. I jumped. Catch Kazarp and his father by surprise. Leave them gaping. Surprise!" the Kzin whispered, and slumped. His eyes closed.

"Hindmost?"

"Ready. Bring him."

Louis set his shoulder in Acolyte's armpit and lifted. Acolyte found the strength to stand, wobbled to the surgery well, and toppled in.

Louis pulled his tourniquet loose and straightened the Kzin a bit. He found the Kzin's severed hand, and the two useless halves of the heavy metal handgun he'd carried. He picked up the half hand.

The Hindmost took it in his mouth. "Close the lid," he said, and fed the hand into another aperture. Then he folded his legs and tucked his heads between his forelegs.

Going into shock, Louis thought. The knobby man said, "Suicide?"

One head came up. "I demonstrate helplessness. This is surrender," the Hindmost said.

"Surrender, good."

The Kzin would likely be in there for days.

Louis might have fainted for an instant.

Agony snapped him awake. The protector's knobby hands were moving the bones in Louis's right wrist. Louis's other hand closed hard on the protector's arm. He moaned and whimpered. Reality came in waves of pain.

Not before the protector withdrew did Louis think to look for the protector's weapons. Just as well. The knobby man's vest bore an amazing variety of pockets, and he saw the shape of the flash in one of those.

Now, what must he do before he fainted again?

Contract. He fished out his notepad and offered it to the puppeteer. "This is what you've agreed to. You should read it aloud, given that our companion has bound himself, too."

The puppeteer took the pad. His other head turned to the knobby man. "Why did you do that?"

"I need allies who are not protectors. Protectors kill each other," the knobby man said. "I can hold you to a formal promise made for mutual advantage. Read."

The Hindmost read.

The knobby man—or woman: he was a bit shorter, a bit more slender than Teela Brown had been after she turned protector. The hairless, leathery skin, the swollen joints, the triangular face and bulging skull, all made it difficult to assign him a gender. Louis thought he could make out traces of male genitalia, but he couldn't swear to that.

Behind the impenetrable wall, a million hologram puppeteers danced. The Hindmost must have thought he'd be back among them before he missed a step.

" '. . . if in his sole judgment the commission involves undue risk—' Sole judgment?"

Louis smiled and shrugged.

" '—undue damage—clear violations of ethics—' Sole judgment?"

The protector asked, "Hindmost, will you bind yourself similarly?"

The Hindmost whistled indignantly. "You speak of enslavement! How can you possibly compensate me? What I offered Louis Wu was his *life*! Point taken, I accept."

Louis could hold back no longer. He asked, "Who *are* you?"

"I have not needed a name. Choose what you like."

"What's your species?"

"Vampire."

"You're kidding."

"No."

Louis was about to faint.

He'd found Teela Brown's medkit welded to the top cargo plate, long ago. He had to stand up to reach it. Grinding his teeth against the pain, he pushed his swollen right hand into the diagnosis well.

The pain went away. A readout asked him questions. Yes, he wanted to remain awake. No, he couldn't replenish supplies of various medicines . . . an ominously long list.

His whole right arm seemed gone and nothing else really hurt. His mind was lucid, free to toy with the pieces of reality and try to put them back together. He had bound himself to serve a protector . . . hadn't he? The *protector* had bound himself to *Louis*, to limitations on his power over Louis Wu. And the puppeteer had bound himself, and was himself bound to the protector, by Louis's contract.

He could hear what the others were saying, but the words slipped through his ears and were gone. "Require most urgently . . . invaders . . . beyond the Arch."

"ARM and Patriarchy ships," Louis said. "Bet." Political entities would invade: it was their nature. He had described the Ringworld for United Nations records. Chmeee had spoken to the Patriarch. What other organizations would know of the Ringworld? "Fleet of Worlds, too?"

"So poorly designed, so ill-protected?" The puppeteer fluted, "Those are not ours!"

"Are these political entities dangerous?" the knobby man asked.

The puppeteer thought they were endlessly dangerous, and said so. Louis's head was bubbling with chemicals; he did not contribute.

"Are they likely to give up their plans?"

"No. I can show you where their interstellar transports hide," the Hindmost said. "Those won't participate in an invasion. Even your sun-powered superthermal laser won't reach the farthest targets. The ships that land will be warships carrying no hyperdrive motors."

"Show me."

"From my cabin."

Louis laughed inside his head.

The unmarked stepping disk flicked only to the Hindmost's cabin, and it wouldn't pass aliens. The Hindmost would be behind an invulnerable wall. What chance was there that the knobby man would permit *that?*

Vampire protector. Louis made his mouth work. "What do you eat?"

"I make a vegetable mash. I have not tasted blood in twenty-eight falans," the knobby man said. "My hunger is no risk to you."

"Good," Louis said, and closed his eyes for a moment.

He heard, "Hindmost, you will only break your contract once. Show me all of the invader ships."

The Hindmost's answer was a warbling, whistling music with overtones in subsonic bass. Louis's eyes popped open to see the dancers disappear, replaced by rotating three-space star maps.

The system looked nearly empty save for the Ringworld and its shadow squares. Color-coded lights blazed far from the Ringworld's arc, and scores of smaller sparks swarmed much nearer. Louis couldn't see motion on this scale, but they seemed to be taking positions around the system, as if just becoming aware of each other.

"I must return to defend the Arch," the knobby man said. "You come."

The puppeteer shied. "But maps are only available here in *Hot Needle of Inquiry!*"

"I have seen them now. Come."

Louis was alone.

And the picture changed as they flicked out. In the captain's quarters was a three-dimensional circuit diagram of some kind . . .

Enough. Louis leaned his head against the stacked cargo plates and closed his eyes.

He dozed, leaning against the stack of cargo plates with his arm in the medkit. Loss of balance snapped him awake from time to time.

Behind the aft wall was the lander dock, nearly empty since Teela burned the lander. Louis couldn't quite remember what else was in there. Lockers for pressure suits and armor, of course, and a stack of stepping disks. He had a vague impression that the Hindmost had made changes, eleven years' worth of fiddling.

To ship's port and ship's starboard the walls were black. *Needle* was embeddded in black basalt: cooled magma.

A network of lines and dots floated beyond the forward wall, like an ant's nest seen by deep-radar. It teased at his mind.

Dots *there* and *there* and *there*. Those two linked, and those three. Here, a network of ten. Way off in the distance, one of the ten appeared to be two dots superimposed. Sketchy contours in the background might shape a map.

The Hindmost must be trying to show him something.

When bladder pressure was stronger than his fear of pain, Louis pulled his hand free and wobbled to the toilet. Evidently he still had a medical problem. Afterward he drank a quart of water. He ate a civilized Caesar salad for the first time in eleven years, left-handed. No more of eating whatever he could find! That, he would not mind giving up.

He examined his hand with meager satisfaction. The swelling was down; the bones seemed to be in place.

He left the machine twice more. The pattern caught his eye again as he left the recycler.

Stepping disks!

His subconscious must have been at work. That map defined the stepping disks the Hindmost had deployed. Several were scattered through the millions of cubic miles of Repair Center. Four in *Hot Needle of Inquiry* itself. One just outside. The double-point must be the refueling probe in Weaver Town, with one disk for transport and another for hydrogen.

The Hindmost had left him this. Louis studied it, fixing it in memory, wondering at the pupeteer's motives . . .

And it all popped back to dancing puppeteers as the knobby man flicked in.

The protector had something in his hand. He blew into it, watching Louis's face. Music fluttered in the air, a woodwind sound.

Louis's reaction must have been unsatisfactory. The protector put the thing away. He examined Louis as a primitive doctor would have, probing here and there to see what hurt. Presently he said, "Not much longer."

Louis had had a notion. He said, "My kitchen wall can be made to dispense blood."

"Will you drink first?"

"No, I won't. I'm not a vampire. Also, the Hindmost will have to rewrite the kitchen program. No, wait, let me try something."

At the kitchen wall Louis popped up a virtual keyboard for kzinti cuisine, marked in dots-and-commas, Hero's Tongue. Louis knew a little of that. He scanned through the extensive menu with the knobby man watching. *Wunderland cuisine—* no. *Fafnir cuisine?* Not under that name. Try *sea life.* There, under the planet's kzinti name, *Shasht. Meat, drink,* too many items. Try *seek: meat/drink.* Four times. Three were soups, with *shreem* as an ingredient, and that left *shreem* itself.

OVERRIDE laws pertaining to Shasht/Fafnir, Earth, Jinx, Belt, Serpent Swarm . . .

A bulb popped into the dispenser port, filled with sluggish red fluid.

The knobby man took the bulb. He took Louis's jaw, faster than he could flinch. His grip was like iron. "You drink now," he said.

Louis opened his mouth, obedient. The knobby man ejected a dollop of sticky red fluid into Louis's mouth. The taste was unfamiliar, but Louis recognized the smell. He swallowed anyway.

The knobby man drank, watching Louis. "You surprise me. Why would you make blood for me?"

For eleven years Louis had been eating what he could catch, or what unknown hominids would offer as food. "I'm not squeamish," Louis said.

"Yes, you are."

In truth, what he had smelled and tasted was making him nauseous. He said, "I have kept to our contract, which calls for me to act in your interest. *You* are in violation. I judge it wrong for me to drink human blood, and I said so."

The knobby man said, "The medkit is through with you, isn't it? You put on your pressure suit. Come with me."

"Pressure suit. Where are we going?"

The protector said nothing.

Louis grinned. He pointed through the transparent wall aft. "Vacuum gear, landing craft, airlock, anything Chmeee and I might need to get out of this ship is in the lander bay. I can't get there except by stepping disk. The Hindmost was holding us prisoner."

"Didn't you have a contract?"

"Not then."

"I learned how to use stepping disks. Come here."

The knobby man had lockpicking tools made of hardwood. He knelt by the disk and lifted its edge.

Louis couldn't see what he was doing. The protector's fingers worked too fast. He saw the stepping disk diagram appear in the Hindmost's quarters, and flicker. Then the protector set the disk in place, pushed Louis onto the stepping disk and followed.

With the lander destroyed, the lander bay was mostly empty space. There were suits for men and kzinti and puppeteers. The transparent walls of the airlock opened into a tunnel that led through several cubic miles of magma, undisturbed since the war with Teela Brown.

Louis glanced at the weapons racks but did not approach them. He pulled out a skintight pressure suit already zipped open along the torso, sleeves, and legs. He wouldn't need the cummerbund. He started to crawl into it, and stopped with a gasp of pain.

Before he could ask for help, the protector was there, easing his half-healed hand and arm into the sleeve and glove, then fashioning a sling from the tie that had been Acolyte's tourniquet. He zipped up Louis's suit, screwed a helmet onto the neck ring, and set an air rack on his back. They waited for the suit to contract to Louis's own shape.

The knobby man worked the controls of the big stepping disk, the cargo disk. Louis began his checklist. *Helmet camera, airflow, air recycler, CO_2 and water vapor content—*

The knobby man pulled him through.

Chapter Twenty

BRAM'S
TALE

The Map of Mars stood forty miles high above the Great Ocean, a north polar projection at one-to-one scale. From the Ringworld's underside there was no sign of the Map of Mars, because the entire forty-mile-high pillbox was hollow.

Louis had seen vast spaces inside the Repair Center, but he had never been inside this one. It was huge and dark. Skeletal chairs equipped with lap keyboards rode on long booms. The ellipsoidal wall was a display screen thirty feet high. The only light came from the screen: a wraparound view of the local sky.

There were no planets or asteroids in Ringworld system. The Ringworld engineers must have cleared all of that out, or used it as building material. The Ringworld's night-shadowed rim showed pale against the black background. Light-amplified stars glared, and four tiny green circles: cursors.

"I found four more," the Hindmost said. He was at a wall of clumsy, clunky lights and dials and switches. Now Louis recognized where he was. This was the system that twisted the sun's magnetic field. He had seen this array in a holo projection, eleven years ago, when the Hindmost manipulated the Meteor Defense.

The air here must be soupy with tree-of-life spores.

It was a tidy place, except—hmmm?

Across that great width of floor, a shadow-shape was standing in near darkness. A shape of motionless menace, skewed from the human shape, too thin and too pointy in spots. Bones. Bones mounted in a pose of attack.

In the shadows beyond those standing bones, gear seemed scattered at random.

Later. Louis said, "I should finish my checklist. Do you need me instantly?"

The knobby man said, "No. Hindmost, show me."

No Belter would have yanked a man into a vacuum before he had checked his pressure suit. That would be murderously rude. Had the protector read the readiness of his suit at a glance? Louis wondered. Was the protector testing his attitude? His equipment? His temper?

The Hindmost was riding one of the cargo plates. He lifted by a yard; his heads dipped among the controls. The skyview zoomed on an orange near-sphere marked in black dots-and-commas. A kzinti ship, probably centuries old and retrofitted with hyperdrive.

The view shrank, and moved, and expanded. This next ship looked big, a long, slowly rotating lever with a bubble at the near end. Louis didn't recognize the type.

The view shrank and moved and expanded to show a gray and black object like a diseased potato seen through fog. The Hindmost said, "The Ringworld engineers left only the most distant comets. Too many to destroy them all—"

"Air reserve," the knobby man said. "To replace air lost over the rim walls."

"... Yes. Now note this ..." A blinking green circle

marked a crater on the proto-comet. The view expanded, then shifted to deep-radar, with a blurred view of structure in the ice below the pock.

The knobby man asked, "What species built that?"

"I can't tell," the Hindmost said. "Mining projects always have that look, like the root system of a plant. But here . . ." Another rotating lever, a ship of the same make, viewed from the side. Familiar little stubby-winged aerospacecraft were strung all along its length.

"These are United Nations craft made by Louis's species."

Louis had finished his checklist. The suit would keep him alive for weeks, maybe months.

"Very good. Allow me," the knobby man said. He stepped on another cargo plate, and rose. His hands were dexterous where the puppeteer's mouths had been unsure. A second screen lit with a darkened view of the sun.

Minutes passed. Then a bright plume began to rise, twisting in magnetic fields.

Louis said, "You're going to kill them, I take it."

"Such are my directions. They came as invaders," the Hindmost said.

"So did we."

"Yes. Are you healthy?"

Louis wiggled his bound hand. "Healing. It's a waste of time, anyway, if I'm going into your magic 'doc. What have you been doing?"

"We've destroyed six carrier ships and a fleet of thirty-two landers. Those were the ships closest to the sun, the most vulnerable. These last are so distant that we may do no more than enrage them. I'm inclined to ignore the installation in the comet. We would only boil ice. I found an Outsider ship on one of the farthest comets—"

"Tanj! Knobby man? You didn't shoot down an Outsider, did you?"

"The Hindmost advised against."

"Good. They're very fragile, but they've got technology we can't even properly *describe*. For that matter, they don't want anything we've got, and what they want, they buy. There'd be no point to hurting an Outsider."

"Do you like them?"

That was a somewhat surprising question. Louis said, "Yes."

"What would they be doing here?"

Louis shrugged inside his suit. "The sky is full of planets. There's only one Ringworld. Outsiders are curious."

The solar plume was still rising. "Observe and criticize," the knobby man said to the Hindmost. Fingers like strings of walnuts danced over the wall.

The puppeteer watched. He said, "Good."

It all seemed very leisurely. The plume would take hours to form. The superthermal laser effect would be propagating for minutes before it left the plume. The targets looked to be hours away at lightspeed.

Louis had already discarded the notion of a last minute rescue.

Louis Wu owed nothing at all to the United Nations or the ARM. He wasn't obliged to protect kzinti ships either. Disarmed and injured, he was no match for a protector of any species. He knew he'd be lucky to keep his life, now that he was back in this dance of powers.

His contract didn't bind him to rescue the knobby man's prey. And they *had* come as invaders.

"I pointed out a monitor station, too. One of mine," the Hindmost was saying. "The Conservatives will never miss it."

"Right. Knobby man, I'm tempted to call you 'Dracula.' Dracula was the archetype of story vampires."

"Follow your whim."

"No. Trite. You're a protector, a prime mover among vampires. Let's call you 'Bram.' Can you tell me what you want of me?"

"I want what is best for my species. Vampires face three threats, and each threatens all beneath the Arch including yourselves."

The knobby man watched Louis's face as he spoke. "First, if vampires become numerous, we deplete our prey. Intelligent hominids might even find a way to exterminate us. *I* don't want any species of vampire getting too much attention. *You* don't want us spreading."

"The vampire slayers, were they yours? No, that's crazy. They're your own species."

"No, Louis, they're not. There must be a hundred separate species of vampire on the Ringworld."

"Ah. Where do yours live?"

Bram ignored that. "Louis, I did not shape the Shadow Nest Alliance. Their solution was elegant, wasn't it?"

"Yah."

"Second, these invaders from space threaten the Ringworld structure itself."

Louis nodded. "An interstellar warship can always use a meteoroid impact for a weapon. Watch for falling comets."

"The third threat is protectors, for the duels they fight."

Louis asked, "Just how many protectors have we got already?"

"Three or more involved in repairing the rim wall installations. Each would seem to have its task, but all will bear watching."

"What species, can you tell?"

"It's an important question, isn't it? Those who rule would be vampires. Any others would be servants drafted from local species. Louis, one can argue—"

"How the tanj did the Ringworld come to be infested with vampire protectors?"

"That is an intricate tale, but why should I tell it?"

Louis had carefully *not* bound himself or the Hindmost to reveal secrets. How could he urge Bram to reveal his? He said, "It's your call. First decide what you want. Decide if we can give it to you. Then decide how much we need to know to do it right."

The knobby man's hand danced over the wall. He said, "You keep secrets. Why should I tell mine? You are bound to obey regardless."

Try this— "You've been shooting down ships. Stet, but suppose you miss one? You've no way to judge what they'll do next. We three, I and Acolyte and the Hindmost, are the only aliens at hand. You expect to watch us and extrapolate what invaders would do. But we don't react if we don't know anything."

The bright plume pulled from the sun had been arcing over, but now it started to straighten, to narrow. Bram said, "Hindmost?"

"The prominence is nearly in place."

"Will you complete the maneuver?"

"Destroy all four sources?"

"Leave the comet. Louis, how can you react properly if you know you're being watched?"

"When I'm being watched, I watch back. Take it into account. Bram, who *are* you? How did a vampire get into the Repair Center?"

"I mapped my way in."

Louis waited.

"Louis, have you seen how hominids behave when they drink the fuel the Machine People make?"

"I've done it myself."

"I never have. Now you must imagine that you have drunk fuel beginning with your mother's milk. Tens of falans later you wake sober for the first time, sober and buzzing with energy and ambition.

"I was born . . . I was *shaped* 7,200 falans ago. Corpses lay all about me, tens of my kind, days dead, and one strange shape that was all knobs. I was all knobs, too, sexless, and cold and hungry and gashed by fighting, but I was solving the world like a great puzzle. Three others were waking, changed like me."

Louis asked, "You *trapped a protector?* Vampires aren't that intelligent."

"This one was born trapped, made to be a servant."

Made by . . . ? "Go on."

"The city stood on a vertical cliff and one great stilt. I was born in its shadow. We were always hungry. A ramp wound up the stilt to the smell of prey, but iron lace stung us when we tried to climb the ramp or the mountain face. Transport flew to and fro. The ramp was never used. After we became protectors, we guessed at the reasons our lives ran as they did. I think we were a defense—"

"Moat monsters," Louis said. "Invaders would have to face vampires before they reach the real guards."

"Plausible," the knobby man said. "There came a famine, when no more produce flowed into the city. A lost war, political games, bandits on the roads, who can tell? We vampires knew only that the flow of garbage slowed to a trickle, and water and sewage, too. What ate of the garbage went else-where, and we who survived partly on scavengers' blood began to starve.

"Many days later the iron lace barrier lifted and great boxes rolled down the ramp. We tried to get them open, get to the blood within. Their wheels rolled over us. A fantastic warrior danced about the vehicles and killed all who came, and stayed after the vehicles were gone, killing all who would follow. She would not heed our pleading—"

"Pleading?"

"She was immune to our scent and ignored our body lan-guage. That enraged us. We had never seen a protector. We were stupid and angry and hungry. We brought the knobby one down at last, swarmed her and took what blood she hadn't lost in the fight, and were still hungry enough to drink from our fallen. Then others fell into a sleep like death, and so did I.

"When I woke, I was changed. But I remembered, and that was already a new thing.

"Many of us tasted protector blood that day. Some died in their sleep. Four protectors woke. By her scent, one was my favored mate, and so we knew each other."

"I wondered. Vampires are monogamous?"

"Say?"

"Mate once."

"No, Louis. When a hominid doesn't have the scent, that is prey. I drink her veins empty while I rish. Her scent may mark a woman as my kind and make her safe. But we were *starving*, Louis. She and I, my mate, what shall I call her . . . ?"

It surprised Louis, the fervor with which Bram told a tale he'd had to be goaded into. Was this the first time he'd ever had listeners? He said, "Anne?"

"Anne and I had the will to keep our mouths shut while we mated. Of course we never mated after we woke changed, but we remembered that we trusted each other."

The memory took him by surprise, and Louis shuddered. *Trust a vampire?*

She had seemed an angel in rut, supernaturally desirable, the vampire who attacked Louis Wu twelve years ago. His hands in her ash-blond curls had found too much hair, too little skull capacity. It was not possible for another hominid to judge what a Ringworld vampire really was.

Louis could see the Hindmost listening: one head cocked toward Bram and him, while the other worked at the board. He said, "Stet, go on."

"We four explored, with ten breeders too young to make the change. My mind made maps as we went. Wedge City was a triangle, the base supported by a mountain face, the point resting on the great stilt, the stilt rising farther to form a tower. We battered down doors and smashed windows, but the only hominids in the city were imprisoned in the tower. When our breeders had been fed and the edge was off our hunger, we followed a scent trail to a better protected place, a place where two protectors had lived above a hidden store of yellow roots. You know of these roots?"

"Tree-of-life."

"We saw their nature. Anne and I, we saw that the root was our blood now. We would starve without it. We killed the others."

"That first protector—"

"I studied her body," Bram said. "She was smaller than me. Her jaw was massive, specialized to chew tough branches that grew locally. Her tools were primitive. She rescued breeders of her own local species, fought to cover their passage out of the city and through the vampires, and sacrificed her life in the act.

"Louis, most life, most animals, most *hominids*, can only survive in one locale. Imagine that your species is restricted to some one stretch of river, clump of forest, isolated valley or swamp or desert. As a protector, you become more flexible, but everything you cherish is in one place. A protector of a less restricted kind can destroy it all if you don't obey her commands."

"Did you see any sign of—"

"Yes, of course, clues were everywhere, they crawled up on our shoulders to bite our necks! Two protectors dwelt in the house of the roots. One served the other. We found bodies, breeders of the servant's species. The master was of another kind, near eighty thousand falans old, protector of a species that has since changed or become extinct. I knew the smell of him thousands of falans later. The famine drove him from Wedge City. The servant stayed to rescue her species."

"Her *blood* made you a protector."

"Evidently," Bram agreed.

"The virus. The gene-changing virus in tree-of-life root. It's in the blood of protectors, too." Louis found that amusing. *Vampires become immortal by drinking an immortal's blood!*

But it did not amuse him to be at the mercy of a vampire protector.

Now the plume from the sun stretched tens of millions of miles into space. The Hindmost rode a cargo plate near the rounded ceiling, one head cocked to hear. Surely he was too far away. Unless . . . a directional mike?

Louis asked again, "How did you get into the Repair Center?"

Bram said, "Roots to last a hundred falans. We must find

the source or die when we run out. Anne and I taught each other to read. Writings in Wedge City guided us to cities with libraries. We chose a cold climate so that we might hide ourselves under clothing. They took us for visitors from afar. We paid taxes, bought land, ultimately gained a citizen's access to the library of the Delta People.

"There we learned something of the repair facilities beneath the Map of Mars.

"We reached the Great Ocean and crossed it. We had to make inflated cylinders to walk about the surface of the Map of Mars. I prefer your pressure suits. Still, we entered while still alive."

"And you didn't kill each other."

"No. Vampires have no minds, Louis Wu. A vampire protector starts fresh, intelligent from birth, bound by no preconceptions and no old loyalties or promises. If a hominid cannot choose a protector of her own species, a vampire must be her next best choice."

You'd have killed each other for the last tree-of-life root. Louis didn't say it. He wasn't sure it was true. "You found the master protector. How? Why did you fight?"

"We fought for who would best guard the Arch and all beneath."

"But his record was good, wasn't it? Whole species must have evolved and died out during his time, but civilizations rose and flourished until—"

"But we won, Anne and I." Bram turned away. "Hindmost, what progress?"

Louis looked toward a skeleton standing in dimness. He had guessed who that must be. "How did you get to him? He was eighty thousand falans old, you said." Nearly a million Ringworld rotations. Twenty thousand Earth years. "All that time, and then there was you."

"He had to come. Hindmost?"

The puppeteer called down. "I have played the Meteor Defense on three targets. We will not see results for two hours. Three before the installation in the comet can observe and react. Any of the others have hours to move, but who can dodge a beam of light?"

"Your opinion?"

"My people prefer to achieve our aims by giving other species what they want," the Hindmost said.

"Louis Wu, react."

Louis answered. "You've started something you can't stop. You've attacked two war fleets, three if you count the Fleet of Worlds. Political structures get old and die, Bram, but information never gets lost anymore. Storage is too good. Somebody will be testing the Ringworld defenses for as long as there are protons."

"Then the Arch must have a protector, for as long as there are protons."

"At least one. Invaders wouldn't just take over territory. They'd fiddle and test and maybe ruin something, like the City Builders did when they took the attitude jets on the rim wall to make interstellar ships."

The knobby man waited.

"A vampire might be a mistake."

"You have a vampire in place. To fight him might be a far more expensive mistake."

When Louis said nothing—still chewing his thoughts—Bram fished something from his vest. It was carved wood, bigger than the flute he'd played earlier. The windsound was deeper, richer, with a drumbeat that was Bram's fingertips tapping the barrel of the thing. Soothing, despite Louis's irritation.

Louis waited for the mournful tootling to stop. He said,

"You need a meteor watch in the plane of the Ringworld. I don't know how to do that. The solar Meteor Defense can't fire on anything that's hiding under the Ringworld floor."

"Come," Bram said. "Hindmost, come. We'll return later to see what has escaped us."

The knobby man's hand felt like a handful of marbles, and his pull on Louis's good wrist was irresistible. Louis found himself walking rapidly away. He looked back once at bones in a stance of attack. Then Bram guided or pushed Louis onto the stepping disk.

They flicked through into *Needle's* **cargo space.**

The knobby man helped Louis strip the suit off inside out, careful of his injured arm, careful not to release spores that might have accreted on the surface. Where was the Hindmost?

Bram led Louis onto the other disk, flicked them both through into crew quarters. At no time had Louis considered resisting. Bram was just too futzy strong.

The protector knelt before a blank wall. "The puppeteer worked here to summon images into his own quarters. Let us see how well I observed him." He produced wooden picklocks and went to work.

A diagram appeared: the map of the stepping disks.

Then a view of Weaver Town.

The Hindmost flicked in: lander bay, then crew cabin. "Forgive the delay," he said.

"Were you testing my security? Hindmost, wake the Kzin now," Bram said. "Afterward I want a better view of the rim wall where the protectors are working. Send your refueling probe."

The Hindmost glanced at readouts in the autodoc lid, touched something, and danced back as the lid lifted.

The Kzin stood in one fluid motion, ready to take on an army.

Now the knobby man was armed with flash and variable-knife, though Louis hadn't seen him move. Bram waited to see Acolyte relax, then asked, "Acolyte, will you bind yourself to me according to the terms of Louis Wu's contract?"

The Kzin turned. His scars had disappeared and his hands looked fine. "Louis Wu, shall I do that?"

Louis swallowed his reservations and said, "Yes."

"I accept your contract."

"Get out of the 'doc."

Acolyte did. Bram led Louis to the big 'doc and helped him in.

The Hindmost was busy elsewhere. Color-coded dots and rainbow arcs swirled and shifted in the captain's cabin, responding to the puppeteer's music. Suddenly he whistled in discord. "The probe!"

"Speak," Bram said.

"Look! The stepping disk is dismounted from my refueling probe! Wait—" The puppeteer tapped at the wall. The view from the partly submerged probe became a view from the cliff-side webeye. "There! Look, there it is!"

The teleport device that had been mounted on the probe's flank now lay flat on the riverbank beside the Council House.

"Nobody's trying to hide it," Louis said. "The little disk in the nose with the deuterium filter, is *that* still in place?"

The Hindmost looked. "Yes."

"It's almost flattering. Someone wants me back."

"Theft!"

"Yah, but leave it. What you'd better do is bring the probe

here and mount another disk. Acolyte, the Hindmost will read you your contract. Don't harm either of these people. Wake me up when the 'doc is through with me. The kitchen wall has settings to feed a Kzin, and Bram here will be using it, too. Will you be all right?"

"Yes."

"Stet." With no small trepidation, Louis lay down in the coffin-shaped 'doc. The lid closed.

Chapter Twenty-One

PHYSICS
LESSONS

They saw it days ahead: a black line against the vastly more distant starboard rim wall.

Closer, the line became a tremendous and artificial silhouette rising above the desert: a raised platform with bumps clustered near the center.

Closer yet, the Reds could see daylight under parts of the elevation. By then Warvia knew. It was the Night People's goal, and the Sand People's cemetery.

They were traveling through a dry land. Sand wasn't good for the motor. There had been a hungry few days before they ran across the Sand People.

The Sand People went muffled in pastel robes. Small, compact beasts drew their wagons in groups of twelve, and served as meat animals, too. Carnivores! Red Herders and Machine People rejoiced alike.

They made gifts of the cloth they'd taken from the

Shadow Nest. The Sand People killed two of their beasts to make a feast. The several species shared lore and stories as best they could. Only Karker spoke the trade language well enough to be understood, and everything had to be translated.

Rishathra didn't require translation, only gestures. Without their robes, the Sand People were small and compact: as short as Gleaners, with broader torsos and lean arms and legs.

Harpster and Grieving Tube kept to the payload shell.

The cruiser departed at halfdawn.

It made Warvia uneasy to know that the Ghouls below her driving bench were near starving. But their goal was in sight.

They arrived in bright mid-afternoon.

An ancient road half covered with sand rose to the axis of the platform. Three arms splayed out from the center section at 120-degree angles. The arms were wedge-shaped platforms that floated unsupported.

The center section was a forest of mooring posts, metal rails, pulleys, and ropes. The roofed buildings on this structure looked like afterthoughts. They were empty and sandblasted by time: warehouses, a banquet hall, an inn. Running through the axis was a deep well with clean water at the bottom.

On one of the wide paths between buildings, the Sand People had laid out their dead. It looked as if they had been doing that for generations. There were hundreds of skeletons. A double handful at the hub end were more mummy than bone. A few were more recent yet.

"Just as Karker said," said Sabarokaresh. "Warvia, did Karker tell you . . . ?"

Warvia said, "Karker told me how to find a shrieker village. Sand People don't eat shriekers, but I told him we could."

"You were guessing?"

"Well, what choice? Antispin of the funeral place . . ." Warvia waved to antispin, and then looked again. Not thirty paces paces away, the smooth plains became a jumble of mounds. It looked like a crumbling city in miniature.

"We won't wake the Ghouls," Sabarokaresh decided. "Let them wake and follow their noses."

So they set their wagon on the cemetery heights, not too close to the array of corpses, and went out to look over the shrieker village.

It was not the strangest thing Warvia had seen, yet it was strange enough.

Here on the flat plain were hundreds of squared-off mounds. It looked like a half-melted city as built by people a foot high. Every mound had a door in it. Every door faced out from the center of the city.

When the vampire killers walked toward the mounds, an army poured out of the holes and took up station.

The shriekers were of a size to make a day's meal, Warvia thought. Their faces were blunt. They came out on all fours, then stood upright to display outsize claws intended more for digging than fighting, and shrieked. The high pitch hurt Warvia's ears.

"Sticks," Forn suggested.

Tegger waved it off. "If we just wade in and start clubbing them, they'll swarm us. There's a forest of ropes where we left the wagon. Didn't I see a net there?"

The guard took station again to defend their city. Barok and Tegger threw the net. It was of strong, coarse weave, intended to lift cargo. Most of the guard crawled out and attacked. The Reds and Machine People ran then, pulling the net behind them, and paused to flip it over, to trap the few remaining guards. The other shriekers stopped, shrieked at the invaders, and returned to their stations.

Four big ones remained caught.

The Reds had eaten, and the Machine People were cooking their catch, before shadow crossed the sun. The Night People emerged, looked about them, and followed their noses. Warvia and Tegger crawled into the payload shell to sleep.

"Mummified, most of them," Harpster told them at the following halfdawn. "Too far gone even to carry as hardship rations. Most of them died old. Sand People seem to lead a good, healthy life. Never mind, there was a . . ."

"Herder," Grieving Tube finished for him. "Killed by his own beasts, I expect. We rarely starve."

"Good," Warvia said.

The sliver of sun was already too bright for the Night People. They sat under an awning while the others soaked up sunlight and waited for the morning to warm.

"We asked the Sand People about this place," Foranayeedli said. "They grow up in its shadow, but they know nothing of it except as a burial place."

"It's much more," Harpster said. "Our need now is to mount the cruiser and moor it tight. We'll need food for five days for all four of you—"

Sabarokaresh said, "We leave you here."

Warvia and Tegger had known this was coming. Warvia said, "We thank you for staying so long. We would have looked peculiar, Red Herders driving a Machine People cruiser. Have your plans changed?"

"We return to port at our own pace. We'll buy our passage with stories and lore. We'll teach the tribes we pass among to make fuel." Barok squeezed his daughter's arm. "When finally we reach Machine People again, we'll have enough of bounties to make Forn a dowry."

"For the lessons also, thank you," Tegger said carefully.

The girl favored him with a lecherous smile. "You were easy to teach!" She glanced at her father. "Oh, there were things we never yet spoke of—"

"Courting," Barok said.

"Yes. Remember how to court," Foranayeedli said. "Most hominids have courting rituals. Don't try to guess what they are. Stick to your own. It keeps *you* comfortable, keeps *them* amused. Can you remember courting?"

Warvia said, "A little."

Tegger said, "We court briefly and negotiate first. I suppose other hominids consider us shy or cold."

"Hmm, yes—"

Grieving Tube said firmly, "Time runs short. We must mount the wagon. Barok, Forn, you'll help before you leave?"

"We will. We've found livestock, too. What do you intend?"

"The wagon must sit solidly on the vehicle at the end of the starboard platform."

"Is that a *vehicle?*"

It was one of three long floating platforms. Tegger might have taken it for a covered dance floor, tournament field, shooting range . . . The roof was transparent. The floor was flat, and five times as big as the cruiser's wheelbase. Sturdy aluminum loops as big as his torso were recessed into the floor.

They centered the cruiser on the platform. Harpster and Grieving Tube supervised from under the awning while the rest threaded rope through aluminum loops and over and

around the iron payload shell. They used pulleys to put ten-
sion on the ropes, until it seemed no force beneath the Arch
would cause the wagon to shift.

They were done by midday. Barok and Forn began to gear
up for their own journey.

"You'll need food," Tegger said. "Shall we smoke some
shriekers?"

"Good. And I noticed something," Barok said. He led
them to his find: a shallow tray three manheights long by two
wide, with lines trailing from holes at the corners. He lifted it
effortlessly.

Warvia grinned. "Brilliant! You can tow it!"

"Yes. But first . . ."

The shrieker guard emerged to form rank.

First, the nets. They scooped up most of the guard, twisted
the net and threw it aside.

Then the four dipped the edge of their tray into the loose
sandy dirt and pushed and wiggled and pushed until the tray
slid in and under. When they pulled at the ropes, the corners
of the tray came up. They had a section of shrieker city on
a tray.

The guard had been working their way free. What they
saw maddened them. A swarm of them dug straight into the
section of city on the tray, frantic lest it escape. The rest
formed a crescent and screamed.

Lifting it took all the strength of all four, but they only
had to carry it thirty paces. Then ropes and pulleys lifted it to
the cemetery heights, and sliding posts on rails took it the rest
of the way. They set it down aft of the cruiser, and slid the
tray out from under the dirt.

Four shriekers still struggling in the net were pulled loose, killed, cleaned, and smoked over wood Barok pulled from a collapsed building. The Machine People drank as they worked, as much water as their bellies could carry. They left before halfnight.

Warvia and Tegger talked to the Night People while they inspected the work.

"Truly, we thought you, too, would leave us before now," Harpster said. He was looking to spinward of port, where Foranayeedli and Sabarokaresh were tiny shadows.

The Sand People had mapped a path to other tribes. Traveling by night, the City Builders could bounce from one tent city to another until they were in green lands once again.

And where, Warvia wondered, would two Red Herders be by then?

Warvia explained: "Red Herders travel widely. Twenty daywalks is nothing. Where we settle, rumor and questions will catch us up. We make poor liars, Harpster. We must go farther. Best to do without the questions."

Tegger said, "In twenty daywalks we've had rishathra with Machine People and Dryland Farmers and Sand People."

Warvia remembered that her own experience was wider yet. Nobody spoke that truth, not even Harpster. He only grinned and said, "But not Weed Gatherers nor Ghouls. Picky!"

Warvia's eyes dropped. She would rish, but not with a Ghoul, and Tegger wouldn't either.

"But we acted without the encouragement of vampire musk," Tegger said. "There is a restlessness in us—or me . . . ?"

"Us," Warvia said firmly. "Mated we are, but no longer for

each other alone. I don't doubt that we can return to our custom—"

"But we must be far from the rumor of Red Herders who rished with every species along their path! We've nearly left the Machine People empire behind. A little farther—"

Warvia said, "Five days, you said. How does this thing move?"

The Ghouls were at work closing the aft end of the great crystal canopy. Warvia began to feel claustrophobic. It bothered her, how little she and Tegger knew of where they were going.

She thought they would not answer; and then Harpster said, "Like this." He moved a lever that took both arms and a strong back. The platform detached from the dock.

Motion was hard to see, it was so smooth, but the platform was clearly drifting away.

"How far are you going?" Tegger asked.

"Oh, easily farther than the rumors you're fleeing." Harpster grinned.

Grieving Tube strode around the bulk of the wagon. "Is this Barok's work? He did well. Tegger, Warvia, we're going as far as the rim wall. We can drop you off at the next stop if you like, or you can come along and then leave us coming back."

Tegger laughed incredulously. "You'll be dead of old age before you get to the rim wall!"

"Next stop, then," Harpster said agreeably.

Grieving Tube chitter-whistled angrily. Harpster laughed and chittered back, whistling ribald-sounding comments through his teeth.

"Grieving Tube wants you," he told the Red Herders. "She thinks we should travel with people who can look daylight in the face."

"We only need to be outside Machine People turf," Tegger said.

"Leave us when you like. But think! It's serious work we're doing. We're going up the spill mountains and farther yet. No Red Herder has ever done anything so big. You'll have so much to tell when you finally settle that you'll never remember to speak of rishathra."

The desert slid smoothly past. Warvia asked, "What are we riding?"

"It's a Builder thing. I've only heard about them. None of the Night People would use an air sled unless the need was dire, but we have permission and directions."

"How fast does it go?" The landscape was moving faster yet. The receding dockyard had become a dot. A sound was rising, as of wind heard through a sturdy stone wall.

"Fast. We'll be below the spill mountains in five days."

"No."

"So I was told. But the first stop is only three days away."

"I'm frightened." Watching the world zip past was beginning to hurt Warvia's eyes.

"Warvia, there are lines under the land. In drawings they look like a honeycomb, and they lift and move Builder things. We can only stop where the lines come together."

"Three days," Grieving Tube repeated.

Far across the desert, a caravan of hominids and beasts popped up and was gone so quickly that Warvia couldn't even identify the species. The air sled was still accelerating.

The payload shell smelled of Ghouls. It hummed. Warvia huddled against Tegger in the dark and didn't speak of what was happening outside. They mated with an intensity backed by fear, and for that time Warvia entirely forgot where she was. But then the whisper of motion was back, and Tegger's voice in the darkness to drown it out.

"What was Karker like?"

"Strong. Strange to hold: strangely shaped."

"Down here . . . ?"

"No, not *here*. His body was broad, shoulders and belly and hips. I think every man is alike *here*. And he was very eager to talk, to try his skill at trade language."

"You only talked?"

Warvia giggled. "We rished. It was his first time. Imagine, Tegger! I was his teacher!"

"Did you tell him—"

"Of course. The only Red Herder woman who ever engaged in rishathra, and all his for the night. He loved it. Who were you with?"

"Hen—no, *Hansheerv*. I made sure I got her name right. She was the tall one, almost my size?" Warvia laughed at that, and he said, "The old leader's widow, though she's about my age. Of course we couldn't talk. We tried to rish in the dark, but we couldn't *gesture* that way, so we went outside and did it by Archlight."

"I wonder if the Night People were watching."

"I wondered, too," Tegger said. And then the whisper of uncanny speed was in their ears and souls.

They dozed. When each knew that the other couldn't sleep, they mated again. And tried to sleep again. When the outline of the door was a white glow, Warvia asked, "Are you hungry?"

"Yes. Are you going out?"

"No."

The door opened on halfdawn light. The Ghouls shambled in. The door closed. "We're moving well along," Harpster said, and Tegger heard relief and fatigue in his voice. "Warvia, Tegger, are you all right?"

"Scared," Warvia said.

Tegger asked, "Shouldn't someone be steering?"

Grieving Tube said, "The air sled rides lines buried in the scrith. We can't get lost."

Tegger said, "If the air sled went astray, it would kill us so fast that we'd barely know it."

"You'll get used to it."

"How do you know?"

Harpster growled. Grieving Tube said, "Let us sleep."

Since they'd left the vampires behind, the Night People had been sleeping in the payload shell. The smell was rich. Warvia huddled against her mate and tried not to think of the smell of Ghouls, or her hunger, or the vibration in the iron around her.

She uncurled and stood up. "I'm going to hunt up a meal. Shall I bring you back something?"

"Yes."

They had left the eternal clouds far behind. The day was ablaze. The land streamed past, pulling Warvia's eyes with it. Warvia dropped from the cruiser and loped over to the piled sand, keeping her gaze always toward her feet.

No shrieker guards came.

Warvia found an entrance hole and tickled it with a stick. A fat shrieker popped out and screamed at her. She snatched it, broke its neck and ate voraciously.

She couldn't keep from looking. The land had become a vast forest. The tops of huge trees were all far below, all converging and disappearing behind the sky sled. The motion threw her balance off, making her dizzy.

She made herself circle the cargo tray and tickle another opening. When a defender appeared, she snatched it and wrapped it in her skirt.

She was stepping onto the running board when she heard a voice speak her name.

The shrieker fell and scampered free. Warvia jumped straight backward, her spear poised to kill. That wasn't Tegger, and the Ghouls were fast asleep . . .

The deck was clear. Whatever had spoken must be aboard the cruiser.

Or under it? The space under there was black. Warvia adjusted her stance, a bit farther from the cruiser. Had she imagined . . . ?

"Show yourself!"

"Warvia, I dare not. It's Whisper."

Whisper? "Tegger called you a wayspirit. He thought he imagined you."

The voice said, "I will not speak to Tegger again. Warvia, I hope you will not babble of me to Tegger nor to the Night People. I could be killed and the Arch itself may fall if anyone takes notice of me."

"Yes, my mate said you were secretive. Whisper? Why tell me?"

"May we talk a little?"

"I'd rather be inside."

"I know. Warvia, we're traveling at just under the speed of sound. That's not very fast at all. When an object strikes the world from outside, it moves three hundred times as fast, with ninety thousand times the energy."

"Really." The thought was shattering. But why? Had she thought the speed of sound was instantaneous?

"Light travels much faster than sound. You've seen that yourself. Lightning, then thunder," the voice said.

It didn't occur to her to doubt a wayspirit. Anyone who could speak such things must really know what she was talking about. She asked, "Why not go faster than sound? Couldn't we hear each other?"

"It's the speed of sound in air, Warvia. If we make the air go with us, the sound in the air goes with us, too."

"Oh."

"The air sled is doing what the universe says it must. It can go to only one place, and then it will touch softly as a feather."

Warvia asked again, "Why tell me?"

"When you know what is happening, it can't frighten you. Of course there are exceptions, but the sky sled isn't one. It flies in a kind of invisible groove, a pattern of magnetic fields. It cannot lose its way."

"Pattern of . . . ?"

"I will teach you about magnets and gravity and inertia. Inertia is the force that pulls you against the inside of the spinning ring so that gravity will not pull you into the sun—"

"Is that real, too, what the Night People say? The Arch is a ring?"

"Yes. Gravity is a force you need hardly notice, but it holds the sun together so that it can burn. Magnets allow the sun's rind to be manipulated, to defend the Arch against things falling from outside. I will teach you more, if you come in daylight."

"Why?"

"You and Tegger are frightened. If you understand what's happening here, your fright will go away. If you lose your fright, so will Tegger. You will not go mad."

"Tegger," she said, and looked around her. "Tegger must be

starving." She couldn't find the shrieker she'd dropped. She went back to the shrieker village, holding her eyes to the deck. Nearly the speed of sound: how fast was that in day-walks?

A shrieker came when she tickled a tunnel opening, and she bagged it. She climbed into the payload bay, and no voice stopped her.

Chapter Twenty-Two

THE

NET

HOT NEEDLE OF INQUIRY, A.D. 2893

... Coffin!

Louis tried to push the lid away. The lid didn't want to move that fast. He pulled his knees up to set his feet and thrust upward, then roll-dived out from under the half-raised lid. Hit the floor. Kept rolling and stood up in a crouch.

Not a coffin, he remembered, but he was on an adrenaline high, with good reason to stay in motion. What had been happening while he was in the box?

His ankle stung. He'd kicked something. *Ignore it.*

The strangest thing about his waking was the way he felt.

In their early twenties, Louis and a dozen friends had run an ancient martial arts teaching program. A few dropped out when the computer had them hitting each other in the face. Louis had stuck with it, play-fighting for ten months. Then it all turned stale, and two hundred years went by, and . . .

It didn't feel like waking from sleep or surgery. He felt more like a fighter halfway through a *yogatsu* match he knows he can win. Absolutely charged up, seething with adrenaline and energy.

Great! Bring 'em on!

Motion! He whirled around. His hands felt naked.

Beyond the forward wall, rocky rolling terrain flashed past on either side, too fast for detail. *Needle* must be moving like a hypersonic shuttle at ground level. And the view was toward the captain's cabin—

Only a picture. None of those great rocks was about to mash him into jelly. The black basalt walls to left and right, the lander bay behind him, were all quite motionless.

The thing he'd kicked was a block of stone in the forward-starboard corner of crew quarters. He'd never seen *that* before. It looked completely inert and harmless: a roughly dressed granite cube as tall as his knee.

He was alone.

Louis understood why Bram had left Acolyte in an induced coma until he could attend to him. Waking alone, a Kzin might set traps and barriers, or force the wardrobe and kitchen systems to produce weapons. But Louis did not understand why Bram had left *him* to wake alone.

How fast *did* a protector learn? Bram had observed him for . . . hmm? Up to three days, if he'd tapped into the webeye camera at Weaver Town. *Could Bram already know me well enough to trust me?*

Not likely! Bram hadn't done this. The Hindmost must have reset the 'doc to open when his treatment was finished.

Now, what was the Hindmost trying to show him? Louis wondered. Did the protector know what kind of show the Hindmost had running here?

The hologram view streamed past him. Distant trees flashed past, an extensive forest of what looked like pines. Dead ahead, mountains and cloud patterns seemed infinitely distant.

The Hindmost could hide anything in the captain's cabin, and his crew would see nothing but this bounding, lurching hologram projection. Maybe *that* was the point.

The bouncing lower rim was dark wood: the front of an alcohol-burning Machine People cruiser. Under that, a bit of a curved rim of gleaming metal or plastic.

The webeye camera that the Ghouls had mounted on a Machine People cruiser now rode something that flew.

Blocks of rock protruded from fringes of forest. The vehicle flew no more than two hundred feet up. The speed? Subsonic, but not by much.

What kind of hominids could tolerate such speed? Louis wondered. Even Disney Port didn't run rides this fast. Most Ringworld hominids would die if they merely traveled beyond their local ecologies. A ride like this would stop their hearts.

What was he supposed to *do* with this?

How much time did he have to play?

Trapped in a bungalow-sized box buried miles deep in cooled lava, he was hardly a free agent. Stepping disks would get him out, but they would only take him to where his masters waited.

Louis knew that he was reacting instead of acting, like a good dog trying to guess the will of his masters. He was seething with new youth, and he couldn't *do* anything.

Sit down, he told himself. *Relax. Distract yourself. Eat?*

The kitchen menu was running. It showed kzinti script and a picture: some kind of sea life. Alien sashimi! Better not. Louis reset it for human metabolism, Sol, Earth, *français, pain perdu,* added *café au lait,* and called it breakfast. And while he waited ... hmmm?

Using the stepping disk would lose him his options.

Examining the stepping disk ...

He lifted the rim as he'd seen Bram do.

The racing landscape blinked out, replaced by an abstraction: the diagram of the stepping disk network.

More links had been added. Several networks had merged into one. The restricted flick from crew quarters to the captain's cabin was still isolated, and so were a few other pairs. Still, the Hindmost had given up some security for greater convenience. Bram must have made him do that.

The diagram measured distance on a logarithmic scale. At and near *Needle*, detail was fine enough to discriminate between crew quarters and the lander bay. There were flick points all through the Repair Center. Louis picked out Weaver Town, hundreds of thousands of miles distant. One point was far to starboard of *Needle*'s position, almost to the rim wall, half a million miles away or more. The most distant point must be a third of the way around the Ringworld's arc: hundreds of millions of miles.

Brighter lines would indicate links that were currently open. If he was reading this right . . . open circuits ran from *Needle*'s crew quarters to *Needle*'s lander bay to the far point on the Great Ocean. Bram must be exploring.

Had he taken the Hindmost? Or had the Hindmost returned to his cabin?

Knowing *that*, Louis thought, would tell him exactly how much trust was between the Hindmost and Bram. In his cabin the Hindmost would be next to invulnerable, with General Products hull material between him and any enemy. Locked off from his grooming aids, he would grow scruffy and uncomfortable—

Ding. French toast with maple syrup. Coffee with foamy steamed milk appeared a moment later. Louis ate rapidly.

Then he tried using the fork on the stepping disk controls.

The tines bent and broke.

Humming, Louis dialed *Earth, Japan, assorted sashimi.*

The *hashi* felt like wood. They even had a grain. He cracked one along the grain to get a point. He began moving whatever would move in the stepping disk controls.

Bright lines faded, others brightened, as links opened and closed.

A slide turned everything off. Moving the slide back the way it had come got him a blinking half brightness: the system wanted instructions.

He kept playing. Presently he had a bent ring of seven bright lines, and a virtual clock, and weird music playing in the background. He couldn't understand the musical puppeteer language, and he couldn't read a Fleet of Worlds timepiece, but he saw how to set it for *fast.*

If he'd read this right, the circuit would take him to the lander bay; then to Weaver Town, to see what had changed. Pick up a pressure suit in the lock, or else he'd be sniffing tree-of-life when he flicked to the Meteor Defense room! Keep the suit on when he flicked to the surface of the Map of Mars, and thence to the farthest point on the diagram, which seemed to be on the rim wall. On to the mystery point at the far shore of the Great Ocean, and back to *Needle.*

Second thoughts? This shouldn't take him more than a few minutes, unless he found something interesting.

He set the sashimi plate on the stepping disk.

Nothing happened.

Of course not: the rim of the stepping disk was still lifted, exposing the controls. Louis pushed it down. The sashimi plate flicked out.

The network blinked out, too. Louis had to shy from sudden motion. The racing landscape was back, and mountains beyond, spill mountains with the rim wall as backdrop. They were nearby, by Ringworld measure, a few tens of thousands of miles away.

Louis thought of matters he would like to study, if he could access the ship's computer. He'd have to ask the Hindmost later. He *must* review what was known of protectors. *Where was that sashimi plate?*

Running through a yoga set allowed him to curb his impatience. How fast was *fast?*

Forty-five minutes later the plate hadn't come back.

His companions might be at one of these points—probably were—and Acolyte might have snatched the sashimi. Still: *rethink.*

The far point in the diagram had drifted a little.

Drifted a little, yah. Louis's windpipe closed up; he was wheezing. Two hundred million miles up the Arch as measured on a logarithmic scale, and *drifting?* That point had to be moving like an interstellar slowboat, at hundreds of miles per second.

It was the refueling probe, of course. They must have mounted a new stepping disk on its flank and set it orbiting along the rim wall. As for the sashimi plate, it must have burned as a meteor.

Louis pulled the disk up to expose the controls. He began to reset them, swearing and talking himself through it, trying to ignore the orchestra. "Now *this* should reset *that* link . . . tanj. Why not? Oh. Stet, *dark* means *off*, now try *this* . . ."

He dialed up a loaf of bread and set it on the stepping disk. *Flick.*

An hour and ten since he had cut his associates off from *Needle.* He'd cut them off from the entire Repair Center, come to that. It would be open war when they discovered that, and breach of contract, too.

Then again, what could they do about it?

The chuckle never reached his throat. Louis knew puppeteers. The Hindmost would have had auxiliary controls implanted surgically. Louis knew he should be wondering *when* to reset the stepping disks. The Hindmost might tolerate his fiddling, but Louis didn't want to face Bram's wrath.

The bread was back.

The cruiser was flying over water. The mountains were to its left now, drifting minutely to spinward. The platform must have turned . . . turned by sixty degrees. Louis let a slow grin form.

It was following the superconductor grid!

Superconducting cable lay as a substrate beneath the Ringworld floor, forming hexagons fifty thousand miles across. It guided the magnetic fields by which solar prominences could be manipulated. Evidently the cruiser was riding a magnetic levitation vehicle, possibly something worked up by City Builders, more likely something as old as the Ringworld itself.

Did the Hindmost know?

Reacting, he was still reacting. And the bread was back.

Worth the risk?

Louis stepped on the disk.

Pressure suits were missing from the lander bay: one for the Hindmost, Chmeee's spare, and a set meant for Louis. It need not mean that Bram's crew were in vacuum. The protector might be showing caution, using the suits for armor.

Louis stepped off to tuck a pressure suit under his arm, then a cummerbund, helmet, and air pack. Then on to Weaver Town.

Louis flicked in off balance. He stumbled and dropped everything he was carrying. Embarrassed, he looked warily about him.

Full daylight. The stepping disk sat on the mud bank of the Weavers' bathing stream, canted at an angle. Nobody was using the pool. Louis listened for children's voices, but he heard nothing.

He'd stooped to examine the disk when a waspish voice spoke close behind him. The fallen helmet said, "Greeting! What species are you?"

Louis stood up. "I am of the Ball People," he said. "Kidada?"

"Yes. Louis Wu's people?" The old Weaver peered at Louis uncertainly.

"Yes. Kidada, how long since Louis Wu left?"

"You're Louis Wu made young!"

"Yes." Kidada's gape and stare made Louis uncomfortable. He said, "Kidada, I have been in a long sleep. Are the Weavers well?"

"We thrive. We trade. Visitors come and go. Sawur took ill and died many days ago. The sky has circled twenty-two times since—"

"*Sawur?*"

"Since the night you vanished with some hairy creature of legend just on your tail, and only a Ghoul child for witness. Yes, Sawur is dead. I nearly died, too, and two children died. Sometimes visitors bring a sickness that kills others but not themselves."

"I hoped to talk to her."

A gaunt smile. "But will she answer?"

"She advised me well." *Don't wait until you're desperate!*

"Sawur told me of your problem, after you vanished."

"I solved it. I hope I solved it. Otherwise I am enslaved."

"Enslaved. But with tens of falans to free yourself." Kidada sounded tired and bitter.

Louis was becoming aware of how much he wanted to talk to Sawur. He would have stayed to mourn, if he had the time.

Time. The sky had circled twenty-two times . . . two falans plus. One hundred sixty-five of the Ringworld's thirty-hour days. They'd left him in that tank for more than half an Earth year!

And he now was playing catch-up. "Kidada, who moved our stepping disk?"

"I know not what you mean. *This?* It was here the morning you were gone. We've left it alone."

The rim was muddy. Louis could see big fingerprints and scratch marks left by fingernails. Some visiting hominid—not Weavers, who had smaller hands—had been trying to alter the setting.

Ghouls. He might have known. He was glad he'd flicked in during daylight. The Night People wouldn't even know he'd been here.

Louis donned his pressure suit. "Say hello to the children for me," he said, and he flicked out.

Darkness.

Louis turned on his helmet lamp, and a half-seen skeleton was watching him.

He was in the Meteor Defense room. The screens were dark. His lamp was the only light.

These bones had been mounted for study. They weren't attached at the joints: they barely touched. A frame of thin metal rods held them in place.

The skeleton stood ten inches shorter than Louis Wu. All of the bones had a rounded look: weathered. The ribs were improbably narrow, the fingers nearly gone. Time had turned bone structure to dust. Weather in here couldn't be that erosive! But the knuckles still showed large, and all the joints were massive and greatly swollen. Those eroded projections in the massive jaw weren't teeth. They were later bone growth.

Protector.

Louis let his fingertips play over the face. The bone was gritty with dust, and smooth. Smoothed by time, as surfaces turned gradually to dust.

This wasn't an erosive environment. These bones must be a thousand years dead, at least.

The right hip had been shattered, the pieces mounted separately. And the left shoulder and elbow, and the neck: all fractured or shattered.

He might have died in a fall, or been beaten to death in combat.

The Pak had had their origin somewhere in the galactic core. A Pak colony on Earth had failed—the tree-of-life had failed, leaving the colony with no protectors—but Pak breeders had spread over the Earth from landing sites in Africa and Asia. Their bones were in museums under names such as *Homo habilis*. Their descendants had evolved to intelligence: a classic example of neoteny.

There was a mummified Pak protector in the Smithsonian Institute. It had been dug from under a desert on Mars, centuries ago. Louis had never seen it except as a hologram in a General Biology course.

This creature might be a deformed Pak, he thought. But there was that massive jaw.

Protectors lost their teeth. That was a pity, because teeth could have told him a lot. But the jaw was a bone cracker.

The torso was too long for a standard issue Pak.

It was not quite a Pak, and it was also not quite a Ghoul. Louis could guess when it had died, but when had it been born? The protector in the Smithsonian had spent thirty thousand years and more crossing from the galactic core to Earth. Gearing up for the expedition might have taken him that long again. Protectors could live a long time.

Cronus was the oldest of the Greek gods, killer of his children, until some escaped and killed him instead. Call this one Cronus, then.

A vampire horde had killed a protector who must have been Cronus' abandoned servant.

Bram and Anne must have stalked the master for years afterward. Years, centuries, millennia? Pak breeders, Man's ancestors, and the vampires', too, had been cursorial hunters before ever they left the galactic core.

Old Cronus might not have taken vampire protectors quite seriously. Vampires, after all, were mindless animals with disgusting sexual and dietary habits, and Cronus had been a superintelligent being with no distracting sex urge at all.

And so was Bram. It might give him a blind spot, Louis thought, if he could find it.

The breaks at the right hip, left arm, and shoulder, and a crack along the skull, had been fresh at death. Louis found old, healed breaks elsewhere. Cronus had broken his spine long before his death. Did a protector's spinal nerves grow back? His right knee, *that* old injury hadn't healed: the knee was fused solid.

Something else was strange about the spine . . . but Louis didn't understand until he returned to the skull.

The forehead bulged. More: the forehead bone and the

crest at the top was smoother, younger than the rest of the skull. The jagged ridge of growth from the jawbone still had an appearance of worn teeth. These things were *recent* growth. The spine, too, was recent growth: it had gone through a period of regeneration.

If Cronus had won his last battle, he would have healed again.

So think of it as a murder investigation. I know the killer, but to get a conviction in court I need every detail, every nuance. Why did Bram put these bones back together? The enemy was dead, there were none to avenge him—

Or did Bram and Anne fear others like Cronus?

A standing skeleton, and a heap of gear in the shadows beyond. Bram hadn't let him near this stuff.

It had seemed scattered, dropped at random. It was and it wasn't. Stuff had been laid out neatly for study; then something had swept through the pattern, like a vampire protector kicking out in rage.

Some of it had simply disintegrated. Some had left clear patterns.

This had been a wonderful fur coat, and a belt to hold it closed. It stank: just a ghost of the stench of old hide, and a Ghoul who hadn't bathed in thousands of years. On the inner surface, the hide surface, Louis could see the traces of a score of leather pockets in a score of shapes, all empty now.

There were weapons: a knife of old metal turned to black rust, slender and a foot long. Two knives made of horn, each no bigger than a forefinger. There were six throwing knives, nearly identical though shaped from stone, as lethal as the day they were made. A slender pole of some durable metal alloy, the ends sharpened to chisels.

Patterns in the dust might once have been wooden shoes

with heavy straps. Here were a fancy crossbow and a dozen bolts, each slightly different. This little box . . . a firestarter? Louis tried, but he couldn't get a flame started. A stack of paper or parchment: maps?

There was a telescope . . . crude, but very finely shaped and polished, and set a little apart. Hello: these next to it were tool-working tools. Pumice, little knives . . . Bram and/or Anne had set up shop here to duplicate Cronus' telescope.

A hard black lump the size of his fist. Louis bent low to sniff. Dried meat? A thousand years beyond its date . . . but jerky always did smell and taste a bit gamy. Maybe a Ghoul would like that.

How long ago had Cronus died?

Ask?

Louis knew he was playing catch-up here. He'd learn more by asking . . . but he'd learn what Bram chose to teach. And time was constricting around him.

Louis patted Cronus' shoulder bones. "Trust me," he said, and flicked out.

He was glare-blind and way off balance.

He convulsed like a sea anemone, reaching between his knees for anything solid, eyes squinted shut against raw sunlight. His gloved fingers brushed something and closed hard.

The badly tilted stepping disk slid under him by a foot or two. He was gripping the rim of the disk itself, he hoped. He held very still.

His photosensitive faceplate turned smoky gray. Still crouched, gripping the edge of the stepping disk, he looked about him.

The Map of Mars wasn't a very *good* map.

He could see a hundred shades of red without moving, but the sky was the dark blue of high-altitude Earth. The sun was too bright for Mars. Nothing could be done about the gravity either.

Maybe it didn't matter to Martians. They lived safe from sunlight beneath sand fine enough to behave like a viscous fluid. Perhaps the sand would even buoy them against Ringworld gravity.

He'd expected to be at Mons Olympus, and it seemed he was. He was a long way up. The stepping disk rested near the top of a smooth forty-five-degree slope of piled dust, and it was starting to slide again.

What had the Hindmost been *thinking* of, to put it here?

Yah, right. Martians. They'd set a trap.

Sliding faster now, losing all stability. It was a long way down. Miles! Dust must have piled here over millenia in a prevailing wind . . . a Great Ocean stratospheric wind, in a weather pattern huger than worlds. Another flaw in the accuracy of the Map of Mars.

Louis squatted, flattened himself against the stepping disk as it became a sled.

It picked up speed. The disk was trying to bounce him off. His hands had a death-grip and he tried to grip with his boot toes, too. An arcology-sized rock stood in his path. He leaned left, trying to steer. Nope. It was going to swat him hard.

Then he was elsewhere.

And his death-grip became something more, because he was falling into a black void.

He chopped off part of a shrill scream. *But I fixed it! I fixed it! I fixed it!*

He was clinging to a stepping disk welded to a gracefully

curved cigar shape: the puppeteer's refueling probe. Around him was black sky and a glare of stars.

The stepping disk, the probe's hull, everything glowed. There must be light behind him. Without losing anything of his toe-and-finger grip, Louis twisted to look over his shoulder.

The Ringworld was adrift behind and below him. He could see fine detail: rivers like twisted snakes, undersea landscapes, a straight black thread that might be a Machine People highway.

The naked sun was trying to broil him. No problem: the suit was one he could sweat through. Night would be a greater threat. He hadn't thought he would need an oversuit.

He was level with the top of the rim wall, looking down at half-conical spill mountains and the rivers that ran from their bases. A thousand miles up. Far ahead of him he could make out lacy lines sketching a long double cone.

An attitude jet. He could see the twin toroids that he'd thought made up a Bussard ramjet; but they were tiny, forming the wasp waist of something far larger. The Ringworld attitude jet was made of wire so thin that it kept fading in and out of sight. A cage to guide the flow of the solar wind.

This one wasn't mounted yet: it wasn't pointed right.

Louis hadn't felt fear like this in two hundred years.

But I got the bread back!

The probe was coasting . . . was motionless, while the Ringworld rotated below at 770 miles per second.

The system must have reset. I took this one disk out of the link, but it must have reset. I don't understand the Hindmost's programming language. What else have I fouled up?

The sashimi? That was easy. The plate must have drifted too far from the disk. The bread hadn't: it was still in range when the disks cycled.

He hung on, hung on . . .

And the disk bumped against his faceplate.

He clung with his eyes closed. He was in no shape to confront anyone, any creature. In a few seconds he'd be safe and alone aboard *Hot Needle of Inquiry*.

A great clawed hand took him by the shoulder and rolled him over.

Chapter Twenty-Three

THE
RUNNING
LESSON

HIDDEN PATRIARCH, A.D. 2893

The Kzin pulled him to his feet. Louis was gasping, shiv-ering. Acolyte couldn't talk to him while his helmet was closed, and Louis was glad of that.

He was aboard *Hidden Patriarch*, near the stern.

Just another goddamn stunning surprise. He had left the mile-long sailing ship on the Shenthy River. What was it doing here?

Acolyte was trying to ask him something. The Kzin was holding—*tanj dammit*! Louis wrenched his helmet open.

Acolyte said, "I was prowling around the stern when this popped up on the stepping disk. Your visiting-gift, Louis? Preserved fish?"

Louis took the sashimi plate. The sliced fish was puffy and crisp to the touch.

"It's been in vacuum," he said. "Did a loaf of bread come by?"

"I let it pass. Louis, you stink of terror."

What am I doing here?

In a moment he could be safe aboard *Hot Needle of In-*

quiry, floating between sleeping plates while he got through his shivering, got his mind back, and tried to digest what he had and hadn't learned.

Acolyte had seen him. If the Kzin could be persuaded to shut up, then—*Yah, right.* The protector must have been observing Acolyte's body language for half an Earth year. The Kzin couldn't hide anything from him.

Louis said instead, "The *dead* could smell my terror." He dropped his helmet and air pack and began opening zippers. "I thought I had the stepping disk controls figured out. Wrong! Oh, and the Martians set us a death trap. That almost got me, too."

An adolescent's half-bald head popped into view above a hatch. City Builder. The boy's eyes widened in surprise, and he dropped from view.

The Kzin asked, "Martians?"

Louis began stripping off his suit. "Skip it. I've *got* to burn some energy. Can you run?"

The Kzin bristled. "I outran my father after we fought."

"I'll race you to the bow."

Acolyte yowled and bounded away.

Louis's pressure suit was pooled around his ankles. At the Kzin's howl, his every muscle locked and he fell over.

That was a *wonderful* battle cry! Hissing ancient curses, Louis pulled the suit off, rolled to his feet and ran.

Acolyte was still in sight, moving considerably faster than he was. Then the ship structure jogged and he was gone.

Louis had lived aboard this ship for nearly two years. He wasn't likely to get lost. He ran hard, competing only with himself. He had a full mile to cover.

"Loueee!"

The voice was faint and strange, coming from high over-head . . . from a Pierson's puppeteer perched in the aft crow's nest.

Louis bellowed, "Hellooo!"

"Wait!" the voice called.

"Can't!" He felt *good*.

A squarish shadow descended. Louis ran on. It came alongside, pacing him: a Repair Center cargo plate with rails welded around it. Louis called, "Stay clear. I'm in a race."

"I don't understand."

"It's not—an intelligence test."

"How do you feel?"

"Wonderful. Disoriented. Alive! Hindmost—don't use—the Olympus stepping disk."

"Why?"

"Martians—they're alive—set a trap." Louis drew a deep breath and blew it out. Salt air on his taste buds: wonderful! His breath was holding, his legs were holding. He pumped harder. "They'll set another."

"Two can play that game. What if I dropped a disk in the sea and began flicking water to Mons Olympus?"

"You ask me? Don't exterminate—anything. You might need it—later. It's the reason—you didn't kill off—the kzinti!"

"More or less," the puppeteer acknowledged. A one-eyed head dipped toward a puff of orange glimpsed far ahead along the top mid-deck. Acolyte.

"Louis, your advent is opportune. We have much to catch up on."

"Where's Bram?"

"Cooking our dinner."

His heads were arced around to look into his own eyes.

Was the Hindmost joking? Maybe that was puppeteer laughter and maybe it wasn't.

"Bram has a sensitive nose," the Hindmost added.

Louis asked, "How goes the dance?"

"The dance! It proceeds without me. I'm tanj sick of using your recycler, Louis! I haven't even had time to redesign it."

"Thank you for that." *Keep it casual.* But if Bram didn't trust the Hindmost enough to let him take normal exercise or use a toilet and shower designed for puppeteers . . .

Then the Hindmost might be ready to take back his life.

The top mid-deck ended. Louis clambered through lad-ders and corridors. Kzinti ladders were heavily tilted and the rungs were too far apart, but Louis went up and down like an ape on steroids. He kept expecting to pass Acolyte. Worse, he expected Acolyte to leap out at him from some alcove. He stayed to the heights.

In his mind he tried to map his way around the garden. It would take too long. At the end of a corridor he ran up a flight of hardwood steps to the top of a wall, along the wall to avoid a thicket of big yellow puffballs with impressive thorns, and dropped ten feet into dirt.

It had been a kzinti hunting park. For two years Louis and the City Builders had tended these plants. They had been growing wild when he arrived. Once they must have fed herds for kzinti sailors. The herds were gone, and he didn't expect to find animals now, unless Acolyte was about to leap out from some citrus thicket.

But he never saw the Kzin.

There were eight tremendous main masts and uncountable sails, and the winches that moved them could only be worked by a Kzin. Or a protector? This mast was the foremast, with the fore crow's nest at the top. Louis was blowing hard. His legs felt like overcooked noodles.

Someone was waiting in the bow.

Louis cursed in his mind. He didn't have breath to spare. A moment later he recognized the protector shape.

Louis slowed. Bram waited like a statue. Louis couldn't tell if he was breathing at all.

"I think you win," Louis gasped.

"Were we racing?"

Bram wouldn't have known of an intruder until the City Builder boy found him in the kitchen, or until he heard feet pounding across the deck overhead. He *must* have run. Louis said, "Whatever. I needed exercise."

Before him was a mountain range ... an un-Earthly mountain range. Conical mountains, spaced wide apart and varying in size, ran left and right. Without a horizon, he had no real grasp of their size. Most were tall enough to have ice-white peaks, but below the ice they were all green patchwork.

Then his eye/mind perceived what loomed above them.

They were *tiny*.

Wait now, the rim was a thousand miles high. Of the twenty or thirty mountains he could pick out, five or six were mere foothills leaning against the rim wall, but two or three might match Everest.

The Hindmost drifted toward the bow. Behind him, a puff of orange pulled itself into view.

The Kzin plodded up. He was done, winded. Louis said, "Thank you, Acolyte. I really, really needed that. I was carrying enough adrenaline to run a war."

The Kzin panted, "Father. Let me win. Didn't want to. Kill me."

"Ah."

"How. Did you pass me?"

"Must have. Maybe in the garden."

"*How?*"

"Bram, *you* must know about cursorial hunters?"

"I don't know the term," the protector said.

"Stct. Acolyte, most hunting creatures miss their jump eight times out of nine. If the prey runs away, they pick something slower. Only a few kinds of meat eaters pick their prey and follow it until they run it down. Wolves do that. So do humans.

"Big cats aren't cursorial hunters, and kzinti aren't, either. Your ancestors learned that they'd better track down an enemy or he'll turn up later, but that's your brain talking. Your evolution hasn't caught up—"

"You knew you would win."

"Yah."

The Kzin blinked at him. "If we had run only as far as the garden?"

"You would have won."

"Thank you for the lesson."

"Thank *you*." That was nicely phrased, Louis thought. Who had taught him that?

Bram said, "Louis. Look around you. React."

React? "Impressive. All that green! From the foothills to the frost line, all green. I shouldn't be surprised. Those mountains are all seabottom muck, all fertilizer."

"More?"

"Some of the pipes have stopped delivering flup. That would account for the lowest mountains. What's left of them must be fairly hard rock by now. The highest ones must have a lot of water ice in them, at least at the peak. I can see rivers running from the foothills. Those mountains will get the Ringworld's only regular earthquakes."

"A difficult environment?"

"I suppose. Bram, we saw all this fifty falans ago. Have you seen signs of life in the mountains?"

"Once around your world would mark the distance to those mountains, but yes, we have. Louis, I have a meal to tend. Hindmost, Acolyte, take him to the dining hall. Show him."

The Hindmost had sprayed webeyes on all four walls of the dining hall.

One was not in use: a mere bronze spiderweb.

A window shaped like a pool of spilled water looked out upon a row of dark green cones capped in white.

Another showed the edge of the rim wall drifting slowly past: a view from the refueling probe.

And one showed a score of muscular, hairy men using ropes to guide a square plate big enough to be the floor plan of a six-room bungalow. The plate floated above them. It might have been a big cargo plate, or part of a floating building. The men were pulling it toward Louis . . . toward the Machine People cruiser and its stolen webeye.

"I left you a record taken six days ago," the Hindmost said, "to watch when you woke. But this is in present time."

"What are they doing?"

The Kzin answered. "They're approaching the rim wall any way they can."

"Why?"

"I don't know that yet. Bram might," the Kzin said. "While you were in treatment, Bram found your City Builder friends and set them aboard *Hidden Patriarch*. They obey Bram as my father's slaves obeyed their lord. They had the ship moving to starboard within a day. Bram is studying the rim wall."

Louis asked again, "Why?"

"We were not told," Acolyte said.

The Hindmost said, "I have never seen Bram show fear, yet I think he fears protectors."

Louis saw the connection. "The attitude jets need replacing. Otherwise the Ringworld slides off center. Any protector who sees *that* will be found mounting attitude jets on the rim wall. Right?"

"If the theory holds."

"Why isn't Bram there?"

The puppeteer made a short, sharp sound, as if a clarinet had sneezed. "If protectors knew that three offworld species have mounted invasions and a fourth is in wide orbit to study the effects, they would swarm the Map of Mars instead."

"Give them decent telescopes? No, they'd still—Ah."

"Ah?"

"Bram has to be on the rim wall, too. He's preparing. The other protectors will kill him if they can."

The puppeteer's eyes met. He said, "In any case, we have *Hidden Patriarch*'s view of the local rim wall. My refueling probe has been in solar orbit for more than a falan now, skimming along the rim walls, recording. We've learned a great deal, Louis." The Hindmost whistled a brief trill.

All three views began a slow zoom.

From Hidden Patriarch's *fore crow's nest:* The spill mountains expanded until only one was in sight. Pale green and dark green, grass and forest, reached up to ice-white. At the very peak a black thread dipped into a compact knot of black fog. Seabottom muck fell steadily from a spillpipe a thousand miles overhead.

From the probe: The rim wall blurred past. Louis tried to keep his eyes off it.

From the stolen webeye—Louis began to laugh.

Now the Machine People cruiser was bobbing gently, twenty feet up. Beyond the edge of the floating plate was rolling landscape, hummocks like a thousand sleeping behemoths.

Ropes were pulling the cargo plate. Thirty-odd men of a species unfamiliar to Louis were pulling the ropes. The men wore light packs, but nothing else. Straight black hair covered their heads and their backs to below their buttocks. Perhaps hair was all they needed for warmth.

They were running uphill toward a ridge, and toward thirty hairy women waiting below the ridge. The women were waving, yelling encouragement. Among them was a small red woman, a Red Herder, attempting to guide them with wide motions of her arms.

The way grew steeper; the men weren't running anymore. As they neared the crest, the women ran alongside them. They were as hairy as the men. More or less smoothly, they added themselves to the ropes. There was general laughter and brief conversations held in gasps.

The women pulled. Some were running backward. They had strong legs, Louis noted, as strong as the men's. They were over the crest now and starting downhill. The runners were behind the window now, trying to slow the craft.

The Red Herder ran to snatch a rope and climb it.

The viewpoint moved faster and faster over the rounded land. By now all the runners must have let go. The hummocks grew larger ahead; grew mountainous. Streams ran among them and converged ahead. Louis realized that he was looking at the foot of a spill mountain.

The swaying of the plate was making Louis motion-sick. "They're going to get themselves wrecked," he said.

Acolyte yowled: kzinti ridicule.

"I don't consider them sane myself," the Hindmost said.

The view from *Hidden Patriarch*'s bow was expanding, too. Now the peak of the spill mountain was lost overhead. A third of the way up the slopes, Louis began to see colored dots and blinking lights.

Blinking lights? "Heliographs."

"Very astute, Louis."

"A Ghoul child told me about this. He thought he was being cryptic. Their whole empire must be linked by heliographs in the spill mountains. How do you suppose they do it? Ghouls can't stand daylight."

"At night they see flashing mirrors from daylit mountains. Easy enough, but how do they send? Louis, they must buy message services from locals."

"Somehow. And bargain with the Spill Mountain People, too, somehow. I bet they don't use rishathra."

"They don't need many. We only see the glitter from a handful of spill mountains. A few thousands of message stations on the surface would be enough to knit their empire together."

"What about the—what are those, balloons?"

The Hindmost trilled again. The zoom stopped; the mountains began to drift sideways. A score of colored dots were adrift against the ice, a mile to a mile and a half up. Louis saw more of them in the wide spaces between mountains.

"Hot gas balloons, Louis. We see them flowing between the spill mountains everywhere we look."

"How much variation—"

Harkabeeparolyn and Kawaresksenjajok entered bearing platters, and stopped in their tracks.

The Hindmost whistled. The hurtling rim wall and the bouncing foothills faded into bronze spiderwebs. It was a wonder the City Builders hadn't dropped everything and run screaming, Louis thought. But Harkabeeparolyn was still staring, and Kawaresksenjajok was watching her and grinning.

Me. Louis said, "It's still me. I've had some medical work done."

Harkabeeparolyn turned to her mate and spoke. Louis's translator said, "You knew!"

"Zelz told me."

"I'll get you for this, you little zilth!" But Harkee was laughing, and so was Kawa.

They set their platters down: a heap of brown and yellow roots and a bowl of pink fluid. Harkabeeparolyn settled into Louis's lap and studied his face from an inch away. "We've been lonely," she said.

It felt natural, as if they'd been doing this forever. It felt as if he had come home.

He said, "You weren't lonely where I left you."

"We were told to come." She nodded at the kitchen.

They had obeyed a protector. That, too, must have seemed very natural. Louis asked, "What were you told?"

" 'Sail to starboard.' " She shrugged. "From time to time *he* comes and looks about and alters our course, or tells us of wind and water currents, or ways to catch and cook fish or warm-bloods or tend the garden. He says we don't eat enough red meat."

"That might be his ancestry speaking."

"Louis, you look as young as Kawa. Can you . . . ?"

The puppeteer answered. "Only for Ball People and the

Ball Kzinti. To heal local hominids or local kzinti or any other species, a thousand of my kind would need a lifetime of study and testing."

Harkabeeparolyn scowled.

Kawaresksenjajok and Bram entered with more platters. Here were six big, surpassingly ugly deep-sea fish. Two were still twitching. The others had been broiled with strange looking plants . . . kzinti vegetables. The bowl of raw vegetables was also from the kzinti hunting park.

Louis looked at the other bowl and asked, "Fish blood?"

Bram said, "Whale blood and a vegetable puree. It would not feed me long. Your kitchen was a wonderful find."

They sat. Kawaresksenjajok went, and returned with a two- or three-year-old child. She had a full head of orange-blond hair. Louis wouldn't have taken her for a City Builder. The older boy was not in evidence.

Bram's cooking was *good*. A little strange. Bram must have been cooking for City Builder tastes using plants from the hunting park. There would be crucial diet components missing or in short supply.

Louis asked, "How long would this keep me alive?"

Bram said, "A falan before your behavior would begin to deteriorate." He sipped decorously.

Acolyte had already disposed of the raw fish. Louis asked him, "Are you still hungry?"

"It's enough. One who satisfies his hunger grows fat and torpid."

The little girl was crawling toward the edge of the table. Louis pointed; Harkee turned; the child reached the edge, slipped, and clung by her fingers. She had a grip like a monkey or a Hanging Person.

"Thought she'd fall? Hah!" The City Builder woman was

laughing at him. "Wrong species." Abruptly she asked the protector, "May we keep Louis for a time?"

In the instant before he replied, Bram's glance touched all their faces, judging, deciding. He said, "You may have each other until midday tomorrow. Louis, we should return to *Needle* soon. We can learn no more until we take the probe over the rim. Hindmost, is that why you let Louis wake?"

"Of course. I've had little chance to brief him."

Again Bram's eyes took them all in. He said, "I must know the spill mountains and the rim. The protectors on the rim wall must not learn of me. The central question is of protectors. I must know where they are, how many, what species, their intentions and methods and goals.

"I have learned what I can without acting, and avoided attention when I could. The pilfered webeye moves ever closer to the rim wall. The Ghouls must intend to show us *something*. Kawaresksenjajok, Harkabeeparolyn, you have shown me spill mountain activity far from the working site. You of the Ball People have brought me recordings made at one of the spaceports. I know more of the rim wall now than I guessed was there to learn. Soon I must show myself. Advise me."

Acolyte spoke. "If others see the probe, they will guess at interstellar invaders. You should prepare to defend the Repair Center—"

"Yes, but the probe implies the puppeteer, not me. I have prepared. Hindmost?"

Louis was thinking: He chopped Acolyte off pretty hard. Why is the kit taking it?

The Hindmost didn't speak.

Chmeee's son came to me as my student. Bram has had too long to impress him. Maybe I've lost a student. If I'd known I wanted the kit's respect . . .

I'd have raced him and beat him. Hah! What's my next step?

Bram asked, "Harkabeeparolyn, what do you know of protectors?"

She had been a teacher in the floating city's library, where Kawaresksenjajok had been a student. She said, "I remember pictures of armor collected from tens of thousands of daywalks around us. They all looked very different, fitted for different species, but all had the crested helm and oversized joints. Fanciful old tales tell of saviors and destroyers fearsome to see, with faces like armor, big shoulders, knobby knees and elbows. Neither men nor women can fight them or tempt them. Bram, do you want to hear old stories?"

"When I know what I must hear, I can learn it," Bram said. "When I ask, 'What have I forgotten?' I can only hope for a useful answer. Louis?"

Louis shrugged. "I'm still two falans behind the rest of you."

Bram looked at them. His hard face permitted little expression. The Hindmost and City Builders watched him anxiously. Acolyte seemed relaxed, perhaps bored.

Bram picked up a chair and moved it to . . . a skeletal structure in an unused corner. Tubes and metal domes and wires had been fixed to a wooden spine in a manner that seemed not quite useful, not quite random. There had been too many distractions, but now that he came to look at it, Louis would have placed it as representing some brief ancient fad in sculpture. It had that kind of esthetic unity.

But Bram was moving it into place between his knees, plucking the strings . . .

The Hindmost asked, "Did you finish the Mozart Requiem?"

"We shall see. Record."

The puppeteer whistled chords of programming music,

speaking to the fourth webeye. Louis shrugged his eyebrows at Harkabeeparolyn sitting in his lap. This nonsense was burning up time they might spend together ... but the City Builder woman whispered, "Listen."

The protector's fingers were suddenly everywhere, and the air exploded with music.

Acolyte strolled out the door and was gone.

The music was strange and rich and precise. The puppeteer was singing accompaniment, but Bram held the structure of it. Louis couldn't remember where he'd heard anything like it.

It was *human* music, paced for human nerves. No sound shaped by aliens could have done *this* to his central nervous system. He felt a roaring optimism ... a godlike calm ... wistful longing ... the power to conquer worlds, or move them.

The music he knew was shaped in computers, not made by toenails softly kicking or stroking stretched surfaces or a bronze plate, fingernails strumming wires, a lipless mouth blowing into pipes with holes in them.

It was making him horny as tanj, and Harkabeeparolyn was half melted in his lap. He thought, *You were right,* but he wouldn't interrupt even to whisper that in her ear. Instead he settled back and let the vibrations flood through him.

And when the sound had finally died away, he sat stunned.

"I think we have it," Bram decided. He set the orchestral sculpture aside. "Hindmost, thank you. Louis, can you describe the effects?"

"Stunning. I, ah ... no, I'm sorry, Bram, it's nonverbal."

"Might it be used as a tool of diplomacy?"

Louis shook his head. "Tanj if I know. Bram, had you thought of mounting a webeye in Fist-of-God Crater?"

"Why? Ah, to point it *down.*"

"Yah, down, *out*, for a view in the plane of the Arch. Fist-of-God is a hollow cone the size of a moon—well, *big*, with a hole in the peak. You could mount a sizable fortress in there if you could anchor it in the Ringworld floor material—"

"The scrith."

"Scrith, yah. A volume a tenth the size of the Repair Center and at least as well hidden."

"Defend the plane of the Arch from inside Fist-of-God?"

Louis hesitated. "I'm sure you can do your spying from there. Defend? Any enemy is bound to think of hiding in the shadow of the Ringworld. I'm not sure you *can* defend that. If you fight from the rim wall, it's the same problem. The Meteor Defense can't fire *through* the scrith, can it?"

"We cannot split our defense. I must command the rim wall, and its protectors, too," Bram decided. "We'll put the refueling probe in place tomorrow. Louis, when did this notion come to you?"

"Just popped into my head. Maybe the music distracted me and my brain went on without me."

"Did your brain pop up anything else?"

"I don't know enough about protectors," Louis said. "There was a skeleton in the Meteor Defense room. You didn't let me get close, but that was a protector, wasn't it?"

"I will show you. Tomorrow, after we place the probe."

The Machine People cruiser was an uncontrolled toboggan now, running up the side of a green hill, veering away. Hell of a ride. The plate's bobbing rim gave him glimpses up the higher, more distant spill mountain. Louis saw blinking brilliance above the snow line. The empire of the Night People was here, too.

Chapter Twenty-Four

THESE
BONES

They flicked from cloudy daylight to the pinkish artificial light of *Needle*'s lander bay; thence to the crew cabin
and a webeye view of the rim wall zipping past in vacuum-
harsh sunlight.

Bram arrived last. He set down his orchestral sculpture
where Louis had dropped his pressure suit components, and
went straight to the kitchen dispenser. "Get us an update on
the probe, Hindmost. How long until we can dock?"

The Hindmost spoke orchestral chords. Equations wrote
themselves across the air in Interspeak symbols. "We could begin to decelerate now at two gee and dock in fifteen and a
half hours."

"You've told me the probe can take ten gee."

"I prefer a margin of error."

"Hindmost, the probe's drive is a powerful, conspicuous
X-ray source. We'll give an enemy minimal time to track it
down. Wait, then decelerate at ten gee."

"At high thrust a fusion drive becomes *brighter*, more
conspicuous."

Bram said nothing.

"Wait, aye aye. Decelerate at ten gee beginning in six hours. Dock in just more than nine hours. May I return to my cabin to eat and bathe and dance and sleep?"

The protector sipped from a squeezebulb. The Kzin's nose wrinkled, though Louis couldn't smell anything. Bram said, "You can do all of that here."

"Bram, I must enter my cabin when the time comes to decelerate the probe. Let me go now."

"Show me your cabin."

The Hindmost whistle-chirped. The rim wall faded out, and they looked into the Hindmost's cabin.

The light was yellow shading toward orange, but the decor was the infinite greens of a cold weather forest. There were no corners, no edges. Floor and wall, table space and storage space, it was all curves.

Bram instructed, "Leave it thus. Bathe and sleep. If you dance, dance alone—"

The Hindmost snorted like an angry horn section.

"If I see a hologram where I should see the Hindmost, I must act. You want me to feel safe, don't you?" Bram stooped with bent knees above the granite block. He lifted, swung around, and set it down.

Oh.

The Hindmost stepped where the granite had been, and was on the far side of the bulkhead.

The contours of the cabin shifted as he moved. A bowl formed from the floor and took on shades of peach. The puppeteer stepped daintily into it. It grew like a flower until it had almost closed above: a high-sided bathtub much like those used in lunar cities.

Bram must have noted Louis's rapt gaze. "What strikes you, Louis?"

What struck Louis was that the Hindmost wasn't going to be much help to Louis Wu. Bram had had too much time to intimidate the puppeteer. Louis said instead, "I had an insight. The Hindmost's cabin, what does it look like to you?"

"A womb, perhaps."

"How about the interior of an animal?"

"Are we playing word games?"

"There's a difference. It might matter. Female puppeteers don't have a womb. A . . . prey animal evolved into a symbiote so long ago that they think of it as the puppeteer female, but it isn't. Nessus had an ovipositor. Bram, get into the Hindmost's records and see if he has a file on *digger wasps*."

"Digger wasps, stet," Bram said. "We have some nine hours to play with. You were going to lecture me about protectors."

Louis asked, "Shall we go look at bones?"

"Lecture," Bram said.

Louis complied. "Our ancestor was the Pak breeder. The Pak evolved on a planet near the galactic core, say a hundred and thirty thousand falans from here at lightspeed." Thirty thousand light-years and a bit. "Some of them tried to set a colony on my planet, on Earth, long ago. There wasn't enough thallium to support the virus that grows in the yellow roots, and that's what turns a breeder into a protector.

"The protectors died off. They may have cleared off some predators first to give the breeders room to expand. The immature Pak, the breeders, evolved on their own, just like they did here. They spread over Earth from landing sites in Africa and Asia."

"Speculative?"

"We have bones of Pak breeders from Olduvai Gorge and other sites. There's a mummified Pak protector in the Smithsonian," Louis said. "They dug it out from under a desert on

Mars. I never saw it myself. Even at my age you can't do everything. But we studied a hologram of the thing in General Biology."

"How did you come by that?"

"He came to rescue the old colony. That's hearsay evidence, Bram, from a Belter who ate the yellow roots, but the Hindmost probably has it in memory. Ship components, Brennan's tale, the dissected mummy, chemical—"

"Let us not disturb the Hindmost. But you studied this mummy?"

"Yes."

"Let us look at bones."

The knobby man's hand felt like a handful of marbles, and his pull on Louis's wrist was irresistible. Acolyte followed, suitless. Kzinti needn't fear the smell of tree-of-life. Louis found himself walking rapidly toward a skeleton looming in amplified starlight.

Bram brought them face-to-face, stepped back and said, "React."

Acolyte circled the skeleton. "It died in combat," he murmured. He sniffed, then followed his nose to Cronus' array of tools and clothing.

Louis ran his fingertips over the eroded edges where bone was broken. Would Bram guess that he'd been here before? Louis said, "Well, it looks thousands of falans old."

"Near seven thousand," Bram confirmed.

"Beaten to death. You?"

"I and Anne."

Acolyte turned, his ears up. "Tell us the tale. He challenged you here?"

"No, we hid our existence."

"How did you find him? How did you lure him?"

"He had to come. We waited."

The Kzin waited. But Bram didn't speak again, so Louis said, "This could almost be a deformed Pak protector. Still, the jaw's a bone cracker. The skull doesn't have much brow ridge. The torso, I think it's too long for a standard issue Pak. Bram, I think you have here a carrion eater."

Back came Acolyte to see what Louis was talking about. Bram asked, "On what basis?"

"Jaw built to crack bones. A predator would have teeth to tear open big arteries or an abdomen. The long torso gives him a gut long enough to deal with a difficult meal. The missing brow ridge—well, he could be going out only at night, or maybe he had bushy eyebrows for eyeshades, but—"

Acolyte asked, "Might he be a Night People protector? Distort the skull, expand the joints—"

Louis shook his head. "I saw a Ghoul child at the Weaver village. I saw adults among the Fearless Vampire Slayers, and more adults in the fungus farm under a floating city, once upon a time. I would swear they were all the same species, and this isn't it.

"Look, the Ghouls at the fungus farm were my height and a bit. He's four inches shorter. No teeth, of course, but look at the hands. Ghoul hands are bigger, thicker, they can tear anything apart. More to the point, Acolyte, the current species is identical across two hundred million miles of distance."

Acolyte watched, saying nothing. It was rare to see a Kzin so still.

"But it's obvious," Bram said patiently. "This is the old one, the species that became the People of the Night."

Louis said, "Cronus?"

"Precursor god of the Greeks?"

Louis was startled, and showed it. "You've been studying."
Tanj, that's where he learned the music!

"They're meddlesome, aren't they, these puppeteers? The
Hindmost has a hundred generations of human literature,
kzinti oral history, kdatlyno touch-sculpture sequences, even
some trinoc vengeance tales. From your nineteenth and twen-
tieth centuries I've viewed entertainments based on Bram
Stoker's *Dracula*, including Fred Saberhagen's and Anne Rice's
work. But why not reserve the name 'Cronus'? This individual
can't have been the first, Louis. Shall I make blurry word-
pictures for you?

"Eighty thousand falans ago there was a dead Pak protector. He might have been hundreds of falans old already. For all
we know, he might have helped build the Arch. Call *him*
Cronus. Archaic Night People came and ate his flesh. If the
meat of a protector didn't bring on the change, then they
found yellow roots the protector carried. They became protectors. If there were many, soon there was one."

Louis slapped the dead protector's clavicle. Dust puffed.
"Bram, *this* is the oldest protector we'll ever know anything
about. Maybe there *were* gods before Cronus, that the Greeks
didn't know about—"

Bram nodded. "As you will. Cronus."

"Stet. Cronus' species might have been eating carrion
for thousands of years after something like the Fist-of-God
impact—"

"Must you speak every trivial truth aloud? Ah, you have a
student. Acolyte, do you see Louis's point?"

"In truth, I see something," Acolyte said. "The numbers
are ridiculous unless something was guiding Ghouls in one direction across large, very large distances. *One* empire. Ghouls

must be the same along the entire two hundred million miles. Perhaps everywhere on the ring."

"Yes! It was Cronus tending his species like a herder. Bram? Doesn't a protector try to preserve his own genetic pattern?"

The Kzin jumped on it. "Yes! How could Cronus guide his own descendants? Even a good change smells wrong. Wait, what if he chose other, similar carrion eaters? No, they would rule his own breed!"

Acolyte was learning how to solve puzzles.

Bram said, "He was a Ghoul. A carrion eater's sense of smell is altered by evolution. What to approach, what to touch, what to put in his mouth, each is a conscious choice. A Ghoul may be more free than other protectors. He may guide his kind toward what he sees as perfection."

They looked at the old skeleton. *He had to come*, Bram had said. *Near seven thousand falans*, he'd said. One thousand seven hundred years? And if Louis's dawning suspicion had any basis in fact, he'd best not ask directly.

Try something indirect. "Your mate, is she still in here?"

"Anne may be dead. When we became aware that the Arch is unstable in its plane, that there must have been motors on the rim, Anne went to fix it. I was able to track her for a time. These others now at work on the rim wall may have killed her."

"Bram, she would have had to *make* those other protectors."

"Anne felt no such urgency when she left me. She would have worked alone. These late-blooming protectors might be the work of the recent one, the Ball People protector—"

"Teela."

"Teela Brown. *Your* mate," Bram said. "The Hindmost has records of her, too."

"Were you here when Teela came?"

"Yes. It was more difficult to hide from her than from the Hindmost. I watched her learn to use the Meteor Defense. I was sure she intended what a protector must: she would save the Arch from impacting the sun. What was her true intent, Louis?"

"Teela was a protector. I can't read a protector's mind."

Bram asked, "If not hers, then whose?"

"You saw the records. Teela was strange."

"Two came into the Repair Center," Bram said. "They ate of the root. One died. The other fell into the coma that leads to the protector state. I had time to hide my presence and set up means to observe her.

"Your Teela wandered the Repair Center. It was a pleasure to watch her. She discovered things I hadn't noticed, and ultimately came here. She played with the Meteor Defense and the telescope display.

"Then she left. I was able to track her a little as she moved to the rim wall. She used a magnetic transport system on the rim wall, much faster than the system we used, but she had an advanced pressure suit."

"Timing?"

"Some extrasolar object impacted the sun twenty-two falans past. Storms of subatomic particles threw the Arch off balance. Louis, Teela was in a great hurry."

Twenty-two falans ago: the Ringworld began sliding off balance about five years before *Hot Needle of Inquiry*'s return. "She was educated on Earth," Louis said. "With a protector's brain and basic physics classes, she must have seen the situation quick enough. She went to fix the attitude jet system. What would she find? Anne?"

"Anne would hide," Bram said. "She would watch Teela. At the first sign of incompetence, she would kill Teela."

"Mmm."

"You knew her—"

"As a woman. Bram, nobody *knew* Teela. She was a statistical fluke, a woman who was lucky every time luck was called for, up until Nessus drafted her for the Ringworld expedition. Any kind of normal life must have been just out of her reach."

Acolyte said, "My father speaks of Teela sometimes. He never knew what to make of her. To the puppeteers, she was part of a breeding program, breeding for luck. Chmeee believed they succeeded."

"No," Bram said.

Louis said, "She's dead, Bram. She's no threat to you."

"But what might a protector leave behind to shape a future she desired? We plan far ahead. Louis, have you seen what you needed to see?"

"Yah."

Bram flicked in, calling, "Hindmost, wake!"

But the Hindmost was awake and dancing in his cabin . . . dancing with three ghosts, three puppeteers too translucent to hide him. "Bram, I thought of something cute. I made a brief burn an hour ago to put the probe below the rim, out of sight of invading ships."

"Numbers?"

The Hindmost whistled. Equations wrote rainbow lines.

Bram studied them. It was the first time Louis had seen him freeze up like that, but the equations looked complex, far beyond his own abilities. Then Bram said, "Good. Begin deceleration now."

The Hindmost chirped. The racing rim wall opened behind him—"Stet?"

"Yes, stet, if it doesn't hide you from me."

—rim wall moving at a blur, its edge far above, the tops of the spill mountains far below. The probe must be about three hundred miles up, Louis thought.

The Hindmost chirped. Louis looked for results, but he couldn't see—wait, now. Night-shadowed, the passing rim wall had picked up a blue highlight: the reflection of a small fusion drive. Floating equations told it better: some of the numbers were reeling down.

Three ghosts still danced with the Hindmost, and Louis knew them. Their hairstyles differed, but they were all Nessus.

Acolyte was gnawing on something that dripped red. It was not an appetizing sight, but Louis was suddenly starved. He tapped at the kitchen wall with one eye for the holograms.

Bram asked, "Hindmost, what do you know of Teela Brown?"

The Hindmost sang like a bronze bell. A third hologram opened behind the Hindmost: a table of contents, as best Louis could tell. The cabin was crowded with images.

Bram flared in anger. "Come here. Come here now!"

The Hindmost didn't hesitate. He stepped and was beside them. "I intended no harm."

"I prefer you here. Louis, Hindmost, Acolyte, I'm trying to paint a picture of a protector in my mind. I have my murky view of Cronus and I knew Anne intimately, but Teela Brown is an alien protector. Soon we must face alien protectors. Hindmost, what have you shown me?"

"These are records on the Lucky Human Project. My administration felt that human allies could do us good. Humans are lucky. We would make them effective by making them luckier. The experiment was local to one planet, Earth. We added a lottery to the formal qualifications that earn a birth-right. We kept track of babies born through luck. We financed a social network so that the children might meet and breed."

"Was she lucky?"

Louis wasn't listening, definitely wasn't listening. When he'd fought free of the Ringworld, Teela had stayed behind by her own choice. Louis had had forty years to avoid thinking about Teela Brown.

"She was a sixth-generation lottery winner, but Teela was not lucky for puppeteers, nor for her associates. I cannot think she was lucky for herself. Any creature seeks homeostasis. Teela lost her mate, then her gender identity and shape, then her life. But luck is a thing of dubious interpretation."

Acolyte spoke. "What if she sought a cause worth dying for?"

Louis gaped. Acolyte added, "Or what if she only wanted to be more intelligent? Like my father. Like me. Luck gave her those things."

Bram said, "Louis?"

"Maybe. Interesting interpretation." Forty years, and he'd never seen what was obvious to this eleven-year-old cat!

"Anything further?"

Louis closed his eyes. He could see her, touch her. "A freak accident took her away from us. Luck. When we found her, she'd found Seeker. Big, brawny explorer type, a wonder-ful guide, and I guess she was in love with him, too—"

"Was she your mate or his?"

"Serial polygamy. Skip it—"

"She left you for him?"

"Not *just* for Seeker. Bram, she'd found this—this *huge toy*. It never would have occurred to Teela that it was beyond her, too big to play with. That *anything* was beyond her."

"She wanted to play with the Arch? Without destroying it, of course. And only a protector can do that?"

Louis rubbed his eyes.

"So you left her on the Ringworld. And then?"

"Seeker must have led her to the Map of Mars, or told her enough that she could guess the rest. She knew going in that she was entering a strange place, a place of secrets.

"She ... let's see ... she wakes as a protector. Seeker's dead. Teela's a protector in the Repair Center. She plays around. She finds out how to turn the sun into a superthermal laser. Blasts a few comets?"

"She did that."

"She learns how to display telescope views with the Meteor Defense setup. She notices that the Ringworld has a wobble to it. She finds attitude jets on the rim wall, but most of them are gone. Any protector could predict the results of that.

"She goes to the rim wall. Bram, did she take roots with her?"

"Roots and a flowering plant and thallium oxide."

"She finds City Builder ships built around the rim attitude jets. Anne may have replaced some of those ... yah. That's what your Anne was doing: intercept every City Builder ship as it comes back from the stars, tear out the Bussard ramjets and mount them on the rim. It's just another thing Halrloprillalar never told me. She and her crew must have been evicted from their ship, sent back through the rim wall by an angry protector."

Bram waited.

"Poor tanj Prill. That could twist a person's mind."
Waited.

"So there's already a few attitude jets back in place, but all Teela sees is that the ship builders haven't stolen them all yet.

She takes over Anne's job. It's urgent. She turns some breeders into protectors. She told me about those: a Spill Mountain People, a vampire, a Ghoul. They all start pulling motors out of returning ships and remounting them.

"They had twenty in place and no more ships in view, and the motors didn't have enough power by themselves. Teela left the other protectors tending the motors. She came back to the Repair Center. She must have known what she was going to do next. She didn't see *Hot Needle of Inquiry* coming at her until she was using the Repair Center telescope again."

Acolyte said, "She must have had a telescope on the rim, Louis."

"Sure, and it must have been good enough to see the big City Builder ships coming in. *Needle*'s much smaller."

"Would she recognize *Needle?*"

"A General Products number-three hull? Sure."

Bram asked, "How could *Needle* affect her plans?"

"What did I tell you about reading a protector's mind, Bram?"

"But you must try."

Louis didn't *want* to try. "Here's what Teela told me. She just couldn't make herself kill a trillion people even to save thirty trillion. Protector intelligence and Teela Brown empathy: she could feel their deaths. She knew it had to be done, and she knew we'd figure out how, me and Chmeee and the Hindmost, and she couldn't let us do it, either. She was inviting us to kill her, Bram."

"I watched her fight. I could have fought better while dead."

"Yah. It was the fight of my life, but nobody outfights a protector."

"If she knew she couldn't play a plasma jet along the rim

wall, why did she return to the Repair Center?" Silly question. Bram didn't wait for an answer. "What did she really want?"

Louis shook his head. "What do protectors want? That's one thing we learned about you. Your motives are hard-wired. You protect your genetic line. When the line dies out, you stop eating and die. Teela didn't have children on the Ringworld, but there were hominids. Relatives, if you close one eye and squint a little. She *had* to save them. Why wait? With the Ringworld sliding off balance—"

Bram brushed it away. "She waited for *Hot Needle of Inquiry*, for puppeteer-derived computer programs. I watched you use them and was glad I had not interfered."

Oh. "But why not just say so? Tanj dammit, why the fight?" Wait, now—"Bram, did Anne leave just after you killed Cronus?"

"She took several days to prepare."

"And that was just under seven thousand falans ago?"

"Yes."

"Around twelve hundred A.D., my calendar. Did she take roots? And does she have to come back for more?"

"Anne took roots and a blooming plant and some thalium oxide. She planted tree-of-life but the crop failed after a time, so she came back near five thousand falans ago. She stayed with me for not long. I haven't seen her since. Either she grew a better garden or she's dead."

"Yah. Teela had the same idea? Roots, plants, thallium oxide. If there's a good place to plant all that, then Anne's garden was in it. Teela would know what it was."

"Anne would hide it well."

"You can't hide plants from sunlight. She couldn't put it where any passing hominid would sniff it. She'd want it within her reach, on a spill mountain, in a place even hot-air balloons couldn't invade. A fissure, a steep valley, maybe. And now we have to *guess* whether Teela saw it."

"And if she did?"

Louis sighed. "Bram, what have you got on *living* protectors?"

"Hindmost, show him. I propose to bathe."

Chapter Twenty-Five

DEFAULT

OPTION

A hundred miles above the spill mountain tops, the probe accelerated. The Ringworld raced toward and past it like a frozen river bigger than worlds, but no longer at 770 miles per second. The probe was catching up.

Louis asked the puppeteer, "Are we in view of that comet installation you didn't blast?"

"Yes, it's far enough above the Ringworld plane, but we will have landed before the light reaches the comet."

Acolyte reclined, huge and silent. Chmeee had sent him to learn, and he had been learning from Bram for these past 2.2 falans. Teaching him *wisdom* would be a neat trick, Louis thought. Protectors had intelligence coming out of their ears, but *wisdom*? Could a Kzin see the difference?

"And you've blasted everything else that can see us."

"Yes."

"Stet. Show us the rim."

"I can't really show you protectors, Louis. It's what Bram asked, but I cannot magnify so greatly."

"What have you got?"

The Hindmost had months, falans, of observing the rim

wall and the spill mountains. Winking heliographs were everywhere, not just on the rim wall. Several times the probe had caught daylit flashes from—one presumed—client species on the flatlands.

A village flashed past, and the Hindmost froze it for their eyes: a thousand houses spreading out from one side of a magnificent waterfall, eight to ten thousand feet high. On the other side of the falls, a dockyard for hot air balloons, marked by a cliff splashed with bright orange paint. Below the dockyard, clustered factories and warehouses ran down the ice and rocks to another orange boulder and a lower landing pad. Come in high or come in low, travelers would find refuge.

The Hindmost jumped the view to another village fifty million miles away. It spread across a shallow green hillside: houses with sloped sod roofs, and a vertical row of industrial works with orange-marked landing pads above and below.

Louis said, "Acolyte, you've seen a lot more of this than I have. What am I likely to miss?"

"I can't guess what you might miss, Louis. They have no more problem with garbage disposal than a school of fish. They—"

Louis laughed widely, white teeth showing. Acolyte waited it out. "Their houses differ but their placement follows a pattern. Balloons and factories are alike everywhere. Bram and I surmise that the Night People mirrors can relay designs, maps, weather alerts, perhaps written music: a trade in ideas."

"Trade between stars is like that."

The rim wall was a continuous sheet of scrith, of Ringworld floor material as strong as the force that held an atomic nucleus together. Even that force wasn't as strong as a meteoroid moving at Ringworld speed, and Louis noted a punch hole high up on the rim wall, a few million miles antispin from the *other* Great Ocean. Otherwise the great empty mountings stood three million miles apart along a featureless rim, and a slender thread ran along the top for a third of its length. They'd seen that eleven years ago: a maglev track, never finished.

Twenty-three of the mounts now held motors. At highest magnification, the tiny pairs of toroids were just visible.

"Here is what they look like firing." The puppeteer jumped the view, fast-forward.

The change was not great. Hydrogen fusion radiates mostly X rays. A fusion motor radiates visible light because it is hot, or because working mass has been added to increase thrust. When a rim wall motor was firing, the wire outline glowed white-hot, and flexed against the plasma's magnetic fields. The toroids were the wasp-waist constriction in an hourglass of white-hot wire, and an indigo ghost flame ran down the axis. Twenty-two of those in a row.

The Hindmost displayed successive views of work around the twenty-third motor. There were cranes and cables big enough to see, and flatbed things that might be used for magnetic levitation, but not a hope of seeing anything man-sized.

And all Louis could think of was his need to talk where Bram couldn't hear.

The protector was using the bath setup in the crew cabin. No doubt that equipment had kept Chmeee and Louis sane, and Harkabeeparolyn and Kawaresksenjajok, too. Still, it was cramped and complicated and primitive. They could hear the whisper of spray through the wall.

Louis said, testing, "Given he bathes at all, I'm surprised he didn't use your cabin."

"Louis, I wish now that I *could* show you my cabin. The dedicated stepping disk is hardwired. It *cannot* move an alien."

The Kzin rumbled, "You value your privacy greatly."

"You know better. I want company," the Hindmost said. "Louis or even you, if I cannot surround myself with my kind. We follow our fears. I followed my fear when I shaped this ship."

"You persuaded Bram of that?"

"I hope so. It's true."

The probe was an hour short of matching the Ringworld's spin. Louis said, "We're going to have to use pressure suits. Let's do something about them."

"I keep my own well-maintained," the puppeteer said.

"Stet. Send me and Acolyte to the lander bay."

"I should come," the Hindmost said. "There's other equipment I should see to."

They flicked out.

"We cannot be heard here," the Hindmost assured them.

Acolyte snorted. Louis said, "Suppose a protector-level intelligence *really* wanted to hear us?"

"No, Louis. I intended to spy on you and Chmeee and—" Harkabeeparolyn hadn't made the cut. "I made this my listening post. No entity could add a spy device in the lander bay without signaling me."

Maybe. "Hindmost, aren't you safe when you're in your own cabin?"

"Bram has a way to attack me there."

"Can you block it?"

"I haven't worked out what he has."

"A good bluff? Bram's had a long time to work on you. He has you terrified."

The Hindmost's gaze converged on Louis: binocular vision

with a baseline of three feet. "You have never understood us. The hidden protector frightened me from the first. I remain frightened. However you plan to circumvent Bram, I may accept the risk or reject it, but only on the odds. I do not turn my mind from danger."

"I don't expect to break my contract."

"Excellent."

There were pressure suits and air racks designed for humans. He and Bram would need two of everything. Louis checked pressure zips on the suits and the racks. He emptied waste recycler reservoirs and filled nutrient reservoirs, flushed the interiors of the suits and the air and water tanks, topped off the air, charged the batteries.

Acolyte was tending his own suit. The Hindmost was inspecting a stack of stepping disks.

Louis said, "I know why Teela Brown died."

The Hindmost said, "Protectors die fairly easily, when they no longer feel needed—"

Louis shook his head. "She found something. Maybe it was Anne's garden, maybe just fingerprints on the rim wall motors. Whatever, she knew there was a protector in the Repair Center. She had to get *Needle* into the Map of Mars, but when she did that, she made us hostages. The only way to make us safe was to die. But—"

"Louis, we don't have time. What do you want of us?"

"I want to change the stepping disk pattern without Bram knowing. Then I may want to change it back. I'm not sure I'm right yet. I need a default option."

The Kzin asked, "Default option?"

The Hindmost answered, "Decide in advance what you will do if you don't have time to decide."

"Like the first move you learn in fighting with a Kzin dagger, a wtsai," Louis said. "If you're attacked too fast to think, there's your training."

"The disembowel."

"Whatever. I just knew there must be one. Epees and hand-guns and hand-to-hand and *yogatsu*, it doesn't matter: you train the moves into your reflex arcs so you don't have to make up something while you're being attacked. Likewise, you instruct a computer on what to do if you don't tell it what to do."

"Clever notion," said the Kzin.

"Hindmost, I don't quite understand your stepping disk network . . ."

They discussed it. The system wanted to know that you really meant the change you'd whistled or typed in. *Push the edge of the disk down.*

"Stet. Now I can do this and you cannot notice. We have deniability. Acolyte, I'll need a distraction."

"See if you can describe it," Acolyte said.

"I haven't the faintest bloody idea. I only need it for about two breaths."

As they flicked through to the cabin, the Hindmost was saying, "Louis, are you aware that you were dying?"

Louis smiled faintly. "Tradition says that everyone is dying. Exceptions may be made for puppeteers and protectors. Hello, Bram. Any change?"

Bram was in a rage. "Hindmost, amplify the light and zoom. The village!"

The probe was moving through shadow; but much closer than the distant oncoming band of daylight was a glimpse of pattern crusting the dim snow-colors of a passing spill mountain.

The Hindmost sang flute and strings. The pattern brightened and began to expand.

The spill mountain village looked like a great blotchy
cross seen from almost overhead. Houses were white of a different shade from the snowfields: sloped roofs under a snow
blanket, strung out along ledges on a background of naked
rock and snow laced with dark paths, sparsely patterned along
twenty miles and more. Factories and warehouses crossed that
band vertically, much more closely clustered, running from six
to ten thousand feet high. At top and bottom were angular
blobs of bright orange and bits of other colors, too.

Bram's temper was under tight control. "You were needed.
I feared the probe would pass before you returned. Can you
see why that might be a concern?"

"Not . . . yes."

Then Louis saw, too. Three bright silver squares: three of
the oversized cargo plates. One was bare; one was loaded with
cargo, hard to see for what it was. The third, a brown square
with a bright rim: the Machine People cruiser still riding its
cargo plate. It was tethered at the upper dock next to a naked
rock cliff painted bright orange, and two patches of yellow
and orange and cobalt blue: deflated balloons.

"That was a quick ride," Louis said.

Daylight swept upon them at 770 miles per second. The
view flashed bright, then dimmed to truer colors.

Acolyte reminded them: "They have their own webeye."

The Hindmost popped up a window next to the probe's—
four now. They were now seeing through the bow of the
cruiser.

Here were Red Herders muffled in lovely furs striped gray
and white. Louis only glimpsed red hands in long loose
sleeves, flat noses and dark eyes deep within hoods, but who

else could they be? The Fearless Vampire Slayers. Several larger furry shapes must be Spill Mountain People. Their hands were broad, with thick, stubby fingers. Glimpses of faces inside hoods were silver-gray, like the hands.

They panted out puffs of frost as they worked. Red hands and brown hands gripped the fuzzy edges of the window, and the view wobbled.

The Hindmost said, "The probe will be well past before we can slow. Shall I bring it back for another view?"

Bram said, "Why? We have our view. Hindmost, we're closing on the near end of the rim wall transport rail, and possible witnesses. Take the probe over the rim when you can."

"Aye aye. Twelve minutes."

The probe was in full daylight now, leaving the village far aft. The dismounted webeye was in jerky motion, carried along footholds and handholds chopped in stone. Windows overlaid on windows.

Bram asked, "Where have you been?"

Louis answered. "The time to check a pressure suit—"

"Yes. Report."

"—is before you're breathing vacuum—"

"You used a checklist. I use my mind."

"And your first mistake will be memorable."

"Report."

"I can't speak for a puppeteer's suit. Ours will keep us alive for two falans. We refilled and recharged everything fillable and chargeable. The Hindmost still has six stepping disks not in use, and we can recycle some of what we're using now. We can put webeyes anywhere. There aren't any weapons in the lander bay. I assume you've stored them somewhere. You decide what you want us to be carrying. We couldn't think of anything else to check."

Bram said nothing.

Hidden Patriarch's crow's nest showed no change, and the Hindmost whistle-bonged that window off. The refueling probe ran along a rim wall touched with violet. The next window over rolled wobbling along a path that had become more than a rock climb, downhill toward rectangular patches of snow.

The Hindmost said, "You were dying."

"Did you see . . . never mind," Louis said. "Show me that medical report."

The puppeteer chimed. Louis Wu's medical record partly blocked both windows. "There, it's in Interspeak."

Chemical . . . major restructure . . . diverticulosis . . . tanj. "You can get used to what age does to you, Hindmost. Old people used to say, 'If you can wake up in the morning with nothing hurting anywhere, it's a sign that you have died in the night.' "

"Not funny."

"But even an idiot might guess something's wrong when he starts pissing gas with his urine."

"I would have thought it rude to observe you at such a time."

"I am much relieved. Even so, would you have noticed?" Louis read further. "Diverticulosis, that's little blowout patches on your colon—*my* colon. Diverticuli can hurt you lots of ways. Mine seems to have extended far enough to attach itself to my bladder. Then it got infected and blew through. That left a tube connecting my colon and my bladder. A fistula."

"What did you think?"

"I had the medkit. It was giving me antibiotics. For a couple of days I hoped . . . well, bacteria can get into a human bladder and make gas, but antibiotics would have cleared that up. So I knew I needed a plumber."

Acolyte didn't usually stare directly into anyone's eyes, but he did now. His ears were folded out of sight. "You were dying? Dying when you refused the Hindmost's offers?"

"Yes. Hindmost, if you'd known, would you have accepted my contract?"

"Not a serious question. Louis, I'm expressing admiration. You are a *scary* negotiator."

"*Thank* you."

Bram said, "Please restore our view from the probe ... *Thank* you. In six minutes we'll move up the rim wall and cross to the outside. I trust we won't lose the signal, Hindmost."

"Scrith stops a percentage of neutrinos. Implied is some kind of nuclear reaction ongoing in the Ringworld floor, but the signal will dwindle predictably and I can compensate."

Bram said, "Good. Is *my* suit in order?"

"It's my spare, after all," Louis said. "Take whichever suit feels lucky to you. I'll take the other."

The probe was slowing, slowing.

"Now?"

"Now."

Chapter Twenty-Six

THE

DOCKYARD

The cruiser and its cargo plate rose through the night. Warvia and Tegger clung to each other in the payload shell. Fear of heights was a terrible thing. They both shrieked when they felt the bump, then laughed because they were still alive.

Leaving the protection of the payload shell was an ordeal. They gasped and shivered in the thin, cold air. The sun was just peeping around a shadow square.

The Ghouls blinked in the growing daylight and crawled into the payload shell to sleep.

Harpster had brought them down at the higher of two orange-splashed cliffs, alongside another floating plate and three baskets attached to collapsed balloons.

The village was stirring. Downslope and to the sides, furred shapes moved out from snow-roofed houses to forage in the tilted lands beyond.

Even to a nomad like Tegger, this wasn't a large village. Then again, it was nearly invisible. The roofs were rectangles of snow on a snowfield; you picked them out by their shadows.

Five locals were trudging uphill to meet the visitors from below. A raptor-beaked bird circled about them. The Red Herders watched them come, but they couldn't see anything inside their furs. They carried water bags and more furs.

The water was heated. It tasted wonderful. Warvia and Tegger struggled into furs in frantic haste, pulling them closed until only their noses showed. That and their gasping seemed to amuse the Spill Mountain People.

"Na, na, it's lovely day!" Saron sang in a nearly impenetrable accent. "You walk in blizzard. Teach you respect mountain!"

They walked around the wood and iron cruiser, paying no attention to the floating plate it rode on.

The five Spill Mountain People looked like barrels sheathed in layers of white-and-gray-striped fur. Saron's fur was different: striped white and greenish-brown, with a hood that had been some ferocious creature's head. Her rank must be distinctive, Tegger thought, and decided that Saron was a woman. She was the smallest of the five. Her voice gave no clue and her furs hid all details.

Saron was studying the bronze spinnerweb and its stone backing. She asked, "Is this the eye?"

Warvia said, "Yes. Saron, we don't know what to do next."

"We were told Night People would come. Where are they?"

"Sleeping. It isn't night yet."

Saron laughed. "My mother told me it was only a way of speaking. They come out at night?"

The Reds nodded.

The bird hovered above them, riding the wind, then suddenly dropped far downslope. It struck talons first, and rose with something struggling in its beak.

Deb asked, "What must the eye see?"

Tegger and Warvia had no idea. This must have been obvious, and Deb answered herself. "The mirror and the passage. Take the eye with us. Does it talk?"

"No."

"How do you know it sees?"

"Ask Harpster and Grieving Tube."

Warvia said, "I'm going to cover them. They could freeze to death up here."

"Good," Jennawil said, and they carried furs into the payload shell.

Harreed and Barraye were at work dismounting the bronze web and its backing. Tegger had decided they were men. Though they peered out of their hoods in frank astonishment at the Red Herders, they were silent. It seemed the women did all the talking.

Tegger tried to help them. As he scuttled sideways carrying one edge of the stone-backed web, he found himself gasping, suffocating. Deb and Jennawil moved in to help. Tegger got out of their way, fighting for breath.

"You're feeble," Saron decided.

Tegger tried to quiet his gasping. "We can walk."

"Your lungs don't find enough air. You will be stronger tomorrow. Today you must rest."

The four picked up the web and began to climb, angling downhill, toward the snow-roofed houses. Saron walked ahead to point out footholds to Warvia and Tegger, ready to steady them if they slipped.

The bird dropped onto the leather pad that crossed Deb's shoulders. Deb staggered and swore at it in some alien language, and it rose again.

Spill Mountain People seemed incredibly surefooted.

Tegger and Warvia walked with their arms around each other, trying to stay upright. They'd been in motion too long.

The mountain seemed to sway beneath them. The wind searched out every tiniest gap in their furs. Tegger peeped out of his hood through slitted eyes, blinking away tears.

He had some of his breath back. He asked Deb, "That was your own tongue, yes? How did you learn the trade speech?"

Deb's vowels and consonants were distorted. He had to catch the sense above the shrilling of the wind. "Night People say, tell you everything. But you, you tell the flatland *vishnishtee* nothing. Keep our secrets. Yes?"

Tegger didn't know the word, but Warvia caught it. She told him, "*Vashnesht*," enunciating it properly, and told the others, "Yes."

Vashnesht: protectors. Keep secrets from the protectors from below the spill mountains. "Yes," said Tegger.

Deb said, "Teela came from below, from the flats. A strange person, all knobs, could not resh. You understand, reshtra? Could not. Nothing there. She let us look.

"She taught us to speak. We knew the speech of the mirrors, but we spoke it wrong. Teela taught us, then told us teach the people who ride the balloons.

"Then she went through the passage. Came back seventy falans later, no change in her. We thought she was a *vishnishtee*, but now we *knew*."

They were passing houses now: rectilinear houses made of wood that must have been imported from the forest below. They'd picked up an entourage of curious children: eyes peeking out from fur hoods, and chattering that came in puffs of fog. Warvia was trying to answer them.

Tegger asked, "May we speak to this Teela?"

"Teela went below again, since forty falans or more," Deb said.

"More," Saron said flatly.

Jennawil asked, "What do you know of reshtra?"

Tegger looked at Warvia. Warvia temporized. "How can you know of rishathra? Do you have other visitors from below?"

The locals laughed, even the men. Deb said, "Not from below, but from sideways! Folk visit from nearby mountains—"

"But they're all Spill Mountain People, aren't they?"

"Wairbeea, the people of the mountains are not all one kind. We are High Point. Saron—"

Here, a door. Tegger eased Warvia in ahead of him. The bird settled on Deb's shoulder as she entered.

This narrow space was not the house proper, only a tiny anteroom supported by wooden beams and lines with hooks for furs. Doors at the far end opened opposite each other.

Now the furs started to come off. The two species stared at one another, fiercely curious.

High Point People were broad through the torso, broad across the face, with wide mouths and deep-set eyes. Their hair and—on the men—beards were curly and dark. Beneath their furs was cloth enclosing their torsos to the elbows and knees, and below the cuffs, a good deal of curly hair.

Deb was a strong woman in middle age. The bird, Skreepu, belonged to Deb. So did the identical-looking young men, Harreed and Barraye: they were her sons. Jennawil was a young woman mated to Barraye.

And Saron was a woman, deep of voice, old and deeply wrinkled. Something about her jaw, her hands: Warvia asked, "Are you of High Point?"

"No, from Two Peaks. A balloon carried us to High Point, far past Short One, where we wanted to visit. The wind blows wrong here. We could not return. The rest flew on, exploring, but I found my man Makray persuasive. He cannot have more children, I have had mine, why not?"

While Deb removed her fur and hung it, Skreepu clung to the leather patch. When Saron led the rest into the main house, the great bird lifted and followed them.

The ceiling was high. Furniture was minimal. There was a high perch for the bird, two low tables, no chairs. This was half of the visitors' house, divided from the other half by the long anteroom. Tegger wondered if he would meet whatever visitors were living on the other side.

The men propped the bronze web against the wall. Then the High Pointers settled cross-legged in a circle that left space for their visitors.

"This is your place, the visitors' house," Saron said. "It is warm enough for most who come, but you may want to sleep in fur."

Jennawil waved about her. "We are High Point. Next spinward call themselves Eagle Folk. Noses like beaks. They're smaller than we are and not as strong, but their balloons are best we have seen, and they sell balloons to other folk. We can get children with them, but so rarely that we resh with little risk.

"To antispin are Ice People. They live higher and the cold hurts them less. Mazarestch got a boy by an Ice People man. The way she tells it, their exertion moved mountain. The boy Jarth can forage higher than any of his peers.

"Visitors come from far spin and antispin. We welcome them all and resh with them, too, but we get no children together. They tell us it is the same for them. Reshtra is for different kinds, mating is between two of a kind. Folk of near mountains can mate, those from too far cannot. Teela told us that our foreparents must have traveled from mountain to mountain, changing as we went.

"And you?"

Warvia was laughing too hard to speak, less amused than embarrassed, Tegger thought. He tried to put an answer together. "On the flat land travel is easy. We have all species mixed. We see every possible way of rishathra. We Red Herders travel with the animals we tend, for all of our lives. We cannot rish. We only mate once."

He could not tell how they were reacting to that: their faces were too unfamiliar. He said, "But some kinds rish for pleasure, some for trade contracts or to end a war or to postpone a child. We hear of Weed Gatherers, near mindless, who rish very nicely, convenient for ones who won't take the time to—to court. Water People will rish with anyone who can hold his or her breath for long enough, but few there are—"

"Water People?"

"Live under liquid water, Barraye. I guess you don't have many of those."

Laughter. Jennawil asked Warvia, "You don't rish, but only you listen?"

"What else is there for my kind when visitors come? But you'll want to speak to the Night People when they wake."

Tegger saw Jennawil trying to keep a straight face.

"Please understand," Saron said, "we have only resh with species from near mountains. Spill mountain species, all of us, all very like each other even if we cannot get children. You . . ." She searched for words and found none.

A bit strange? Very queer? Demons from below? Before the silence could grow yet less comfortable, Warvia said, "We hear that protectors can pierce any secret. How can you hope to hide anything?"

"From flatland *vishnishtee*," Deb said.

Saron explained. "*Vishnishtee* are a danger. Teela told us so, the Night People tell us, and the legends tell us, too. But the passage belongs to High Point. The passage is of interest to *vishnishtee*. The passage pierces the rim wall. They can go out of the world through the passage if they wear their balloon suits and helms with windows. The Night People don't like to draw attention from *vishnishtee*."

"You have protectors here?"

It seemed clear that Saron was speaking for the bronze web as well as Tegger and Warvia. "Three flatland *vishnishtee* rule the passage. More: they have taken some of us away, older ones, and some of those come back to us as *vishnishtee*.

"When the Death Light shone, the flatland *vishnishtee* showed us how to hide. Sod or rock is enough to stop the light that shines through fur and flesh, but better was to hide in the passage itself. Makray was hunting when the Death Light shone," Saron said. "Half a day from shelter, and no *vishnishtee* to tell him he wanted it."

Deb said, "Many of us went to hunt, or were caught out. One of every three died. Odd and feeble children were born after. All the mountains about tell the same tale, and only we and the mountains nearby had *vishnishtee* to give warning. Flatland *vishnishtee* are not wholly evil."

Tegger asked, "Death Light?"

But none of the High Pointers chose to hear, and Tegger didn't ask again. Saron said, "High Point *vishnishtee* serve the flatland *vishnishtee* to keep us safe. But they will not tell the flatland *vishnishtee* where we have the mirror, and those will not learn of themselves. They are good at knowing secrets, but the mountains are not theirs."

Warvia sighed. "The Night People will be very glad of your answers. We've traveled vastly to find them. No doubt they'll have better questions."

"And Louis Wu," Deb said. "Or is he only a tale?"

"Where did you hear it?"

"From message mirrors and from Teela."

Tegger said, "Louis Wu boiled an ocean. The City Builder Halrloprillalar traded and rished with him. Louis Wu is real, but is he on the other side of that spinnerweb? Deb, I need sleep."

Warvia said, "Yes!"

Jennawil expressed the others' surprise. "It is the middle of the day."

"We worked through the night. *Breathing* is labor," Warvia said.

"Let them sleep now," Saron ordered. "We go. Teegr, Wairbeea, will you wake when the Night People do?"

Tegger could hardly keep his thoughts together or his eyes apart. "We may hope."

"Food behind that door. Flup, we forgot! What do you eat?"

"Freshly killed meat," Warvia said.

"Behind those little doors—no, never mind. Skreepu will find you something. Sleep well." The High Point People filed out.

They *had* to look behind the little doors, and that let half the heat out of the house. Opening the little doors revealed food—visitor food, plants and old meat, not Red Herder food—and snowscape seen through wooden slats. Bars to keep away predators, and the great outside to keep food cold.

Warvia and Tegger curled together, fur beneath them, fur above. They'd set their clothes aside to air. They were warm enough, but Tegger could feel the cold at his nose. He could hear knocking behind the wall as the High Pointers donned their furs.

He was near sleep when Warvia said, "Whisper would have better questions."

He said, "Whisper was only my madness."

"Mine, too. Whisper taught me things—"

"What?"

Warvia whispered in his ear. "She was with us on the air sled, beneath the cruiser. She taught me about speed so that our speed would not drive me mad. She keeps herself a secret, Tegger. I don't want the web to hear us."

They'd propped the web upright against a wall. Tegger looked at the web, propped against a wall with a view of the whole room, and laughed. "If the web is no more than a slice of stone—"

"We will all seem great fools."

"What does Whisper look like?"

"I never saw. Perhaps a wayspirit with no body at all."

"What did she teach? No, don't tell me now. We should sleep."

"Why did you say we cannot rish? Was it the way they look?"

"No. They're no stranger than Sand People. My mind saw me in Jennawil's arms, gasping like a beached fish—"

Warvia laughed deliciously against his ear.

"Then I remembered that they talk with—talk *for*—the Ghoul empire. We would be famous. Did you want to settle somewhere, someday, where no Red Herder has heard of Red Herders who rish with every species under the Arch?"

"We never did that!"

"Tales grow in the telling. They are mighty tellers, the Ghoul empire, and these Spill Mountain People speak their words for them, and you and I destroyed the biggest nest of vampires beneath the Arch."

"Yes."

"You were thinking—"

"They are new to this. They have only rished with peoples very like them. Love, would you like to *teach* rishathra, if only once?"

They slept.

Chapter Twenty-Seven

LOVECRAFT

The probe tilted over and rose at ten gravities straight up, closing on the rim wall. The blue highlight converged, then went out. The probe coasted, rising.

The Ringworld's edge was narrow. The probe rose a few hundred feet higher, and arced over. A puff of fusion flame halted its fall and set it drifting toward the shadowed back of a black wall that seemed to reach to the heavens.

It slowed. Hovered. The probe spat.

A window popped up to overlay the others. It showed the probe hovering on indigo flame; then the probe dropped away and it showed only starlight.

The Hindmost said, "I give you a webeye window beyond the rim wall."

"We need a view from the underside. Get us that," Bram commanded.

"Aye aye." But the Hindmost was doing nothing.

"Hindmost!"

"The probe already has my instructions. Motors off. Rotate. I want a view."

The probe was turning as it fell. The view turned: black

rim wall, sunglare, starscape . . . a silver thread was shining against the star-spattered black below the falling probe.

"That!" Louis said. "See it? You need a burn or we'll hit it."

"Burn, aye aye." A burst of woodwinds, then, "What is it?"

"Not a spaceport ledge, it's too narrow."

They waited through the lightspeed delay. The silver thread was growing larger, clearer. Now it seemed banded, like a silver earthworm. Eleven minutes . . .

The probe's spin stopped. Window displays tremored: the probe was thrusting, flaring in X-ray light.

Nova light blasted through the hologram window.

Louis, with his arms thrown over his eyes, heard music from hell, then a voice that had lost all human traits. "My fuel source is destroyed!"

Bram's voice was cool. "My concern is for the enemy that fired on us."

"We are challenged! Arm me and send me through!" A bestial bellow, all madness. *Acolyte's idea of a distraction? Or are we locked in with a mad Kzin?*

"Let me through to my cabin," the Hindmost pleaded. "I must see what is still working."

"What could be working? Your probe is destroyed and we are attacked, we are known. Could an invader react so quickly, or was that a protector?"

"The stepping disk at least should be safe."

Louis opened his eyes. "Why?"

"I'm not a fool!" the Hindmost bleated. "I opened a stepping disk link as we crossed the rim. A plasma blast, kinetic weapons, any threat should go straight through."

"Straight through to *what?*" Louis blinked. He was still seeing spots.

"I linked it to the stepping disk at the map of Mons Olympus."

Louis laughed. It was probably too much to hope for, that a thousand Martians were setting a new trap when the stepping disk sprayed star-hot plasma over them, but heyyy . . .

Big claws closed on his shoulders; warm red meat breathed in his face. "We are at war, Louis Wu! This is not a time for distractions!"

Distractions. Stet. "Acolyte, go suit up. Get my suit, and a webeye sprayer, too, and my cargo disk stack, wherever Bram—Bram?"

"Dining hall aboard *Hidden Patriarch*," Bram said.

"Hindmost, route him there first. Bram, get him some weapons. If we have a working stepping disk on the probe, we should use it."

Bram said, "Go."

The Hindmost rattled/chimed/bonged. Acolyte stepped and flicked out. The Hindmost stepped where the granite block had been and was gone, was in his cabin, his tongues licking out at what looked like an alien chess set but must be a virtual keyboard. One head rose to say, "We have a link. The stepping disk still operates."

"Try the webeye sprayer," Bram ordered.

"Spray what?"

"Vacuum."

Eleven minutes later the blacked-out window lit again: a revolving starscape with a slow ripple to it. Louis could picture a webeye falling free through vacuum, spinning a little— was the probe spinning too?—drifting gradually away from the probe. And while the protector was worrying about the Kzin and trying to watch the puppeteer and all *four* hologram windows, Louis knelt above the stepping disk and lifted the edge.

A tiny hologram of glowing sticks rose just above the disk itself: the map of the stepping disk system. A larger display would have given him away, but the Hindmost had fixed that. Louis tapped his changes in quickly and pushed the rim down.

"Do you see?"

"Hindmost, explain to see me how we could have missed *that* until now!"

Bram and the Hindmost sure as tanj weren't watching *him*. Louis turned.

As viewed through the free-falling webeye, the silver thread had become a silver ribbon with raised edges, a shallow trough not unlike a miniature of the Ringworld itself. Slender toroids arced over it.

Unmistakably, it was the transport system: the magnetic levitation track that ran along the top of the rim wall for a third of its length. Teela's repair crew must have led it over the rim wall and down the outside.

Louis said, "Well, *I* haven't been watching the rim wall for a good half year."

"We should have looked closer," the Hindmost said.

The silver rail swept past. Now there was only starscape. The fluttering webeye was below the Ringworld floor, falling into the universe.

Louis said, "I might have guessed. You, too, Bram. What else would Teela's crew use to move their reclaimed ramjets?"

"The terminus is far to spinward, perhaps on a spaceport ledge. We're in the wrong place to be looking for a factory."

Stacked cargo plates flicked in, with pressure gear and a webeye sprayer added to Louis's clutter. Louis shouldered the floating mass aside to leave room for Acolyte.

The Kzin flicked in wearing full pressure gear: concentric

clear balloons and a fishbowl helmet. He tipped back the helmet and asked, "Are we ready?"

Louis gestured at a rippling starscape. "You don't want to flick into *that*."

Unexpectedly, the Hindmost said, "The link is still open and has stopped moving."

Louis said, "What . . . ?"

Bram snapped, "Sprayed with plasma flame, dropped for a thousand miles, and it *still works*? Improbable!"

Louis took the webeye sprayer off the stacked cargo plates. "Try it."

Heads turned. They didn't get it. Louis said, "Hindmost, I want to spray a webeye through the stepping disk link. Set me up. We'll just see what it hits."

The Hindmost whistled. "Try," he said.

Louis sprayed a bronze net at the stepping disk and saw it vanish.

They waited. Acolyte used the time to take a shower. Thirty-five degrees of Ringworld arc: five and a half minutes in transit, and the same again before they'd *see* it arrive. Transfer booths didn't work faster than lightspeed, and neither, it seemed, did stepping disks.

"Signal," the Hindmost said as his other tongue licked out. A fifth window popped up.

They looked up at stars crossed by the rim wall. A fuzzy bulk at the edge might be the probe. A lousy view—but the probe wasn't falling. It had landed on a tiny target, the maglev track.

Bram said, "Acolyte, take the sprayer. Go through. Spray us a camera where we might see something interesting. Return instantly and report. Don't wait for danger. We know it's there."

Too fast. Louis was just beginning to pull his suit on. Acolyte would be gone before he was ready. He said, "Hold it. Bram, he's got to be armed!"

"Against protectors already on site? I prefer Acolyte to be conspicuously unarmed. Acolyte, go."

The Kzin flicked out.

Louis finished getting into his suit. They'd have eleven minutes to wait.

Did Chmeee really think an old man like him, Louis wondered, could restrain and protect an eleven-year-old Kzin male?

It had been four minutes, and something was in view.

They watched a dark blur moving around the blurred edges of the window, inspecting the probe at its leisure. Then suddenly it was clear and close, an elegant alien pressure suit with a bubble helmet, and a near-triangular face with a mouth that seemed to be all bone. A single fingertip came closer yet, and traced curves Louis couldn't see. It had found the webeye.

It snapped around quicksilver-fast, and still wasn't quick enough. Something fast and black brushed across it and leapt away, out of range, gone.

The elegant intruder's suit was slashed wide along the left side. It lifted a weapon like an old-fashioned chemical rocket motor. Violet-white flame lashed after the attacker. It must have missed. The elegant one bounded after, holding its suit almost closed with one hand, firing with the other. A ghost-trail of ice crystals followed it.

Bram said, "That was Anne."

"Which?"

"Anne was the killer, Louis. They're both vampire protectors, but I remember how Anne moves."

"How do we warn Acolyte?"

"We cannot."

Louis caught himself grinding his teeth. Acolyte was nowhere: a signal, a point, an energy quantum moving at light-speed toward where one protector had killed another and was ready for more.

"Your Teela was too trusting," Bram said. "She made a vampire into a protector, and that one must have changed others of his species before Teela killed him. But Anne and I are of another species than theirs."

"Signal," the Hindmost said as his other tongue licked out. Now they had two windows placed on the maglev transport track.

Acolyte had arrived; had sprayed a webeye on . . . Louis couldn't tell. On something above his head. There was no sign of another intruder. The Kzin posed with the probe just behind him. It looked half melted and somewhat battered, and it was blocking the track.

Any protector would have to remove that blockage.

Acolyte, get out!

The track receded into infinity. It looked to be around two hundred feet across, and geometrically straight.

Acolyte was turning slowly, taking it all in. He sprayed another webeye, then stepped back to the probe and was gone.

The Hindmost said, "He flicked out."

"Well, where is he?"

"Do you assume I want fusion plasma spraying through my cabin?"

"Where's the link? Where did you flick him?" The Hindmost didn't answer, and Louis knew. "Mons Olympus, you freemother?"

He lunged toward the stepping disk, stopped himself, and scrambled onto the stack of cargo plates instead. He led a line through the handholds, then around his tool belt: a poor man's crash web. "Chmeee will have my ears and guts!" He set the cargo plates aloft and eased them onto the stepping disk.

Flick, and the sky was half stars, half black. Silver fractal filigree under his feet and stars showing through that.

Marvelous.

He looked up and down the maglev track. It was peaceful as hell. Nothing moved at all.

Silver lace. Where had he seen this kind of fractal pattern? He'd expected the maglev track to be a solid trough, but you could see stars through the mesh.

Hah! It was the Pinwheel, the old orbital tether they still used to transfer bulk cargos between Earth and the moon and Belt. The fractal distributed the stresses better. But never mind that—

"Bram, Hindmost, the maglev track is *lacework*. Can you see it? If I had the sprayer, I'd put a webeye on it right now. Look through the lace and see whatever tries to hide in the Ringworld's shadow."

They'd hear that in five and a half minutes. *Hot Needle of Inquiry* was that far away at lightspeed.

An ink blot pulled itself over the edge and walked toward Louis . . . a bulk like a sack of potatoes painted black, with a flared bell held negligently in one hand.

Louis touched the lift throttle.

The cargo plates didn't move. There was a maglev track under him, but it wasn't giving him enough lift.

"I'm looking at an ARM weapon," Louis said. They'd hear him and know the rest: ARMs must have landed on a spaceport ledge and found protectors there.

How do you activate stepping disks when you can't step off first? I'll be dead when they hear all this. Should have brought an orchestra—or a recording of the command.

The protector-killer examined Louis Wu with a proprietary air. It—Anne—She was a slender shape in an inflated suit designed for something a little taller—recessed eyes peeped over the chin readouts—and much wider—

Flick, he was upside down and falling through red light.

It was red rock all around him and below his head, and hundreds of feet of smooth lava running down, down. The cargo plates surged upward, and Louis hung head-down over red rocks. He could feel the ropes slipping, in the moment before the plates' inherent stability turned him upright.

Louis's brain and belly and inner ears were whirling. Moments passed before his eyes could focus.

No Martians were there to watch.

He was hovering alongside a glassy-smooth stretch of lava that dropped almost straight for . . . futz . . . a thousand feet before it eased toward horizontal like a ski jump. Louis could see a splash of orange at the bottom: Acolyte in his translucent suit. He might even have survived such a fall . . . or not.

Louis decided he needn't fear Martians.

This time the Martians had mounted their stepping disk upside down at the top of the highest cliff they could find. Then the flame that destroyed the Hindmost's refueling probe had flooded through the stepping disk. Any Martians watching the trap must have been crisped. The cliff side had melted and flowed, forming a slide.

Louis landed the cargo plates, loosed the lines, and jumped down.

Acolyte lay at an angle on hot red rock.

Louis got a shoulder under the Kzin. Not enough, and he pulled to roll the Kzin over him. Acolyte was an inert mass. Louis could feel broken ribs shifting.

He could have used Martian gravity about now.

He tightened his abdominal muscles, knees and back, grunt and lift. Lift! A nearly grown male Kzin, pressure suit and all, rose just high enough to roll onto the cargo plate.

Louis crawled aboard. Tied the Kzin down. Took the cargo plates up. He used the little thruster to put him just under the stepping disk. Lifted until his shoulders touched.

Flick, they were upside down in *Needle* with the cargo plates on top of them.

Bram did the rest: rolled the cargo plates off, opened all the sealstrips that held the Kzin's suit together, and pulled him out. The Kzin's eyes blinked, focused, found Louis. Otherwise he seemed unable to move.

Bram eased Louis out of his suit, stretched him out next to Acolyte, and examined him. That hurt. "You've torn some muscles and tendons," he said. "You need the 'doc, but the Kzin needs it more."

"He goes first," Louis said. If Acolyte died, what would he say to Chmeee?

Bram lifted the Kzin with no apparent effort, rolled him into the 'doc and closed it. An odd notion: had Bram been waiting for permission?

Not so odd. Louis was starting to hurt in earnest now, and it wouldn't do to let Bram know. Louis was a hominid and Acolyte wasn't, and a protector might *need* a breeder's permission to heal an alien first.

Bram picked him up and set him on the cargo plates in one smooth motion. Pain flashed through him, blocking his breath, turning his scream to a squeak. Bram hooked up leads and tubes from Teela's portable 'doc. He said, "Many of the reservoirs here need filling, Hindmost. Can your larger 'doc make medicines?"

"The kitchen has a pharmacy menu."

The port and starboard walls glowed with orange heat.

In another window he saw a black, baggy shape roll over the rim of the maglev rail. Then nothing, only a silver path receding to infinity.

The pain was receding. Louis knew he wouldn't be lucid much longer.

He felt lean and knobby arms around him. Hard fingertips probed him here and there. A rib felt distant pain, then eased. His back cracked, and again lower down, and a hip joint, and his right knee.

Bram spoke near his ear, but not to Louis. "The Night People went to some effort to show us a spill mountain village, one out of tens of thousands. Why?"

The Hindmost replied, "Didn't you see the way . . ." and Louis was asleep.

Chapter Twenty-Eight

THE

PASSAGE

"Feel that?"

"Yes," said Warvia.

The room was trembling, a tiny vibration in all the walls and the rock below.

Riding weird vehicles had left them dizzy and disoriented, but they'd had hours to sleep that off. This was something else. Tegger hadn't noticed at first. Now Warvia's breathing and the endless tremor were the only sensations in the dark room.

"Any idea—"

"Seabottom mulch. It's pounding on the peak, and we feel it all the way down here."

Tegger stared at her in the dark.

"Pipes pump it up the back of the rim wall. It falls fifty daywalks from the edge of the rim," Warvia said. "It falls on all the spill mountains. It's what *makes* the spill mountains. Without the pumps, all the soil beneath the Arch would end up in the seas. Whisper told me all about it."

"You got more out of Whisper than I ever did."

"I wonder where she is now."

"She?"

Fingers caressed his jaw. "I'm guessing. I asked, but she wouldn't say. Do you know what that seabottom muck is called?"

"What?"

"Flup."

Tegger belly-laughed. "What? You mean all this time— Flup, everyone I *know* thinks he knows what flup means. Seabottom?"

"This mountain is made of it. Pressure turns it into rock—"

White light flooded them. A voice said, "Hello."

They leapt to their feet, wrapping fur around them. The High Point People had left them a fur like Saron's, relic of a green-spotted sloth with a damaged head. On Warvia it looked quite lovely.

Warvia had other concerns. She whispered, "That was no High Point accent—"

"Hello? You hear the voice of Louis Wu. May we talk?"

Tegger blinked against the painful light. Details weren't there, but he could pick out a man's shape and something stranger.

"You have invaded our privacy," he said.

"You were not sleeping. Ours is the spy device you carried for so long. Will you speak or shall we come another time?"

Something rapped on the wood beside the skin door. A woman's voice called, "Teegr? Wairbeea?"

"Flup! Come in," Tegger ordered.

Through the skins came Jennawil and Barraye and a smell of blood. "We hear voices," the young woman said, "else we would have left this in the anteroom. It's a gwill. Skreepu killed it for you."

The gwill was a big lizard. Its tail still twitched.

"Your timing is good," Tegger said. He hefted the gwill. Its skin felt armored. It would have to be skinned. To the glare in the web and the monsters within, he said, "You speak to Jennawil and Barraye of the High Point People. They know what we only guess. Jennawil, Barraye, we meet Louis Wu at last."

Dozing with his chin on the portable 'doc, Louis heard himself speaking. "You hear the voice of Louis Wu. You see my associates, Bram and the Web Dweller. We have kept silence because we have enemies."

"We are Warvia and Tegger," a high-pitched alien voice said. Louis's eyes were open now, and he recognized the red-skinned vampire slayers. "Why do you break silence now?"

"We must ask questions." That was the voice of Louis Wu, all right, but it was coming from the Hindmost.

A High Point man said, "We are to show you the hidden mirror and the passage through the rim and anything else you desire."

"Thank you. Are you prepared to go through the passage?"

Jennawil jumped in shock. "No! There are *vishnishtee*—" Louis's translator hesitated an instant. "—protectors moving constantly through the passage."

Louis decided not to speak. He was feeling mellow and foolish, and pain lurked if he wanted to feel it. He wouldn't make sense, and what would they make of two "voices of Louis Wu"?

The Hindmost said, "Tell us what you know about protectors."

"Of two kinds they are. Protectors of our own kind would keep us safe, but they obey flatland protectors—"

"May we speak to a High Point protector?"

"I think not. Keeping secrets from flatland protectors is near impossible, and protectors are conspicuous. I can ask."

The puppeteer asked, "Will Whisper speak to us?"
Huh?

The Red Herders looked at each other. The woman said firmly, "Whisper will not."

"What can you tell us of Whisper?"

"Nothing."

"What lies beyond the passage?"

Barraye said, "Poison, we think."

Jennawil explained: "Protectors wear suits that cover every part of them when they go through the passage. They carry a great bulk of tools back and forth. Rumors say they are building something out there, something monstrous."

The red woman said, "Louis Wu, it was the massed might of the Night People that moved the eye here. Come night, you may speak to them."

"How long until night?"

Jennawil said, "Two tenths."

The voice of Louis Wu said, "We wait," and sang like a bass string quartet.

Bram asked, "Did you hear, Louis?"

"Some of it. Good act, Hindmost, but you need better makeup."

"Louis Wu is *vashnesht*. Wizard. He remains out of sight," the Hindmost said, "while his weird servitors speak for him."

"Stet. Who's Whisper?"

"Anne is Whisper," Bram said. "I've seen your tapes of Whisper guiding the red man. She used the cruiser's mission for concealment."

" 'Whisper' fits her," Louis said.

The Hindmost turned from the window. "Louis, what do you think? Where is Whisper? Will she interfere?"

Louis was watching the people in the window. There wasn't quite enough anesthetic in him to knock him out. "Bram, you're the only one who might guess what she wants."

"Yes."

"I'm too groggy to think. I think I want my voice back."

"As you will," said the Hindmost.

Warvia stripped the gwill with a knife. Tegger said, "Red Herders have to eat meat freshly killed. Watching may distress you."

Warvia tore the gwill apart and gave part to Tegger. They ate. The High Point couple seemed fascinated and appalled. Tegger wondered why they were still here, now that the window was only a bronze web again.

Bones only. Tegger looked the question; Barraye pointed to a receptacle.

Jennawil said, "Tegger, Wairbeea, we noted that you did not speak of reshtra until you saw what was under our furs."

Ah.

"Our people mate once, for life," Warvia said, and looked at her mate. Something passed between them, and she added, "A thing happened to us, to change us. But we don't *need* rishathra. What changed was only that we have a choice."

Tegger had thought it through. "Barraye, Jennawil, there are no tales of Red Herders who rish. What if your talking mirrors spread that tale all across the flatlands? Where could we live? Who would mate to our children?"

The High Pointers looked at each other.

"You saw the Night People, Jennawil," Warvia said. "What if it is told that you rished with red-skinned visitors from below? What will the Night People expect?"

Barraye nodded. "They would think to resh with us. How curious are we, my mate?"

She was whacking his massive shoulder, lightly and open-handed, and laughing. Tegger suspected that was a no. "Not their shape alone. Their *smell*!"

Barraye patted her rump reassuringly. "Well, then, we must keep yet another secret."

Fun stuff. Louis watched in passive prurience. A show like this would be a success, he thought, on pay channels on every world in known space. And of course it was being recorded . . . for that matter, how many senses did the webeyes record? Not just sight and sound. Smell? Radar for a kinesthetic sense?

Somewhere in there he fell asleep.

Hours later, it seemed, he woke and stared in astonishment at himself looming above him.

No: at his pressure suit, angular like fractured bones where a human would be smooth. Bram tipped the helmet back and asked, "Are you well?"

"I'm pretty sore." The medkit was dripping stuff into him, but he could feel where the pain was waiting.

"Two ribs were out of place. I set them. No bones are broken. You've abused muscles, torn ligaments and mesenteries, slipped a spinal disk that I reset. You would heal with no more than your own defenses and the portable medkit."

"Why are you wearing my suit?"

"Reasons of strategy."

"Too complex for my tiny mind? All right, Bram. You'll notice that we have more visitors. If you'll disconnect me, the voice of Louis Wu can show a face."

The Hindmost and Bram waited to either side of Louis and a little behind. On the other side of the webeye window, the Reds huddled under a fur, letting the Ghouls take center stage.

The Ghouls were shivering. The lanky woman said, "It's

cold out there! Well, I am Grieving Tube, this is Harpster. Is your box making sense of my voice?"

"Yes, it's fine. How did you know about my translator?"

"Your companion Tunesmith seems to have departed, but his son Kazarp spoke of your visit to Weaver Town."

"My regards to Kazarp. Grieving Tube, why did you move two manweight of poured stone over such a distance if you could have spoken to me through Tunesmith?"

The Ghouls laughed, showing *way* too much teeth. "Spoken, yes, but what would we say? The rim wall is in the wrong hands? We don't know that. You, are you a *vashnesht?*" *Protector*, the translator said.

Bram said, "Yes."

Tegger started to get up; Warvia held him back. The Ghouls, too, had flinched, but Harpster made himself speak to the protector. "We know enough to know our helplessness. These are vampire protectors. They take the High Point Folk as meat from a herd. Some return as protectors. Many simply disappear."

Bram said, "They are repairing the Arch."

"Do they do more good than harm?"

"Yes. There are too many, and they'll fight when the repairs are done. We hope we can improve the balance."

"How do you expect to help?"

"We must know more. Tell us what you can."

Harpster shrugged hugely. "You know what we know. High Point will show us more, come dawn."

The Hindmost fluted. The window shrank to background size.

"We wait," he said. "Louis, we recorded earlier conversation. They know much of protectors and something of Teela Brown. Or shall we serenade you?"

Bram was reaching for the instrument package he'd brought from *Hidden Patriarch*.

"A little dinner music would go nicely," Louis said politely. "And I'm starved."

Louis was trying to do some stretching. Lifting Acolyte had pulled some serious muscles and tendons. Bram's attentions had helped, but he had to move carefully.

Many hours had passed. Now the window at High Point was rotating bumpily across night-darkened mountainscape. A mixed bag of hominids were rolling the stolen webeye like a wheel over the worn paths of the village. When they left the village and began moving uphill over rock, the motion began to jar his stomach.

Louis turned his back on the display, trusting the others to alert him when the webeye got somewhere interesting. What was taking the Kzin so long? Anyplace in known space, he could at least have used a 'doc! The medkit wouldn't do anything for him except inject chemicals, and he'd need it again in a few minutes.

Four High Point People carried the web and its backing. They climbed uphill in the charcoal night. Saron moved ahead of the Red Herders and Night People to point out footholds for them.

The Ghouls had tried to help carry, but they were doing well just to catch their breath.

"Sunlight soon," Warvia said to the Ghoul woman. "What will you do then?"

"I was told we would come to the passage. Shelter."

There were no roads here. What paths there were, were only scuff marks on hard dirt and rock. The High Village People moved up and up across a tilted land, on and on, miles above the infinite flatland.

To spin was the oncoming terminator line, and daylight.

Close up against the spill mountains the land below was a relief map, like the map the Ghouls had made for them outside the Grass Giants' hall. A view like this may have given them that notion. Farther away, all detail was lost. A thread of silver linked by puddles might have been the Homeflow, or any other body of water, or something else entirely.

Warvia may have been thinking similar thoughts. "The lands the Red Herders move through, are they even big enough to see? How will we ever find Red Herders again?"

Harpster said, "That's not the problem at all—"

Grieving Tube said, "Our people know the routes of the Red Herders. They'll map—Forgive me." She had to stop for breath. "They'll map a path for us—by mirror-speech. You'll find a new home—as quickly as you came here."

"Oh. Good." Then Warvia laughed. "Your solution was extreme! We didn't need to travel quite so far."

Tegger wouldn't show weakness with Warvia watching. With dying strength he followed Saron. The old woman moved more slowly now. He could hear the other High Point People gasping as they carried the web's weight along the hill.

Day swept toward them from spinward. As the first edge of sun peeped around the shadow of night, Harpster pulled from his pack two rolled-up hats with gigantic brims. Now only the Night People walked in shadow.

"We should be on the fringes of Red Herder turf," Warvia said, "as far as possible from stories that must have started already."

Harpster said, "No. Warvia, Red Herders aren't all the same species."

"Why, of course we are!"

Tegger said, "We woo our mates from other tribes at the feasts, when the herds cross. We've done it since before anyone can remember."

Harpster said, "Good idea—"

"But you don't always," said Grieving Tube. "You and Warvia, you have the same accent—"

"Yes, we both were born into Ginjerofer's tribe, but others mate across the lines."

"Some tribes have given it up. Some just don't push it, like Ginjerofer's people. Tegger, the farther you go from Ginjerofer's tribe, the less likely your children will find mates who can give them children. It wouldn't matter so much if you didn't mate for life."

"Flup," Tegger whispered.

Something flashed at them as they rounded a barrier of crumbling rock.

Tegger had tried to imagine what a mirror might look like. Now he couldn't see it. What he saw was himself, Warvia, the Ghouls and High Point People, the sky and the rim wall. A mirror was a flat window that showed what was behind the viewer. It stood as high as a Red Herder man, and three men wide.

They set the web and its backing carefully in place, flat onto the mirror. Saron and the men went to the ends of the mirror, and the Night People went with them.

Harpster began to talk, spitting his consonants, as if he were addressing a crowd.

The men began to tilt the mirror up and down. It was mounted on hinges. Jennawil stood behind Tegger and pointed along the rim.

Toward the next spill mountain.

A highlight played on the mountain's flank, falling and rising as the men tilted the mirror.

Tegger asked, "How does it work?"

Jennawil laughed. "Ah, the Night People haven't told you everything! Sun mirrors flash a code known to us and Night People. They carry news between mountains, but also news of flatlands to mountains and back to flatlands."

That explained much. The Ghouls had always known too much about the weather, the Shadow Nest, the bronze spinnerweb itself.

The four took up the eye of Louis Wu again. "Around this jut of rock," Saron said, "and up."

"We've been discussing your problem, Grieving Tube and I. We think we have an answer," Harpster said.

Tegger had been thinking, too. "It's like being crushed between two bulls. If we go too far, we doom our children. If we settle too close to Ginjerofer's route, we'll hear tales about ourselves."

"We're too conspicuous," Warvia said, "too easy to recognize. When visitors tell of the vampire slayers who learned rishathra, that will be us."

Harpster was grinning with all his spade teeth. "Suppose there was an old story," Harpster said. "Once upon a time all hominids were monogamous. No man looked at a woman who was not his mate, and she would not look aside from him. War happened when hominids met.

"Then came two heroes who saw that hominids could live otherwise. They invented rishathra and ended a war. They spread it like a ministry—"

Warvia cried, "Harpster, was there really such a tale?"

"Not yet."

"Oh."

"The Night People are selective about whom we speak to, but you must not think we're silent. You've seen the sun mirrors. Those are our voice. You know that every priest must know how to dispose of his dead. Priests must talk to us."

The route had become steeper, and they were all huffing now. "We can spread the tale from several directions," Grieving Tube said. "Only the old women remember the legend, or the old men. The tale tells of heroes of their own species who invented rishathra and ended war, and it tells that their own species has practiced rishathra ever since. Details are different among different species. When a variation appears in which the heroes were Red Herders who ended a war to gain allies against vampires—"

"It's just a story." Tegger laughed. He was starting to believe it would work. "Only a story. Warvia?"

"Maybe," she said. "Maybe. It's worth a try. We can lie, love, as long as we don't have to lie to each other."

A rock as big as the tallest city building had split vertically, and the High Point People were leading them through the split. Ribbons of color ran through the rock. "Ice did this," Deb said. "Water soaks into rock. Freezes. Melts and freezes again."

The wind shrilled through, icy, tearing at any bit of exposed skin. Tearing at eyes. Tegger walked blind, feeling his way, following Warvia, though her eyes were closed, too.

A big hand on his chest stopped him. He opened his eyes into slits.

Finally, here it was, a place to hide from the wind: a rock tunnel into the mountain. But they'd stopped within the cleft, with the tunnel's mouth barely in view. From the cleft a slope of shattered rock ran up to a rough rock entrance.

Barraye spoke for the first time. "Teegr, that is not shelter."

He asked, "Why not? Monsters inside?"

"Yes. *Vishnishtee.*"

They set the web on its rim and propped it to face the opening. Barraye had gone silent again. Saron said, "Louis Wu, can you see?"

The bronze web spoke. "Yah, barely. How deep is that thing?"

"We think that this is passage through the high mountain. None of us have gone that far."

"You've been inside?"

Deb spoke. "Most of High Point and near a hundred of airborne visitors hid in the passage when the Death Light shone. We could only hunt at night. After the Death Light faded, we were cast out and forbidden to return."

A breathy voice said, "Describe the *vishnishtee.*"

Tegger's eyes met Warvia's. That voice from the web must be the *vashnesht*, Bram, but it sounded very like Whisper.

"The *vishnishtee* cared for us," Deb said, "but none of us ever saw one."

"What, never?"

"But sometimes one of us would disappear. There was a limit to how far we could go down the passage. We knew there was death in the passage, but there was death outside, too."

"Couldn't you make your own shelters? Rock would stop radiation ... stop the Death Light."

"We knew that. Hide in caves, the *vishnishtee* said. Make houses of rock? The mountain would shake rock down on our heads!"

The voice of Louis Wu said, "My companions are showing me a picture taken from tens of daywalks above you. It's amazing how much detail you can see when you're far enough away, Deb. The mountain you live on is kind of a flat cone, but around that tunnel, it's like a sand castle piled against a wall with a pipe poking out of it."

They waited for Louis Wu to make better sense.

"Yah. What I mean is, the passage is older than the mountain and a lot stronger. Made of scrith, I bet. The mountain gradually settles under its own weight, but the passage stays right where it is, and *vishnishtee* have to keep digging the entrance again. Can you take me through?"

"No!" said Barraye and Saron and Jennawil.

Deb said, "We were cast out! If we're seen, we will die!"

Saron said, "We have stayed on broken rock. We left no footprints and no scent. If a *vishnishtee* learns that we have come bearing *this*, we will die."

It was Harpster who protested. "The eye of Louis Wu has come far to see so little."

"That is as it is. Harreed, stay behind. If you find sign of us, conceal it. Harpster, are you strong enough to take Harreed's place?"

And a voice said, "Leave the web."

Nine hominids froze. Tegger could see no tenth. And—that was not the voice of Whisper, nor the protector Bram, either, but it had the same breathy speech impediment.

The High Point People were quietly moving back through the cleft in the rock and downslope. Tegger and Warvia followed, leading the Ghouls, who by now were nearly blind in the black shadows of their hats. They left the bronze spinnerweb propped in the cleft and didn't look back.

Chapter Twenty-nine

COLLIER

They were four in *Hot Needle of Inquiry*'s crew cabin: Bram and the Hindmost and Louis Wu, and Acolyte, in a great black coffin where their exercise space used to be. They all used the same shower and the same kitchen wall.

Sleeping arrangements weren't a problem. The Hindmost wanted the sleeping plates, but that was all right. They'd moved the cargo plates beside the water bed. Louis used that.

He was sitting cross-legged on the bouncing surface, eating something crunchy and nutrition-free. Boredom had him eating too much. He might be getting too much painkiller, too.

Bram didn't want him exercising alone in the lander bay. Louis had healed enough to want that. He had offered to take Bram along, teach him yoga or even some fighting techniques. Bram refused. He intended to be *right here* when . . .

What the futz was Bram expecting? Louis wondered. For most of two days he'd watched the wreckage of the refueling probe. It lay smashed on the maglev track in a window that overlaid six others—five, now—and Bram stood before it, watching.

Louis was getting cabin fever.

To ship's port and starboard the glow of dying coals had faded to the black of cold basalt. In space that would have been stars, an infinite universe spread to either side.

Futz, he *had* stars. One webeye lay on the maglev track, looking down at the universe through the filigree surface. Another starscape, from the webeye Louis had sprayed onto the vacuum, had fuzzed out only hours ago.

In another window the stolen webeye moved into a smooth-bore tunnel, stopped in what was clearly an airlock for several hours, then moved on through several doors, past piles of strange equipment vaguely glimpsed, and stopped again. Louis had never seen what was carrying it, nor heard that voice again.

The flight deck was windows overlaid on windows, a perspective that could cross the eyes and twist them in their sockets. One was a graph like a constantly wiggling mountain range, purpose unknown. Three were replays: High Point Mountain swept past the refueling probe; the probe maneuvered until it was smashed by violet light; a protector died, his suit slashed open to vacuum.

Nothing was happening where the ruined probe lay on the maglev track. The window held Bram like a dark Dali silhouette, say *Shades of Night Descending*.

Louis closed his eyes and sagged back on the water bed.

Popped them open again. He'd seen blue-white light flash from one of the windows.

The light was out now, but the wrecked probe was glowing cherry-red. Something tiny was coming down the maglev track from far away, running straight into the window.

It came at astronomical speed, a foot above the track: something like a floating sledge. It decelerated savagely. Something manlike dropped off the back and rolled out of view as the vehicle eased to a stop inches from the window.

The Hindmost moved up beside Bram.

The probe cooled to murky red, darker, black.

That wasn't a sled. It was a shallow box. The bottom was black like wrought iron. The sides were so transparent as to be barely visible, but Louis could pick them out by the knobs embedded for tiedowns. Lines held tools against the sides of the box: a wand with a handle, maybe a line saw; a wide-mouthed thing, gun or rocket launcher or energy weapon; a pry bar; stacked boxes; skeletal metal stuff.

A window behind it showed starscape and, rising into view, a nearly empty flat surface. Louis glared and looked away. The stolen webeye had left the tunnel and entered some kind of open elevator, at the worst possible time.

Louis heard, "I do not understand war, but I feel Louis might."

"Even drugged?"

"Ask."

"Louis, are you awake?"

"Of course I'm awake, Bram!"

"This is a duel among protectors—"

"Medieval Japanese," Louis said thickly. Despite what he'd said, the drugs had him wanting to doze. "Hide and stab. Win any way you can. They didn't duel like Europeans."

"Yes, you understand. Do you see why this second intruder is still alive?"

"No . . . wait." The newcomer moved in a crouched and jerky strut, examining the slagged probe. It was the knobby shape of a Ringworld pressure suit, and wide through the torso, like the one Whisper was wearing; but it *fit*.

The newcomer found marks on the probe where a stepping disk had been attached. Its head snapped up, and in a flash it was gone.

But Louis had glimpsed its face. "Spill mountain protector. Whisper must see that, too. It's a slave, stet, Bram? There must be a master, the protector in charge of the maglev track. The master sent him."

A window lurched, then rolled over and over, showing the black underside of the Ringworld, then stars streaming past, Ringworld, stars . . . The protector's servant had cleared the maglev rail by rolling the ruined probe into space.

Now the main window was backing up. The spill mountain protector jumped free.

Louis said, "The first one, the one that died, he left a maglev sled on the track. Acolyte sprayed his webeye on the sled. That's what we're watching. Somebody has to get the probe and the sled off the track. So here's a spill mountain protector to dump the probe, and he's sent the first sled back where it came from, down to the spaceport ledge. Problem solved. Now he's boarding his own sled . . . there it goes back up the track to wherever *he* came from."

Bram said, "You do understand."

"Whisper's started something she can't stop."

"She's guessed that I sent the probe," Bram said. "She doesn't want my enemies to study it."

"She can't know how many there are."

"She might extrapolate. Begin with Teela Brown—"

"Yah. It all begins with Teela." The pain had gone far away. Louis felt himself floating. Better disconnect himself from the medkit, clear his head.

The webeye window's motion stopped. Then it, too, began gliding up the track.

Whisper was using it to follow the other sled.

"Teela made protectors to help her mount motors," Bram said. "A spill mountain protector might be trusted, because Teela could hold his species at ransom. A Ghoul protector might consider that his species already owns all beneath the Arch, and act only to preserve it. A vampire—"

"Starts fresh. A protector born with a blank mind, and Teela right there to teach. *You* said that."

"Yes. Shall we call him Dracula?"

"Mary Shelley."

"Why am I lecturing a drug-stupefied breeder?"

"I think Teela would pick a woman to be a protector. Three women."

Bram shrugged widely. "Stet. I don't know the name, but stet. Mary-Shelley made blood-children, protectors of her own vampire species, and hid them from Teela. When Teela returned to the Map of Mars, two protectors followed. Only the Ghoul remained on the rim.

"Mary-Shelley must have known that her brood would kill and replace the Ghoul. She would rule the rim through them. The spill mountain protector may have guessed that Teela planned to bathe the rim in solar flame. He fought to protect his kind. But Teela killed both.

"Now we must ask, how many are Mary-Shelley's brood?"

The Hindmost said, "Manufacture, acquisition, transport, mounting, supply."

"Three, I think," Bram said. "Manufacture would use repair facilities already in place at a spaceport. If a ship comes, manufacture becomes acquisition. As for supply, no protector would allow another to control what he needs. Stet? Three. Lovecraft to build, Collier for transport, King above them all to mount the motors."

Louis smiled. *Bram had remembered who Mary Shelley was!*

The Hindmost said, "My kind would be a hundred strong, for the company alone."

"And my kind," Bram said, "would each design his own domain to run without his help. There were Spill Mountain People at hand. Let them build and move and mount, while Lovecraft and Collier and King lurk to pounce."

Louis asked, "You think they were expecting Whisper?"

"Whisper, or each other, or me, or invaders from the stars. Do you think us too stupid to extrapolate planets from what we can see of the universe? Anne perceived protectors in place on the rim, each ready to kill her. Wherever she's been or whatever she's done since, she's reached the rim unnoticed by me or by them. She's killed Lovecraft already."

"She makes a pretty good target for Collier, though. Hindmost? Can you read the back of a webeye camera?"

"Louis? I don't unde—glass, he sprayed it on glass." A pipe organ cried in pain. "Done, but wait eleven minutes."

Eleven minutes later the window suddenly faced *back* along the maglev track, into the bed of the sled.

Louis made out some dim shapes suggestive of tools. Nothing big enough to hide a protector. Where was Whisper?

The picture reversed again—and the first sled was slowing.

The second sled began to slow, too.

Louis heard woodwinds scream, and saw the Hindmost's heads jump bolt upright. That wasn't the Hindmost's song. It was Bram and his musical sculpture, and he was already setting it aside. He went to the stepping disk and flicked out.

Louis said, "Did you see that?"

"He's gone," said the Hindmost.

"Where? Why?"

"You tell me. Louis Wu understands duels, stet? Would you take food?" The Hindmost stood beside him, holding a flask.

Louis took it and sipped. Broth. "That's good."

Sanity check: the granite block was back in place and the Hindmost was in the crew cabin, still trapped, like Louis himself.

Louis said, "He's gone where he'll need a pressure suit. For now he's nowhere. Hindmost, if you turned off the stepping desk system, where would Bram be?"

"Safeties prevent me."

"What if we just blast the system with a flashlight-laser? Tanj, no, he's *got* the flash *and* the variable-knife—"

"The system is buried in the hull, Louis."

"Then shift his flick to Mons Olympus! Where does he *think* he's going, anyway? He may be there already. Summon up that map."

The Hindmost made music.

Nothing happened.

"I'm locked out," the Hindmost said. "Bram has learned my programming language. He's wrested control of the stepping disks from me." His legs folded under him. His heads tucked under his forelegs.

Louis tried lifting the edge of the stepping disk. It wouldn't move. Bram had taken full control. Those tanj concerts weren't entertainment. They were Bram practicing with his handmade instruments until he could duplicate the Hindmost's musical speech.

Something was happening: the webeye window jittered and shook. Louis shouted, "Hindmost! Turn the picture around! It's looking the wrong way!"

The puppeteer didn't move.

The window skewed sideways, hit the side of the track, and bounced away spinning. Whatever had attacked the sled was having its effect.

The puppeteer was unfolding himself.

The maglev sled hit the other wall hard. The picture juttered and slid. When it came to a stop, it was looking at nothing but silver filigree.

The puppeteer whistled and the picture reversed. Now starlight showed them walls of shattered crystal. Bullets had chewed the sled into lace, and the tools in the bed had been showered with glass slivers.

Most of these things had been unrecognizable. Now they were junk, with one exception.

Seeing Acolyte and him flick in and out, Louis thought, would have told Whisper about stepping disks. She must have ripped the stepping disk off the probe and tossed it into the sled, for there it was, unharmed.

Three pressure suits leaped into the sled in the same instant. Two fired sprays of projectiles at anything big, then hurled anything hurlable in a rapid search for a protector hiding in wreckage. But Whisper was nowhere.

Two protectors picked up the stepping disk and held it on edge so that the third could inspect its underside. They turned it to show the upper surface. The vampire must have thought it more dangerous than useful, because he adjusted his weapon and fired a bright, narrow beam at it.

The beam lashed straight up out of the cabin's main stepping disk and began to char the ceiling.

Though Louis couldn't remember jumping for cover, he and the Hindmost were now curled intimately behind the recycler wall. The Hindmost didn't look like he intended to uncurl.

Louis poked his head around.

The vampire protector had picked up the stepping disk and was trying to hurl it over the edge of the track.

The disk was suddenly too heavy, as an intruder's weight slammed it down.

The intruder—Bram!—lashed out as the other leapt away. The other vampire—Collier?—fell and separated, cut in half by six feet of wire in a stasis field. Both ends of him spewed fog. But Collier's torso still had arms, and one came around with the bulky light-weapon.

Bram's variable-knife licked out again. The light-weapon fell.

No telling where Whisper had come from, but she was there. Two spill mountain protectors faced two vampire protectors.

The puppeteer was still in something like a catatonic state. Louis tried to follow what was happening in the webeye window. It wasn't simple.

The spill mountain protectors hadn't attacked.

Whisper was wearing one of their suits; she'd be able to talk to them. Louis could hear Bram's breath huffing with recent exertion, but *he* wasn't talking. He wouldn't have the right kind of suit radio.

He was blinking his helmet lamp at Whisper.

Tanj, that must be the Ghouls' heliogaph language! Louis realized. And now the others were using helmet lamps, too.

It went on and on, and presently an agreement was reached.

The spill mountain protectors picked up the ruined sled with some difficulty. Bram gave his weapon to Whisper and helped them throw the sled over the rim and into space.

They dropped the stepping disk into the undamaged maglev sled. The two vampire protectors got in, then the spill mountain protectors. The sled began to move back *down* the track. As the sled began to pull away, Bram puffed a webeye onto the track, then another onto the sled.

Then Bram sang the song of an orchestra being gunned down by terrorists.

He stepped on the disk and flicked out, gone, *here*. As the light through the webeye window showed his going, Bram walked off the stepping disk, lifting his helmet. Something like a fat burl flute was in his hard beak of a mouth.

When a puppeteer is upset, he loses control, not of speech, but of emotional signals. The Hindmost's song was as pure as wind chimes. "You've learned my programming language."

Bram put the flute away. "Our contract does not preclude such a thing."

"I am disturbed."

"Did you follow what you saw? No? Of Mary-Shelley's blood-children, we've killed Lovecraft and Collier. Collier's servants tell us that Lovecraft's servants are ready to load cargo. We expect that they will aid us. Now only King remains. When King is dead, Whisper will control the rim and I the Repair Center, and *then* we may accomplish something."

The kitchen delivered a flask, and Bram drank deeply. Louis noticed he was carrying the big light-weapon. That thing would probably kill everyone in the cabin if it was fired.

Bram looked at him. "Louis Wu, what would you do now?"

"Well, she's *got* to kill King. Too late for anything else. Me? My suit would keep me alive for two falans, so I don't have to board a sled and rev it up to seven hundred seventy miles per second and then let King shoot at me. I might come back to this side of the rim, then climb up the wall from here."

"You would lose all surprise."

"He still—"

Bram waved it away. "Anne's suit won't last that long."

"Mph." *Cargo*, Bram had said. "Well, if I had something King wanted, I could put it on the sled with me. Of course he'd have to *know* I had it. What does King want?"

"Never mind, Louis. I thought it worth seeking a different viewpoint." Bram whistled at the stepping disk system, then flicked out.

"*Now* where's he gone? Hindmost, are you still locked out?"

"I can't use stepping disks. I can find him."

"Do it."

Two windows showed moire patterns: webeyes destroyed in the battle. The Hindmost sang them out, then popped one up in their place. It began flicking past other views. Weaver Town. *Hidden Patriarch*: the foremast crow's nest.

The Hindmost sang flutes and percussion. He said, "I've begun a search program. If invaders come using familiar craft, we'll know it in minutes."

"Good." Louis pointed at the window half obscured by that one. "I hope you were recording that."

"Yes."

The stolen webeye had reached the spaceport ledge. Tiny starlit pressure suits walked through vacuum toward a structure too huge to show its shape. It took them forever to round the curve of it.

Bigger yet: a pair of golden toroids mounted on tall gantries. It took Louis a moment to see the rest of it.

Cables were growing out of the toroids, spreading like a growing plant, narrowing at the ends to invisibly fine wire.

"Stet. They're actually making new motors."

The Hindmost said, "I've wondered if the wire frames are an innovation. My records show no more than the toroids."

"Interesting notion, but maybe the City Builders took just the toroids. That wire frame could be awkward if you wanted to land a ship."

The shifting window showed *Hidden Patriarch's* aft crow's nest; then the kitchen and two adult City Builders and three children. Where had the older children been hiding, Louis wondered, that he hadn't met them? But they were all moving out the door. And now they came chattering back with Bram between them.

Bram had stripped off his suit. He stretched out on a bench. Harkabeeparolyn and Kawaresksenjajok began a massage.

Bones and swollen joints and no fat anywhere. "He looks like a tanj skeleton *now*," Louis said.

Bram seemed asleep.

"If Bram thinks there's time for that, he's likely right. Hindmost, let's get Acolyte out of that box and me in."

The puppeteer whistled up a window. "Louis, the nanotech devices are still repairing damage to his spinal cord. He should be free in a few hours."

"Tanj!"

"Leave him?"

"Yes!" Louis curled up on the water bed. "I'm going to sleep."

Chapter Thirty

KING

Louis uncurled slowly. Pain is a great teacher. Still, he moved more easily than he had these last four days.

The medkit had been giving him diet supplements, but he'd turned off the pain drip. Louis disengaged himself and went to the fore wall.

Here: in *Hidden Patriarch*'s dining hall, Bram was speaking to the City Builders. The webeye windows in the walls were active, and one was the same as this second window—

Here: the vast width of the spaceport ledge. The nearly finished rim wall motor was gone, completed and moved somewhere. Here passed a huge floating sledge with skeletal towers and alien waldos at the corners. A tower with a spiral decor ... more than decor: it was bending over like a silver tentacle, and its tip was an infinite bifurcation. It englobed the picked-over hull of a City Builder starship and lifted.

Beyond the edge of the ledge was a line of vertical rings: the deceleration track for incoming ships.

Here: a blur of maglev track with stars showing faintly through. Whisper must have set her sled moving, Louis decided. Built up considerable speed, too, while he slept. It had to be Whisper; who else would have sprayed a webeye?

Here: a sluggishly drifting starscape seen through a filigree maglev track, and a tiny green blinking cursor. "I found a spacecraft," the Hindmost said.

"Show me."

The puppeteer sang and the view zoomed hugely, to a blurred view of something more crowbar than ship. Little winged spacecraft ran its length like aphids on a twig. At the near end, a big drive cone and/or plasma cannon drifted past.

"Another ARM ship," Louis said. "Good catch."

Bram had left the dining hall.

The Hindmost noticed motion along the maglev track. He chimed. The window reversed to show the other side of Whisper's webeye.

That wasn't the sled Whisper had been using. It was a vast dark plane. Cable rose in loops of varying thickness and varying curvatures, branching like arteries, reaching around and up and out of sight. A slender pillar rose out of the center.

Whisper's handhold was on the narrowest of these loops. She was floating in close foreground, with one hand on a cable as thick as her fist.

It seemed a fantasy, like some ancient book cover. The only item Louis could recognize was welded just behind Whisper: the stepping disk off the refueling probe.

Louis realized that his mind wasn't tracking. What he needed was breakfast.

Muscles in his back, groin, right hamstring, and some transverse muscles under his ribs protested when he moved to the kitchen wall. Lifting a Kzin, even a Kzin not quite grown ... "Remember, I'm a trained professional," he muttered. "Don't try this stunt in Earth gravity." He dialed up a pastiche omelet, papaya, grapefruit, bread.

"Louis?"

"Nothing. Is Acolyte ready to come out?"

The Hindmost looked. "Yes—"

"Wait." Louis tapped an order. "Let's pacify him with a haunch of mammal."

Acolyte sat up fast and found himself looking at a rack of beef ribs. He took it and found the Hindmost behind it. He said, "Your munificence as host must be legendary," and began to tear ribs apart.

The Hindmost said, "Your father came to us as an ambassador. He's taught you well."

Acolyte waggled his ears and kept eating.

The puppeteer dialed up a big bowl of grassy stuff, but it only stopped one mouth at a time. For Acolyte's benefit, he described the deaths on the maglev track, singing up visual displays, with Louis filling in a word here and there. The puppeteer didn't grasp strategy. One thing Acolyte *wasn't* hearing was that Bram had begun treating his alien serfs as prisoners.

Acolyte dropped a big white imitation bone into the recycler. "Louis, are you healthy?"

"I'm not ready to race you again, not just yet."

"You did well. What it cost you . . . you did well. I think my main nerve trunk was broken. Shall I put you in the 'doc?"

"No no no, it's all coming to a head! Look—" Louis waved through the webeye window, at Whisper floating motionless above an infinite field of superconductor. His mind had had time to digest a little of that weird picture, and he spoke for the puppeteer as well as the adolescent Kzin. "Whisper's in free fall. That means we're looking at a vehicle moving at seven hundred seventy miles per second, antispinward. It's a vehicle even if it has to stretch the full width of the maglev track. Two hundred feet wide and maybe longer than that.

"Those loops—Acolyte, you were in the 'doc when Bram was hinting around. You're looking at the barest fringes of a rim wall ramjet. Lovecraft's team had one all ready to go. Whisper's holding it hostage."

Whisper was looking back, watching the webeye. Bram must have told her what it was.

Bram flicked in. He was wearing Louis's pressure suit with the helmet back. He looked at his allies; glanced into the windows; then turned to the kitchen. "Louis, Acolyte, Hindmost. What news?"

"As you see," the Hindmost said. "An ARM carrier vessel orbits a hundred million miles out from the Ringworld's underside. How will you deal with it?"

"Not yet." Bram turned back to the windows. Now Whisper was clinging like a frightened monkey to the loop of superconductor.

"She's begun deceleration. Acolyte, do you understand? We hope that King will consider a rim ramjet and the large sled too valuable to destroy."

"Louis explained."

Bram said, "Whisper expects me. What do you need of me before I go?"

The puppeteer bleated, "Give me access to the stepping disks!"

"Not quite yet, Hindmost."

Louis asked, "What kind of opposition . . . ?"

"King has a long supply line. He'll have a few spill mountain protectors. He will rotate them frequently unless he prefers to watch them die. They must scent their own kind, to know whom they protect, or else protect all beneath the Arch. King reserves that for himself."

"Not many, then."

"None, it may be. King's own hands may serve him. The

rim wall ramjet motors cannot be moved by muscle. In any case, I don't fear the High Point protectors. If they see a clear victory, they will finish the loser. The victor holds their people ransom."

Louis said, "Give us a hint. If you and Whisper are killed, what do we do?"

"Your contract. Protect all beneath the Arch." Bram lowered his faceplate and fixed it in place. He was gone, a virtual particle in motion, and the port and starboard walls were glowing bright orange with the heat of the momentum exchange.

Tiny bottles popped into the kitchen well. The Hindmost inserted them one by one into the little medkit on the cargo plate stack. "Antibiotics," he said.

"Thanks, Hindmost. I must have been clean out."

More bottles. "Pain blockers."

Whisper wasn't in sight on the barge. She'd been conspicuous enough until now. She'd shown herself to King's telescopes, with King's treasure displayed vastly behind her. What was she playing at now?

Was she high in that cone of superconducting cable? How well did vampires climb?

Under the maglev barge?

The view ahead hadn't changed. The track ran on and on. The barge and its unwieldy cargo might be decelerating, but even at high gee it would take awhile. Louis wondered if Whisper was planning to ram the terminus. King might be wondering the same thing.

Nah. In ten hours at 770 miles/second, she'd covered around twenty-four million miles. But the track ran for two hundred million miles, and where in that length was her target? She couldn't give King that much time to shoot at her.

Where, for that matter, was King? The vampire protector could be anywhere, if he'd trained High Point protectors to mount the ramjets for him. *What was that?*

Maglev sled, the small variety, almost lost on the vast track. Coming straight toward the window. Now veering from side to side, and slowing . . . matching speed with the barge . . . *contact*, and five matching pressure suits were past the webeye before Louis could blink. The Hindmost whistle-chimed, the view reversed, and . . . gone. They had already disappeared into the maze of coils.

Five matching pressure suits would be five spill mountain protectors, stet? They'd guard the ramjet, protect it from stray effects of a battle, serving both sides. For King, they would also serve as a distraction.

And anyone who had ever watched a magic act might guess that one of the five was King himself, his suit bulked out with additional weapons or armor.

Where were they?

Action far aft. Louis couldn't make it out. This was going to be frustrating, he thought. He glanced at the Kzin: would Acolyte freak out? But he was watching with the patience of a cat at a mouse hole.

Traces of motion, distant flashes of light . . . and two maglev sleds were weaving through the coils! Sporadic flashes of light followed them. They dipped below view, then rose. One struck a coil and rebounded into an actinic blast, crashed into another coil and was out, over the edge of the track, gone. The other . . .

"Clever," Louis whispered, and lowered his gaze to the bed of the barge. But there was nothing to be seen.

The Hindmost said, "Louis?"

"Whisper had the little sleds following the barge, right aft where King couldn't see them. I only saw two, but maybe there were more, all slaved to the one she was in, and which one is that? Now she's dipped them and rolled clear and sent them up again for King to shoot at. Even if King's figured it out by now, it puts her in two places, and Whisper knows where *he* is. And I could be completely wrong."

"The barge will stop soon. Then the dueling field expands, stet, Louis?"

"Ye gods, you're right. If—"

Bram flicked in.

Light slashed where he had been, but Bram was among the superconductor loops and firing back with Louis's flash. Light flared among the loops, a storm of energy beams. Bram stood up, holding his suit together with one hand.

The first beam hadn't missed. It was hellishly intense, having gotten through the laser shielding on Louis's suit.

Now two tiny man-shapes were firing among the loops, leaping, firing, chewing up the ramjet.

Louis said, "I just—" and stopped.

"Share it," Acolyte spat.

"Light doesn't hurt a superconductor. They're all *three* using light-weapons. If King had known . . ."

Bram would be dead if he didn't get to safety soon. He'd taken cover behind a thick loop of ramjet and was watching, just watching. Likely Bram had no better idea than he did, Louis thought, as to which man-shape was Whisper, which was King. He'd done what he could.

One combatant flared like a sun and dissolved.

The other flared brighter and was gone faster. Four shapes leaped like fleas, a pincer closing on Bram.

Louis started to laugh.

Bram ran for the stepping disk. He blazed like a sun and then he was gone, *here*, off the stepping disk, throwing back his helmet, pulling in air in great gasps. His pressure suit glowed dull red in spots. He stripped it away, keeping the gloves on until he was clear of the rest, hurled the suit into the shower and turned it on.

Louis was still laughing.

And Acolyte seemed to be smiling widely, but on a kzinti that was no smile. He said, "One of you will tell me what happened."

"Whisper is dead and I am alone," Bram said. "Is there more to know? King's protector servants were to guard the ramjet and the barge while we fought. But we three came to fight war on a superconducting field, under superconducting coils. We all chose energy weapons. Stet, Acolyte? The Arch lives by the rim ramjets! We are protectors!"

Acolyte said, "Stet."

"Four protector servants saw that none of us could harm the transport or the ramjet. Whisper and I thought they would kill the losers. But they saw two dying and one unwary, and they struck to free themselves from us entirely! I must have seemed easy meat," Bram said. "Witless ones. If they saw me flick in, couldn't they guess I'd flick out?"

Bram looked at the webeye windows glowing in the Hindmost's cabin. Four protectors in High Point pressure suits gathered around the stepping disk. Their helmet lights blinked heliograph patterns. One looked up into the window. Then all four eased around out of view.

The window went to moire patterns.

"That won't save them," Bram said, and turned. "Hindmost, why was a link made between Weaver Town and the Meteor Defense room?"

The puppeteer said, "Ask Louis Wu."

"Louis?"

One does not reproach a Pierson's puppeteer for cowardice. Louis barely glanced at the Hindmost. "It's the morals clause, Bram. I've judged you unfit to rule the Ringworld."

Bram's hand was a vise on Louis's left shoulder, lifting. Louis could see the Kzin bristling, trying to decide whether to interfere. The protector said, "By what unjustifiable arrogance could a breeder—It's Teela, isn't it?"

"What?"

"She forced you to kill her. She forced you to kill hundreds of millions of Spill Mountain Folk in order to push the Arch back into place. Of course she had to die to save the hostages she had given me. Of course the Arch would have impacted the sun without plasma to feed the rim ramjets. But why did she impose these tasks on *you?*"

"All right. Why?"

Bram had set Louis on his feet, but his grip hadn't relaxed. "I've read your record from the ship's computer. You open problems, then abandon them—"

Louis believed he was prepared to die, but this was turning weird. "What problems, Bram?"

"You found a dangerous alien species in interstellar space. You opened negotiations, you showed their way to your world, then left professional ambassadors to try to deal with them. Teela Brown you carried to the Ringworld, then left to another's care—"

"Tanj dammit, Bram, she made her own choice!"

"Halrloprillalar you brought to Earth, then allowed the ARM to take her. She died."

Louis was silent.

"Despite Teela, still you have ignored your responsibility for forty-three falans. Only the fear of death brought you back here. But you understood her message, didn't you, Louis?"

"That is *completely*—"

"You must judge the Ringworld's safety. She trusted your wisdom, Louis, and not her own. She was half right, half bright."

The Hindmost spoke from safety behind the kitchen wall. "Teela wasn't wise. Protectors are not wise. Their motives don't come from the forebrain, Louis. She may have been just wise enough."

"Hindmost, that's ridiculous," Louis said. "Bram, I'm naturally arrogant. You're being too clever. Bright people do a lot of that."

"What shall I do about the protectors who killed my mate?"

"We'll ask the High Point People if we can please talk to a protector. We'll tell them they're in charge of the rim. Bram, spill mountain protectors have *every* interest in protecting the Ringworld from *any* danger. Anything that happens hurts the rim wall first, and who should know that better than they do?"

Bram blinked. He said, "Yes. Next. I have ruled in the Repair Center for more than seven thousand falans. How do you judge me—"

"I know what you did. The dates, Bram, the *dates*. You didn't even try to hide them!"

"You talk to too many kinds. You've traveled too far. How could I lie? You might have learned."

"I am," Acolyte said, "bewildered."

Louis had nearly forgotten the Kzin. He said, "He and Whisper searched for the mysterious master protector for—how long, Bram? Hundreds of falans? But it wasn't enough, even using the telescope display in the Repair Center. The Ringworld is too big. But if you know where a protector will be, you can be there first. A disaster lures protectors. Like

Bram. You'll have to do something about that ARM carrier ship, won't you, Bram?"

"Yes."

"Whisper and Bram found a large mass falling toward the Ringworld. That was all they needed. Cronus would have to do something about that. He'd come to the Repair Center. Whisper and Bram would be ready. Stet, Bram?"

Silence.

"Maybe Cronus knew how to stop the impact. Bram and Whisper would have waited, right? See if he could do it. But Bram knew something was wrong—"

"Louis, we think it was his habit. His first move was to set up defenses. We—We couldn't. Couldn't."

Bram's fingers were sinking into Louis's shoulder, drawing blood.

Louis said, "You killed him before he could finish."

"We moved almost too late! He and we stalked each other. He and we had mapped these vast spaces and set traps." Bram was speaking to Acolyte now, telling of a duel to one who loved such tales. "Anne was crippled for a lifetime. I still don't know how he shattered my leg and hip in the dark. We killed him."

Louis said, "And then?"

"He didn't know, either. Louis, we searched his tools, he brought *nothing*."

"Whatever he had, he never got to use it. You and Whisper, you had no ideas at all."

Bram said, "Acolyte—"

"You let Fist-of-God hit the Ringworld!"

"Acolyte! An enemy waits for me in the Meteor Defense room. Here is your wtsai. Go and kill my enemy."

"Yes," Acolyte said.

Bram whistle-trilled into his eccentric flute. The Kzin stepped forward and flicked out. Louis tried to follow, but Bram's fingers were sunk deep in his shoulder.

Louis said, "You bloodsucking freemother."

"You know where I must be, but I decide the rest. Come." Bram and Louis were on the stepping disk and gone.

Chapter Thirty-One

THE

RINGWORLD

THRONE

They flicked into the gloom of the Meteor Defense, and Louis was flying, hurled away.

He tried to land rolling. He glimpsed Bram flicking out in a burst of mad flute-oboe music. Something monstrous and shadowy was leaping at Louis, and something much faster scuttled toward them both.

Louis landed on his right shoulder, where a vampire protector had sunk dirty claws deep into the sinew and muscle. Louis cried out and kept rolling, and the first attacker landed almost on top of him. The second fended off a reflexive kick from an orange-furred leg and was at the stepping disk. He played a snatch of flute-oboe music and was gone.

The first attacker swept him up and rolled them another ten feet into shadow. "Louis?"

Louis's shoulder was screaming. He pulled in great lungfuls of air. His nose was full of the smell of Kzin. "Acolyte," he said.

"I intend to kill Bram," the Kzin said.

"He may be dead already." *Smell of Kzin and something else. What?* "Did that other one try to kill you? You were supposed to die to distract him. So was I, I think."

"I didn't scent him until he leapt. He must have judged me harmless."

"Are you offended?"

"Louis, where is Bram?"

"Anywhere. Bram controls the stepping disks. There must be twenty or so scattered through the Repair Center."

"Yes, he whistles them up, but that other got through before Bram could change the flick, don't you think?"

"What I'm thinking," Louis said, "is that Bram went through and then changed the flick to Mons Olympus, or the rim, or Hell. Then the other one copied Bram's command and changed it back."

"Then we're missing a fine battle."

What was he smelling? Flowers, something flowery, pulled at Louis's attention and made it hard to think. The Kzin's smell was far stronger . . . and his fur had hard lumps. Wait, now, that was a throwing knife, and that was a long metal pole with chisel-sharpened ends.

Louis said, "You probably can't kill Bram. For that matter, wasn't he teaching you?"

"Louis, shouldn't I kill my teacher?"

Oh? "I'll keep that in mind." Louis sat up.

"No, not you, Louis! I came to you for wisdom, but Bram made me his servant. I learned from Bram by listening until I was ready to learn by freeing myself. See, I have these."

Cronus' weapons.

Louis said, "Most appropriate, but Bram—"

Bram fell from the ceiling. It was thirty feet to the floor, and he landed hard, rolled, and came up with two feet of blade. He tried to balance it on end as another man-shape dropped toward him.

The other's arms swung forward. Bram leapt away as sharp

objects rattled across the floor. *Shuriken?* The blade fell over. Bram's enemy slammed down, rolled and bounced to his feet. He seemed made of knobs, bigger than Bram, with one arm clutched against his chest and sharp metal in the other.

Louis's mind was still trying to catch up.

Bram must have turned a second stepping disk upside down and fixed it to the ceiling. Copying the Martians? Now the vampire protector had nearly reached the first stepping disk, with his larger attacker a long jump behind, as Acolyte surged from cover. Acolyte jabbed the iron pole at Bram's ribs.

Bram didn't turn. He braked for an instant. The pole went past his navel and Bram had the end. He pulled and twisted, the pole bent, and the other end cracked Acolyte across the forehead.

It slowed Bram just enough. The other was on him. He chopped at Bram's wrist, at the foot that came at his face, elbow, the other foot, the other arm.

Bram went down flopping, with bones or tendons cut in all four limbs.

His attacker had vanished. He spoke in the trade language as spoken around Weaver Town, distorted by a protector's usual breathy speech impediment, and Louis's translator was only a moment behind.

"Furry People, you must stay back for now. You shall be satisfied, but this seems a good time to talk."

Acolyte was sitting up, dazed. "Louis?"

If the other protector was still afraid of Bram, so was Louis. He couldn't see any way to drag Acolyte to cover. His own cover wasn't good, but he stayed where he lay. He called, "Stay back, Acolyte. I brought him here."

"Yes," said Bram's attacker. The walls reflected his voice, masking its origin. "Louis Wu, why have you done that?"

Bram sat in a spreading pool of blood. He could have been trying to tie tourniquets, but he wasn't. He'd left his weapons lying. It came to Louis that whatever was done for him, Bram would stop eating now and would be dead shortly thereafter. Protectors do that when they lose their reason to live.

Louis called into the dark. "You'd be Tunesmith?"

"And you'd be Louis Wu who boiled an ocean, but why have you made Tunesmith into *this*?"

Bram broke in. "My time runs short. May I borrow yours? Come, I swear you're safe. Louis, Tunesmith has asked *my* question. Why did you open a stepping disk for a Ghoul whom you have never seen?"

"Forgive me," Louis Wu said. He was having trouble concentrating. That flowery smell! He remained where he was, on his side, nursing his ruined shoulder.

He said, "Bram, you know why I judged you and Anne unfit to hold the Repair Center. I haven't heard you say I was wrong. We could argue before Tunesmith and let him judge. Bram?"

Silence.

"Tunesmith, did you examine the skeleton?"

"Yes."

"I've been calling him Cronus. Cronus was your ancestor. I think even Bram saw the implication. Cronus had eighty thousand falans to breed his genetic line toward the traits he wanted. He shaped an empire with communications that reach all the way around the Arch—"

"Ring. It's a ring," said Tunesmith.

"Cronus extended his breeding program through an area almost too vast to describe. The Night People must number tens of billions. They're all one species, as the vampires are not. He shaped you to be ideal protectors."

Tunesmith said, "I see possible improvements."

"So? Bram here is a vampire protector. We have recordings of Bram in better health, and you'll see them. You're his clear superior. Bigger brain. More versatile. Less reflex, more choices. Bram?"

Bram said, "He beat me. Bigger brain? He was intelligent as a breeder, of course it's bigger now. Louis, he knows nothing. Invaders threaten. You are obliged to train him!"

"I know, Bram—"

"Contract violation or no, you must teach him. Tunesmith, trust his intent, question his judgment. Learn from the Web Dweller but do not trust until he gives you a contract."

Louis asked, "My turn?"

"Speak."

"Tunesmith, protectors do immense damage when they fight. Bram and his mate fixed a problem, and the protectors in charge of the rim wall right now are a local spill mountain species. We need them there. I'll show you why when we get—" The smell. "—get back to the ship." It was tree-of-life. "Get me out of here, Tunesmith. I can't stay here!"

"Louis Wu, you're much too *young* to respond to the smell of the roots. It's faint here, too."

"I'm too old! The root would kill me!" Louis rolled to his knees. He couldn't use his right arm. "Last time I smelled this I barely got away." With Acolyte's help he was on his feet, and he lurched toward the stepping disk.

He had beaten current addiction once. The tree-of-life smell had turned off his mind in a moment, but he had beaten that, too. It had been much stronger eleven years ago. Only a reformed current addict could have walked away from it.

A hand like a fistful of walnuts had his wrist. "Louis Wu, I heard him use three chords and I followed him through each time. One leads to traps and a weapons cache, one to a fall from the ceiling, and the last flicks us to where we fought. Whole fields of tree-of-life grow there, where an artificial sun—"

Louis began to laugh. The smell of tree-of-life was in his brain, and the way out led to where he had fought Teela Brown!

Tunesmith watched him. He said, "Too old, but something was done to you."

Bram was trying to laugh. It sounded awful. "I saw records. Nanotechnology. Experiment stolen from Earth, stolen again, bought by General Products from a thief on Fafnir. It's the puppeteer's autodoc, Louis!" His voice wasn't built for it and his lungs were collapsing, but he laughed. "Eighty falans, Louis. Ninety. No more. Remember me!"

Tunesmith and Acolyte were both looking at Louis Wu.

The scent was in his nose, but it wasn't pulling him. His mind was his own. But that meant . . .

He told them, "I was very sick. The autodoc must have healed me very thoroughly. Changed everything. Every cell." Bram was right. Twenty years, twenty-five tops.

"You could become a protector," Tunesmith said.

"It's only a choice."

Bram was dead. Maybe a protector could will his heart to stop. His last words were suspiciously apt.

"It's an *option*," Louis repeated. The strength was draining out of him.

"You're ill," Tunesmith said.

The Kzin helped him lie down. Tunesmith's knobby hands probed him. The portable medkit hadn't magically healed anything. Tendons, mesentery, a hamstring. His shoulder was badly swollen around five deep puncture wounds. Tunesmith's arm was worse, puffed out and immobile in a sling, but the protector ignored it.

"I don't know your kind. I don't think you can walk, and you may have a fever soon. Louis, what would you normally do for medicine?"

"Back to the ship. Into the 'doc. Heals everything."

Tunesmith went away, taking the Kzin with him. They were back quickly. They lifted Louis and set him down again. He rose into the air, lying flat.

"This will carry you. Signal the magic door."

The Ghoul protector had invented the stretcher? No, they'd gone for a cargo plate and rope to pull it. Louis said, "I can't sing the Hindmost's programming language."

"We're trapped?"

"Not quite."

They set him down. Tunesmith said, "Louis, what shall I do to find my son?"

"Oh . . . tanj. I totally forgot Kazarp in all this. Would he hang around the Weavers? Does he have relatives in the area?"

"There were Night People with us when I flicked in. They can return him to his mother. My fear is that he may have followed me."

"Aw, futz! No, wait, you'd smell him. Knowing your own gene line is built into your brain. Tunesmith, he'll know me. Better send me. Don't go yourself."

"I would terrify him. Louis, shall I play random chords?"

"And test them how? Bram set traps. Tunesmith, we don't need the stepping disks. I led us back to Needle once before, on foot, without the Hindmost's help. Dug a tunnel. That's still in place."

"How long?"

"A few days. You'll have to tow me. We'll need water and food."

"There's water at the tree-of-life farm," Tunesmith said. "Food—" He and Acolyte moved toward Bram's body, and stopped. Tunesmith said, "I was taught that others should not see me eat."

"He's not yet carrion," Acolyte said.

"My teacher's friend, few there are who will discuss cuisine with the Night People, but I see you have an interest. We can eat the freshly dead. We often prefer it, but some are too tough at first, and this was a protector. I could put him on a second cargo plate and pull him along with a longer rope—"

"I'm hungry now, Tunesmith. I would not offend you by eating in your presence."

"Take what you need."

Louis turned his back on what happened next, but he couldn't help grinning. The sounds told the story. A kzinti kitten must have to fight for his food. Now Acolyte was trying to wrench his hard-won portion from Bram's body. Now he used his wtsai, *thuk!* and retreated with whatever that got him.

Tunesmith approached and settled cross-legged. "A child's habits aren't easily broken. Will Acolyte listen to me after this?"

"It's a good start."

"There is food for you, too, Louis Wu. I see no risk in your eating boiled tree-of-life root."

The thought made him flinch, but, "Yams and sweet potatoes are nearly the same species. We roast them."

"It means?"

"Build a fire. Put the roots in the coals where it's not too hot."

"We'll find something to burn in the tree-of-life farm." Tunesmith called toward sounds of grinding teeth and yowling rage. The Kzin was still trying to chew nourishment from the corpse of a protector. "Acolyte, there is prey in the tree-of-life farm. Little animals, and quick. I don't think anyone but a Night People protector will ever eat Bram, and then not today."

"Well, let me hunt, then!"

"You'll need me to get back." Tunesmith fluted, and they flicked away.

Tunesmith came back with an armful of yellow roots. "Acolyte hunts alone. I whistled in the return flick to use when he wants it." He set the roots in the fire. "How do you like your water?"

"Clean. Any temperature, really."

"Cold, too?"

"Sure."

Tunesmith flicked out, and back again with a slab of ice. "Easier than choosing an appropriate container."

"Where did you get that?"

"Miles above us, where air is thin and cold." He soaked a swatch of cloth in dripping ice water and draped it around Louis's neck. "How long do you cook tree-of-life?"

"An hour," Louis said, and he showed Tunesmith the timepiece in the skin of his hand. "This tells tides, too. Not much use here. This makes it a calculator. This is a game, you move the numbers around like—tanj, you're fast."

Acolyte flicked in, his mouth bloody, something dripping from his hand. He set to work with the wtsai. "I looked for anything from the Map of Earth. Nothing quite fit, but this is much like a rabbit, don't you think?" He cleaned the beast and skinned and splayed it butterfly fashion, and perched it above the coals to roast.

Louis said, "Some fun, huh?"

Acolyte thought it over. "Yes. But I'm not wounded."

Acolyte's forehead was swollen and the yellow fur was soaked with blood. Louis said, "We're all wounded. Victors don't have to pay attention to that. Acolyte, tell us a story."

"You first. You fought the lucky protector, Teela Brown."

"I'm not quite proud of that. Let me tell you how I boiled a sea."

He did. Then Acolyte told his father's tale: his arrival at the Map of Earth with a kzinti assault boat and puppeteer tools. The war. Friends and enemies, the deaths, the matings arranged to bind allies. Learning to talk to females.

Chmeee had sired three children in his few weeks on the Map of Kzin. A local lord had contracted to raise them. When he could, Chmeee had retrieved his eldest son from Kathakt—amicably—and brought him to the Map of Earth. Acolyte had seen his first human being at twelve falans.

The eldest son of a lord trained hard. Enemies and friends, whom to watch, whom to almost trust, how to talk to possible mates. *Don't* talk to female diplomats, they'll have your hide—

"This grows boring," Tunesmith said.

Acolyte said, "Yes, it grew boring until I wanted to scream. One day I screamed challenge and fought my father. He let me go. I've been injured and I've starved and I was slaved to a vampire protector, but that diplomatic flup is out of my life. Tell us a tale, Tunesmith."

"I'll sing it. Then we should sleep, and after, Louis can lead us to safety."

Tunesmith sang of a thing of fiery magic abandoned by Louis Wu, who boiled a sea. Five Night People, greatly daring, had dismounted a magical door. They didn't know where it led and they couldn't make it work.

One night Chime was gone.

The rest promised to hold his son from following, and Tunesmith went through the door alone. A scent pulled him toward what he could only perceive as the promise of Paradise.

He woke in the garden of tree-of-life. The woman who had gone through ahead lay dead beside him. Chime had been too old.

He explored. He found the Meteor Defense and the telescope. He created a physics to explain what he was seeing. He and Louis discussed that, with Acolyte listening. Tunesmith had deduced not just worlds, but black holes, too. He had guessed at the existence and nature of other protectors.

"What did you eat? Dead rabbits?"

"Well, Chime, of course, but I haven't been awake long enough to get very hungry."

Louis tried to talk about what a protector needed to know immediately. Invader ships: it was time to take some prisoners, see what their policy actually was. *Hidden Patriarch* and its crew: there must be City Builders everywhere, easily found. The children would need mates in not many years. The Web Dweller—

"A contract is an unambiguous promise, stet, Louis? But why should the Web Dweller offer me such a thing?"

Acolyte said, "Through fear, but he often reacts badly to fear."

"Better if you have something he wants," said Louis. "Tunesmith, what if you offered him the four hundred and first rim wall ramjet?"

His own dinner was ready by now. He explained while he ate. Bussard ramjet, attitude jet, hydrogen fusion. Tunesmith already understood the law of reaction and the Ringworld's instability.

"There are only four hundred mountings. When you build the four hundred and first motor, we'll mount *Hot Needle of Inquiry* at the axis. It's a General Products hull; radiation can't touch it. At sublight speed it'll take the Hindmost a thousand years or so to match with the Fleet of Worlds . . ."

Acolyte stalked away from the smell of politics.

Louis said, "I don't expect that'll bother him. The Conservatives are in power in the Fleet of Worlds. Nothing will change. They may even want him back. Anyway, we can offer."

"He likes power games, does he?"

"Stet."

"Let him play. If he gains more power, we'll offer him the two hundredth ramjet. It's clear we don't need them all. Acolyte! Do you wonder how you lived?"

Acolyte stalked back. Tunesmith sang of finding the skeleton and weapons of Cronus. Clues there told him that he was challenged. He chose his lurking spot and waited.

A monstrous shape of orange hair flicked in and surged away. Tunesmith stalked it, but he sensed no harm in it. "It may be my kind hasn't grown up frightened of your kind's smell."

Acolyte thought that over. Tunesmith said, "But now I knew my enemy would use others for bait. When two hominids appeared and one threw the other flying—"

The Hindmost flicked in.

He squeaked like a smashed piano and was instantly gone, but Tunesmith was faster than that. He went through with the

Kzin on his heels and Louis screaming, "Wait! What if it's Mons Olympus?"

He'd reached his feet, but they were gone. Louis said, "Idiots," and limped to the stepping disk and flicked through anyway.

Tunesmith was in some kind of weird weaving defense pose. Acolyte was not quite a safe distance away, trying to talk him down. Tunesmith ignored the Kzin. "I want to talk to your leader," he said firmly.

Thousands of three-legged, two-headed creatures were watching them through the forward wall.

"We say 'Hindmost,'" one of them said. "I'm the Hindmost. Speak your desire."

"Teach me."

The granite block had been set aside.

Louis limped past Kzin and protector. The pain in his shoulder was a part of his anger. He asked the Hindmost, "Now how did you do that?"

"I braced my forequarters against the wall and pushed with my hind leg. Bram felt the strength in my leg. He should have known."

"Lucky for us—"

"Where is Bram?"

"Dead at our hands. Tunesmith, the teaching aids are all here aboard *Hot Needle of Inquiry*. Those pictures especially. They're made by bronze webs like the one on the cliff at Weaver Town."

Tunesmith said, "I follow Bram's advice. Web Dweller, teach me. I am not to trust you until we have a contract."

"I'll print out my people's standard contract for service."

"Only for my amusement, I hope. Louis, my son needs . . ." Tunesmith looked again. "You, into the 'doc, now. Is that it?"

Acolyte was lifting him.

He was in the big box and Tunesmith was examining the readouts doubtfully. "How long?" the Ghoul protector asked.

The puppeteer said, "Three days, maybe less."

Louis talked in haste. "Don't anyone sign anything. Hindmost, I don't know how to feed a Night Person. Try aged beef. Try cheese. Tunesmith, I hope you won't destroy that last ARM spacecraft unless they do something dreadful—"

"Nearest possible mates in this universe?"

"Well . . . that, too. Now, the High Point protectors hold the rim wall, and at this point they may be scared out of their minds. Talk to them through that window, with the black sky and the big strange shapes? Ghouls stole that web from a vampire nest, carried it maybe two hundred thousand miles plus two miles straight up—"

"The sunlight network told us about it."

"Tell the spill mountain protectors they're in charge of the rim. *Mean* it."

Acolyte was closing the lid on the big box. Louis laughed suddenly. "Hey. Remind you of anything?"

He heard the voice of Louis Wu telling a hairless face with red skin, "We'd like to talk to a protector, please. We want to propose a contract."

And the lid closed and he could rest.

GLOSSARY

ARM: once the Amalgamated Regional Militia, now the United Nations armed forces.

antispin: direction opposite the Ringworld's direction of spin.

collier: 1. A ship used to carry coal. 2. A merchant who transports or sells coal.

cziltang brone: alleged to be a device to allow solid objects to penetrate scrith.

cruiser: a Machine People vehicle.

elbow root: ubiquitous Ringworld plant, a kind of natural fence.

daywalk: varies by species, but usually means a serious effort consistent with foraging and health. One daywalk for Machine People is about ten miles; for a Grass Giant, less, but they can keep it up forever. Gleaners can do one and a half Machine People daywalks for a couple of hours.

Fleet of Worlds: the homeworld of the Pierson's puppeteers, and four worlds sequestered for farming.

flup: seabottom ooze.

Outsider hyperdrive or **hyperdrive**: a means of faster-than-light travel, common in known space.

Patriarchy: the kzinti empire.

Repair Center: ancient center of Ringworld maintenance and control housed beneath the Map of Mars.

payload shell: the locked iron housing on a Machine People cruiser.

rishathra (reshtra): sexual practice outside one's own species but within the intelligent hominids. Not a useful term beyond the Ringworld.

scrith: Ringworld structural material. Scrith underlies all of the terraformed and contoured inner surface of the Ringworld. The rim walls are also of scrith. Very dense, with a tensile strength on the order of the force that holds an atomic nucleus together.

spill mountains: mountains standing against the rim wall, the outflow of the rim spillpipes. One stage in the circulation of flup. The spill mountains have their own ecology.

spin or **spinward**: in the direction of rotation of the Ringworld (against the rotation of the sky).

star or **starboard**: to the right as one faces spinward.

stet: leave it alone, no change, that's exactly right.

tanj: an expletive. Initial slang for "There Ain't No Justice."

thruster: reactionless drive. In known space, thrusters have generally replaced fusion rockets on all spacecraft save warcraft.

vishnishtee/vashnesht: wizard or protector.

weenie plant: ubiquitous Ringworld plant. Edible. Grows in damp areas.

webeye: puppeteer technology, a multisensory probe.

R I N G W O R L D

P A R A M E T E R S

30 hours = 1 Ringworld "day."

1 turn = 7.5 thirty-hour days = 1 Ringworld rotation.

1 falan = 10 turns = 75 days

Mass = 2×10^{30} grams

Radius = $.95 \times 10^8$ miles

Circumference = 5.97×10^8 miles

Width = 997,000 miles

Surface area = 6×10^{14} square miles = 3×10^6 times the surface area of the Earth (approx)

Surface gravity = 31.7 feet/second/second = .992 gee

Rim walls rise inward, 1,000 miles

Repair Center = 40 miles high by $.56 \times 10^8$ square miles area = 2.24×10^9 cubic miles

Near Great Ocean = 600 × surface area of Earth

Star: G1 or G2, barely smaller and cooler than Sol

CAST OF CHARACTERS

MACHINE PEOPLE

Valavirgillin (Vala, "Boss")—hired the caravan. Represents Farsight Trading

Foranayeedli (Forn)—Barok's daughter. Kaywerbrimmis's crew

Sabarokaresh (Barok)—biggest male. Kaywerbrimmis's crew

Kaywerbrimmis (Kay)—Valavirgillin's Wagonmaster

Anthrantillin (Anth)—wagonmaster

Taratarafasht (Tarfa)—female, Anth's crew

Whandernothtee (Whand)—wagonmaster

Chitakumishad (Chit)—Whandernothtee's crew

Sopashintay (Spash)—Whand's crew

Himapertharee (Himp)—Anthrantillin's crew

High Rangers Trading Group—died but for Valavirgillin, forty-three falans ago

Tarablilliast (Tarb)—Valavirgillin's mate, taking care of their children, far to starboard

GRASS GIANTS

Paroom—male sentry

Thurl—alpha male, the Bull

Moonwa—female, the Thurl's primary wife
Beedj—male, the Thurl's probable heir
Tarun—male
Wemb—female
Makee—male, Wemb's son
Heerst—male
Twuk—small Grass Giant female

GLEANERS

Perilack—female
Silack—beta male
Manack—alpha male, hairier
Coriack—female

REDS

Tegger hooki-Thandarthal—ambassador
Warvia hooki-Murf Thandarthal—ambassador
Anakrin hooki-Whanhurhur—messenger
Chaychind hooki-Karashk—messenger

RIVER PEOPLE

Wurblychoog—female
Borubble—male
Rooballabl—speaks trade language
Fudghabladl—old one, remembers

BALL PEOPLE

Louis Wu
The Hindmost (the Web Dweller)
Chmeee

WEAVING PEOPLE

Parald
Strill
Sawur
Kidada

FISHERS

Shans Serpentstrangler
Hishthare Rockdiver

SAILOR

Wheek

NIGHT PEOPLE

Kazarp
Tunesmith
Harpster
Grieving Tube

KZINTI

Acolyte—Chmeee's eldest son
Kathakt—a lord of the Map of Kzin

SPILL MOUNTAIN PEOPLE

Saron—older woman
Deb—middle-aged woman
Skreepu—bird, belongs to Deb
Harreed—Deb's younger son
Barraye—Deb's older son
Jennawil—younger woman mated to Barraye

PROTECTORS

Cronus
Bram
Anne
Lovecraft
Collier
King
. . . and others, nameless.